Zee Locked-In
OVR Worlds Online
Book 1

Justin Monroe

For my loving wife and my awesome dad. Without them this book wouldn't exist.

ACKNOWLEDGMENTS

Writing a book is seemingly a solitary effort, but in actuality it isn't. There are far more people that have helped me along this path than I can possibly name. First of all, my wonderful wife. She has tolerated long stretches of me tapping away on a keyboard in the evenings while only half paying attention to the world around me. She doesn't always understand my nerdy ways, but she supports me nonetheless. I wouldn't be here if not for her support.

There are all the test readers that have gifted me with their attention and opinions. Chief among them is my Dad, a writer in his own right, and the person aside from myself that has read my work more than anyone. There are several friends and random readers on Royal Road that read and commented on this work. Along the way, whether I've taken their exact advice or not, they've all helped me make it better.

Then there was the professional assistance that I employed to complete this work. My editor Emily Cataneo of The Redbud Writing Project, was a pleasure to work with and I truly feel she pushed my work to the next level. For any aspiring writer out there that is debating whether to employ a professional editor or not, I can't recommend it enough.

My cover was brought to life by the extremely talented Egil Thompson. He's a tremendous collaborator and vivid artist. Check out more of his work at www.artstation.com/egilthompson.

I've always dreamed of publishing my work, and all of these people, and more have helped me reach this point. I stand on the shoulders of giants and can never express the true depths of my gratitude.

Chapter One

The crowded public bus, operated by Express Trans Inc., hit another pothole and I bounced in my seat. Every inch of my body was sore after a 12 hour graveyard janitorial shift. I shifted uncomfortably on the hard plastic and tried to focus on the episode of *Doctor Who* playing on the cracked screen of my widget. Wearing the vision obstructing widg-glasses in public was a great way to get robbed or stabbed, so I had the battered outdated device strapped to my wrist instead.

It had been a long night at work, and the morning sun was already well over the horizon. My eyes burned around the edges, and each blink felt like fine sandpaper skritching across my eyeballs. The combination of sweat and vapor from my breath made the filter mask over my mouth and nose chafe uncomfortably. More than anything, I just wanted to get home and pass out. As usual, it seemed like this bus ride would never end.

Over my wireless earbuds, the musical score swelled with excitement as the Tenth Doctor, as portrayed by David Tennant, sprinted through the Library, clutching his sonic screwdriver and the voice over by River Song filled my ears. The two parter *Silence in the Library* and *Forest of the Dead*, had aired over 40 years ago - well before I'd been born - but they were two of my favorites. A private smile tugged at my lips, despite my exhaustion. I loved this part.

"Everybody knows that everybody dies, but not every day. Not today."

The Doctor shoved the modified sonic screwdriver into the massive computer and energy crackled. The Doctor grinned wide eyed and gleeful at once again having snatched victory from the jaws of defeat. The scene dissolved to white. The white faded to a new scene to reveal River uploaded into an idyllic virtual reality garden and reunited with her friends, all slain previously in the story.

The episode paused and the picture blinked away as my virtual digital assistant, skinned to look like Dean Stockwell when he played Admiral Albert "Al" Calavicci on *Quantum Leap*, filled the screen.

"This is your stop Zee." Al's image chewed on a cigar as he spoke.

I glanced out the window to see the battered bus was crawling along my street. Another commute smothered to death thanks to classic TV.

"Thanks Al," I said.

I heaved myself up and shuffled towards the doors. Over my earbuds the remainder of River's voice over played out, even though I wasn't watching my widget anymore.

"*...Some days, nobody dies at all. Now and then, every once in a very long while, every day in a million days, when the wind stands fair and the Doctor comes to call, everybody lives.*" I found myself mouthing the lines along with River Song.

As the episode ended, Al automatically switched over to my widge-cast feed, streaming the morning's episode of *Wake the Fuck Up America* by the independent Dread Pirate Robert's Network. The host, who's on air alias was Markey Moron, was angrily railing against the tattered remnants of the US government and the sheeple that had sold off their voting franchise to Mega-Corporations. Markey was an angry and paranoid old nut, but he operated outside the censorship of mass media, and every now and then he stumbled across real news.

The bus finally ground to a halt and the doors creaked open.

"Take it easy Ned," I said to the driver as I climbed down the stairs.

Detecting Ned's response, Al paused Markey's tirade so I could hear.

"You'll tell your pops about that new investment opportunity right Zack? I swear, it's a sure thing!"

With my back still turned to Ned, he couldn't see me roll my eyes. Ned, who was a cousin to one degree or another, was always pitching some half baked get rich quick "investment opportunity" to anyone that would

9

listen, and even some, like me, that wouldn't. I'd figured out most of Ned's ideas were just reskinned pyramid schemes when I was 8, and I'd never risk actually telling my dad about anything Ned cooked up. Without turning I gave Ned a wave goodbye as the doors squealed shut, and let him draw his own conclusions.

The Colorado October morning air was warm, sticky with humidity, and heavy with the rotting smell of garbage and pollution that not even my mask could filter out. The Denver city government had stopped even issuing air quality warnings, it would be breaking news if breather masks weren't advised for once. And even if the air wasn't choked with pollution, the mask protected by the increasingly virulent strains of viruses and bacteria constantly evolving to try and kill us.

There were four hundred twenty-one steps from the bus stop to my apartment building. Along the way, I had to step around the huddled forms of the still slumbering homeless along the sidewalk. I did so with a palpable sense of dread that I could easily join them. Thanks to PrimaTech, the monopolistic Mega-Corporation that owned my hospital, and the entire American healthcare system, my family and I lived barely one paycheck away from eviction.

Overhead, I heard the motorized buzz of several aerial drones. Most were probably delivering online orders, but there were guaranteed to be a few OzCo "Public Safety" drones mixed into the bunch. Denver and the outlying suburbs had disbanded their police departments before I was born, but not because of the Police Abolition Movement of the twenties. The decision was economical, not ethical, so instead they had contracted out all law enforcement operations to the Mega-Corp OzCo, just like the Feds and most every other municipality. As far as I knew, I wasn't on any watch lists, but kept my head down all the same.

Stomach rumbling, I hesitated outside the Vend-o-Mart Express franchise for a heartbeat, contemplating popping in for a breakfast burrito. Then the synthetic intelligence running the ad-screens outside the store scanned my face, despite my breather mask, and lit up with advertisements selected just for Zachary Jones.

The ads included a new online streaming service, widget parts for DIY repairs, *Wild Lords 5* Hollywood's latest rehashed piece of crap, the latest OVR World home immersion pods, and of course the very breakfast burrito I'd just been considering. It was the ad for the immersion pod that kicked me into moving on. After my paycheck cleared tomorrow, I'd have just enough crypts set aside to rent some pod time for a night of virtual clubbing.

At the door to my building, I placed my thumb on the scanner pad just above the door handle. Then looked directly into the security camera lense over the door. The building's synthetic intelligence, SI, security software matched my face and thumbprint to our lease, then the heavy door unlocked with a series of metallic clicks a second later. This relatively

minimal level of building security gave us the illusion of safety, however, I

knew of six different ways to enter the building undetected. The thriving

drug trade being done by Skeet in apartment 2B told me that I wasn't alone

in that knowledge either.

The building's elevator had been out of service since before we moved

in, so I began the familiar climb up the stairs to the tenth floor apartment I

shared with my parents. Graffiti covered the walls of the staircase, and

drifts of garbage cluttered each landing. Half the lights were burned out,

and of the surviving fixtures most strobed out a morse code message of

impending death.

When I finally reached the tenth floor, my chest was heaving and my

skin was sticky with sweat beneath my smothering synthetic janitor's

overalls. Bone weary, I shuffled down the hall to my door, 10E, and

thumbed the security pad above the knob while digging in my pocket for

the key. After our apartment's thumb scanner had been hacked and our

place ransacked for the third time, I'd caved and installed the illegal

deadbolt myself. It was my crowning achievement in DIY home

improvement. When the apartment's security system finally *beeped* its

approval of my identity, I already had my key in the lock and diligently

jiggled it until the pins caught and I could twist it open. Then using my shoulder and full body weight, I shoved at the humidity warped door. It reluctantly gave way and swung up.

Stepping inside the apartment, I gratefully tugged off my mask as an unsurprising auditory assault crashed over me. I slammed the door shut with more force than was strictly called for. Dad, wearing a faded black t-shirt with big *ACAB* lettering and tattered sweatpants, was sprawled out on our stained sagging sofa watching an *OVR Worlds* game replay. The World Series was about a month away, and all eyes were on Dackon Darkblade and Bennette Ogresbane duking it out again for the top rank on Gygax.

"Morning Zack to the Future. How was the night?" Dad's eyes only flicked away from the TV screen for a heartbeat before latching back onto the sword dueling avatars on the screen.

"Same shit, different night. You should try it some time." Not that any legitimate employers would look twice at Dad, a self declared and officially blacklisted Democratic Socialist. I yanked open the fridge to find the filtered water pitcher empty. Annoyed, I yanked the pitcher out and stuck it under the tap to refill. "How'd Mom do last night?"

Dad's eyes were fixated on the screen. After repeating my question and only getting silence back, I chucked an empty beer can at him over the kitchen island. The can bounced off his ample gut.

"Fuck'n hell Zack!" He sat upright and glared at me.

"How was Mom last night?" My tone was heavy with exasperation.

"Wouldn't eat again." Dad bent over to retrieve the fallen beer can, he shook it to see if there was any left. "So I had to order a nutrient boost from that fuckin box."

"Damn it. Another one? That shit isn't cheap." I mentally rolled an hour off my planned pod rental.

"That reminds me, you get paid tomorrow, right? Make sure the entire check gets in the account this time. Those Mega-fuckers want their cut again for rent."

"Yeah…" I scowled at my dad with obvious trepidation.

"Well, the power bill is past due again. And we can't have the power going out on Mom again."

"I gave you the crypts to catch us up two weeks ago! Where'd it go?" If I didn't manage his cash flow, we wouldn't hurt for beer and pizza, but continued electricity and rent were questionable.

Dad just shrugged in seeming bewilderment. Teeth grinding, I struggled to choke down a flood of possible enraged responses. While tomorrow was payday, the majority of that check was destined for KushNet Investments, the Mega that owned and managed every building in our neighborhood. The handful of crypts I'd set aside for my weekend plans had just been gobbled up yet again by my dad's careless disregard of reality.

I stewed silently in the kitchen as the water filtered. Then poured myself a cup and tried to focus on breathing away my rage. The fridge rattled after I returned the filter and slammed the door shut. It seemed to be enough to drag Dad's attention away from the glittering delights on the screen.

"You know, this wouldn't be a problem if you and the others at that Mega-fuck owned hospital you slave away at would just get together and unionize. Then you could demand fair wages and health care and - "

"More like we'd all get our knees shattered for suggesting it."

Knowing that Dad was about to climb up on his rickety old soap box, yet again, I grabbed my water, snagged a bag of chips and retreated down the short narrow hall to the back bedroom to check on Mom myself. Once upon a time, Dad had been a passionate social justice activist and labor leader.

When I'd been much younger, he'd taken me to protests with him. Mom had put an end to that after I got tear gassed at the tender age of 9 and had been almost trampled by the protestors turned fleeing mob. Dad had lost hold of me in the chaos and we'd been separated for over an hour. I still had nightmares about that day.

In the face of an unending global economic crisis, the erosion of our democratic institutions, and a dying ecosystem, there weren't a lot of Dad's type left. Society at large hadn't just abandoned Dad's ideals. He'd been beaten and broken repeatedly until all he had left was spouting nonsense from the safety of our sofa.

Slipping through the bedroom door, I expected Mom to be asleep. To my surprise, she was awake and sitting up in bed. Mom had her decrypted tablet in hand and her glasses perched on her nose. I guessed she was either picking through blacknet message boards or scanning code. Once a hacker, always a hacker she liked to say. Not that she had the energy or coherence to do much of anything these days. She gave me a mock glare of consternation over the top of her tablet as I came in.

"You didn't get him going again did you?" Her voice was just above a whisper, but her gaze was focused and alert. A Red Alert klaxon started going off in my head.

"Like he needed any help." I rolled my eyes at her and she flashed me a wan smile. I moved over to check the readouts on the bulky PrimaTech Auto-Nurse 6500x beside her bed.

"You seem to be feeling pretty good." I didn't hide the foreboding edge in my tone.

"I was thinking I might get up and do a jig later."

"Yeah, that's cause Dad let you pain meds run out again." I clenched my jaw so hard it hurt. "You'll be feeling a lot worse in an hour or two."

"He didn't forget," Mom said. "I asked him not to dose me."

"Mom...what the fu - "

"Language Zack!" she scolded me. Though, I'd heard far worse come out of her mouth.

We'd walked this road before. The various drugs that the Auto-Nurse pumped into my mom's cancer riddled body, kept her in a state that she called "acceptable misery". Mostly they just knocked her out to the point of being barely conscious. But for my bright and quick witted mom that was the real torture. Coming off the drugs created a narrow window of pain free lucidity. However, when the window inevitably closed, the agony would come on quicker than we could get the meds back into her.

"I just wanted to see you this morning and not through a haze," she said softly. Mom set aside her tablet and reached out to grasp my arm. For the moment, her grip was strong and steady. She pulled my hands away from the Auto-Nurse's control panel and guided me to sit beside her on the bed. "I don't know how many more times I'll get to do that Zee."

"Stop it," I said, my voice cracking around the words. "You've got -"

"Shhhhhhh Honey." Mom smiled at me weakly, but her words were laced with resignation. "Why don't you put on *Buffy*? And we can both get some rest."

I had to choke down the lump in my throat before I could reply. "Fine, but at least let me get the meds flowing again. So that it doesn't get too bad."

"Alright." Mom rolled her eyes in mock exasperation.

Opening up the Auto-Nurse's hard plastic case, I replaced the drained pain medicine and saline packs, checked that all the hoses were good, then locked it back up. Satisfied that a fresh stream of meds were flowing, I flopped down in the battered recliner beside Mom's hospital bed. Using my widget, I selected the next episode in our endless cycle of *Buffy the Vampire Slayer* rewatching. We were in the front half of season 5, *The Replacement*. With a flick of a fingertip across the widget screen I cast it up to the small TV mounted on the bedroom wall.

"I love this one," Mom said as the episode began.

"Me too."

With an exhausted sigh, I put up the foot rest of the recliner and pushed back. Before Nerf Herder had guitar shred to the end of the opening credits, I heard gentle snores from the bed. Looking over, I saw that Mom had passed out. Hopefully she'd sleep through the worst of the broken drug cycle. Getting up from my recliner, I pulled the blanket up higher over my slumbering mother.

Plopping back down in my recliner, I turned the volume down a couple notches and tried to settle in myself. Technically, I had a bedroom of my own, but it was still crammed with a mountain of cheap pseudo-science dietary supplements from the multi-level marketing scheme Ned had sold Dad on last year. Most days I ended up passing out right there in the recliner.

"Zee! It's 8:15 PM! You've got to wake up now! Ziggy says there's an 87.3% chance that you'll be late for work again and you'll never leap out of here!" Al shouted over my earbuds.

Groaning, I sat up trying to clear my head of sleep, the recliner squeaked in protest from the movement. I ripped out my earbuds, silencing Al's continuing shouts. Yawning, I checked the display on Mom's Auto-Nurse to make sure she was still supplied. It looked like Dad had actually handled the midday resupply while I slept, a nice change of pace.

On my widget, Al was still ranting at me to get moving. I'd snoozed him four times already and he was going nuclear. I couldn't really blame Al. After all, I'd programmed his escalating tantrum myself.

Even after six months, my body and the graveyard shift did not get along. Sleep came in the form of several short naps spread through the day. When I tried to dismiss the alarm from my widget's screen, Al prompted me to solve a calculus problem before he'd return to normal function. Just to make sure I was *really awake*.

"Al, play my news feed," I said after shoving my earbuds back in.

While the news played, I stumbled up from the recliner and hauled myself into the bathroom. Al hadn't been wrong. I was really going to have to bust a move if I had any hope of getting to work on time. I hoped there was some hot water today.

The latest Top Player standings from the OVR Worlds, Omega Virtual Reality Worlds, (or just *The Game*, as it was almost universally referred to) popped up on the widget screen first and Al recited the standings and relative changes. Being the biggest and most immersive VR system in the world the game now filtered up to the top of everyone's news feed, whether you played or not.

On Gygax, Bennett Ogresbane had bested Dackon Darkblade for the top rank. That had been the duel Dad had been watching when I got home. All the Sci-Fi nerds had gotten together in Zeta Quadrant for a massive battle, to determine "once and for all" which universe had the best ships, *Star Trek* or *Star Wars*. On *Fleming's World* the annual Tournament of Assassins had kicked off, with a surprising upset. The team from Brazil was off to an early lead. Russia was still the hands down favorite this year, if they didn't get busted for another hacking attempt. And the annual *Middle-Earth* race from the Shire to Mount Doom was in full swing with an unfortunately named Dildo_Draggins_69 somehow in the lead.

In real world news, Las Vegas, Chicago and Omaha were still under martial law after the coordinated attacks of the so-called Free Nation Alliance had killed thousands. The Senate, serving at the pleasure of their Mega-Corp electors, had passed more taxes on non-game generated income. I'd be seeing that come out of my next check. And there was another massive hurricane about to smack into what was left of the drowned Gulf States.

Mom and Dad were both in the bedroom when I got out of the shower. There hadn't been any hot water left, so even if I hadn't been in a hurry, it would've been quick. Dad had a bowl of some ultra processed protein mush in one hand and was trying to coax Mom into eating. With her drugs flowing from the Auto-Nurse she was barely coherent, but when her glassy eyes spotted me her slack face lit up with a dreamy grin.

"Hi Honey," she slurred.

"Overslept." I leaned over and gave Mom a quick kiss on the forehead. "Gotta run. Try to eat. OK?"

Mom nodded her head but looked dubiously at the beige slurry on the offered spoon.

"Got your mask?" Dad asked.

I rolled my eyes and held up the breathing mask for him to see. Not that I'd ever seen Dad wear his outside. But I tried to wear mine diligently, because I knew it made Mom happy. I was halfway down the hall when Dad shouted after me.

"Left you some pizza in the fridge! And make sure those assholes don't fuck up your check again!"

With a frustrated sigh, I ripped open the fridge door, grabbed a can of coffee and a slice of beyond-meat-lovers pizza. I tried, with mild success, not to slam the door behind me as I bolted out of the apartment.

"Al, play my *Going to Work* playlist," My widget detected the command and Queen's *Another One Bites the Dust* thumped through my earbuds as I ripped off a bite of the cold pizza.

Breakfast of champions, I thought distastefully.

Feet moving along with the staccato beat, I took the stairs down two or three at a time while I choked down the pizza. When I got outside, I tugged my mask into place and broke into a brisk jog as I chewed the last bite of pizza. My Mega-Corp overlords at PrimaTech didn't look kindly on tardiness, and there were thirty or more suckers waiting for me to screw up mopping floors and scrubbing toilets.

Reaching the bus stop I was breathing hard under my mask and smothering janitor's uniform was damp with sweat. I checked my widget, knowing Al would have already tracked the bus for me. Of course, the bus wasn't on time either, so my rush had been wasted. Leaning against the bus stop pole I closed my eyes and caught my breath. Somehow, I must have dozed off leaning against the pole, because the next thing I knew the silent electric bus was stopped in front of me.

"You coming or what, Zee?" shouted the bus driver.

"Yeah," I grunted and heaved myself into motion. "Sorry, Luke."

I climbed aboard, tapped my widget against the reader to pay the fare, and slumped onto the first open seat. The bus's electric motor whined as we rolled into motion. It would take at least an hour and a half and forty or so stops to get to the hospital.

"Based on the traffic report, it doesn't look good Zee!" Al reported over my earbuds, ironically interrupting *Don't Stop Believing* by Journey.

Despite the hour, the bus was crowded, and as usual, the AC was out of commission. I found myself jammed between two Augmented Reality dopes, reality warping display glasses firmly in place over their eyes. They gasped and their bodies jerked seemingly at random as an overlay of augmented reality beamed in on their glasses to entertain them and blot out the ugly parts of our world. They were probably high too, as most auggers were.

I did my best to ignore them. I opted to check mail on my widget, mostly spam that had slipped past Al. Then I switched to the Pipeline app to stream some OVR World highlights from the day that Al had queued up for me. I'd never have enough crypts to be a player. That would have required at least a personal pod at home, a dedicated fiber optic connection, and the crypts to kit myself out for adventure in one of the various competitive worlds. I was lucky to rent a rig and be an occasional tourist to the virtual world, dancing the night away on a zero-G dance floor, sipping simulated cocktails and possibly a virtual hookup.

However, I still stayed up on OVR World events. It was damn near impossible to have a conversation with anyone if you didn't. In most every way, the virtual reality of the OVR Worlds was the only reality anyone actually cared about these days.

Chapter Two

"You're late Jones! Again!" shouted my PrimaTech supervisor, Raj, as I hurried through the back doors of the Denver PrimaTech Hospital franchise and scanned my widget at the security checkpoint.

"Sorry. I know!" I gasped. "The bus broke down, and the driver said it would be two hours to send a replacement. I ran over a mile to get here. I'm only twelve minutes late."

"You know the drill." Raj didn't even straighten from his slouched position; feet up on the desk, a stim stick vaping between his lips. "Every minute you're late adds ten to the end of your shift. You just added a buck-twenty to your night. We've got some VPs from corporate coming through in the morning, so I want this place glowing by then. Get upstairs and get to work!"

Raj had even more people waiting for his job than were waiting for mine. Clearly Employee Satisfaction *wasn't* a measured metric on his performance eval.

"Your widget will get you into all the Labs on six tonight. Make sure they're spotless!" Raj shouted as I retrieved my cart and started shoving it down the hall towards the elevators.

The labs on six? Generally the day crew cleaned those with the omnipresent PrimaTech Security watching their every move. The extra space to clean would easily add three hours onto my shift, but Raj would no doubt screw me out of any overtime I might have coming. Labor cost was *definitely* a metric on his performance eval.

You'd think by the year 2052 they would have invented a robot that could clean and polish hospital floors and of course they had. But why buy a robot that would require maintenance when you can essentially "buy" a human that can merely be replaced if it breaks down? Dad was always talking about "labor laws" and other crap his "organizers" would reinstitute. I knew the Megas would never release the stranglehold they had on our economy or government.

Just ask any budding Mega-Corp junior executive. According to them, Megas were our saviors. Who else had had the money and resources to rebuild after the complete economic collapse and repeated natural disasters like the Mud Bowl? All the coastal cities flooded by the mid-thirties and storms like Thomas and Veronica had sealed the deal that Harvey and

Maria had started back in the teens. In fact, they were running out of names

for the monster hurricanes that regularly lashed the southern third of the

country in a storm season that never seemed to end. Never mind the

repeated volcanic eruptions triggered by shifting polar ice, the endless

wildfires out west, or the pandemic super viruses.

We'd been in the Denver area for three years now, since I was sixteen.

We probably would have already moved on if Mom hadn't gotten cancer a

year ago. She was just too sick to move, and we were too poor to afford the

treatments she'd need to get better. As it was, we could barely afford the

hospice equipment that was keeping her in a state she only loosely termed

as *comfortable* and drawing out what was left of her life.

It was nearing the end of my normal shift by the time I finally reached

the sixth floor. Normally, I just mopped up the halls and wiped down the

walls. I started there, because it was the easiest and most routine. When that

was done, I used my widget to buzz myself into the nearest lab. As

promised, the door chimed and slid open. I went to work, avoiding any of

the expensive-looking equipment. The phrase "you break it, you buy it"

flashed through my head.

In the second to last lab, my entire world came to a sudden screeching

halt. I couldn't believe my eyes. I had to be imagining what I'd found. A mental image of Admiral Akbar played in my head shouting "It's a trap!" But all the same, I couldn't move on.

Sitting out, on one of the work tables, was an injection module clearly labeled *PrimaTech Nano-Therapy*. I'd seen pictures of the device when researching Mom's cancer online, but I'd never envisioned I would see one in real life. This thing was the magic bullet in cancer treatment.

Treatment was the wrong word. It was a cure. But it might as well have had an eighty-foot neon sign attached to it screaming FOR MEGA EXECS ONLY, it was that expensive. Even if I'd cashed in my Voting Franchise, and sold off any pretense I had of participating in our hollowed-out husk of a "democracy," I couldn't have come close to affording these meds.

One injection, and microscopic robots would flow through the patient's body. They'd devour cancer cells, not only sparing healthy cells, but knitting together damaged tissues in their wake. Supposedly, so simple to administer that it didn't even need a doctor or nurse. Just a shit load of crypts.

Boom. No more cancer.

I found myself standing in the middle of the lab, mop in hand, staring at the injection module. I thought maybe it had already been used, that's why it had been left out. It was trash. Fit for a janitor. But then noticed the blinking green LED labeled *READY*.

Then I became painfully aware of the multiple sensors and cameras focused on me, following my every move. The PrimaTech security synthetic intelligence would already be wondering about my frozen position, calculating my line of sight, seeing the immensely valuable medication on the table and raising the alarm. Or, maybe, it wasn't so smart. Maybe it was a coffee break. I didn't know! All I did know was the stormtroopers weren't rushing in on me. Just cause I hadn't actually done anything wrong didn't mean anything. An SI's calculated probability that I was even considering a crime was enough for them to not only shit-can me, but to rough me up on the way out the door for good measure.

In a flash, I made my decision and something resembling a plan took shape. I started vigorously wiping down the stainless-steel counters and tables like I hadn't seen the miracle sitting there. Then I "accidentally" knocked it to the floor and it went skittering under another table. I kept on scrubbing like I hadn't noticed. Just another clumsy and incompetent corporate drone. My heart was pounding. While I continued to work, I held my breath expecting alarms to blare any second.

Shaking with adrenaline, I finished the counters and began to slosh my mop across the floor, as if, maybe, I was behind schedule and trying to catch up, which had the benefit of being true. I made sure to do a thorough job, working my mop well under each of the stainless-steel tables. Nothing to see here, just doing my mindless menial job.

When I reached the module, I knelt low, feigning for the monitoring SI getting my mop wrapped around a table leg. In actuality, I swept the little miracle towards me. The thing was so small it fit in the palm of my hand. I cradled the priceless device and slid it into one of the oversized pockets on my overalls.

I finished my remaining lab on the sixth floor in record time, my heart threatening to pound out of my chest the whole way. It felt like an eternity. My mouth was dry with anxiety and sweat was streaming down my forehead when I finally pushed my cart into the elevator and pressed the button to return to the basement.

As expected, Raj harangued me about the extra time it had taken and before I even asked, he refused to authorize the overtime. Maybe I should have tried to be more outraged, but instead, I just hurried out the door, then started running the moment I tasted "fresh" air. I started coughing almost immediately. I'd left my filter mask hanging from my cart. No way in hell I was going back for it. I was never going back there. Ever.

Sirens filled the early morning air as I exited the hospital and in my mind, they were all coming for me. I ran harder. I ducked down side streets and doubled back, doing whatever I could to throw off the pursuers I knew must be hunting me. I wasn't a real criminal, so I had no idea how this stuff was done. The shows we all lived on told me I had no chance at all, but as I ran and ducked, and crouched behind dumpsters, the sirens weren't getting any closer. It was possible they'd just been ambulances headed to the ER.

About a quarter-mile into my "escape," I stopped to catch my breath, coughing and gasping for air in turns.

"Al, get me an auto-cab home." I wheezed, hands on my knees.

Al blipped onto my widget screen. *"Are you sure Zee? There's surge pricing for the morning commute. It'll be a pricey ride."*

"Just fucking do it, Al," I snapped. The morning shift of lab workers would be arriving at any moment and would soon realize what was missing. Once they did, it wouldn't take long for the security SI to track me down and send a squad of Mega-Goons after me.

"You got it, boss," Al answered, his tone simulating reluctance and wounded feelings. Al blipped off the screen and a second later a map appeared, showing my approaching computer-driven taxi.

There had never really been a thought in my mind that I might actually get away with this. Not long term. I guessed there was a greater than zero chance of the missing nano-therapy going unnoticed, but the odds were deep in the decimals. My only objective was to get the tech home and into Mom before anyone could stop me. I figured the odds of that were maybe a little better than a coin toss? After that, I didn't really care what happened.

The self-driven cab arrived, and I climbed in. It took off as soon as I clipped in the seat belt. When presented with the option on my widget to pay for Premium Lane access, I accepted. Anxious energy hummed through my whole body as I zipped through morning traffic. Compared to my usual bus route, this was light speed. My left leg kept bouncing with agitation. When we finally pulled up to the curb outside our apartment building, I rocketed out and up the stairs.

"Zack? What's wrong?" Dad asked as I barged into our grubby flat. He was just taking his "breakfast" out of the fridge. A long-neck and a piece of cold pizza.

"Wait right there! Don't move!" I commanded, knowing that the "security system" that inhabited every square inch of – well – everywhere, would be scoured by OzCo's prosecutors. I couldn't have my father implicated in any way. He was better than nothing when it came to helping Mom.

I thundered past him and down the narrow hall to the bedroom. I felt like I was going to throw up. Shaking, I pulled the injector out of my pocket. It was a three-inch tube with an injection patch on one end and a big red button on the other. From what I had read, it didn't really matter what type of cancer it was, the little robots would adapt as needed once they were in her bloodstream.

I heard my dad coming down the hall. "Zee. What's going on? Is everything all right?"

Mom began to stir at the commotion, her dark brown eyes fluttered open, glazed with pain meds. Before I could stop myself, before Dad could enter the room, before Mom could stop me for my own sake, I pressed the injection patch to her forearm and hit the red button. A sharp hiss followed, along with an inhuman electronic voice saying, *"dose dispensed."*

About an hour later, we were sitting in our tiny living room, I in the only chair, my folks sitting on the broken-down sofa. I had laid out everything that had happened to my parents. I figured, if anything, my full and thorough explanation, and their honest in the moment reactions would only serve to exonerate them when the various recordings made by my widget and our smart TV were reviewed.

"I really still can't believe it worked." I said.

"Oh Zee. What did you do?" Mom's face had regained color as I had explained. Her breathing was strong and steady, and her eyes were clear of drugs and pain. But now, she wore an expression of mingled shock and terror.

"Fuck yeah. Way to stick it to those Mega-Fucks." Dad looked proud?

"Jeremy!" Mom scolded. "Your son is going to jail."

"We'll get him a lawyer! We'll stage a protest! This is still America damnit!"

Just then there was a thunderous banging at the door.

"Zachary Jones. This is OzCo Security. We have a warrant for your arrest. Open up!" came a man's booming voice from the other side.

Dad began to stand up, and I could see he was already building up a belligerent head of steam. His youth as a community organizer and activist was about to burst forth at the worst possible moment. I leaned forward and grabbed both of my parents' hands.

"Mom. Dad. Look at me." The door rattled in its frame again, and I waited until both of them turned their gazes back to me. "We can't fight this. There's no point. We'd just rack up a mountain of debt trying, and it would only get tacked onto my sentence."

"That's bullshit!"

"That's just reality Dad. This isn't the America you grew up in. Not anymore. The Megas own my ass now. Hell, they owned my ass before this, this won't be all that different."

Dad opened his mouth to continue the argument, then Mom spoke up, her voice firm and commanding. "He's right Jerry."

"Beth —"

Then the door exploded inward. *Seriously? A breaching charge?* Heavily-armed and armored Mega-Goons pounded into the room, screaming at us not to move. I was thrown to the floor and an armored knee was shoved into my back as my wrists were ziptied.

One of the greatest sights of my life was seeing - out of the corner of my eye, I was still eating carpet - my mom stand up under her own power, and without falter walk towards the door. She was stronger and more coherent than I had seen her in months.

"Zachary William Jones, you're under arrest for grand larceny. A judge has reviewed the security files of your theft and escape and has found you guilty. If you would like to question this verdict you may hire an attorney. If you cannot afford an attorney any expenses you incur in your defense will be added to your restitutions once you are convicted."

Chapter Three

"Inmate 81342." The scrubs-clad OzCo MedTech read the designation from her tablet in a disinterested monotone. The two burly guards stood flanking her in the doorway, arms crossed, casually lethal.

I glanced down at the plastic bracelet around my wrist and read the number under the barcode for the twentieth time. Not me. I didn't know whether to be relieved or pissed. *Just get me jacked in and on with this bullshit.* That was the practical side of me talking. Just as loud was the voice screaming, *What's going to happen to me? How do I do this shit? Which world are they going to stick me in? What does it feel like to die?*

Of course, generally speaking, everyone knew how the OVR World worked. The net was full of headlines every day with stats on all the new quest launches, clan wars, rankings in virtual sports from baseball to Quidditch, and high-level raid scores. Always the looming possibility to come away with life-changing CC for the real world. But I still had a lot of practical questions. Questions I had never really given much thought to since I had never seen my life going in the direction of having money to gamble with and worlds to conquer. And, I had never really planned on becoming and Inmate Gamer either.

"Inmate 81342. You're up!" The MedTech sounded annoyed now. Some dazed, middle-aged dude with glasses, sitting on the bench across from me, jolted to awareness after his neighbor gave him a sharp elbow.

"81342, let's move it!"

Lifting his manacled hands to wave in acknowledgement, the man struggled to his feet. Like the rest of us, he had ankle chains as well. They added to the eeriness of the room as they clanked against the cement floor while he hobbled to follow the impatient MedTech with her guards.

I let out a long sigh through gritted teeth while my stomach gurgled. No solid foods for 24 hours before entering your SimPod. Not that the OzCo cafeteria food at Florence Correctional Institution was anything worth writing home about. *Soylent Green is people!*

I closed my eyes, and let out another long, frustrated breath, trying to keep my anxiety from eating me from the inside out. *At least you qualified for the Gamer Program*, I reminded myself. *You could be in an Inmate Work Camp, drilling for oil in ANWAR, processing nuclear waste at Rocky Mountain Flats, or mining coal in West Virginia. Any of those would have amounted to a very short lifetime sentence.* After spending most of my life with a widget on my forearm, with

24/7 access to the web and entertainment, I found it unsettling to be so

alone with my thoughts. When I opened my eyes, a new batch of prisoners

was being escorted into the room, the racket of their shackles bouncing

about off the cement walls. An apple-shaped girl about my age plopped

down on the bench beside me.

"Shit a dick man! You look terrified. First time jacking in?" The girl

snickered. "Whatever you do, don't barf on me. There's no changing

clothes or showering before you get in the pod."

I let out another deep sigh through my clenched jaw. Surveying my

new neighbor, I guessed she was predominantly Native American, with

long, straight, black hair pulled back in a ponytail, dark rusty brown skin, a

dusting of freckles across her cheeks. At first, I thought she was stoned: her

eyes were dull, her round face slack. But her voice was quick and sharp,

almost cheerful. "It ain't so bad inside. This'll be my fourth jack, and to be

honest I like it better than being out there." She waved her hands around to

indicate, I assumed, the outside world.

"R-R-Really?"

"Yeah, man. You can be anything in there! Way better than the shit

show outside. Better than walking around in your actual body!" she

continued casually, maybe feeling smug about being in the know. "Of

course, they don't take such good care of your body when you're in these

38

prison pods. They wanna keep your brain firing at full capacity but that's pretty much all they care about for us 'cannon-fodder.' If you buy your own pod it's a whole different story, but for us, not so much. Spend enough time in one of these pods and eventually, you won't have much of a body left."

"Well, that answers one of my questions," I admitted, anxious to keep her talking. "I mean, I understand that SI will never match the plasticity of human thought, so the Megas farm any brain they can to generate crypts, but even they have to know that a brain without a body isn't going to live."

"There are plenty of brains out there. New ones being born every minute. But you think I looked like this when I first jacked in?" She leaned back and ran her hands up and down her plump body, inviting me to follow with my eyes. "I used to be in shape, played soccer and ran track. I was H-O-T-T, hot! Now my knees are shot, I got arthritis in my back and I ain't winning no beauty contests. I figure I've got five, maybe six years before I'm all washed up. Might as well spend'm in a body I can choose!"

She fell silent after her tirade, maybe regretting her blunt honesty. I slumped back against the wall and sourly processed what she had laid out there. What sort of life was I looking to have when I got out? I had to make this time worth it then. Aside from paying off my sentenced debt, I had to make as many extra crypts as I could. Maybe set Mom and Dad up for what time they had left. Not to mention myself. Good luck getting a legitimate job with a record of corporate theft and no skills aside from mopping and dusting. We sat silently through a couple more inmates being picked off by a rotating cast of techs and guards.

"How much you owe?" she asked companionably after seeming to shake off the melancholy that had swept over us both.

"Almost five million in restitutions to pay off." My empty stomach twisted and gurgled.

"Shit a dick! What'd you do, rob a bank?"

"Stole some meds," I admitted.

"Didn't take you for a druggy." She looked me up and down and kinda pulled away a bit. "Didn't think they let druggies into the Gamer Program. Not enough brain-power left to farm."

"Not drugs, *medicine*. Nano-bot therapy for my mom."

"Shit a dick." She seemed to use that term a lot. "Where'd you run into that?"

"Right place, right time I guess." With my raw nerves, I couldn't bring myself to elaborate further in that moment.

"And your mom? Did you get the stuff to her? Did it work?" This girl was now fully engaged, her eyes sparkling with this conspiratorial information.

"Yeah and yeah, I got them to her and they worked as advertised," The rapt attention and admiration of this girl I'd just met washed over me and soothed my anxiety somehow. It was the best feeling I'd had since saying goodbye to Mom.

A tech and guards re-entered the room. "Inmate 81348."

"Fuck. That's me."

"Hell yeah. Enjoy it." It was clear she couldn't wait to get jacked back in. But I wasn't ready. There was still so much I didn't know. I needed to stall for time, but that was not the guards' plan. They yelled out my number again as one of them started smacking his palm with his stun baton.

The girl reached over and grabbed my wrist as I stood on quaking knees. "You seem like a good kid. Can I give you some advice?"

"Yes. Please."

"Don't pick a Defender role. They take the most damage. You won't have a perception filter in there so damage equals pain. Go for Striker or Healer. But if you go Striker, pick something that uses Dexterity for defense over armor or specializes in ranged attacks," the girl explained in a rush of words. The guard called my number again.

"O-O-Ok?" I tried desperately to process her words.

She grinned at me, I think she could tell that I was overwhelmed. She rolled her glittering eyes in annoyance as they insistently called my number. She let go of my wrist and I turned to walk away.

"My handle's Macha," she called after me. "I'll see you inside. What's yours?"

"Inmate 81348, get your ass over here."

What's a handle? My name?

"I'm Zack. Zack Jones." I answered over my shoulder.

"Never mind, noob," she giggled. "It'll be your prisoner number until you earn enough crypts to change it. Now go! Don't want to get a beat-down before you even get started!"

Chapter Four

The guards kept an iron grip on my shoulders as the OzCo MedTech escorted us briskly down a long hall cement brick walled hallway. I struggled to shuffle my manacled feet along at their pace. Just another lamb to the slaughter as far as they were concerned.

Chin up and take it like a man. Don't let those Mega-Fucks get you down. I heard my dad's voice in my head. Followed swiftly by what I thought Mom would say, *Don't lose your head. Observe everything and work hard.* The pep-talk lasted about as long as it took to think it.

A door slid open to my left. The two guards hurled me in. Like the hallway, the walls of the cramped room were built from gray painted cement bricks, the floor was a single smooth slab of cement with several small grated drains embedded in it. At the exact center of the room was a gleaming white SimPod, basically a largeish egg-shaped plastic coffin with several touch screen displays mounted to its surface.

The pod's lid was propped open. Inside I saw a vague body outline in the cushions of the base and the lid. I knew enough about the process to know that the cushions hid the prods and rollers that would keep my body "alive" for the years I would be kept captive. A from what Macha had said, the prison pods were designed for just that, to keep the body alive so OzCo could farm my brain activity for their own purposes, nothing more. Nothing like the consumer pods that forced your body into fitness while you played. If you had the means, you could go into a pod a 600 lbs slob and come out a couple months later transformed into a Greek Adonis with washboard abs and bulging arms.

The girl, Macha, popped into my head again. The game had taken its toll on her body. She was my age and had been in three times already. What would ten years do to me? Crap, there had to be another way. *I'm smart, I can figure this shit out!*

All these thoughts took a handful of seconds as the crew around me scanned the plastic bracelet on my wrist, took my measurements from head to toe, shone a bright pen light in my eyes, took my blood pressure and weighed me, all while making minor adjustments to the pod. Dazed and practically limp, I complied with their prodding and orders.

My shackles were removed and my widget strapped to my wrist. Use of my widget and digital assistant, Al in my case, as a resource was one of the few benefits of regular players not automatically denied to me as an inmate. It was an obscure amendment of the Inmate Player Act when it was passed by Congress. While I didn't understand the reason for the egalitarian gesture, I was grateful for it.

I felt a bee sting at the back of my neck as they manhandled me into the pod, my cell, my new home. A wash of warm peace flowed over me. Suddenly I couldn't imagine resisting as they tucked me in and closed the lid.

Ice cold liquid gurgled up from somewhere around my feet, but I didn't care. Or, it wasn't exactly that I *didn't* care, I tried but found I *couldn't* care. Whatever they had shot into me was some powerful shit. It seemed I would soon drown and I wouldn't mind a lick.

The pod was dimly illuminated by several small LED screens and blinking indicator lights. There were words and numbers on the screens, but I couldn't focus long enough to understand them. Observing from somewhere outside my body, I saw a phallus-looking appendage emerge from the ceiling of the pod and shove my lips apart. I still couldn't care. Ot its own accord my jaw relaxed, letting it enter. I even closed my lips around it as I felt something plunge down my throat.

The freezing liquid was now covering my legs and about to spill across my chest. My nostrils filled with the smell of salt. The phallus now completed its job and sealed off my nose just as the ice-cold brine washed across my face. Fully submerged and serene, I awaited my fate. The last thing I remember was something suctioning against the back of my neck, then painlessly burrowing to my brainstem. Then nothing.

***

I wasn't wearing anything at all, except for my birthday suit. Looking down at the sight, I was immediately disappointed. I apparently wasn't starting with a new body. At least not yet. This was just the beginning, I told myself. Maybe I would still get a chance to power up.

Holding up my hand I examined it in detail. It looked like my hand. Exactly. Down to the little scar I'd gotten from a dog bite when I was twelve. This had to be a digital simulation, but it was so complete, I had fully crossed the uncanny valley. I reached up to touch my face. It felt real, entirely familiar.

Glowing words appeared floating in the air in front of me.

Welcome, Inmate 81348, to Game Management. Your Personal Digital Assistant is being loaded. Please wait...

A light blue pinwheel icon spun in the center of my vision, gradually becoming a darker blue to mark the progress. I stood there, naked, completely vulnerable while I waited for Al's program to sync with the

OVR World's servers. I knew every long-term player used some kind of

Synthetic Intelligence assistant, like Al, to help in their gameplay. However,

like most things having to do with the game, I was clueless as to the exact

details.

Your Personal Digital Assistant has been loaded to your Pod's Memory Core.

The spinning pinwheel turned uniformly dark blue and Al blinked into

existence beside me. He had on his usual garish attire, randomly selected

and appropriate to the fictional character he was based on. Today he wore a

sparkling silver suit jacket and bright orange slacks, with his ubiquitous

cigar between his teeth. In his hand was a multi-colored Ziggy interface to

"the future", the matching prop for Al from *Quantum Leap*.

"Yowzaa!" Al cried. "What a rush, Zee! I've never had so much

processing power!"

Al shivered all over and shook out his limbs. My digital assistant

looked around at the blank space surrounding us. This was the first time I'd

encountered Al in a truly virtual environment. Before this he'd always just

been a shouting face on my widget screen. I'd shifted through a couple of

assistant skins over the years, Johnny 5 from *Short Circuit*, Lt. Commander

Data from *TNG*, Mr. Fantastic from *The Fantastic Four*. In fact. Al had only

been my assistant's skin for a couple of weeks before I got locked up.

Considering how much time he and I were likely going to spend

together in this game, I was beginning to wish I'd had a different option loaded, like *Doctor Who's* Clara Oswald, *Marvel's* Black Widow, or maybe even Caprica Six from *Battlestar Galactica*. Either one certainly would have been more pleasant to look at, and gentler on my frayed nerves. But given that I was still completely naked, maybe it was best that I had the thoroughly unsexy Al.

Too late now, I told myself with a shrug.

"You ready to get to work, Al?" I asked.

"Ready when you are Zee baby!"

"Let's do it then." A thrill zipped through my entire body with the declaration.

"Let's get this show on the road! Beginning Character Generation!" Al pressed a button on his control pad.

A fully three-dimensional hologram of my thoroughly unimpressive body appeared in front of me. A glowing window hovered in the air over my right shoulder.

CHARACTER STATISTICS

Handle: Inmate 81348

Race: Human (default)

Role: Unselected

Class/Level: Unselected/0

ABILITIES

Strength (Endurance): 10 (10)

Strength Skills: Melee Combat, Athletics, Carrying Capacity

Dexterity (Defense): 10 (10)

Dexterity Skills: Ranged Combat, Acrobatics, Stealth, Sleight of Hand,

Open Lock. Reflex

Constitution (Hit Points): 10 (50)

Constitution Skills: Concentration, Fortitude

Intelligence (Arcane Mana): 10 (NA)

Intelligence Skills: Arcana, Investigation. Appraise, Disable Device. Forgery,

Lore

Wisdom (Faith Mana): 10 (11)

Wisdom Skills: Conviction. Perception, Survival, Tracking, Animal

Handling, Medicine, Willpower

Charisma (Inspiration): 10 (NA)

Charisma Skills: Imagination, Deception, Intimidation, Persuasion,

Influence

RACIAL SKILLS: None

RACIAL TALENTS: None

CLASS SKILLS: None

CLASS TALENTS: None

CARRIED EQUIPMENT: None

STORED EQUIPMENT: None

COMBAT STATISTICS

Weapon - Talent Modifier - Weapon Damage - Accuracy - Median Damage

None

ACHIEVEMENTS: None

TOTAL ABILITY POINTS: 5

CURRENT CRYPTOCURRENCY: 0.00

CURRENT DEBTS: 4,720,572.23 CC - OzCo Department of Corrections

CURRENT EXPERIENCE: 0

EXPERIENCE TO NEXT LEVEL: 500

A long, weary sigh escaped my lips as I studied the screen of Character Statistics. I'd played some pen and paper RPGs in middle school, and a few old school video game emulators on my widget. I recognized a lot of the terms in an abstract sense, but I was quite certain that the devil was in the details. I turned back to Al for advice.

"Have you downloaded the game's starter guides yet?"

"Um. Let me see if Ziggy's got that yet." Al frowned down at his glowing handheld Ziggy interface. He jabbed a couple buttons eliciting beeps and chirps from the device, then smacked the side of the prop, causing a squeal of protest. Then he nodded in satisfaction. "Yeah. We've got what you need, Zee."

"Where do we start?"

Al went still and pursed his lips in consideration as he studied his handheld, but also seemed to freeze completely in place - a sign that he was scanning large amounts of data - before answering, "You need to set up your basic character structure first. Choosing your Race, Role, and Class will have impacts for your entire character. Would you like me to provide you with reading material on those three options?"

"Yes, please." I licked my lips in anticipation. Finally, I'd have a chance to absorb some information on the game mechanics. Of course this would be a total crash course, compared to the months of preparation and planning that most gamers undertook.

Al jabbed a button on Ziggy and a flood of pop-up windows filled with text appeared in the air before me. Looking closer, I saw each window contained an in-depth description of a different Race, Class or Role. There wasn't really any order to what Al had presented either. In just a few seconds I saw headings for Centaur, Warlock, Elf, Striker, Bard, Monk, Defender, Dwarf.

"Woah!" I shouted in frustration. "Too much, Al!"

"How would you like this information organized?"

"Entries by category, Role, Race and Class, then alphabetical after that."

There was a flurry in the air as the windows arranged themselves into three stacks in my requested order. There were far fewer Roles stacked up than either Race or Class. So I started there. I found I could pick up each screen like a tablet. It was weightless and paper-thin, but still tactile.

Role described one's general purpose in the game. For example, a Defender was meant to stand up front and take as much damage as possible. A Healer was meant to stand back and cast healing and either buff or de-buff spells. Strikers were offensively focused, meant to do lots of damage, but didn't have the stats to take heavy hits. Controllers shaped the battlefield or influenced the actions of enemies. Unlike your Class or your Race, which were specific to the world you were playing on, your Role also translated to other worlds of OVR World, if I ever got that far. Each Role also came with suggested Classes. There were some Classes that were compatible with multiple Roles, and some that leaned heavily into just one Role.

I thought back on the rush of advice Macha had given me. Defenders were a bad idea, she'd said. Reading the Role description, I could see why. They were expected to stand up front pulling enemy attention or aggro to them and absorb most of the hits, while more fragile characters either did damage or used magic to support. Defenders had extra hit points and special talents to help them fulfill that role, but I could clearly see how being a Defender would literally hurt big time as an inmate player without the benefit of a perception filter.

With that in mind, I settled in and started reading through the much thicker pile of Class descriptions, discarding any Class that was labeled as Defender preferred. I'd occasionally ask Al to define a term or explain a game mechanic. My head started to spin when he started to explain the benefits of having a high Intelligence, Wisdom or Charisma score and how the OVR World SI would provide me with extra information with those statistics.

After several hours of reading and asking questions I finished the stack of Classes. I'd divided the Classes into three piles: *Interested, Maybe,* and *No Way*. Only then did I remember that I was still standing there entirely naked. I'd been standing there for hours and I wasn't at all tired, but I still felt an instinctive dislike for my complete nudity. Especially when Al got to stand there in a suit, an ugly suit, but a suit nonetheless.

"How do I get some clothes, Al?"

"Default threads will be selected for you after you've picked a Class."

"If I pick one now can I change it later?"

"Ziggy says nothing will be set in stone until you approve the final settings," Al answered after consulting his handheld.

"Let's try out being a Ranger then."

The Ranger class was at the top of my *Interested* pile. It was a Striker preferred class, but offered some nice versatility in strategy, letting me fight with a bow or melee weapons.

"You sure you wouldn't rather try a Bard, Zee?" Al inquired, waggling his eyebrows suggestively. "Musicians get all the babes."

"Ranger. Just do it, Al," I replied, sighing.

"You got it, boss." Al pressed a button on Ziggy. Upon making the selection, simple brown and leaf-green clothes appeared on both my body and my mirror avatar.

Next I started digging through the stack of Race options. This time, as I picked up each Race option to read it, the appearance of my duplicate instantly shifted to reflect that option. I got to see what I'd look like as an Elf, whip thin with narrow angular features, or a Dwarf, short and thickly built with a bristly beard. Somewhat disturbing was seeing myself as a Centaur. I thought I looked kind of cool as an Avian with dark feathers covering my entire body, stubby flightless wings sprouting from my shoulder blades, a sharp beak for a mouth and clawed bare feet.

All the races came with different basic talents and abilities, but also different vulnerabilities and weaknesses. I quickly narrowed my choices down to Human, Wild Elf and Half-Elf. All seemed to work well with being a Ranger. Human seemed to be the most versatile of the races, coming with eight extra Ability Points at character generation, and two extra Ability Points at each subsequent level, an extra Class Skill and an extra Talent. Wild Elves got a bonus to Dexterity and Wisdom, but also took a penalty to Strength. They had a heavy emphasis on wilderness settings, with bonuses to the skills for Stealth, Survival and Tracking. They also favored bows and had the ability to see in the dark. And Half-Elf seemed like the best of both worlds. No bonuses to stats, but also no penalties. I'd get five extra Ability Points to start and one extra Ability Point at each additional level, then pick up a shorter distance of night vision and get lesser bonuses to bows and woodland skills than a pure Elf.

I found myself toggling between the three options indecisively. I just couldn't picture myself as an Elf, narrow sharp features, and noticeably long pointed ears. Additionally, the penalty to my Strength seemed like a big drawback. But as a Human, I just looked too much like myself, and I didn't know how much time I wanted to spend customizing my appearance to change that. Half-Elf really seemed like the happy compromise. The default setting left me with a stubbly shadow of a beard, a look I could never manage in reality, and ears that were pointed, but less dramatically than the full Elf. Swallowing down my lingering doubts, I locked down my race at Half-Elf. Step three done.

With direction from Al, I found that when I focused on other statistics, a drop-down list of available options would appear. Many times there was an option to increase or decrease a particular skill, like Dexterity or Strength. All were pre-set at ten, which Al explained was the baseline for an "average human" or half-elf in my case. Al also pointed out that increasing one value, say my Strength, decreased my allotted Ability Points by the same amount, and I only had five points to work with. Also, many of my other stats altered themselves as I futzed with my base Abilities.

Raising my Dexterity would increase my Defense and Ranged Weapon Attack. Changing my Strength changed my Endurance and Melee Weapon Attack, or bumping my Wisdom increased my Faith Mana, my available power for Faith-based magic. I also found I could decrease a stat, all the way down to 1. Each decrease would buy me a corresponding ability point. Al cautioned me against dumping my stats too low, as it had a trickle down effect on all dependent abilities.

When I focused on the Skills or Abilities lines, I found a couple of entries already selected that seemed to come with my Race or Class, but when I tried to alter them a pop-up alert appeared saying *Training Required.*

"Skills will self-adjust as you work through the game. Or you'll be able to spend points on them when you level up," Al explained. "Not that you've ever had much cash, but it's a shame you're doing this as an inmate player, Zee."

"Why's that?" I asked.

"Regular players would be able to buy extra levels, equipment, and ability points right off the bat. Not to mention, you'd have had more world options than just Gygax. You could spend a weekend dog fighting in an X-Wing, swinging around old NYC like Spider-Man, or recovering the Maltese

Falcon. And that's just the action and adventure stuff, Zee! You should see the 'adult content' that the OVR Worlds have to offer..."

Tuning Al out while he spoke, I focused my attention on finalizing my allocation of Ability Points. As I was toggling my precious points from Strength to Dexterity to Constitution, I was pleased to find that as I tweaked my physical attributes, my flabby janitor's body shifted and changed. While trying to decide how pronounced I wanted my six-pack abs to look, I noticed one of the cells at the bottom of the Character Statistics screen changing as well. The Current Debt amount had gone up.

"Al!" My digital assistant was still droning on about all the more x-rated game options I was missing out on because of my inmate status. He went silent at my shout. "Why the hell did my debt increase?"

"Oh! That?" Al waved his hand dismissively. "It's nothing boss, just a bit of loose change."

"But shouldn't my debt be going down now that I'm jacked in?"

"Well yeah, it will. Once you're actually in the game." Al said.

"What the fuck is all this?" I waved my hands around at the emptiness around us. "It's not the real world! That's for sure!"

Al winced and shrugged his shoulders, "Relax, Zee. You're in your pod, but not yet 'in the game'. OzCo charges inmate players for time spent in Game Management. They had a couple of scaredy-cats try to spend their entire sentence in here instead of going out into the game."

"Why the hell didn't you tell me that?"

Staying in here hadn't been my intention - mostly because I just hadn't thought of it. But weren't they already farming the other nine-tenths of my brain that was not currently engaged? Was I not doing my best to get this shit done? Apparently not.

I hurried through the rest of the tweaks as best I could and when I was done, stepped back for one last look. Crap, I had forgotten about my handle. It still read Inmate 81348. I tried to change it, but found I couldn't edit that field. It cost 5 CC, and like all the paid features, I was locked out due to my status. I would have to go into OVR World with a handle screaming "I'm a noob and a low-life".

I reviewed my stats one last time.

CHARACTER STATISTICS

Handle: Inmate 81348

Race: Half-Elf

Role: Striker

Class/Level: Ranger/0

ABILITIES

Strength (Endurance): 13 (16)

Strength Skills: Melee Combat, Athletics, Carrying Capacity

Dexterity (Defense): 13 (13)

Dexterity Skills: Ranged Combat, Acrobatics, Stealth, Sleight of Hand, Open Lock. Reflex

Constitution (Hit Points): 13 (65)

Constitution Skills: Concentration, Fortitude

Intelligence (Arcane Mana): 10 (NA)

Intelligence Skills: Arcana, Investigation. Appraise, Disable Device. Forgery, Lore

Wisdom (Faith Mana): 11 (22)

Wisdom Skills: Conviction. Perception, Survival, Tracking, Animal Handling, Medicine, Willpower

Charisma (Inspiration): 10 (NA)

Charisma Skills: Imagination, Deception, Intimidation, Persuasion, Influence

RACIAL SKILLS: Half-Elf Wilderness Skills: Survival (+1), Stealth (+1), Tracking (+1)

RACIAL TALENTS: Half-Elf Flexibility (+5 AP at Level 0, +1 AP), Nightvision (15'), Elven Bow Proficiency +1 Level

CLASS SKILLS: Athletics (+1), Stealth (+1), Survival (+1), Tracking (+1)

CLASS TALENTS: Archery (Level 0), Two-Weapon Fighting (Level 0)

EARNED SKILLS: None

EARNED TALENTS: None

CARRIED EQUIPMENT: Standard Clothes, Short-sword, Dagger, Short-bow, Arrows x20

STORED EQUIPMENT: None

COMBAT STATISTICS

Weapon - Talent Modifier - Weapon Damage - Accuracy - Median Damage

Shortsword - 0 - 20 - 7 - 59

Dagger (off-hand) - 0 - 14 - 7 - 40

Shortbow - 0 - 18 - 7 - 57

ACHIEVEMENTS: None

TOTAL ABILITY POINTS: 10

CURRENT CRYPTOCURRENCY: 0.00

CURRENT DEBTS: 4,720,602.76 CC - OzCo Department of Corrections

CURRENT EXPERIENCE: 0

EXPERIENCE TO NEXT LEVEL: 500

At least my avatar had a little more muscle on his bones, but I was still not feeling very good about myself when I hit the "Done" button. A pop up appeared before me.

Character Generation Complete.

Are you ready to spawn?

Yes

No

"See you later Al," I said as I focused on the *Yes* button.

"Good luck boss! Go get'em!" Al cheered, far too enthusiastic.

With no other real choice, I selected *Yes* and my vision dissolved in a shower of pixels.

Chapter Five

The short-term pods that I'd used before weren't rigged for deep-immersion like my prison pod. While short-term pods still provided direct neural interface, giving full sensory input, they were meant for quick trips to the OVR Worlds. A night of clubbing with - like I'd done before - usually called for a rental pod. The Megas and the remnants of the government also used short-term pods for their lower level staff to save on time and money. Why bother flying people from all over the globe for face-to-face conferences any more? And working from home took on a whole new dimension when everyone could *feel* like they were in the same office building while in reality they were spread across the world. Most companies preferred podded employees whenever possible; who needs an office building? And the corporate overlords could monitor productivity much more closely when every movement could be played back at will. Big

Brother was most definitely watching when you were a podded Mega-Corp employee.

Details and sensations were never quite as deep or rich in a short-term pod. That said, this convict pod wasn't top of the line either. Let's just say my entrance into Gygax was not smooth. My legs instantly buckled beneath me, my vision jumped and the axis of this make-believe world spun.

I was a mess; the ground felt spongy, the air refused to enter my lungs and an overwhelming sharp odor filled my nose. Slowly, very slowly, things began to steady. I caught a full breath of crisp clean air, the dirt below me seemed to solidify and the spinning eventually came to a halt.

Sitting still, I focused on breathing and registering the sensations around me. Warm sunlight on my face. A sky above me so blue it was almost unrecognizable, I'd never seen the real sky look so pure. Fat, billowing clouds floated up there too, not the constant brownish grey haze that I was used to. This world was completely alien and scary, yet somehow beautiful at the same time. And there were trees. Thick towering trunks with leaves spanning every shade of green. Don't get me wrong, I'd seen trees before. But these things were glorious giants. And so green, and everywhere, surrounding me. Nothing like the stunted sticks that passed for trees in the "city parks." Primordial trees like these, I'd only ever seen in movies and TV. They reminded me of Fangorn Forest from *Lord of the Rings* or Sherwood Forest from one of the Robin Hood films.

Feeling a bit like Bambi, I stood on shaky legs and marveled at the virtual world. I'd had no idea it would be so...complete. Even down to the, yeah, the smell. I just about choked on it; it felt like it was going to eat my nose up. It was just the combination of actual fresh air and pine trees. Air so crisp and pure that my lifetime spent surrounded by cement, steel and garbage had made entirely alien to me. My feet finally under me, I could breathe cautiously through my mouth and my muscles seemed to respond to my demands.

"All right...where the hell am I?"

So far, all I knew was that I was standing on a narrow dirt path, thick green vegetation covering the ground on either side. Gentle sunlight, filtered by the thick canopy overhead, illuminated the area. A soft, cool breeze rustled the leaves and whispered across my skin. In the distance, I could hear gurgling water, the songs of birds, and the breathing life of wilderness. At first, it seemed frighteningly quiet compared to the heaving mass crammed into Denver, but as I stood there, it started to sound like gentle music all around me.

Kneeling down on the path, I reached out to run my hands through the leaves of a lush fern. They were smooth and pliant in my hands. Even when I knew they weren't, they looked and felt entirely real. Even when clubbing I had always felt the difference between real and simulated. But here? *Sure feels real to me.*

As I looked around, ghostly icons appeared on the periphery of my vision. When I focused my attention on the icons they became more solid and slid into focus. I found colored bars measuring my Hit Points, Endurance, Mana, and Experience. There were also menus for Inventory, Map, Character Stats, and Quests.

I took my first few steps in this new world when without warning a window popped into my vision, almost completely blocking my view.

Welcome, Inmate 81348. You have entered the World of Gygax and are located in the Orientation Zone of Rowling Valley. You are currently in Greenwood Forrest, the Spawn Point for all wilderness themed character classes.

Lethal Player-vs-Player Combat is disabled in Rowling Valley. However, beware of Monsters, Animals and Natural Hazards. They can kill you if you are not careful!

Maximum Player Level: 5 - Once you reach Level 5 you will graduate from the Orientation Zone and will be required to leave.

Warning! *You have connected as an Inmate Player. You will not have access to Perception Controls until you are released from incarceration and your Character is converted to regular status.*

Good Luck!

I swiped at the window as Al had shown me. The hovering text vanished. I pulled up my Inventory screen, styled like a backpack, and chose a short sword and dagger. The items appeared in my hands, while the scabbards for both appeared on the belt around my waist. Al had also told me I could designate five items for quick access. I designated my short-bow and arrows. Immediately I felt the string of the bow across my chest and the curve of its shaft across my back as it was magically slung over my shoulder. I could also feel the leather strap for my quiver over the other shoulder.

Experimentally, I swung my sword and dagger and grew accustomed to their weight and feel. I'd never handled anything more dangerous than a kitchen knife before. Even the dagger was considerably longer and more dangerous-looking than I had imagined. Without really knowing what I was doing, I tried to mimic some of the movie moves, like from *Gladiator* or *Lord of the Rings*. I jumped into one balletic move after another, imagining downing one assailant, then his imaginary buddy. Thankfully, I managed not to cut myself with any of those initial clumsy thrusts and slashes. I definitely wasn't Aragorn. Fuck, I wasn't even Frodo.

After my impromptu performance, I scoured up and down the path, hoping I hadn't been observed. When the coast appeared clear I gazed out through the woods all around me. Out in the real world, I had often felt lonely, but there had always been people packed densely around me. *Here, I'm alone! Really alone!* I thought with a thrill of excitement followed by wonder as I realized I didn't mind it.

Both directions of the path, out into a meadow and deeper into the forest, had absolutely no other people. Not a soul, not a building of any kind, just birds flying in a blue sky, a squirrel leaping from one branch to another, and the rustle of branches from a gentle breeze.

The elation was short lived, though, as I suddenly shuddered at a thought. Was there a monster around the corner on the path ahead of me? Had I landed in the wrong place? Was there anyone else in this world? I focused on the Map menu in my vision and to my relief, a circular map popped up before me.

There was a blinking icon with a miniature "me" in the center, the path I was on leading up and to the right, as well as down and to my left. There didn't seem to be much shown on the map other than the path, trees and a creek up in the right-hand quadrant. I sheathed my dagger and sword to free my hands. I reached up to the map with my right hand and pinched my fingers together, hoping the map would zoom in. It did. I spread my fingers apart and the map obligingly zoomed out.

Various icons appeared as the map expanded. Mountains showed to my left, a lake appeared at their base. Off to my right, there were a number of icons. I concentrated on one. "Orc Nest" popped up with a cartoonish rendition of monsters I had no desire to meet at the moment. I checked another. "Goblin Cave" did not seem any more inviting than the orc nest. I turned my head to the right and the map moved with me, gaining additional details as I shifted my view. What appeared to be the valley floor lay further off to my right and as I continued to turn a number of paths and roads seemed to be converging. I continued my visual sweep and found a destination that I hoped would offer comfort and security. It appeared to be a nice little walled-community. The icon read "Village of Elmore." I scanned the map for the most direct route. It seemed a simple enough path with no "nests" or "caves" too close. Re-arming myself with my sword and dagger, I headed down the trail, determined to reach safety before nightfall.

As I walked, I studied my surroundings in more detail. I found that if I focused my attention on any particular plant or tree, my Survival Skill would activate and identify the specific type of vegetation and notable qualities. That was pretty cool, though everything I'd looked at so far indicated that it was inedible and, believe it or not, my stomach was growling like I was hungry. I also noticed that after I'd climbed up a particularly steep incline along the path, my Endurance bar had decreased. When I stopped and rested for a moment, the bar slowly refilled.

As the map had indicated, I soon reached a small stream. The path crossed the water, apparently using several large flat stones as a crossing. At the bank of the stream, I noticed several tracks in the soft, damp earth. I knelt to examine them closer and my Tracking Skill activated. Text appeared next to the marks identifying them as deer tracks. The tracks began to glow with yellow light and as I looked around, several more prints illuminated off in the direction the deer had approached from and then left by.

I considered following the deer. I was a Ranger, after all. From what I'd read during Character Generation, hunting wild game seemed like it should be comfortably within my wheelhouse, and not too dangerous for my first encounter. While I contemplated the option, I heard a sudden chorus of shouts in the distance, along with the clang of metal.

Was it a battle? I used the flat stones to hop across the stream and headed off towards the sound at a slow jog. I crested a short hill and saw that the trail I'd been following wound down and connected with a wider graveled road. Down on the road, I saw what I guessed was a farmer's wagon, loaded with baskets of produce. A trembling boy stood up on the seat of the wagon with a loaded crossbow. On the ground, the farmer wielded a pitchfork, trying to fend off four short creatures with leathery green skin, massive, pointed ears and clawed, bare feet, all swinging crude looking stone axes.

As I focused on the creatures, red text appeared above each of their heads.

Goblin Bandit Level 1

There was a small, red bar beneath the text, and when the farmer lunged forward and managed to stick one of the goblins with his pitchfork the bar beneath the struck goblin's name shortened by half. I focused on the farmer then and saw blue text over his head, Farmer Hoggins. There was a red bar under his name as well, but it was nearly gone.

The farmer jumped back from his attack and narrowly avoided the ax swings of the attacking goblins. A window popped into my vision.

Quest Offer

Goblin bandits have attacked a local farmer on the road to Elmore. Will you help him?

Exp Reward: 25

CC Reward: 5

Accept

Decline

Without hesitation, I reached out and tapped the "Accept" option. Tightening my grip on my sword and dagger, I took a nervous gulp of fresh air then charged down the trail toward the fight. Immediately, I was distracted by a ghostly, grey image running just ahead of me. It seemed to be mirroring my movements, but as I read the text that appeared in the top of my vision I started to understand.

Mimic the movements of your Combat Training Guide. Your Combat Guide will calculate your optimal movements and strikes to defeat your foe based on your combat rankings.

I stopped short, processing this new feature. The guide kept running for a step or two, then zipped backwards to surround my body. It now had a green tinge that stood out about an inch all around my limbs and body. I raised my sword arm and the green haze went along with the movement until I stopped. The green shadow kept rising, quickly changing from green

70

to grey to red. Instinctively, I raised my arm higher to match the movement of this new ghost. As I did, the shadow turned to grey, and when I had matched the shadow completely it turned green. Obviously, the objective was to stay in the green for my best chance at survival.

Like the old Dance Dance Revolution or Guitar Hero but for fighting, I thought.

Thinking I might miss out on the battle, I resumed my charge toward the conflict, all in green. My guide slowed as I reached the road, so I did as well. The goblins were apparently not very observant, as none of them sensed my approach. My guide "told" me to raise my sword arm high while jutting my dagger out into what I figured was a defensive stance. I did my best to match the guide's movements and with a minimum of grey or red, I managed a massive if clumsy strike against one of the goblins. Bone-jarring force shot up my arm while oily brown goblin blood splattered across my face, vanishing almost immediately.

My guide kept moving in anticipation of a new attack as I watched the results of my first killing blow. My initial instinct was to look away, but there was suddenly nothing to look away from. The bloody creature I had cleaved was just a pile of dust in the already dusty road. Text appeared before my eyes.

Goblin Bandit Killed: 25 Exp

Achievement Earned: First Kill 5 Exp

Achievement Earned: Backstabber - Surprise Attack Talent Unlocked!

Astonished, I looked around for my guide. It was two feet behind me, all in red, with its sword arm at shoulder height and its dagger out slightly from its body, protecting its midsection. With arms and knees rattling, my vision blurred and my head spinning, I stepped back and tried to get into the green. Before I managed, however, two of the remaining goblins turned on me yellow pointy teeth bared in snarls.

Instinctively, I fell back even further. I was pleased to see my guide stay green as long as I kept my sword high and my dagger covering my midsection. Maybe it was for the best that both goblins disengaged with the farmer and without hesitation rushed me. I didn't have time to think about the gore my first strike had caused or the nausea that was rising in my thankfully empty stomach. I had to fight.

I'll admit, I was in the red for the rest of the battle. My footwork was not even close, my strikes were late and lacked the follow-through. Maybe I should have started with just one weapon out? One of the goblins managed to land a heavy blow to my leg, knocking away a third of my HP. Sharp pain lanced up my leg and I cried out. The other goblin struck two glancing blows to my arm and midsection, taking a few points away with each hit. Teeth gritted against the pain, I soldiered on. As soon as the second was dispatched a text box appeared in the upper right-hand of my vision.

Goblin Bandit Killed: 25 Exp

HP: 10 HP Lost. 31 of 70 HP Remaining!

Distracted by the text, I was completely out of position when my guide turned towards the final goblin. *Crap, isn't the farmer going to do anything?* I wondered while scrambling back, but the goblin's hatchet-sized ax ripped into my forearm.

Goblin Bandit Attack: 15 HP Lost. 16 of 70 HP Remaining!

I stumbled, trying to ignore the pain and regroup. The ghostly red image of my guide dissolved and reappeared to mirror my current position. My guide had its weapons raised up, while mine were down by my side. Lifting my weapons, I mirrored the guide's position.

Just in time! The goblin's next attack clanged against my sword. I followed my guide to sweep the attack away, then started to get the hang of the fight. I lunged forward to stab with my dagger, staying in the green for once. I clipped the goblin in his shoulder and his health bar dropped by a quarter. My guide continued to glide through the strike and step forward, crowding the goblin so he couldn't make any hefty swings with his ax. My guide showed me to block the goblin's ax-wielding hand with my sword while I stabbed and sliced up close and personal with my dagger. I devoted all of my attention to mirroring my guide and soon the final goblin was dust on the ground.

As the last goblin fell, more text appeared.

Achievement Earned: Goblinslayer 5% Bonus Damage when fighting Goblins

Achievement Earned: Good Samaritan - +20% to Charisma skills when interacting

with Friendly NPCs

Quest Complete: Save Farmer Hoggins 25 Exp, 5 CC

I dismissed the text as another window appeared.

Loot

Stone Hatchet x4 - Estimated Value 0 CC

Rotten Hide Armor (small) x4 - Estimated Value 0 CC

12 CC

I touched the screen for the twelve CC and it was added to my account, along with the five CC I'd earned from my Quest. I also stowed one of the stone hatchets in my "backpack" inventory. I doubted I'd fight with it, but figured I might need to chop firewood or something. Then I swiped the window away. Farmer Hoggins was standing by his wagon waiting stone-still for me to finish.

"Thank you, kind adventurer, for aiding my son and me. You saved our lives! How can we repay you?" Farmer Hoggins exclaimed when I finally gave him my attention. His words sounded stilted and scripted to my ear.

The farmer must be an NPC, a Non-Player Character. NPCs, controlled by the OVR World Synthetic Intelligences, populated many of the virtual worlds in the game. Players wanted to be heroes, or villains, not wenches, blacksmiths, or farmers. It occurred to me that what I'd just gone through was probably a pretty standard "beginner's quest."

"I…." Just then I realized I was breathing hard from the fight, and my Endurance bar was nearly empty. "…I was happy to help…ummm…good farmer. If you're traveling to the village of Elmore, maybe I can hitch a ride?"

Farmer Hoggins smiled. The smile was off…just wrong. He looked real enough. His skin was tan from the sun, with crow's feet around the eyes and sweat on his brow from the heat of the day and exertion of battle. Hell, I even picked up the slightly sour smell of body odor. The farmer walked and talked, if a little woodenly, but his chocolate brown eyes had no depth, no sparkle…no intelligence. A shudder crept up my spine and I found myself praying this was just the economy model NPC, developed for the less engaging parts of the game. So much for overcoming the uncanny valley.

"Joyfully! We would happily accept your company! Please join my son, Billy, and me on the wagon!"

I saw now that the boy had blue text over his head labeling him Billy Hoggins. Billy smiled at me. His gaze also lacked that genuine human spark. I suppressed another uncomfortable shiver, and favoring my injured arm and leg, climbed up on the driving bench with the farmer and his son.

Chapter Six

The wagon ride to Elmore proceeded without further incident, though OVR World continued to impress me with its beauty and shocking realism. After hearing my virtual stomach growl - damn realism - Farmer Hoggins offered me an apple from his load. I gratefully accepted the apple and crunched into it, juice spilling down my chin. The flavor, bright and crisp, filled my mouth like no apple I'd ever eaten before. I devoured the fruit while the wagon bounced down the road. Shock absorbers clearly hadn't been invented yet. When I finished the apple, a new notification appeared.

Apple consumed. 15% Bonus to Endurance Regeneration for 5 minutes!

With the new buff in place my Endurance bar began to recharge itself noticeably faster than when I'd just been sitting idle. Hoggins offered me another apple and I eagerly accepted it. The buff didn't stack to 30%

recharge, but the second apple added another 5 minutes onto the duration of the buff.

While I was munching away, we passed from under the canopy of towering trees and into a rolling countryside of green hills dotted by smaller, broader trees. The sky overhead was an infinitely deep blue, specked with fluffy white clouds. *The programmers must have taken artistic license with the beauty of something as simple as a clean sky. Or did we really fuck up the real thing that bad?*

Farmer Hoggins told me that we'd be safe now that we were out of Greenwood Forest. Taking the NPC's word for it. The tension I'd been holding in my shoulders ever since killing the goblins released. I tossed away the second apple core and began to explore more details of my user interface. I needed to find the settings menu and make some tweaks. For one thing, the text notifications in the center of my vision were pretty distracting. I ended up finding the visual settings accidentally when I went to swat at a fly that had landed on my forehead.

The menu screen popped up in the air in front of me and I found a list of options that I could adjust. Looking over at Hoggins and his son, I wondered if the NPCs could see the screen. However, they didn't seem to take any notice. After some exploration, I found the notifications menu and adjusted the opacity, size and placement of my text alerts. Now, instead of popping up dead center in my vision, they'd scroll across the bottom of my vision, and would automatically fade after repeating three times or after I consciously dismissed them. There were more settings including Audio, Chat, Combat Guide, and Parental Filters, but I left them alone for now. I took note that the Perception Filter menu was entirely grayed out and unselectable.

As we drew closer to the village I closed the settings and marveled at the detail of this contrived world. We passed small farms, with NPC peasant families tending crops and hanging laundry to dry. Almost all stopped in their boring simulated lives to give us a wave and a friendly greeting. On the crumbling urban streets I'd left behind, or in the dark musty halls of my apartment building, no one was nearly so friendly. In my neighborhood, you generally avoided making eye contact with anyone you didn't already know. The less I knew about my neighbors and the less they knew about me, the better.

Further on we came upon a sleepy flowing river and a moss-covered stone bridge. Upstream from the bridge, I could see a few short falls and the slowly turning water-wheel powered mill. The closest point of comparison I had to the mill were the shuttered and crumbling factories or the barely maintained wind turbines.

We eventually began to encounter other players. I could tell they were players from the white text that hovered over their heads denoting their handle, level, class and race. Reactions from the players that saw me ranged from glares of distaste to quick dismissal to cautiously friendly nods of acknowledgement.

For my part, I couldn't help but stare at most of the players I encountered. Almost to a one they were decked out in amazing costumes and even more outrageous bodies. I saw a massive centaur paladin with a shining breast plate and matching barding for his horse body. Then a prancing gnome wizard wearing purple flowing robes with glittering stars sewn across the fabric. There was an eye-catching Nordic goddess in what seemed like an impractical chainmail bikini. And a stocky dwarven druid with a massive wooden club and a green beard woven with twigs and leaves.

Even closer to town, I saw other inmate handles, but even more custom handles. Some handles were entirely on theme with the setting, like *Sir Roderick Trueheart*, or *Idus the Wise*. Others were clearly attempts to get a popular name through creative spelling. It was like trying to decrypt vanity license plates, a wizard named *M3rl1n* or a ranger named *4r4g0rn or 4r4th0rn*. That one was a stretch. There were handles that were complete compromises to popularity, like *DreadPirateRoberts_3871011*. There were also handles that were entirely out of place or seemingly random like *Jellybean6969* or *Fart_M4st3r*.

The narrow dirt road that Hoggins and I had been bouncing along, merged with a wider cobbled highway and the traffic (foot, mounted and wagon) grew thicker. I started trying to guess at a player's class or race

79

without looking at the text over their head. I quickly grasped that robes and a lack of heavy weapons marked magic users, and that armor, swords and bows were indicators of a warrior-class. Something else became obvious as I saw more NPCs. Farmer Hoggins and his son were not alone when it came to that dullness in their eyes. I could easily spot NPCs at a distance. Oftentimes their movements seemed stiff or jerky. And up close that spark of genuine humanity was always missing from their gaze. Like staring into the face of a mannequin.

A wooden palisade, probably fifteen feet tall, surrounded the village of Elmore. NPC guards in studded leather armor, carrying ax-headed polearms, stood sentry at the gates while a near constant stream of player and NPC traffic moved past. The farmer drove us through without being stopped.

Inside the walls, Elmore looked like a Disney version of a medieval village. I half-expected to see some starry-eyed pretty princess dancing around singing about her heart's desire, with the rest of the town as chorus. Wood-framed houses with thatched or mossy wood-shingled roofs framed meandering roads with no seeming patterns or organization. The village smelled considerably better than I imagined a medieval village actually would have. Woodsmoke, fragrant flowers, and clean humanity took the place of rancid meat, rank body odor and open sewage. The village was filled with the sounds of people hustling about, a mix of both players and NPCs.

Towards the center of the village, I started to see sturdier stone buildings that appeared to be various merchant shops and a two-story tavern and inn named the White Horse Inn. The inviting scent of roasting meat drifted to me from the establishment and my stomach rumbled again.

"I'll get off there, at the Inn," I instructed Farmer Hoggins.

Hoggins nodded and pulled his wagon to a halt in front of the Inn's doors. "You have my gratitude, Inmate 81348. If you ever need anything from me, just say the word."

I felt the urge to correct Hoggins and give him my actual name, but shrugged it off. What was the point? "I just did what anyone would do. Thanks for the ride."

I hopped to the ground and little Billy Hoggins waved goodbye as the farmer coaxed his ox into motion. I waved back on reflex, only feeling a little silly a heartbeat later. Sure, they weren't real, but it didn't hurt to be polite.

Turning toward the White Horse Inn, I heard raucous voices and fiddley music coming from the windows. Really, it smelled and looked nicer than most restaurants I'd seen in the real world. Of course, restaurant dining usually involved visiting some Mega-Corp chain for me.

The heavy wooden doors of the Inn swung open and three players emerged. White player tags appeared over their heads as they stepped through the doorway. I immediately noticed a small circled C, like a copyright symbol, next to each of their handles. I'd noticed it on several other players previously, but hadn't yet found out what the marks denoted.

Lute Eveningstar ©, Level 2 Wizard, Elf

Brother Marl Rockport ©, Level 2 Cleric of Ares, Dwarf

Markus Atrius ©, Level 2 Fighter, Human

Lute was a strikingly attractive Asian woman with amber skin and raven black hair pulled back from long tapering ears. She wore forest green robes and carried a gnarled wooden staff that looked to be a thin tree branch. Marl had a hard-as-weathered-granite expression, with pale skin and rosy cheeks beneath a fiery red curly beard. He wore a bulky mix of plate armor and chainmail on his stout frame, and carried a massive war-mace, slung over one shoulder. Markus wore a full suit of glittering chainmail and carried a massive halberd in one hand. Markus had dark black skin, a short but thick black beard, and a shaved scalp.

Marl and Markus surveyed me in a glance, while Lute stared off unconcernedly over my head. I don't know if it was my Level 0 standing or my inmate handle, but the cleric and fighter seemed to immediately dismiss my existence. The three players moved down the stairs to the street and without a word flowed around me like I was a rock in a stream. I shrugged and moved up the stairs and caught the door before it had fully swung shut. I stepped into the inn, more than a bit anxious as to what I was getting into.

The room had surprisingly high ceilings. But as I took stock of my surroundings, the ceiling height instantly made sense, standing at the bar or loitering in the crowd, of clearly non-human races, including a chestnut centaur and white furred minotaur, who were well over seven feet tall. I swallowed hard and tried to ignore that new detail. There was no Player-vs-Player violence allowed here, right? Should be safe. This wasn't the *Mos Eisley Cantina*.

Sturdy wooden tables with a mix of benches and chairs filled much of the room while more intimate booths lined the walls. To my left was a massive fieldstone fireplace burning merrily along. In the middle of the room was the large, U-shaped bar. On the back wall I saw a swinging door leading back to what I guessed was the kitchen, and beside that a narrow staircase, probably leading to the guest rooms above. The large, crowded room smelled of woodsmoke, alcohol and food mostly, and once I got over my initial intimidation, I decided it had a warm, almost homey feel to it.

There were probably thirty or more players in the room, individually or in small groups, along with a number of NPCs moving about, delivering drinks or clearing tables. I noticed only the NPCs had names floating over their heads, but for the first time, there was no text over any of the players' heads.

Several players throughout the room took note of my arrival and then quickly dismissed me. It wasn't nearly as blatant as the dismissal I'd received from the trio exiting the bar. Just another new face, not recognized and written off. Clearly this wasn't *Cheers* or at least I wasn't Norm. No one knew my name here.

I spotted an open stool at the bar and took the seat. A heavy-set human NPC with a stained apron and the name Travis the Innkeeper in blue letters over his head moved over to me. Travis had a balding head but a thick wiry salt and pepper beard down to his chest. His cheeks were plump and rosy. The picture of a hospitable fantasy innkeeper.

"What'll it be?" Travis asked, his accent vaguely British.

I glanced around for menus and didn't see any. "Umm...what's good?"

Travis laughed boisterously. "If you ask me wife, everything! She does the cookin. So don't let her 'ear you say different."

"Cheeseburger?" I wondered if the game's meat would taste like the vat grown "miracle meat" I'd grown up eating.

Travis looked confused. "Cheese what?"

I frowned at the flat-eyed NPC's confusion. Clearly I was missing something. Were there really no menus in this place? My stomach gurgled again. Then I felt the light touch of a hand at the small of my back and felt someone step up close beside me.

"Maybe I can help, sweetie," purred a soft feminine voice.

I looked over to find sparkling red eyes - definitely the eyes of a player - set in an Aphroditesque face with dark black skin, framed by long sterling silver wavy hair. When I said her skin was black, it wasn't any shade of human skin tone that I'd ever seen in life or on screen. Equally disconcerting and enticing, it was black like polished obsidian and seemed to drink in the illumination around her. Tapering pointed ears poked out of her lustrous hair. She smelled, enticingly, of crushed lavender and spices. This was a special type of elf that I'd just read about hours ago in Character Generation, but for the life of me I couldn't remember the name of the subrace in that moment. I licked my lips reflexively at the puckered pout on her painted red lips and tried to find some charming words.

"Uhhh…" That's me, *Captain Smooth Moves*. Mothers, lock up your daughters!

"You just got here I take it? First timer?" the woman asked. She stepped in closer to me, her arm snaking around my waist and soft supple breasts covered in a low-cut silky purple blouse pressed to my side.

"Ummm…." This was just turning out to be pathetic. I really didn't have much practice at this.

She giggled and I felt her ample chest heave gently against my arm.

Finally my brain sputtered to life again and I discovered my long lost linguistic skills.

"Yeah!"

Too loud! I cleared my throat and tried again, my cheeks flushing. "Yeah...yes...yup. Just jacked in this morning."

"Wonderful!" Her thick pouty lips spread in a wicked, implication-laden grin. "I love virgins."

"Well I'm not…" I instantly felt compelled to set the record straight on that count but lost the train of thought as the girl giggled breathlessly again.

"I'm Zack?" I finally managed to choke out.

"Are you Zack or not?" the girl teased.

I grit my teeth and tried to get some control over myself. "I'm Zack. And you are?""

"Dirzbryn Baenmtor." She delicately traced the tips of her fingers up and down my spine. I shivered with pleasure. The longer I looked at her, the more I thought that there was something vaguely familiar about her face, beneath the exotic skin tone and elvish features. I wondered if she'd modled it after a real person.

"D-D-Dir-zzz-b-b-bryn?" I asked. The name, which had rolled off her tongue so effortlessly, felt clumsy and very foreign in my mouth. "Where's that name from?"

"It's Drow, dark elf. It means 'Dream Assassin' of the House 'Blessed by the Abyss'. Catchy. No?" The tone of her voice made it sound like I was incredibly slow, but adorable, like an untrainable puppy. Her gently glowing red eyes glittered and she winked at me. "No real names in here, sweets. You can just call me Bryn."

Oops. Couldn't really unring that particular bell.

"Bryn?" I tried the name out and managed not to stutter this time.

"That's it!" Bryn leaned in and gave me a soft kiss on the cheek. Then she whispered in my ear, her lips grazing my skin, "I'll give you *lots* of practice saying my name if you want."

Her teeth bit down on my earlobe and gently tugged. Apparently despite my skin being virtual, I could still get goosebumps. I also discovered an entirely new sensation when my pointed ears burned with flush. On an instinctual level, I felt like an insect caught in a web, and this Bryn was the spider.

"Your tips are bright red, sweetie," Bryn purred, one nimble finger teasing the pointed tip of my ear. "How cute."

"Uhhhhhh…." Yup. My language center had crashed again. Damn it, I may not have ever been a cassanova, but I wasn't usually this big of a spaz! But then, I'd never had a woman just walk up and start hitting on me either.

Still toying with my sensitive pointed ears, Bryn turned her glowing eyes to Travis, who was silently waiting for us. "Maybe we should have some Spring Wine to celebrate your first day? Something dark and rich!"

Travis looked at me expectantly. Head spinning, I was about to nod my head when I heard the clomp of heavy boots and felt a looming presence behind us. A hand roughly pulled Bryn's hand from my hip. She hissed at the intrusion. I heard the ring of coins hitting the wood floor beneath my stool.

"I doubt he can afford that, Brynny. Even if you weren't about to pick his pockets clean," said a stern male voice.

Bryn stepped away from me and I turned to see her red eyes glaring at a tall blond human man with a action movie star handsome square-jawed artfully grizzled face. The man had on sturdy leather armor, a gleaming metal breastplate, and a massive two-handed sword like Mel Gibson's in *Braveheart* - a claymore? - slung over his back. One of the man's leather gauntleted hands was clamped around Bryn's slender wrist.

"Lemorak!" Bryn seethed. "How dare you--"

"How dare I?" Lemorak demanded, cutting her off. "How dare I keep you from taking advantage of some poor unsuspecting noob before he's even got his head on straight?"

"It's none of your business!" Bryn snapped back. "Who made you the protector of every noobie that stumbles through town?"

Lemorak shrugged his broad shoulders and grinned. "I guess I did. Care to take a swing at discouraging me?" He dropped her wrist and jutted his chin at her. "Go ahead, Brynny. Give me your best shot."

The entire common room had gone silent as everyone stopped what they were doing to watch the confrontation. Bryn stood there for another heartbeat, her small fists clenched and her entire body trembling with rage. I was more than a little confused. Wasn't player on player combat forbidden here? How was she supposed to hit him?

"You're such a spoilsport!" Bryn said. "One of these days someone will rip that stick out of your ass, and you might just like it."

Finally, Bryn closed her blazing red eyes and pulled in a deep breath. I tried to not get distracted by the swelling of her chest in that low-cut blouse. Calm serenity settled over her beautiful face and she licked her lips and opened her eyes. "He barely had anything worth picking anyway. I'll earn my *Pickpocket* Achievement somewhere else."

Then she turned and stormed out the door. I'd like to say that I didn't watch the sway of her hips and tight round butt encased in black leather pants as she went, but I'd be lying. However much time she'd spent designing the look of her avatar, it was time well spent.

Shaking his head, Lemorak turned to face me. "Sorry about that. She's not exactly the best welcome Elmore has to offer. She's just another thief class trying to train up her Pickpocket skill by picking on noobs. Doesn't help that she's sunk a shit load of points into her Charisma to dazzle you with her glam." Lemorak settled in on the empty barstool beside me and clapped me on the back. "Let's get you off on a better foot. Have you ordered?"

"N-n-no. Not yet." I turned back to face the bar where Travis stood with inhuman patience awaiting further interaction. After sliding off the barstool to reclaim my purloined crypts, represented in the game as a handful of gold coins, I decided to take another stab at ordering some food.

"Steak?" I'd never actually had real beef from a cow, just tofu seasoned imitation or the cloned stuff grown in a vat. This wouldn't exactly be real either, but I figured with the detail of the simulation, it might be as close as I was ever going to get.

Travis laughed and then feigned a bow. "Oh, yes yer Lordship. Of course. At'll be seven gold."

"Seven crypts!" After my rewards from the goblin encounter I only had 17 CC to my name, and that had just almost been stolen. On the outside 17 CC would have been a decent amount of money. At my job in the hospital, mopping floors, I'd only made 9 CC a week.

"It's a themed menu," Lemorak explained with a sigh. "Travis, just bring us the day's stew and trenchers, and get the noob some ale. Put it on my tab."

Travis moved away chuckling to himself.

"And don't forget to give me the noobie discount for this guy," my neighbor shouted after the Innkeeper.

"Thanks for that. I'm…"

"Please!" He held up his hand to cut me off. "Not your real name."

Right. I'd just about done it again. I paused to consider. Did that mean Macha hadn't given me her real name? I dismissed the question and fumbled for something to call myself. I really didn't want to be *Inmate 81348* when I didn't absolutely need to be. At the same time, I didn't have a readymade alias already thought up. All the same, I couldn't think of anything but my long-standing nickname. "....I'm Zee."

"Nice to meet you Zee. I'm Lemorak. How long have you been jacked in?"

"I'd guess eight or ten hours? I haven't seen any clocks." No wonder I was starving, even after the apples that Hoggins had shared with me.

"Didn't bother with a training class on the outside before jacking in?" Lemorak asked.

"It wasn't really an option," I answered with as little inflection as possible.

Travis returned with a bowl of dark brown stew for each of us. Chunks of potato and vegetable floated in it along with some stringy-looking meat. He also left a small round loaf of coarse dark bread and a tankard. I watched Lemorak rip out the center of his loaf of bread and dump his stew inside like a bowl. I followed his example.

"I think it's goat tonight." Lemorak lifted his tankard. "Cheers." I hurriedly lifted my own and we clinked them together. "Now shut up and eat. I have some emails to write."

Lemorak's eyes shut, but he also began mechanically eating his stew and taking occasional sips from his tankard. From my previous clubbing trips, I knew that closed eyes on an avatar was the universal sign in the OVR Worlds that a player was accessing other menus or screens without logging out.

I turned my attention to my stew and drink. At first I wasn't sure what to make of it. It was different from anything I'd eaten in reality. Then my stomach rumbled as the first couple bites reached it and decided that it didn't care what I thought of the food. I began shoveling the stew and soaked bread down as fast as I could slurp and chew.

Goat Stew consumed. 1% Bonus to XP Earned for 12 hours!

Ale consumed. +1 Bonus to Charisma for 30 minutes! -1 Penalty to Dexterity for 30 minutes!

After the apple that Hoggins had given me, I was beginning to understand that any food or drink I had in the game came with bonuses or potentially penalties. I'd have to see if Al could dig up a list of what foods and drinks did what. I was just finishing the meal when Lemorak opened his eyes again. His meal had been completed for several minutes, and when it was done he'd sat there entirely still, eyes closed. He watched me finish stuffing the remnants of the bread bowl into my mouth and wash it down with my last bit of ale.

"Come on, Zee. I'll show you to the Noobie Shelter for the night," Lemorak said before he pushed himself up. His armor clanked and rattled. I got to my feet as well, a little woozy from the ale. Lemorak steadied me as I swayed on my feet.

"Noobie Shelter?" I asked, my words a little slurred.

"Yeah, it's where most the level 0s spend their first few nights. And other levels that have a run of bad luck and no party to back them or enough ranks in Survival to camp out. It's attached to the Temple. You could've gotten a free meal there too," Lemorak explained.

"I hadn't really thought about sleeping or eating when I jacked in," I confided in him.

"Your pod will take care of your actual body, but the Game simulates most of the burdens of living on your avatar. For the sake of authenticity, I guess. Let's just be glad they skipped all the bathroom functions. Although, I guess there are some players that are into that sort of thing too. You can purchase an add-on patch that'll remove the need to eat, but it costs.."

We stepped outside. The sun had set and it had gotten considerably darker and cooler. White text immediately appeared over Lemorak's head.

Sir Lemorak, Level 4 Paladin of Triumph, Human

I saw Lemorak's eyes dart over my head and could tell he was reading my handle, class, level and race. If he cared that I had an inmate handle, he didn't let it show. He ushered me off into Elmore.

As we walked, a notification scrolled across the bottom of my vision.

New Friend Request! From: Sir Lemorak

Accept

Decline

I quickly accepted. Lemorak's player tag turned from white to green.

Walking through the streets of Elmore, Lemorak and I passed several other players despite the town being shrouded in darkness already. True to the fantasy setting, there were no street lights to illuminate the simulated town. Yellow glows spilled from the windows of some buildings, and occasional passing players carried torches or candles, but compared to the electric lit streets of the modern world I'd always known, Elmore at night felt awash in darkness.

Overhead, the night sky was filled with more stars than I could comprehend and a brilliant silver full moon. More than once I tripped or bumped into an obstacle, having been distracted by the sight. The moon in particular was a dazzling sight compared to the pale sickly yellow object, more often obscured by smog than not, that I had always known.

"Nice, huh?" Lemorak observed, having taken notice of my distraction. "Hard sight to find on the outside. Saw it look that good once or twice when I was in the sandbox."

"Hard to believe the sky was ever this clear," I muttered, my voice tinged with awe.

"There isn't much light pollution here to begin with, but if you get away from town, it's even better."

"Almost feels like an alien world."

"When they first launched Gygax in the OVR Worlds, they really played up the fantasy setting. There were four moons of different colors. It freaked some people out too much, though, so they dialed it down to something more Earth normal. All bets are off when it comes to the sci-fi parts of the game like Vulcan or Arrakis, though, or if you go to one of the themed fantasy worlds like Krynn."

"Fucking crazy," I said. I really couldn't keep my eyes off the crystal-clear night sky filled with stars and a gorgeous moon.

My new friend kept silent for the rest of our walk, allowing me to soak in the scenery. He even stood silently and waited for my awe to wear off once we reached our destination. He bid me farewell at the door to what he called the Noobie Shelter. As we were parting, as if in afterthought, he offered to meet me in the morning to help get me further oriented. I eagerly

accepted his offer and asked him when and where he would like to meet.

"Clocks haven't yet been invented in Gygax. I'll wait for you out front

here, an hour or so after sunrise."

"S-Sure," I stammered. "I don't want to put you out. What if I'm

late?" I waited for a response, but when I got nothing but a smile and a

shrug I continued. "It makes me nervous, setting a meeting time when I

can't tell if I'll make it."

Lemorak sighed, but still smiled. "If you're late I'll wait. If I'm late I

guess you'll wait instead. Or not. I guess we'll just have to see how it works

out. You'll get used to it."

He turned and marched away down the narrow street.

The Noobie Shelter, according to the sign out front, was officially

named the New Adventurer's Lodge. It was a long, squat, stone building

attached to a larger domed temple, on one end of a small, grassy village

square.

After Lemorak vanished into the deepening night, I turned and made

my way into the Noobie Shelter. Upon entering I was greeted by a friendly,

but dead-eyed, NPC Cleric, Brother Patrick. This kindly cleric immediately

took note of my wounds from the goblin battle. Truth be told, after the

initial pain of receiving them, the wounds hadn't bothered me much at all.

If not for my nearly empty HP bar, I would have forgotten. Brother Patrick explained that since I was still level 0, I was eligible for free healing.

I accepted his offered healing. The NPC Cleric muttered a short prayer in a quasi-Latin sounding language and one of his hands began to glow with a golden light. He touched my wounds in turn. A pleasant warmth radiated from the touches and I watched the HP bar on my HUD rise back to full.

When I was fully healed, Brother Patrick showed me into the shelter. Just past the entry vestibule proved to be a good-sized dining hall. A massive cauldron of something simmered over a wood fire. Long tables with benches filled the room. The dining hall was lit by plain-looking cast iron chandeliers burning candles. A couple of players hunched over their bowls of food. I noticed their character details didn't hover over their heads, just like in the White Horse. The Cleric asked me if I needed to eat and I told him I already had.

"Then I will show you the accommodations." He ushered me across the dining hall and through a door at the far end.

We proceeded down a long narrow hall, with several other similar halls branching off of it, all with doorways spaced evenly along each wall. Within moments, I was disoriented and completely lost. It took a while, but eventually I realized that the interior of the shelter had to be much larger than the outside indicated.

"Is this place bigger on the inside?" I felt silly asking the question. I started to wonder if a madman with a sonic screwdriver was going to come walking around the next corner or if I'd hear the *vrrrworp* sound of the TARDIS in flight.

Patrick smiled serenely at me. "Blessed are the stones of this hall. We never know how many new adventurers may need accommodation. The Lodge expands and contracts to meet our needs so that we may fulfill our purpose."

I took in the information and filed it away. The fact that the game's programmers were willing to play with some pretty basic geographic structure could prove relevant in the future. Clearly, they could always handwave any discrepancies as "magic."

The cleric stopped at one door and opened it to a small room, probably about ten feet by six feet. There was a small, simple bed about the size of a long twin-sized mattress. There was also a small, wooden chest on one wall, with a little oval mirror hanging from the wall in a wood frame, and a plain wooden chair. A small glass window looked out into a night-shrouded courtyard. The chamber smelled clean and untouched.

Patrick explained to me that the chamber was enchanted to only open for me or one of his fellow clerics once I entered. He also said that anything I stored in the chest would be kept safe for me, even if I left the shelter.

"May I offer any further assistance to you, Inmate 81348?"

"No. Thank you."

"Sweet dreams."

I stepped into the chamber and closed the door. I hung my weapons from a couple of wooden pegs I found on the wall and then flopped down onto the bed. It felt surprisingly soft and comfortable and I almost immediately drifted off into an exhausted sleep.

Interlude One

It didn't feel like a dream. Somehow, I was standing alone on the starship bridge of the USS *Enterprise NCC-1701*. I imagined James Doohan saying *...no bloody A, B, C or D*. The original Enterprise. Kirk's Enterprise! I could feel my feet on the humming deck and feel my heart pounding rather alarmingly in my chest. I reached out to steady myself on the back of Captain Kirk's famous center chair.

What was going on? Could this be some sort of glitch in the game? I knew there was a Star Trek section of *OVR World*, multiple, in fact, one for each pivotal era, but how had I ended up here?

Every detail of the helm console before me seemed a perfect replica of the bridge I knew so well from binge-watching the Original Series a thousand times. This wasn't one of the updated visions from the films, from JJ Abrams, or from Discovery.

The bridge was entirely abandoned. All the stations had screens up and running, control lights shone or blinked as I assumed they should and on the big screen in front a barren red Mars-like planet floated peacefully on a bed of twinkling stars. The hum and tones of the classic Star Trek bridge filled my ears as I slowly turned in a circle, taking in my surroundings. Gingerly, I reached out and touched the back of Captain Kirk's chair again. It felt entirely, even impossibly, real.

Glancing down, I realized that I was wearing a gold uniform tunic with sewn-on command emblem badge. Black trousers and black leather boots completed the uniform. Around the cuffs of my tunic sleeves were the rank stripes of a captain.

"Cool…" I whispered.

There was a whooshing hiss of turbo-lift doors opening and I spun around, startled. Off of the turbolift strutted a man in a battered and incongruous blue pinstripe suit and a long brown trench coat, with a neck tie loose around his throat. One hand was tucked into a pocket and the other swung free, holding a buzzing, slender, pen-like device with a glowing blue tip. He wore a mischievous, crooked-toothed grin and had wild, brown hair, with a direct intense gaze. I recognized him instantly.

"The Doctor?" I blurted in confusion. Someone had gotten their classic sci-fi jumbled.

"Who?" The man asked looking around curiously and spoke with a gentle British accent. "Where'd he go?"

"You!" I shouted and pointed at him accusingly. "You're the Tenth Doctor!"

"Me?" the man pointed at his own chest, seemingly puzzled before he looked down at himself. He spun around wildly, looking for a reflective surface. The metal doors of the turbo-lift seemed to give him what he needed. "Well, would you look at that?"

He spent several seconds probing his face experimentally, with a look of amused amazement. "Right. Well then. Now that we know who I am," the Tenth Doctor spun to face me, eyes bright with excitement, "let's talk about who you are, Captain!"

"I'm sorry, but I've got to ask why the Doctor would be on the bridge of the *Enterprise*?"

The Doctor shrugged, his grin widening. "I have no idea. It's your head, Zee. Why don't you tell me?"

"My head?" I asked, my voice shrill.

"Exactamundo!" The Doctor started casually strolling the bridge, idly poking at buttons and flipping switches. Each action produced a chirp or beep or whistle. "Your gorgeous, brilliant, little human head! I'm tapping into your juicy little subconscious in order to establish communication."

"So you're not actually the Doctor?"

"Well that wouldn't make much sense, would it?" He had paced around until he was standing in front of the viewscreen.

"I guess not?"

"Of course it wouldn't! Aliens aren't real! Well..." The fake Doctor trailed off for a moment, then shook his head, derailing whatever train of thought he'd veered onto. "No, I'm a subprogram within OVR World's governing SI. Mostly, I'm something of a self-repairing or antivirus program, but that makes me well-suited to watch out for anomalies. When anomalous players connect to the game, I establish a connection with them. Your subconscious chose this location and my form. So if this is confusing, you only have yourself to blame."

"Anomalous players?" I asked, suddenly feeling woozy and not so sure I wanted the answer.

The Doctor scrunched up his face and shrugged his shoulders high around his ears. "Well. That's hard to explain right now. Suffice it to say, not everyone's brain can handle such a direct connection to the game's interface. I'm mostly here to provide you with guidance as you progress through the game, answer some questions, and occasionally provide you with special quests."

Head spinning, I dropped down into the Captain's chair and slumped back. I closed my eyes and tried to sort through the information. "I must have really snapped."

"Easy there, Captain!" the Doctor urged me. "Deep breaths. This is just an introductory meeting."

Gritting my teeth, I forced a breath in through my nose and blew it out through my mouth. "This is for sure the weirdest thing that's ever happened to me."

"Well, I would hope so! I'd say someone has been watching too many reruns."

"So, you can just pop into my dreams whenever you want? Will you always look like this? Will we always be here?"

The Doctor's avatar laughed merrily. "Well I suppose I can keep appearing like this if you like. Where we meet will mostly depend on your subconscious."

"What should I call you?"

"Why not The Doctor?"

Lacking an obvious alternative, I shrugged and nodded. "Anything else I need to know?"

The Doctor's smile turned mischievous. "Tons! More than we have time to discuss now. Like I said. This is just me popping in to say hello. You've got a long road ahead of you, Zee."

The Doctor's image strode around the perimeter of the bridge again until he reached the doors to the turbo-lift. I slowly pivoted in the Captain's chair to watch him. The doors of the lift whooshed open at his approach.

"It's a pleasure meeting you, Zee."

"Ummm...you too?"

The Doctor winked and stepped through the doors to the lift. They began to hiss shut behind him, but he spun around at the last instant and caught it with his hand. He stuck his head back out and said, "Oh! One more thing, Zee. Don't tell anyone about me. Not even your new friend, Lemorak. Like I said this is kind of a unique arrangement. They won't really understand."

I shook my head. "Sure. Yeah. That makes sense." I didn't really understand, so how could I expect anyone else to?

Chapter Seven

I awoke to dim morning light peeking through my small window. The memory of my dream on the bridge of the *Enterprise* and the conversation with the Doctor was bright and vivid in my mind. Definitely not a normal dream.

"What the hell was that?" I asked the empty room as I rubbed the sleep from my face.

I couldn't tell how long I had slept, but I felt fresh and ready for the day. In fact, as I got up, I realized that I felt too fresh. There was no lingering scent of body odor, no morning breath, no little crusties around my eyes and I didn't have to piss. *I could get used to this.*

Meeting up with Lemorak jumped to mind. Had I left my new friend waiting? Rolling over, I looked up at the small window to try to gauge the time. The sky outside was lightening to blue with the approach of dawn.

Raring to go, I jumped up, and was reaching to snatch up my weapons when I caught sight of my reflection in the mirror. The strange sight brought me up straight. It wasn't my face! Ok, well, it was my face, but it didn't have the instantly familiar features that I'd recognize as my own. Up until that moment, I had forgotten all about my race selection. It was a bit like having a stranger staring back at me. Maybe a stranger that was related to me, but a stranger all the same.

Leaning in close to the mirror, I studied my appearance for the first time. My hair was still a dark brown, but was longer than in the real world, falling in gentle curls around my slightly pointed ears. Brown scruffy stubble covered my cheeks. I ran my hand over it noticing the alien sensation for the first time.

"Fucking hell," I muttered. "This is weird."

Taking a deep breath, I yanked my gaze away from the mirror. I belted on my weapons and took the few steps to my door. When I opened it, I was surprised to find Brother Patrick standing stock still in the hall. The NPC stirred as I stepped into the hall.

"Good morning, adventurer. How may I assist you?" His smile was pleasant, but a little creepy. I had seen my fair share of horror movies and this would have fit in nicely. He was like a pod person. Had he been standing outside my door since - when? Since I went to bed last night?

"I've got a friend waiting for me, how do I get out?" Then my stomach grumbled for attention. "And, where can I get some breakfast?"

"Of course," he answered. "Please follow me. I think you will find our breakfast service to your liking. And," he intoned as if it was our little secret, "it's free. We understand you might be a little short on coin, being new to this world. And we want you to get the best start on your day."

As we walked, I noticed a number of other NPCs standing outside of other doors. After several turns down identical halls, I quickly decided it was a really good thing the cleric was there.

I saw several other players as we walked, each being led by their own NPC cleric. Each cleric looked eerily similar to Patrick. It was like the programmers had gotten lazy and just made a template for them, then tweaked the features just a little. This disappointed me and got me hoping this wasn't going to be a trend in the entire game. The hype was that *OVR World* was the cutting edge and this was definitely feeling a bit algorithmic.

A couple of the players seemed to be just arriving, dusty from the road and eyes half-lidded with exhaustion, while other players seemed on their way out bright-eyed and bushy-tailed like me. Like at the tavern, none of the players had tags over their heads. I felt relieved that within the shelter my inmate status wouldn't immediately put me on the wrong foot like it had with the trio I'd met the night before.

Upon reaching the dining hall, Brother Patrick gave me a quick run-through of the buffet set out for us and politely set me to it. I got in line for some oatmeal being served from the black cauldron by another vacantly smiling Stepford Cleric, who also shared Patrick's general appearance.

The oatmeal was much closer to the meals I was used to back home than the comparative feast I had been treated to the night before. It was warm, simple and quite bland. Nothing to write home about, but it filled my stomach and gave me an hour long 5% buff to Experience Points earned. When I was done, I got up and left the shelter in a bit of a rush. Outside, sure as shit, Lemorak was patiently sitting under a wide shade tree in the village square.

"How was your first night?" Lemorak asked as he stood.

Memories of my weird dream came rushing back and I shoved them aside. "Fine, I guess."

"Good, let's get on a roll." Lemorak headed off at a brisk pace.

Lemorak ushered me off on a quick tour around the town of Elmore. He showed me some of the more common spots to pick up quests from NPCs, the Mayor's residence, the Guard House, the Guild Halls, and the NPC Class Trainers. Lemorak had me stop to talk to the Ranger Class Trainer, an NPC human ranger named Aldris Strongbow, stationed outside the provisioner's shop. After a brief chat, the grizzled middle aged ranger assigned me several quests meant to hone my ranger skills.

"The rewards are pretty basic for the intro class quests," Lemorak told me when I stepped away from Aldris. "But completing them unlock better ones down the road."

After talking to Aldris, Lemorak's tour continued. He pointed out the Bank, though he added that most of its functions were off limits to me as an inmate. Then there were various merchants that I might need while in Elmore, once I had gold to spare. NPCs and players alike were up and moving about as the tour progressed, though unlike yesterday afternoon and evening, the population was decidedly skewed towards NPCs.

"Where are all the other players?" I finally asked.

"It's a weekday, so most of the players on right now are full timers, and not everyone hangs around Elmore all the time. All the gold and experience are mostly outside the walls. There won't be many Casuals jacked in till it starts to be evening on the East Coast. Even then, it won't really be crowded around here until the weekend. Then it can be a real goat rodeo." Lemorak shuddered in mock horror to punctuate his words.

"But the OVR Worlds are global, why would it matter what time it is outside? If this is an Orientation Zone, shouldn't it be packed with new players from all over?"

"Damn Zee. You really are new, huh?" Lemorak chuckled and shook his head ruefully.

"Weren't you a noob too at some point?"

"Fair point." Lemorak's handsome face split in wide grin and he laughed a little harder than I felt the quip deserved, but then he sighed answered my question. "Rowling Valley is the Orientation Zone for North America and just the world of Gygax. Sure, every second new players are jacking in for the first time all over the globe, but they don't all pick Gygax, and depending on where they call home, they go to the OZ relevant for their continentinent in the real world. Not to mention regular players that pick non-human races can choose alternate OZs based on their character race. Understand?"

I nodded my head as I digested the information. "Makes sense. Thanks."

"That's what I'm here for! Come on, let's get you a quest and some EXP."

We exited Elmore through a gate in the palisade at the opposite end of town from where I'd entered with Farmer Hoggins the day before. Lemorak directed me to stop and talk to one of the guards on duty to get a quest for the day. As I approached, the NPC guard idly shifted his weight from foot to foot and adjusted his grip on his pike. Even as he stiffly turned his head towards me, it didn't really feel like he was looking at me.

"G-G-Good morning?" I felt awkward talking to the oddly lifeless guard.

"No time to talk. I'm waiting for the Captain to come. We just had a farmer come in and say he was attacked by kobolds on the road," the Guard cried, his demeanor instantly shifting from placid stiffness to animated melodramatic alarm.

I glanced back at Lemorak and he made a rolling *Get on with it* gesture with his hand. Sighing, I turned back to the guard.

"Um....K-kobolds attacking? Is that...uh...something I could help with?"

The guard gave me a skeptical once over. "Kobolds aren't usually just a nuisance. I suppose you could fend them off. Dispatch fifty of the little monsters to teach them not to stray from their village. My Captain'll pay one gold for each kobold tooth you bring back. They're lucky we don't wipe them out!"

Text appeared in my notification bar.

Quest Offer: Kobolds have attacked an Elmore Farmer. Slay 50 Kobolds to teach them a lesson. The Guard Captain will pay you 1 coin for each Kobold tooth you bring him!

Exp Reward: 100

CC Reward: 1 CC for each Kobold tooth you turn in

Accept

Decline

I accepted the quest and turned back to Lemorak. We walked for about an hour down a gravel road while Lemorak kept up a constant lecture about what I needed to do and when I needed to do it to survive and then thrive in this world. Though I nodded and grunted affirmative sounds every once in a while, I got the impression that he would have carried on even if I'd suddenly fallen into a pit of lava.

Finally, we crested a short rise and saw what looked like a crude collection of mud huts in the distance. Tiny creatures scuttled from hut to hut.

"This Kobold den is the best Level 0 'Exp farm' in the area, especially if you have a higher level to back you up," Lemorak explained.

We advanced down the hill at a more cautious pace. When we were still about a mile distant from the kobold den, which I now saw marked on my HUD's map, Lemorak guided us off the road and into the sparse trees.

"For now, this is going to be a bit of a grind for you. I can generally one-hit these Kobolds. So I'll be here to back you up if you pull too big of a mob, but otherwise you'll be on your own. If all goes well, you'll have enough CC to buy some starter armor, and we'll have you at level 1 within a couple days," Lemorak explained. "Ready?"

I drew my short sword and dagger and nodded.

Lemorak grinned at me, then started banging his metal bracers against his breastplate, making a loud clanging sound. After several seconds of this racket, Lemorak stepped back and casually leaned against a nearby tree. I stood waiting with my weapons drawn, not knowing what to expect.

Within a minute I heard something rattling through the thick brush. Then a diminutive, under three feet tall, lizardlike creature with short horns, pinkish purple scales for skin and a stubby nub of a tail came charging at me with a stone spear out of the brush. A text alert scrolled across the bottom of my vision.

A Kobold Hunter, level 0, is attacking you!

My shadowy combat guide activated, and I frantically matched the guide's stance. Following the movements of my guide, I batted aside the kobold's lunging spear strike with my short sword. The kobold and I circled each other warily. I mimicked my guide when it found an opening and lunged forward, the tip of my short sword leading and my dagger warding against the spear point. My sword found its mark and I stabbed the kobold through the throat. A glowing red aura flashed around the kobold's body.

Critical Strike! Double Damage!

Kobold Hunter killed: 8 Exp

I pulled back and the kobold corpse fell to the ground and dissolved before my eyes. I checked the Loot screen, collected a bronze coin, which amounted to 0.01 CC, and the kobold tooth shown there, then discarded the rest of the stuff the little monster carried.

"Here comes another!" Lemorak called just as I was dismissing the Loot screen.

I did my best to follow my guide through the next encounter. Though I took a spear butt to the gut and lost 3 HP, I dispatched that Kobold Hunter with some well-placed footwork and decisive stabs and slashes, all courtesy of my combat guide. When the monster was down and dust, I was glistening with sweat and breathing heavy, but grinning at my conquest.

The day proceeded pretty much exactly like that. Kobolds, up to three at a time, would emerge from the brush to attack me. Lemorak would stand back while I took the lead and though I suffered the occasional glancing blow or slice, it was nothing that slowed me down. I was having too much fun.

As I fought, my Endurance bar slowly drained with the exertion. I noticed that as it got lower, I sweat more and breathed harder. Once I stopped to rest, my Endurance bar would slowly recharge. When my Endurance bar was full, my Hit Points would slowly start to regenerate. Scratches and bruises that would take a week or more to heal in the real world stopped hurting within an hour here. This gave me great confidence to soldier on through the hits I was taking, despite the pain. Lemorak told me that my HP would continue to heal after resting, so long as I didn't fall below 50 percent. After that, I'd require attention from someone with the Medicine skill or magical healing.

As the day progressed, I observed on another break that my Endurance recharged slower. When I commented on this, Lemorak told me that would continue to happen until I ate and slept. A little after noon, I'd earned a new achievement.

Achievement Earned: Kobold Slayer - 5% bonus damage when fighting Kobolds

It was late afternoon when eight of the little shits exploded from the brush to charge me.

"Frak me!" I shouted in alarm and fell back under the rush of spear points.

Exhausted at this point I quickly fell behind on the advanced moves needed to ward off such a throng. Spinning and striking as best I could, I was soon surrounded. The creatures slashed and bashed me from every direction while I did little damage of my own. One of the Kobolds behind me struck hard with the shaft of his spear. Pain lanced up my back as I fell to the ground under the blow.

The Kobolds shared an instant of hissing victorious laughter as they moved in for the kill when I heard Lemorak cry at the top of his lungs "OORAH!"

The paladin charged in on the circle with his massive sword in a two-handed grip. Out of the corner of my eye I watched two kobolds turn to dust as he cleanly sliced through one and cleaved into the next. The last Kobold Hunter was falling to the ground and dissolving when I finally managed to heave myself up from the ground.

My entire body ached and I was missing over half my HP. Lemorak grinned at me as he sheathed his sword and picked through the various Loot screens. Then he tossed a handful of coins to me.

Lemorak has given you 4 CC

Accept

Decline

I grudgingly accepted the Crypts, since I wasn't really in a position to turn any down. I'd collected a total of 15 CC through the day, including what Lemorak had just tossed me, though that didn't take into account the payout I was expecting from turning in all the kobold teeth I'd collected.

"Hold on, and I'll heal you up." Lemorak made a gesture in the air and muttered something under his breath. His hand began to glow with purple light and he laid it on my forehead. Soothing warmth ran through my body and my HP bar rose to just under full.

"Thanks." I rolled my shoulders, still a little sore, then leaned back against a tree to catch my breath. "Why the fuck hadn't you been doing that all day? You can just heal me?"

"You didn't need healing until now," Lemorak responded. "If something like that happens again and I'm not here to save your ass, run. You're faster than the kobolds. You can always run back to town or gain some distance. Then pick them off with your bow as they come running. Your melee training guide will always try to find a way to fight to victory, even if there isn't one. It's just an SI you're a human. Sometimes your good sense has gotta take over. That includes knowing when to run."

"Alright," I responded sheepishly, as if he was calling me stupid and I was agreeing. I quickly altered the route of the discussion. "I actually haven't used my bow at all. What's that like?"

"There's a separate training guide for ranged combat. It'll activate once you pull out your bow. We can give it a shot, so to speak. I'll pull the kobolds' aggro and you can stand back and take some shots. I'll cut down anything that gets too close. Sound good?"

"What if I hit you?"

Lemorak shook his head. "Even if we weren't Friends, we're in the OZ; no lethal Player vs. Player combat here. They'll just bounce off if you hit me."

"Let's do it." I pushed myself off the tree, sheathed my melee weapons and unslung my bow.

Lemorak proceeded to hoot and holler until a Hunter came out of the brush. I had retreated about 30 feet behind him with a tree to my back so nothing could easily sneak up on me. Fumbling, I eventually fit an arrow to the string and raised my bow. A misty, glowing trail of yellow light ran from the tip of my arrow along the projected arc of a shot. With almost no tension on the string, the line fell quickly to the ground. I flexed and pulled back on the string. The aiming guide lengthened and moved as I swung the bow around.

When I eventually put the target on the Kobold, the guide turned green, but I almost instantly lost the green as I failed to track the monster's movement. I loosed the arrow anyway, hoping it would at least be close. It thumped into a fallen log about ten feet away from the Kobold.

Cursing, I notched another arrow and drew it back to aim. By then Lemorak was casually batting aside the Kobold's spear thrusts. I let out a long breath and struggled to line up the shot. The good thing was, now that Lemorak was fighting the Kobold, the little monster wasn't moving nearly as much. I got my targeting guide to turn green and released my arrow. It flew downrange and sunk into the Kobold's arm. The Hunter howled in pain as about two-thirds of his HP bar dropped away.

As Lemorak parried and side-stepped the Kobold's attacks, I fired a third arrow, which whistled harmlessly past the pair. Taking another deep breath I held it and focused on aiming. I hit this time and the kobold dusted at Lemorak's feet. The EXP notification scrolled across my vision as another of the little buggers ventured out to attack Lemorak.

We spent the rest of the afternoon practicing my archery. We took occasional breaks so I could rest my arms, since firing my bow still drained my Endurance. I started to pick up the knack of using the Archery Guide, and I started dropping the kobolds quicker. I certainly liked fighting at a distance. Other than a growing blister on my fingertips it didn't hurt at all, and I was gaining EXP points quickly.

The sun was sliding down the sky into late afternoon when I dropped another Kobold with a carefully aimed shot. I heard a blaring of trumpets and bold text in all caps scrolled across my notification bar.

LEVEL UP!

LEVEL 1 RANGER REACHED!

ARCHERY TALENT IMPROVED TO LEVEL 1

TWO-WEAPON FIGHTING TALENT IMPROVED TO LEVEL 1

SKILL IMPROVED: ATHLETICS +1 -> +2

SKILL IMPROVED: SURVIVAL +1 -> +2

SKILL IMPROVED: STEALTH +1 -> +2

SKILL IMPROVED: ANIMAL HANDLING +1 -> +2

SKILL IMPROVED: TRACKING +1 -> +2

INCREASE TO HIT POINTS +20

INCREASE TO MANA +10

2 ABILITY POINTS AWARDED

+1 ABILITY POINT FOR BEING HALF-ELF

NEW RANGER TALENT UNLOCKED - LIGHT ARMOR

PROFICIENCY

Lemorak was standing next to me when I finished reading the notifications. His eyes were bright with excitement. "Well, now that that's done we can pack it in. Good work today. You've earned some ale. Come on. First round is on me."

"I thought you said it would take a couple days of this for me to level?" I asked as we headed back to the road.

Lemorak shrugged his armored shoulders. "Like I said, this is a good EXP farm. We pulled better today than I was expecting."

A nagging suspicion in the back of my mind said that Lemorak was hiding something. I didn't want to accuse him of lying to me. He was the one person I'd found willing to give me the time of day. And I still had very little idea of what I was doing. So I didn't push the matter any further

Reaching the road, we started the walk back to Elmore. As we walked, Lemorak told me how to set my avatar to follow him automatically so I could enter Game Management and look at my Level Up options. I did as he instructed and selected the Level Up button that I found hovering at the bottom of my HUD - that's what Lemorak called it - and found myself suddenly in the same featureless white Game Management area where I had completed Character Generation. In the upper right corner of my vision was a small screen showing my avatar proceeding on auto-pilot following Lemorak.

Al blinked into existence beside me. His outfit had changed: he wore baggy tangerine pants with a more subdued black dress shirt under a silver bomber jacket. His ever-present cigar smoldered odorless between his lips.

"Zee! That was insanely fast!" Al said. As he spoke, my mirror image avatar appeared before us. "Well done!"

"Thanks Al. What have we got?"

"Level 1 baby!" Al crowed. "Ziggy says that means three fresh ability points to spend! And some of your existing skills and talents get a bump as well. You'll also now be proficient with light armor when you can afford some. Gotta get that Defense up, Zee!"

A window appeared with some choices that I could spend my three Ability Points on. I found that now that I was at Level 1, I could use my Ability Points on more than just my six basic Abilities. I could also use them to upgrade my Skills or purchase extra Talents that I met the prerequisites for (which weren't many). On the Skill side, one Ability point actually equaled a +4 modifier to the Skill I decided to apply it to. The cost for Talents depended. Most cost one Ability Point, but several cost two or three. I read through the options and asked Al some clarifying questions.

In the end, I decided at this stage I was better off just bumping up base Abilities. I put one point each in Strength, Dexterity and Wisdom. Strength improved my melee attack accuracy and damage, Dexterity improved my defense and ranged attacks, and Wisdom improved some of my critical skills and would boost my Faith Mana, which Al said I would need when I got access to spells at Level 5.

"All set, Al," I told the digital assistant.

CHARACTER STATISTICS

Handle: Inmate 81348

Race: Half-Elf

Role: Striker

Class/Level: Ranger/1

ABILITIES

Strength (Endurance): 14 (19)

Strength Skills: Melee Combat, Athletics, Carrying Capacity

Dexterity (Defense): 14 (15)

Dexterity Skills: Ranged Combat, Acrobatics, Stealth, Sleight of Hand, Open Lock. Reflex

Constitution (Hit Points): 13 (85)

Constitution Skills: Concentration, Fortitude

Intelligence (Arcane Mana): 10 (NA)

Intelligence Skills: Arcana, Investigation. Appraise, Disable Device. Forgery, Lore

Wisdom (Faith Mana): 12 (44)

Wisdom Skills: Conviction. Perception, Survival, Tracking, Animal Handling, Medicine, Willpower

Charisma (Inspiration): 10 (NA)

Charisma Skills: Imagination, Deception, Intimidation, Persuasion, Influence

RACIAL SKILLS: Half-Elf Wilderness Skills: Survival (+1), Stealth (+1), Tracking (+1)

RACIAL TALENTS: Half-Elf Flexibility (+5 AP at Level 0, +1 AP), Nightvision (15'), Elven Bow Proficiency +1 Level

CLASS SKILLS: Athletics (+2), Survival (+2), Stealth (+2), Animal Handling (+2), Tracking (+2)

CLASS TALENTS: Archery (Level 1), Two-Weapon Fighting (Level 1), Light Armor Proficiency

EARNED SKILLS: None

EARNED TALENTS: Surprise Attack (Achievement)

CARRIED EQUIPMENT: Standard Clothes, Short-sword, Dagger, Short-bow, Arrows x20, Stone Hatchet

STORED EQUIPMENT: None

COMBAT STATISTICS

Weapon - Talent Modifier - Weapon Damage - Accuracy - Median Damage

Shortsword - 1 - 20 - 9 - 64

Dagger (off-hand) - 1 - 14 - 9 - 44

Stone Hatchet - 1 - 10 - 9 - 54

Shortbow - 1 - 18 - 9 - 63

ACHIEVEMENTS: First Kill, Backstabber, Good Samaritan, Goblin

Slayer, Kobold Slayer

TOTAL ABILITY POINTS: 13

CURRENT CRYPTOCURRENCY: 41.00

CURRENT DEBTS: 4,713,110.73 CC - OzCo Department of

Corrections

CURRENT EXPERIENCE: 548

EXPERIENCE TO NEXT LEVEL: 2,000

Since I hadn't made any payments towards my OzCo debt, I was

surprised to see it had decreased from the 4,719,052.68 CC the last time I'd

checked to 4,713,110.73 CC. Since I hadn't sent any of my CC from

adventuring towards the debt - which was the traditional way to get out fast

- that meant the decrease was entirely due to my brain activity processing

data and generating CC in the background.

When the world markets collapsed during the Mudbowl and other

global warming-related disasters, like annual monster storms and never-

ending wildfire seasons, it was the Mega-Corps that funded the rebuilding

of civilization. Their efforts also lead to the death of government-backed currency, in favor of various cryptocurrencies, of which BitCoin was one of the earliest progenitors. These new currencies were derived from computing power instead of the gold of other tangible world commodities. At first, each Mega tried backing their own form of crypto-currency, but the conversions were confusing and the markets too volatile. Which led to the unification into one coin of the realm, just called CryptoCoin, Crypts, or CC. The world's first global currency.

In the beginning, the Mega-Corps were the only institutions with the super computers needed to mine for Crypts. But what's the best and cheapest supercomputer around? An engaged human brain. That's what led to their early investment in OVR World. You couldn't just plug a brain into a pod, give it no stimulus and get a return, though. Engagement in a virtual reality was the best way anyone had found to keep the human brain engaged and producing CC through background mental processing. It had the added benefit of letting us all escape the dark and dreary mess that was the real world.

After OzCo, which had started out as a massive ISP and cyber security firm, had branched out into policing and then private prisons, and eventually the entire Criminal Justice system, they'd started looking for every possible way to turn a buck on the venture. For the truly unskilled, that had led to labor camps. For those with specialized and valuable skill sets (Coders, Lawyers, Doctors etc) they'd created Indentured Employees.

And since they own most of the tech and infrastructure that powered the OVR Worlds, that had also created the Inmate Gamer Program. No more pesky prison population to feed, house and secure, and best of all the crypts generated by Inmate Gamers created massive profits for the Mega-Corp.

Sure some regular, paying, players complained about inmates being out in the rest of the population. However, after much testing and piloting, OzCo had found it to be the most profitable model. With OzCo holding an absolute monopoly on not only the tech and software, but the world's communication's infrastructure, they really didn't have to care too much about customer satisfaction.

I did some quick arithmetic in my head based on how long I thought I'd been in the game. I was generating an average almost 260 CC per hour from background processing. I pushed that out and figured that meant at my current rate of production, I'd only have a little under two years in the game even if I didn't throw any of my adventuring rewards at the debt. That seemed entirely too fast given the 15 year sentence that had also been attached to my imprisonment. While waiting to jack in, I'd done the math based on published averages and had thought I might be out in ten years instead of 15 by playing, and if I was very lucky and earned very well then maybe around eight years.

I asked Al to review my calculations.

"Ziggy says all the math checks out," Al confirmed.

"What the hell is happening?" I demanded, to which my digital assistant just shrugged.

Chapter Eight

At the gates of Elmore, I turned in my collected Kobold teeth to the guards. Without keeping track, I'd killed fifty-six kobolds throughout the course of the day. A notification appeared for the EXP and CC award for completing my second quest.

Quest Complete: Push back the savage kobolds

100 EXP Awarded!

You killed 56 Kobolds! Bounty Awarded 56 CC

The sun was sinking below the horizon as we walked through the gates. Lemorak led me straight to the armorer's shop where we selected a basic suit of brown leather armor for 55 gold, basically the entire bounty I'd collected for the Kobold teeth. I still had a good amount of coin left over from what I'd picked off the corpses, though. All the same, 55 crypts seemed incredibly expensive to me. Then I saw how much some basic chainmail, a breastplate like Lemorak's, or the full suit of platemail cost and thought I was getting off light. I equipped the armor and it materialized on my body feeling snug as a glove, a perfect fit.

Lemorak told me that I could purchase a handle change from any merchant. In Elmore the price matched with Character Generation, five CC, but he said it would be more once I left Elmore. Eager to relieve myself of my inmate designation, I dipped into my looted coin and purchased the handle change from the NPC Armorer.

Conscious that I'd been cautioned against giving out my real name, I decided I couldn't name myself Zachary or even Zack. As much as I was embarrassed by my inmate designation, I really didn't know what I wanted my handle to be. I'd never wanted a different name. Seeing one obvious option I tried Zee, but it was taken, and I didn't want to be Zee495364. I wouldn't be a number anymore.

"Hey Lemorak. Where'd you get your handle?" I asked.

"Sir Lemorak was a lesser known Arthurian Knight. Not a popular one like Lancelot or Percival, so I got lucky and it was still available."

"Know any famous Rangers?"

"I'm sure Aragorn is taken." Lemorak quipped.

I rolled my eyes, but I checked anyway. It was.

"How do you feel about masks? Zorro was kind of Ranger-like. Or I guess there was the Lone Ranger."

"You're not helping." I sighed but tried both. Zorro and the Lone Ranger were already taken.

"Who said I was trying to help? I can't believe you signed up for the game, even as an inmate, and didn't have a decent handle in mind."

I spent several more minutes fussing over various options. Anything I remotely liked was already taken and had a slew of numbers after it.

"At this point you seem like a total Zero," Lemorak chimed in.

I tried Zero. Also taken. Of course.

"That's it. Let's get going. Now that you've purchased the add-on you can redeem it whenever you want. It's time for food and ale."

Reluctantly, I dismissed the window. I noticed it didn't close entirely. A little envelope symbol appeared on my HUD. Lemorak was trying to hurry me out the Armorer's door when Bryn stepped into the shop. I managed to keep my tongue from flopping out onto the floor to trip up my feet, but it was a near thing. Now outside of the tavern, I could finally read the player tag over her head.

Dirzbryn Baenmtor, Level 2 Assassin, Dark Elf

The gorgeous dark elf, who had had her hands all in my pockets the previous evening, appeared geared up for battle. She was sheathed in studded black leather armor that deliciously hugged every one of her substantial curves, not at all obscured by the purple half cloak that hung around her neck. A long slender rapier hung from one shapely hip. From

131

the other hip dangled a delicate-looking hand crossbow in a holster and coiled a black leather whip. Her long shimmering silver hair was pulled back in a tight braid. The dark elf's red gaze flashed with merry mischief and her thick crimson painted lips spread in a matching grin as she saw Lemorak and me.

"Hello boys. Did you have a thrilling day?" I'd never felt someone undressing me with their eyes before, but the slow deliberate once-over that Bryn gave me felt exactly like that. "Someone's looking rich."

"Ummmm…." God damn it! What was wrong with me? How could another player's high Charisma effect my own ability to speak or think coherently? I made a mental note to ask Lemorak about it later.

I could practically hear Lemorak's eyes rolling as he replied. "We did fine, Brynny. I see you're still in one piece."

"I trust you're taking good care of the sweet noob."

"He's in good hands. Better than yours," Lemorak said.

Bryn stepped up close to me and said softly, "Is that right sweetie? Is Lemorak taking good care of you? Did you see all the sights?"

"Y-y-yeah." I stammered. "T-toured the town. Then just killed kobolds all day."

Bryn rolled her eyes, then reached up. The nails of her ebony fingers were painted a deep purple. She traced a sharp fingernail down my cheek as she purred, "That hardly sounds like *all the sights*."

She stepped around me, bumping her hip against mine. "Would you like me to show you everything you're missing?"

My mouth opened to respond but no words came out. I felt the points of my ears begin to practically glow red. What the hell was it with this woman?

"Your tips are blushing again, sweetie." Bryn gave me a playful wink, dashing any hope I'd had that she hadn't noticed.

Lemorak noisily cleared his throat, and one of his hands came down on my shoulder. "Come on Zee. Let's get you a drink."

"Bye Zeeeeee," Bryn caroled as Lemorak hauled me stumbling out the door.

As the door swung shut, I received a friend request notification.

New Friend Request! From: Dirzbryn Baenmtor

Accept

Decline

After only a brief debate with myself, I accepted the request without mentioning it to Lemorak. I didn't know how long I'd be in Rowling, and spending some time with the assassin might be fun. Potentially fun in a *50 Shades* kind of way, but why the hell not give it a shot?

As if reading my mind, Lemorak said, "She just likes toying with noobs. Keep in mind. You have no idea if she's really a guy or a gal IRL. Something worth thinking about. And don't forget to check your pockets."

"Wait…" Lemorak went striding on, laughing at the no doubt stunned look on my face. I ran after him. "Wait, a guy?"

It was quiet at the White Horse when we arrived, so Lemorak and I sat up at the bar again. Lemorak ordered stew in trenchers again for the both of us and a round of ale. As Lemorak ordered, I glanced around at the other common room occupants. It was still a little jarring to me, the sheer variety of forms that players had available to them here.

My neighborhood in the real world was fairly diverse, but out there regardless of skin color or physical attributes at our most basic level, we were all still human. But in the OVR Worlds, I could be sitting in a pub watching a poker game with a table populated by a fairly normal looking human with dark black skin, a towering dappled centaur, a pale two foot tall gnome, and a green skinned tusked half-orc. What's more, you knew that everyone had at some level chosen to look the way they did. It was pointless to stigmatize anyone by the way they looked, because it wasn't their real body anyways.

But then it was also jarring to consider that each of these players was probably far better off then me in a socio-economic sense. They probably all had fairly well paying jobs with Megas, inherited wealth, or some other leg-up that had let them afford this experience. In a flash, I remembered the repeated glares I'd gotten from other players after they'd noticed the inmate handle floating over my head.

"Gonna catch up on some correspondence, try to stay out of trouble." Lemorak told me before his avatar's eyes closed to mark him as navigating system menus.

Our drinks arrived and I forwent further people watching to open the screen for the handle change screen again. I sipped at my ale and futzed with various notions. Nothing felt right. Why was this so hard? When Lemorak began to stir beside me, I closed the screen in frustration.

"Any luck?" Lemorak asked, having guessed what I'd been doing.

"Don't want to talk about it," I grumped.

Lemorak smirked and shrugged his shoulders. Our dinners arrived at that moment and we both leaned in to the steaming hearty stew. Between bights, Lemorak rattled off several real world news updates to me. At first I figured Lemorak was just trying to do me a favor, being that I was an inmate, he knew I didn't have regular net access like he did. However, after summarizing several stories he started asking me probing questions too. Asking me what I thought about certain things.

The news seemed oddly irrelevant to me given our current setting, but I indulged Lemorak. I'd be stumbling around blind in the game if he hadn't taken an interest in me. If he wanted to know my opinion on politics and current affairs, it seemed a small price to pay. He didn't argue or debate with me, just occasionally nudged me to elaborate. After a while, I got the distinct impression that he was judging my answers, but he had a good poker face and I couldn't tell exactly what he thought.

"Shit man, I don't know." I sighed exasperated and pushed aside the remnants of my dinner. Lemorak had been probing my responses after telling me about a protest in Minneapolis that OzCo Security had put down violently or decisively. "It's not like it's anything new you know? Do I like it? Fuck no, but what is anyone supposed to do about it? The Megas have stacked the deck. The whole damn system is corrupt. My dad tried to fight it when he was young, and it never got him much but scars and broken bones. I've always just tried to survive and not make too many waves. And what does any of it really matter in here anyway?"

I waved my hand at the crowd of fantastical players around us. Over in one corner a bard player was playing a flute while generating an illusionary lightshow with his music. There were literally seven dwarves gathered around one squat table drinking and throwing stone dice. And in a shadowy booth an elven wizard and human warrior were passionately making out and inappropriately groping each other.

Lemorak pursed his lips and studied me for a handful of heartbeats. I could see thoughts churning behind his eyes, but I also thought that he could sense I'd hit some sort of limit. My new friend lifted his tankard of ale from the bartop and let out a long sigh.

"The only thing necessary for the triumph of evil is for good men to do nothing," he intoned solemnly, then brought the tankard to his lips and tipped it back to drain it.

Trying to drown the surge of frustration that had led to my snapping at him, I lifted my own tankard and killed it as well. Lemorak had a slightly wooden but friendly smile on his lips as I finished off the ale and set my tankard back to the bar. He waved off Travis as the NPC bartender came over to dutifully refill our drinks.

"Let's call it a night Zee."

"Lem I'm sorry, I didn't -"

Lemorak waved off my apology as he heaved himself up from the barstool. "Don't worry about it. I pushed you to it."

I followed Lemorak out of the White Horse and we walked through the quiet simulated town towards the newbie shelter in uncomfortable silence. Had I just alienated the first friend I'd managed to make in here? When we reached the town square, the windows of the newbie shelter glowing gently with lit candles on the far end, Lemorak came to a stop.

"See you again tomorrow?" I asked.

Lemorak chuckled and his shoulders seemed to relax almost imperceptibly. "If you want."

My head was nodding agreement before I'd really even considered.

"I'd be totally lost without you Lem," I said earnestly. "I can't thank you enough."

"Don't worry about it," Lemorak said and waved off my words. "It's kind of what I do."

Puzzlement briefly flashed over my face. *What did that mean?* I wondered.

"Meet you outside, same time tomorrow. We'll grind out some more kobolds. You won't get a level, but you gotta start somewhere." Lemorak spoke before I could question his previous statement.

"Sounds like a plan. Have a good night" I said with a shrug.

"You too Zee."

Shoving aside any lingering questions, I headed off across the square towards the newbie shelter.

Chapter Nine

The next day went much the same. Lemorak had me stop at the same town gate and speak to the same guard to be assigned the same quest. He explained to me that most quests were refreshed each day, and the minor ones that didn't have much story to them, were usually repeatable.

We hiked back out to the kobold village and set to drawing in small bands of the little critters again. I noticed almost immediately that now that I had leveled up, the kobolds were noticeably easier to kill, but they also awarded me less EXP. That said, my new armor kept me from getting damaged nearly as often, and since I could slay the monsters faster, I was able to handle slightly larger groups.

Lemorak didn't have to jump in and save my ass at all which was gratifying. Instead he just stood back and tossed out helpful pointers occasionally. Then at about midday we switched things up like before, so that I could get some more bow practice in.

After completing the quest to kill 50 kobolds, we made the trek back to town almost an hour earlier than we had the day before. I turned in the quest to the guard at the gate and Lemorak and I headed to the White Horse.

"Dinner's on me tonight," I insisted, feeling a little flush with crypts for the first time in my life.

The White Horse's common room was packed when we arrived, but we lucked out: a couple of players recognized Lemorak and offered us their table in front of the big fireplace as they were leaving. Despite the crowd, no one objected to us snatching the table after just walking in.

"Helped them get rolling in their first days too," Lemorak said with a wink. "Tika! Ale for me and my boy Zee!"

Ale arrived moments later, carried by a curvaceous young barmaid with a tumble of thick fiery curls, named Tika. Lemorak and I took the tankards and then the paladin proposed a toast. "To Zee the Unnamed!"

I rolled my eyes and banged my tankard into his. I really needed to pick a new handle!

Lemorak proved to be quite popular; several other players stopped by our table to say hello to the paladin. It soon became clear to me that Lemorak had been in Elmore for quite awhile, and had been Mr. Miyagi to many newbies. I couldn't decide how I felt about that. It meant I wasn't that special to Lemorak, and this might be a short-term friendship. At the same time, Lemorak seemed well respected, and I was clearly benefiting from his attention. And of course, several of Lemorak's old friends felt compelled to buy us drinks, which was nice.

Deep into my fourth - or fifth? - ale, I still hadn't come up with a new handle. Lemorak had stopped even remotely trying to help me out after our second round. Instead he was giving his own "Turing Test" to Tika, by shamelessly flirting with the buxom redhead NPC, her ample cleavage quivering as she tittered at his flirtatious lines to test her responses. I would have died of embarrassment if I'd tried even saying the most tame of the lines that Lemorak was casually throwing at the NPC.

But then, Charisma is an important stat to Paladins, I reminded myself through a haze of ale. *Lemork probably doesn't have to worry too much about the NPC Barmaid, or any Barmaid reacting negatively to him.*

Outside, a storm had rolled in over Elmore and it had begun to pour. Players started streaming in and soon the White Horse's common room was stuffed from wall to wall with bards, clerics, fighters and wizards of every stripe. Out of the crowd emerged the three players I'd briefly encountered when I'd first arrived at the White Horse, Marl, Lute, Markus. All three were drenched and had sour expressions on their faces. Before I knew it they loomed expectantly beside our table.

141

"All right, Old Timer. It's time for you and the convict to move along. We need the table," Markus said.

Lemorak glanced over from bantering with the tittering Tika. He leaned back in his chair and slapped his booted feet up onto the table. "Move along, Marky Mark and take the Funky Bunch with you." Lemorak raised his hand and made a shooing wave. "My friend and I are having another round. Or ten."

"Stop wasting space, Sir Turtle-a-lot. Some of us don't have time to loaf around," rumbled Marl.

"You corporate stooges aren't paid hourly? Tough shit." Lemorak folded his hands behind his head and grinned at the trio. A growl rolled out of the dwarf like two boulders grinding together.

"Come on, guys. They're not worth it," Lute said in a bored tone.

Marl seemed ready to press the matter. Cool and collected I could practically see gears turning behind Markus' eyes as he weighed their options. "She's right, Marl. Let the old timer and his noob pet finish their drinks."

Markus and Lute both turned away while Marl glowered at us for another heartbeat before flipping us the bird and joining them. Lemorak was looking at me as he spoke his next words, but his voice was loud and clearly pitched to follow the trio.

"Damn Mega-Fucks think they own the place. I've talked to smarter NPCs than those three."

There was a roar from Marl as he spun back around, fists balled. Having been told that there was no player-on-player violence in Elmore, I was surprised when the dwarf stomped over and took a swing at Lemorak's face. Lemorak pushed his chair further back and as he fell to the floor his booted foot nailed Marl on the chin. "Oops," Lemorak laughed as Marl stumbled back, stunned. A sudden and heavy hush blanketed the White Horse common room. Text rolled across my notification bar.

Tavern Brawl Initiated by Marl! All Damage is Nonlethal! Fists and Improvised Weapons Only! No Magic!

I had just finished reading the text when Lemorak howled in delight and launched himself to his feet, his fists swinging at the stumbling Marl. The crowd in the common room broke into cheers as the tall paladin and stocky cleric began to trade blows.

Out of the crowd came Markus barreling towards me. I scrambled to my feet just in time to receive a punch to my gut. The air in my lungs exploded and I doubled over in pain. It wasn't as bad as the weapon damage I'd taken, it sure felt a lot like a real punch.

Markus dealt 10 points of unarmed nonlethal damage to you!

90 of 100 HP remaining.

I fell back a step and gasped for air. Markus followed me step for step as I frantically threw my arms up to block his incoming blows. Stunned and gasping, my attempts at defense were less than effective. Where was my Combat Guide?

In rapid order I took another 48 points of nonlethal damage, leaving me at 42 HP. I had no idea what would happen if - or when - I hit zero. I managed to land a punch or two of my own, but it wasn't an even exchange. I had never been a street-fighter and it was showing. I had hardly made a dent in Markus's HP bar.

A crack, and pain crashed across my back as splintered chair legs tumbled past me. I went down, all fight leaving me as I crumpled to the ground. Groaning, I rolled over onto my back and saw Lute standing over me with the remains of a shattered wooden chair. The crowd exploded into fresh cheers at the spectacle. The text of Lute's attack scrolled across my vision.

Lute dealt 37 points of nonlethal damage to you with an improvised weapon!

5 of 100 HP remaining.

"Get up, Zee!" Lemorak shouted from where he held Marl in a headlock with one arm, smashing the dwarf in the face repeatedly with an empty metal tankard.

Markus's booted foot came down hard on my chest when I tried to rise, pinning me to the floor. The fighter leaned over me, his dark brown eyes drilling into mine. "You need to learn your place, convict. Hope this hurts."

Before Markus could deliver another blow, his head snapped to the side as a bare foot came from nowhere and connected hard with his face. Markus stumbled to the side, shook his head and turned to face this new combatant. I was surprised as a figure, dressed in billowing orange robes, face wrapped in a strip of orange cloth, stood silently in a defensive stance, dark eyes glittering from between a gap in the head wrap.

Lute began to say something to Markus, but the figure spun into motion. Another barefoot swept up in a crescent kick and connected with Markus's face again. He dropped to the floor in a clatter of chainmail. Whoever this was, they'd just put Markus down with essentially two hits!

Lute jumped into the fray, broken chair legs raised as improvised clubs. When Lute swung, the orange-clad figure spun away in a blur of motion and the broken chair legs whistled through empty air. Gracefully, my savior continued the motion of their dodge and another bare foot came lashing out in an axe chop kick that connected with Lute's elegant slender nose. Lute stumbled back. Markus pushed himself to his feet to rush the figure in orange, but both of orange robe's fists lashed out in rapid succession, battering through the fighter's raised arms and then pummeling his face with a flurry of blows.

Markus went down under the barrage and the orange figure followed him, pressing the advantage and raining fists down on the fighter's face. Lute was stumbling forward now to get the orange figure off her friend. I surged up from where I was lying on the floor and hit her with my best football tackle (as if I had ever actually played football).

Lute and I tumbled across the floor exchanging blows and grappling for a hold. The mage seemed a bit helpless without her magic and though she continued to struggle I soon had her pinned. Someone else must have joined the fight, because out of nowhere I felt a blinding pain at the back of my head. Just before my vision dissolved to black, a notification appeared.

D4vidtheGn0m3 dealt 7 points of non lethal damage to you!

No Hit Points remaining!

You are unconscious!

When I awoke, I was in Elmore's village square on a bench. The rain had stopped and the night air was cool on my skin. My head was throbbing. Lemorak sat on the bench at my feet and I muzzily heard him talking to someone. I groaned and rolled onto my side. My eyes still closed against the lingering pain, I read the Achievement notification waiting for me on my HUD.

Achievement Earned: And Stay Out! - Be thrown out of a Bar, Tavern or Inn for

fighting - 500 Exp

"Sleeping beauty awakes!" Lemorak chortled. His speech was noticeably slurred. I dismissed the notification and reluctantly opened my eyes.

"Fuck a duck! That gnome tinker rung his bell good," said an oddly accented unfamiliar female voice.

"What the hell was that gnome prick doing? Once you jumped in the odds was evened up. That was a perfectly kosherized brawl. Very unsportsmanly of him." I heard the slosh of liquid and looked over to see Lemorak taking a swig from a large clear bottle of dark brown liquid.

"Gnome? Tinker?" My voice was hoarse and throat raw. "What happened?"

"You..." Lemorak burped. "You, my friend, lost your first tavern brawl!"

"How did I get here?" Woozy, I pushed myself up to a sitting position. The square around me spun.

Lemorak looked at me like I was very slow. "I carried you." He took another swig and then offered me his bottle. I waved him off.

"You'll be fine in an hour or two," said the female voice. I looked around for the source and saw the orange billowing robes of my hero. She leaned against a tree several feet away, deep shadows leaving all but her bright orange clothes visible. "Nonlethal damage is just meant to slow you down. Not incapacitate."

"What happened to the others?" I asked.

"Well, after that damn Gnome jumped in, the whole thing turned into a true brawl. The guards showed up and cleared out the White Horse. We're on the ban list for 24 hours," Lemorak explained, his tone making it clear that he believed the ban to be a grave injustice. He took another long swig, then shouted at the top of his lungs, "Damn Mega-Fucks!"

"Go sleep it off, Lem. Tomorrow's another day." The woman in orange stepped out into the moonlight. "Plenty of EXP and Crypts for all."

After she stepped into the light I saw the Player tag in white over her head.

Macha, Level 0 Monk of the Stalking Tiger Way, High Elf

In my dazed state, it took me a second to realize that Macha was the handle of the girl from the waiting room. With the CC adding up on my debt in Game Management, I hadn't taken any time to customize my avatar. Being that Macha had played before, she'd likely had more time to make tweaks instead of reading Class descriptions. Or she just hadn't cared how much debt she racked up. Her avatar shared traits with her real body, but only in the most general sense. Had her real body and avatar been standing side-by-side I wouldn't have even guessed they were connected.

Her skin was the same deep rusty brown, and her hair was still jet black, but was in a short pixie cut now. Of course she was an elf here, so her ears were long and delicately pointed now. Her dark eyes and crooked smile still had the same self-assured confidence. Her face was strikingly attractive, distinctly thin and delicate. I wondered how long she'd spent adjusting each facial feature to create something so purely symmetrical and yet exotic. I hadn't seen her standing in the real world, but Macha's avatar easily matched my six feet and might have beat me by an inch. Her orange robes were loose and billowing, but I got the impression that the body beneath was whipcord thin and strong as steel.

"Good to see you again, 81348." Even though she knew it, I noticed she didn't use my real name. "I told you to look me up. How'd you wind up with this jackass?" She waved at the drunken Lemorak.

"That's Sir Jackass to you missy." Lemorak slurred. "And I have taken young Zee under my wing, like I once did with you. I believe someday he will make a fine squire!"

"I didn't exactly know what I was doing when I jacked in. Lemorak and I met on my first night when I ended up at the White Horse. He's been showing me around and helped me level up," I told Macha.

"A fine squire he will be!" Lemorak chortled and slapped me on the back.

"You've been in for three days and you're already Level 1? Impressive noob," Macha said, her eyes directed just above my head, appraising my player tag.

"Is it?" I looked over at the drunken knight, who appeared to have fallen asleep. He had said it might take a few days for me to level. I'd just thought I'd done really well.

"Fuck yeah! This is my fourth spawn. I know what I'm doing and I'm only an eighth of the way to level 1 at this point. Lemorak is hardly a prime example of a Power Leveller either."

"What do you mean?"

"Lemorak has been in Elmore longer than any other player. He's been here, hovering at Level 4, every time I connected in the last seven years," Macha explained.

"Why would anyone do that?"

Lemorak's eyes snapped open and his sharp blue eyes locked with mine. The drunken glaze that had filled his gaze a moment before was entirely clear. "I've been waiting for a player like you, Zee."

Chapter Ten

"A player like me?"

"Player like him?"

Macha and I spoke in surprised unison. Lemorak held up a hand to forestall us and looked deliberately at Macha. "Would you excuse us?"

Macha glowered at Lemorak, clearly curious and reluctant to leave. Lemorak just stared at her, his blue eyes placid. Finally, with a reluctant sigh, Macha relented. "Fine! None of my fucking business."

She stomped off into the night towards the Noobie Shelter. I couldn't help but admire her as she walked away. Was there a fetish for being into elf girls? Because if so, between Macha and Bryn, I might have unknowingly stumbled into it. *What does that say about me for picking Half-Elf as a race?* The thought was interrupted by a notification.

New Friend Request! From: Macha

Accept

Decline

There was also a message with the request. *Let's kill some shit together. ;-)*

I fully intended to do just that. I accepted Macha's friend request after reading and closing the message.

Lemorak waited several long minutes for Macha to gain some distance and then looked suspiciously around us at the shadows filling the village square. He closed his eyes and whispered some nonsensical words under his breath, then waved his arm around overhead in a circle. A glittery screen of silver light descended around us. The soft murmur of the night-shrouded village faded and Lemorak and the world outside suddenly felt very far away.

"So what? I'm Neo and you're Morpheus?"

Lemorak blinked at me in confusion for a heart beat then smirked ruefully and shook his head. "Shit that was an old reference. No you're not *The Chosen One.* But I do believe you have the potential to be very disruptive to the status quo."

I couldn't help but snort in skepticism at the assertion. "Disruptive? Me? How?"

"How many crypts have you generated towards your debt since jacking in, Zee?" Lemorak asked me after opening his eyes.

I checked for the latest number. My debt was at 1,985,802.36 CC. I did some quick mental math.

"Around 14,500 and change at the moment," I told him after checking the latest number.

Lemorak squinted. "Around 200 an hour?"

"About 250," I corrected.

"Do you know how much crypts the typical brain generates?"

"Based on the brochure I read? Between 50 and 60 CC an hour after OzCo takes their cut for pod rental, utilities and 'player upkeep.' What does it mean that I'm generating over 200 an hour?"

Lemorak considered the question for a long moment and then shrugged. "I don't really know, to be honest. Anyone that tells you different is probably a liar. But it's rare. Very rare. Players like you are about one in several billion."

Silence fell between us as I processed what he'd said.

"Is that why Macha said I got to Level 1 really fast?"

"EXP awards are connected to CC generation, though only OVR World's architect really knows how, but yes, you'll level up much faster than other players."

"And why have you been waiting for a 'player like me'? For years?"

"That's...complicated," Lemorak said carefully. "I don't know that you're ready for the entire story now. I'll say that you're not the first such

153

player I've encountered. I'll also say that I represent a group of players that have always tried to help players like you. As far as we know, you're the first player to join the game through the Inmate Program. I'm worried that you might be in a great deal of very real danger."

"Why would I be in danger?"

"Can you imagine how valuable a brain like yours would be to OzCo? Especially if they could learn to duplicate your processing power? If they figure out what you are, they might never let you out of their pods. Or if they did, it would only be to experiment on you."

"That sounds bad for me, but hardly worth you sitting around Rowling for years with your thumb up your butt."

"Money makes the world go round Zee," Lemorak intoned. "And the OVR Worlds, for better or worse, are the foundation of the global economy. I think the system could use a little disruption. More than a little."

I took a moment to digest Lemorak's words. He wasn't wrong. A familiar memory of Dad pounding his fist on the arm rest of the sofa, red faced and railing at a news broadcast flashed through my mind.

"OzCo owns my pod and my debt, can't they already tell how much Crypto I'm generating?"

"Officially OzCo developed the OVR Worlds, but most of the code was written by one man, Adam Huxley. OzCo has high level access to the game's admin SI, they can make updates, add patches and create new worlds for players to access, but they can't access much of the underlying code. Huxley was a complete privacy nut. He coded protections for player information while they're jacked in with layers of SI controlled encryption. OzCo has tried but they've never been able to crack that particular nut. For the moment, you're isolated from their monitoring. A black box. Your pod will automatically open when your debt is paid off, but for the moment, OzCo can't tell how much CC you're computing."

Another long silence fell between us as I digested what Lemorak had told me. I'd known something was weird the day before when I'd leveled up and seen how fast my debt was falling. But I'd had no idea what it meant. Lemorak, to his credit, patiently waited for me to consider everything.

"You knew. When you came up to me and Bryn in the White Horse. How?"

"I suspected. I didn't *know* until you leveled up yesterday."

"How? How could you if my pod is isolated from monitoring?"

"I have a dedicated SI running on my pod," Lemorak said after a long hesitation. "All of the members of my group do. It's programmed to look for certain indicators, aberrations in the code that players like you cause, but we have to be in relatively close proximity for it to work. I got pinged as soon as you entered Elmore that day. That's why I've stayed in Rowling

Valley for so long, so that if a new player was detected, I could help them. Help you."

Something else clicked into place.

"And last night at dinner, all your questions about what I thought about the news and politics. That was some kind of test?"

Lemorak blew out a long breath then shrugged his shoulders. "Of sorts. I needed to make sure you weren't a privileged little boot licker or a self centered asshole."

"So, what?" I knew I sounded angry, but I couldn't help it. "I passed?"

"We don't agree on everything," Lemorak winced at the edge in my tone, but held his hands up as if in surrender. "But you seem to know right from wrong, and friends don't have to agree on everything."

"What a ringing endorsement."

Oppressive silence stretched between us as my mind churned to try and catch up. Was there anything else I was missing? What else wasn't he telling me? In the end, I decided there was really only one way to find out.

"So…" I looked around at the glowing privacy screen around us. "What now? How can you help me?"

"Elmore is too small for you to stay for long." Lemorak hadn't hesitated.

He clearly already had a plan in mind, I rolled my hand in a *get on with it* gesture.

"We need to power level you to Level 5 and get you out to the rest of Gygax as quickly as possible. We also need to train up your skills above your level so that other players will underestimate you. Once you leave you'll be open to PvP. We'll avoid Mega-Corp employee players like the Three Stooges from tonight. Your debt will be paid off way quicker than anyone will expect. Once it is, your pod will open and you'll be released from prison. It won't take long for OzCo's techs to examine your pod data and figure out what happened. Here's the important trick, you can't afford to die and respawn like everyone else. Even after we leaving Rowling and Respawn becomes available. A character death triggers an immediate logout while the 12 hour re-spawn timer runs. Normally, a player just logs back in after the timer and re-spawns or creates a new character. But for you, it will open your pod and break the protections on your personal data. You can't risk leaving your pod until OzCo will release you from prison. For the sake of cost savings, their discharge process is very efficient and fast. You'll need to disappear when that happens. The CC rewards you earn from those big quest in the game will have to set you up on the outside when that happens."

"And you'll help me?" My head was spinning with the intricate plan.

"If you'll let me. That's what I've been kicking around the OZ all these years for."

Lemorak and I headed our separate ways to get some rest after he quickly outlined his plan to power level and train me. He headed to the boarding house where he rented a room, and I headed back into the noobie shelter. A different NPC Cleric greeted me at the door. I didn't bother to note his name. What was the point? However, he took note of mine.

"Inmate 81348." I tried not to wince as he rattled off my inmate designation.

"A young *lady*..." Despite being an NPC, he infused his tone with a notable degree of forced politeness with the word. "...left this note for you."

He held out a small rolled parchment to me, tied with a strip of black silk. I took the scroll and unrolled it to find a handwritten note from Bryn. Her handwriting was delicate and graceful.

Zach,

Saw you get your bell rung at the White Horse. Hope it didn't hurt too bad, sweetie. Sorry I didn't jump in to help, but the distraction of your little show made for some easy pickings on the spectators. I owe you a drink. Heading out tomorrow to quest for awhile. Don't let Lemorak suck all the fun out of your game in the meantime.

XXX

Bryn

After reading the note twice, I rolled it back up and stowed it in my inventory. I had no idea why Bryn seemed so interested in me. Every time we'd met I'd turned into a bumbling tongue-tied idiot. I had the distinct impression she enjoyed watching me squirm. After my conversation with Lemorak, I was certain that she was probably more trouble than she was worth. I was beginning to feel very uncomfortable that she knew my real first name. At the same time, my love life hadn't exactly been booming on the outside. Bryn seemed like a bad decision that I might enjoy, at least for a little while.

I asked the Brother at the shelter door to show me to my room. Shortly after, I was on my narrow bunk and staring up at my Handle Change screen. I tried not to think about the cleric standing outside my door. Lemorak had told me to pick a new name by morning. He'd also reminded me that it didn't need to be permanent. I'd be able to change my handle as often as I wanted once I had the CCs coming in.

Exhausted, I tried random names that struck my fancy and checked availability. Picking a name, a new identity just felt weird to me. In one sense, it was like picking any new online username. However, the virtual reality was so realistic, that choosing a new name felt more serious than that. Finally, I found a new handle that I could stand and that was available. I selected accept.

Player's Handle Changed to: Zee Locked-in!

Congratulations Zee Locked-in!

Players on your Friend's List have been notified.

Handle finally changed, I drifted off to sleep with only a few hours of darkness remaining.

Chapter Eleven

When I walked out of the shelter the next morning, Lemorak sat waiting for me in the same spot as the previous mornings. After exchanging pleasantries we headed directly out of the village and into the countryside. Lemorak led me to a stretch of gravelly beach along the river. The water gurgled slowly by us while upstream I could hear the creaking of the mill water wheel.

Lemorak talked me through on how to disable my Combat Guide in the game settings. He said that in a real fight I would likely still need it for a while, "...but the elite players all consider it a crutch for noobs and casuals. For training purposes it only gets in the way."

Then Lemorak began to instruct me in the basics of sword work. While demonstrating a form to me, Lemorak explained that the game monitored "player learning." It would award skill and talent levels if I acquired the training organically or demonstrated any skills I had in real life. I didn't think my proficiency with a mop would be very relevant.

"Our bodies are just simulations here," Lemorak said while guiding me through a structured dance of sword work. "Without your character stats regulating everything, the only real limitation on your body would be your ability to mentally picture what you wanted to do. You could easily do an Olympic class gymnastics routine, as long as you could imagine it exactly. But you have the Acrobatics skill and your Dexterity score regulating your capabilities. Your stats limit you from what your mind is capable of executing. Training or demonstrating skills is slower and tedious compared to just leveling up and spending your ability points. Most casuals don't bother with it, but through this method it's possible for skill ranks to far outpace your actual level."

"Is that what you've been doing all this time?" I asked as I struggled to precisely match the movements he was showing me.

"I'm a level 4 paladin, but because of my in-game training and demonstrating skills and knowledge I have in reality, I have skills and talents not typical for my level or class. Many of my skills and talents are at ranks closer to a level 10 or 12 character that only spent Ability Points to improve."

We worked and trained the morning away. After breaking for lunch, hard cheese, jerky and thick crusty bread, which Lemorak produced from his inventory, we went into the woods and Lemorak had me work on my Ranger skills. Stealth, Survival and Tracking were all on the agenda that the class trainer had given me.

With my shortbow in hand, I stalked various animals for several hours. It was during this experience that I came to appreciate another benefit of my Half-Elven race selection. I found I could peer into deep woodland shadows, seeing more clearly than I felt mere human eyes would have allowed.

"Wait till you try it in a cave, better than even the best night vision goggles." Lemorak said when I remarked on the effect.

After hours of hunting, and scaring off several animals, I brought down a small deer with a single clean arrow shot. After missing every unassisted shot I'd taken that afternoon, I had finally resorted to switching my training guide back on for the killing shot.

The slain deer didn't dissolve into dust like a killed monster did. It fell to the ground in a very realistic fashion. Lemorak helped me heft the carcass over my shoulders and had me lug it back to the beach where we'd started our training.

"Shouldn't we be heading back to town?" I asked as the sun got low in the sky.

"Better we give Elmore a break for a bit after last night. Besides, serious players tend to only head into town to pick up or turn in quests, sell off loot, rest up, or team up with other players. There's way more EXP and CC to earn out here."

At the pronouncement, I tried not to let my disappointment show at the realization that I probably wouldn't be seeing Bryn or Macha for a while. Next, Lemorak showed me how to use my Survival skill in less obvious ways. Closing my eyes, I activated the Survival skill and mentally told the game that I wanted to set up a camp. To my surprise my avatar's body began to move automatically, without input from me. It was a strange sensation even though I found I could interrupt an action with a conscious effort, but otherwise my body was on autopilot.

Before the sun had set, I'd constructed a simple lean-to from fallen branches and built us a fire ringed by stones. When I applied my Survival skill on the deer carcass, my hands instantly and skillfully skinned and butchered the carcass while the constituent parts were deposited into my inventory. Using the fire, Lemorak and I cooked some of the venison and had ourselves dinner under the open night sky. When I checked my Character Stats that night before falling asleep, my Stealth, Survival, Tracking, and Athletics skills had all improved from +2 to +3.

The next day we rose with the sun, ate a breakfast of cold leftover venison, then broke camp and hiked several miles deeper into the wilds of

Rowling Valley. My muscles burned from the previous day's exertions, and a night camping on the hard cold ground had left knots in my back.

"That'll get better as your Athletics skill improves," Lemorak told me after I griped about it. "A good Athletics skill will also slow the drain on your Endurance."

By mid-morning the exercise had worked all the kinks out, so we stopped and began practicing sword work again. I felt more comfortable with the stances and movements Lemorak had shown me the day before, but my exacting mentor still called out a litany of my errors.

After a foraged lunch of berries and fruit, courtesy of my Survival skill, we continued our walkabout. Lemorak had me exercise my Ranger skills at every opportunity. I used Tracking to trail wild game, Stealth to remain undetected and my Survival to identify useful plants and herbs.

While hunting I snagged a couple of rabbits, thanks to my archery guide again. That night I broke a new camp. With the increase to my Survival skills, the process went faster than the day before and the simple lean-to I constructed was a little sturdier.

Lemorak and I proceeded like this for over a week. When we saw signs of other players, we adjusted our path to avoid them. While we hiked we looked for any excuse for me to practice my various skills. He also shared with me knowledge and tips for the OVR Worlds in general, and Gygax specifically.

Whenever we stopped hiking we'd work on combat abilities. My swordwork improved enough that Lemorak and I could engage a sparring mode that allowed us to fight each other at full speed and force. The damage from sparring was *non-lethal* and still stung, but the Hit Points that I lost instantly replenished as soon as we rested for a few minutes.

Along the way we frequently came across wandering monsters, orcs, goblins and kobolds mostly. If the creatures were low enough level, Lemorak let me fight them solo, only coming to help if an encounter proved too difficult. However, Lemorak consistently avoided dealing the killing blow. He told me he was very close to reaching level 5 and couldn't risk earning too much EXP. Once he hit level 5, the system would require him to depart the OZ, whether he wanted to or not.

Lemorak steered our trip to various NPCs with quests for me. A human wizard that wanted me to kill some rats in his basement that he had accidentally turned into the size of Dobermans. An elven druid that needed help collecting a particular moss. Then the centaur ranger that challenged me to an archery contest. I lost to him four times despite using my archery guide. Lemorak had me repeat the quest - the centaur NPC reset each time I failed - until I finally beat him on the fifth go around. We found a little dwarf girl that had gotten lost in the woods after wandering too far from her clan's stone quarry. And several other quests, ranging from mundane chores to small feats of heroics.

On one of those side quests, Lemorak guided me to a small copper mine in the foothills of the Salvatore Mountains that ringed Rowling Valley. There I talked to a frantic dwarf NPC. He told me that his miners had been chased out by a nest of giant spiders, and I agreed to help eliminate the pests.

"You can handle this one on your own. It's pretty straightforward," Lemorak told me as we stood at the entrance to the mine. "If you get in a bind just retreat out of the mine. Watch out for the Queen in the big chamber at the back, she can be a bitch. She can't fit in the tunnels though, so just avoid her. She's not a win condition for the quest."

I drew my weapons and descended into the mine alone. As the darkness enveloped me fully, my Half-Elven Night Vision kicked in. I found I could clearly see in the darkness out to 15 feet around me, although everything was in black and white. Beyond the 15 feet, my vision was hazed and foggy.

Reaching a fork in the tunnel, I went left on a whim. Almost immediately I began to encounter tomcat-sized spiders, crawling along the floor, walls, and ceiling in ones, twos, and threes.

Giant Spider, Level 0 Pest

When the spiders came at me, my combat guide engaged and I hacked away at them with my short sword and dagger. The spiders smacked at me with their legs and tried to bite at me with slavering oversized mandibles. Fortunately, these spiders didn't have a venomous bite, and while they were creepy as hell, they weren't very tough. I found their legs to be convenient targets for hacks and chops of my short sword. As quickly as possible, I'd dismember the pests, then finish them off with relative ease.

I'd been at it for a little over an hour, methodically working my way deeper into the mine, when I heard a woman's shout echo out from the deeper darkness ahead of me. The cry stopped me in my tracks. Was it part of the quest? A fair NPC maiden that needed rescuing? Little twists of story weren't unusual, but Lemorak hadn't mentioned anything.

Tightening my grip on my weapon, I pushed forward against the insistence of my jangling nerves. The echoing cries and sounds of battle became more frequent and closer with each step. Whatever was happening must have drawn the attention of all the spiders in the area, because I wasn't encountering any as I ran. My tunnel finally opened into a cavernous chamber dimly lit by glowing moss growing along the walls. The illumination allowed my Half-Elf enhanced eyes to see beyond the normal 15 feet radius.

I was at the top of a narrow stone ramp, leading down to the chamber floor. The dim light of the moss reflected off the glistening wet stone of the chamber. Stalagmites and stalactites jutted from the floor and hung from the ceiling. The heaving bodies of several dozen spiders all circled around a lone woman in black leather armor and a purple cloak with the hood pulled up. I immediately saw her biggest predicament: a massive glob of ropey white spider web glued one foot to the floor.

The woman was barely holding the circling spiders at bay with a cracking whip and the broken remains of a snapped rapier. A chittering roar came out of the shadowy gloom beyond my vision and trembled the stone floor beneath my feet. Then, stirring in those deep shadows, I saw the lurking form of a massive spider, the size of a small pick up truck. The Queen.

"Any time you want to jump in and kill some of these shits, feel free!" the woman shouted, and I immediately recognized Bryn's voice. An instant grin tugged at the corners of my mouth as any temptation I might have felt to retreat vanished.

With my short sword and dagger in hand, I moved down the ramp and began hacking and stabbing my way through the mob of spiders. Spiders began dying under my assault. The Queen let out a chittering roar that sent fresh tremors up through my boots and bristled the hair and the back of my neck with a lizard-brain alarm of danger.

Halfway to Bryn's position, I found my Endurance bar was plummeting fast, and it felt like I was barely making a dent in the mass of spiders. I'd only lost a few HP so far on the quest, but that would change if I didn't get a breather. Gritting my teeth in determination, I pushed forward despite the rising risk. I finally cut my way through the spiders and stumbled into the small circle of clear ground that Bryn had held onto.

The dark elf's glowing red eyes widened in surprise as she caught full sight of me. Then a playful smile quirked her full lips,

"Are you following me?" Despite the immediate danger, her tone was light and playful.

"Thought I'd take you up on that drink offer." I grinned at her, then, with my sword, batted away a spider that had dropped off the ceiling. In the back of my mind, I observed that the surge of adrenaline seemed to have freed me of the stuttering fumbling madness that had consumed me every time we talked before. Or maybe she just wasn't laying it on thick with her high Charisma in that moment.

"Fabulous timing, sweetie." Bryn lashed out with several cracks of her long leather whip to drive back a probing rush of spiders. "Watch my back while I cut free of these webs, would you?"

"As you wish." I offered a mocking courtly bow before turning my back to her and following the form of my combat guide, spinning into a series of slashes with my sword and dagger to drive the spiders back.

Seconds later, freed of the webbing, I sensed Bryn step up behind me, her back to mine. The Spider Queen shrieked in fury as her offspring rushed us and fell in droves. Bryn and I circled back to back. We moved intuitively together, almost dancing, our bodies communicating through shoulder pressure, through bumps of our hips and butts. After several seconds, I realized that Bryn was giggling like a jubilant school girl.

The last of my Endurance bar drained away within seconds of our offensive, and I started to lose HP as a result. With each drop of HP, muscle cramps shot through my legs and arms.

"I can't keep this up for long," I shouted to Bryn while plunging my dagger into the multifaceted eye of a spider. A critical strike notification scrolled by my vision, but I was already whirling onto the next attack.

"We're going to have to work on your Endurance if we're…" Bryn's quip was cut off as another chittering cry erupted from the Queen and the tide of spiders stopped moving like they'd all just become statues. Bryn and I stood there back-to-back, chests heaving as we absorbed the change of dynamics.

"This can't be good." The rasp of Bryn's whisper sent shivers up my spine and I wasn't sure if it was lust or fear.

"Maybe we won?" I asked. A notification I'd been ignoring waited at the bottom of my vision.

Achievement earned - Pest Control - Kill 50 giant rats, insects, or other vermin type creatures - 25% bonus damage against pest creatures in the future

171

As if on cue the Queen leapt out of the shadows beyond my night vision. She soared over our heads and landed astride the ramp leading to our exit. Now she was fully lit by the glowing moss for the first time, and I could see her bulbous chitinous dark green body was at least the size of an ox, eight long legs as tall as I was, and slavering clacking mandibles. She hissed out a fresh rage-filled shriek, and in unison her soldier spiders all rippled into movement, falling away from us to scurry back into the mine's tunnels.

Giant Spider Queen, Level 5 Pest

"You were saying?" Bryn asked wryly as we surveyed the Queen.

I was too busy looking for another exit or some sort of solution to quip back. While scanning the ceiling a plan took shape in my head. Gulping nervously, I looked over at Bryn. "Think you can keep her in that spot for a second or two?"

She quirked a silver eyebrow at me in a Spock-like expression, but she nodded her head. "Got a spare blade?"

"I won't need it anyway," I said, holding my short sword out to her hilt first.

Bryn tossed aside her broken rapier and accepted the short sword. With my sword in one hand and her whip in the other, she charged the Spider Queen. Bryn held the short sword out defensively, while she cracked the whip to keep the Queen from rushing forward or skittering from side to side.

Meanwhile, I sheathed my dagger and unslung my bow. I notched an arrow and picked my target carefully among the shifting shadows along the ceiling. Not for the first time, I was thankful for my Half-Elven racial selection and the accompanying night vision. With a grunt of effort, I put a full draw on the bow string and put my aiming guide on target, then loosed. The arrow snapped off the string and cracked into the stone at the base of a cluster of stalactites. Sparks flew from the impact. I hoped it wasn't just wishful thinking, but I thought there was a noticeable quiver in the stone

Dodging a swipe of one of the Queen's front legs, Bryn giggled merrily as she guessed at my plan. "Clever boy!"

Determined or desperate, I drew and let fly three more arrows rapid fire. My second to last shot did the trick. Whether realistic or not, the arrowhead buried itself in the stone with a sharp *crack*. Small rocks began to fall from the ceiling, then stalactites broke free. The pointed stone spears plummeted from the ceiling towards the Queen. I followed the falling stones down with my gaze. Focused on doing her part, Bryn had moved too close.

Driven by instinct, I dove and wrapped an arm around her narrow waist. She howled with exhilaration as I hauled her back. Rocks crashed to the floor where she'd been standing a heartbeat before. I threw her to the ground and came down atop her, shielding her with my own body. Several stones clipped me painfully and knocked away HP, but nothing critical.

The Queen shrieked over the rumble of stone for an instant, but abruptly cut off when she was impaled by multiple falling stalactites. Bryn and I coughed as thick dust billowed around us. Darkness fell as the dust blotted out the glowing moss. We lay there gasping and coughing for several long minutes as dust settled.

I suddenly became acutely aware of the lush leather-clad curves of the body beneath me. Bryn's softly glowing red eyes opened, two flickering beacons in the pitch black of the cavern. They illuminated her alluring still inexplicably familiar face. Then I felt soft hands at the back of my head and she pulled me down into a deep kiss, her tongue shoved demandingly into my mouth. When she pulled away, she bit down and tugged at my lower lip.

"Thanks for the save, Zack." Her voice was a raspy purr.

My head spinning, Bryn elegantly slid out from under me. Seconds later, when blood flow resumed to my brain, I rolled over and got the distinct impression that I was entirely alone in the chamber. "Bryn?"

Silence.

The darkness of the chamber was so thick that my 15 feet of night vision didn't even let me see the walls. I withdrew a torch from my inventory and lit it. The chamber was entirely empty. My short sword lay discarded a few feet away.

The corpse of the Spider Queen had already been looted. Usually only the killer of a monster could claim the loot from a corpse, but during Character Generation I'd noticed Rogues and Assassins both had the ability to steal loot on kills that weren't theirs.

"You sneaky bitch," I grumbled as I retrieved and sheathed my sword.

There was a new achievement notification awaiting my notice.

Achievement Earned - FATALITY! - Kill an enemy using a feature of the environment

- 50% bonus Exp for the Encounter!

Well that's something I guess. Torch in hand and short sword at the ready, I made my way out of the mines. Lemorak met me halfway back on the way out.

"You all right?" he asked. "I saw that snake Bryn come rushing out of the entrance with a shit-eating grin on her face and thought I'd come check on you."

"Yeah, fine," I muttered, embarrassed. Together we made it out of the mine without further incident. I turned in the completed quest to the dwarf NPC and we got on with our day.

***

A day after the mines, I reached level 2 after slaying my first Ogre. I'd needed a little help from Lemorak to survive the experience, but it had been an exhilarating if slightly terrifying experience. The rush of pleasure that the level up sent through my senses was even stronger than reaching Level 1. I wondered how Lemorak had forestalled reaching Level 5 for so many years. I completed my Level Up with Al's assistance.

"Alright Al, tell me how Charisma works."

"Charisma? You don't need Charisma Zee. Ziggy says that's a dump stat for Rangers!" The image of the synthetic intelligence software look at me with confusion.

"I need to understand how other players with high Charisma might influence me." Then I told Al about the flustered dweeb I turned into anytime Bryn batted her red eyes at me. My SI assistant was chortling by the time I was done. I resisted the futile urge to strangle the program.

"The Charisma score mostly helps players influence NPCs," Al said after his laughter subsided under my withering glare. "It makes an NPC more likely to give the player a favorable or pleasant interaction. It also gives them access to several avatar customization features, allowing them to more easily import various templates deemed highly attractive by most people. But for players without perception filters, like you, it can monkey with the player's simulated autonomic responses. Creating general good vibes, a sense of trust, but also an arousal response."

"She can fuck with my head like some kind of sex jedi?" My voice cracked with alarm.

"Nothing quite that bad Zee." Al tried to sound soothing, but it wasn't really what the program was meant for.

"Lemorak is a Paladin, he's probably got a decent Charisma himself. It's mostly just suggestive. Bryn's just got a little more Vava to go with her VOOM. If you know what I mean. She'd probably picked up a seduction talent or something to help." Al wagged his eyebrows at me suggestively and I sighed in annoyance.

"I know all too well what you mean, and I'm sick of it Al. Aside from getting a perception filter, which isn't an option, how can I counter a high Charisma score?" I didn't like the idea of Bryn or anyone being able to screw around with my reactions.

"You're already on your way lass! Charisma might be your dump stat, but Wisdom is the source of Willpower and you've already started beefing it up as one of your secondary stats. Get it high enough and you'll have a clear head against most Charisma based influences."

"Let's get to work leveling up then."

It didn't seem wise to dump all my ability points into improving my Wisdom right then. Most of my time was spent fighting after all, but I made sure to bump my Wisdom a point. I also ordered Al to at least remind me to evaluate Wisdom at each level up.

CHARACTER STATISTICS

Handle: Zee Locked-in

Race: Half-Elf

Role: Striker

Class/Level: Ranger/2

ABILITIES

Strength (Endurance): 14 (20)

Strength Skills: Melee Combat, Athletics, Carrying Capacity

Dexterity (Defense): 14 (15)

Dexterity Skills: Ranged Combat, Acrobatics, Stealth, Sleight of Hand,

Open Lock. Reflex

Constitution (Hit Points): 15 (115)

Constitution Skills: Concentration, Fortitude

Intelligence (Arcane Mana): 10 (NA)

Intelligence Skills: Arcana, Investigation. Appraise, Disable Device. Forgery,

Lore

Wisdom (Faith Mana): 13 (66)

Wisdom Skills: Conviction. Perception, Survival, Tracking, Animal

Handling, Medicine, Willpower

Charisma (Inspiration): 10 (NA)

Charisma Skills: Imagination, Deception, Intimidation, Persuasion,

Influence

RACIAL SKILLS: Half-Elf Wilderness Skills: Survival (+1), Stealth (+1),

Tracking (+1)

RACIAL TALENTS: Half-Elf Flexibility (+5 AP at Level 0, +1 AP),

Nightvision (15'), Elven Bow Proficiency +1 Level

CLASS SKILLS: Athletics (+3), Survival (+5), Stealth (+4), Animal Handling (+3), Tracking (+5)

CLASS TALENTS: Archery (Level 4), Two-Weapon Fighting (Level 5), Light Armor Proficiency, Favored Enemy (Goblin)

EARNED SKILLS: None

EARNED TALENTS: Surprise Attack (Achievement)

CARRIED EQUIPMENT: Leather Armor (+3 Defense), Short-sword, Dagger, Short-bow, Arrows x20, Stone Hatchet

STORED EQUIPMENT: Standard Clothes

COMBAT STATISTICS

Weapon - Talent Modifier - Weapon Damage - Accuracy - Median Damage

Shortsword - 5 - 20 - 14 - 66

Dagger (off-hand) - 5 - 14 - 12 - 45

Stone Hatchet - 5 - 10 - 14 - 56

Shortbow - 4 - 18 - 13 - 68

ACHIEVEMENTS: First Kill, Backstabber, Good Samaritan, Goblin Slayer, Kobold Slayer, And Stay Out!, Ain't Got Time to Bleed, "The dishes are done man.", Marathon Runner, Orc Slayer, Pest Control, FATALITY, Specialist (Survival, Stealth, Tracking), Trained (Animal Handling), Practice Makes Perfect (Survival, Stealth, Tracking), Hunter, Gone Fishin, Camp Cook

TOTAL ABILITY POINTS: 16

CURRENT CRYPTOCURRENCY: 226.58

CURRENT DEBTS: 4,654,207.86 CC - OzCo Department of

Corrections

CURRENT EXPERIENCE: 2,093

EXPERIENCE TO NEXT LEVEL: 5,000

On the tenth day of our hike, we came across a clearing where Macha was fighting a small mob of goblins. I felt a surge of excitement at coming across a familiar player. No offense to Lemorak, but Macha seemed a much more...*attractive* travel companion. And unlike Bryn she didn't seem like the kind to loot and run.

"She's got this. Kill stealing is for assholes." Lemorak put a hand on my shoulder, halting the step forward I took to go help out.

We stood at the edge of the clearing and watched. Macha was Level 1 now. She still wore the same flowing orange tunic and billowing pants, but now wielded a long curved katana. We stood in plain view, but far enough away not to pull the aggro of her opponents. I kept my bow ready, but without any tension on the string. Macha danced, sliced, dodged and rolled her way through the fight with tremendous grace.

Lemorak explained that monks were generally considered a Striker class. Martial artists, they specialized in mostly unarmed and unarmored combat, utilizing flurries of well-placed blows to overwhelm an opponent. They had limited weapons proficiencies, mostly martial arts themed weapons, like the katana or nunchucks, but monks were just as lethal with their fists and feet as I was with blades or a bow.

The whipcord elf-monk was a twirling whirling dervish of goblin death. Each of her movements were smooth and graceful. When she attacked, she used her fists, feet, elbows, legs, knees, and even head about as often as her flashing sword. Watching Macha's fluid movements, I began to appreciate the skills she possessed, even at a Level 1. She wasn't quite at a Jackie Chan or Jet Li level of skill, but I could understand how she had quickly overwhelmed Markus in the White Horse brawl.

When the last goblin fell, Lemorak began clapping and hollered across the distance, "Well done, Macha!"

Macha gave us a wave and while she looted the goblins we walked across the meadow. She gave us her trademark cocky smile as we approached, the sun casting a warm glow on her dark brown skin Sheathing her sword into a scabbard across her back, she stepped forward to shake hands. I noticed her palms and knuckles were wrapped in strips of rough cloth, but her slender fingers felt soft and smooth against mine.

"What've you two been up to?" Macha asked. "Been looking for you around town."

"Just a bit of a walkabout for our Ranger friend here," Lemorak explained.

"Level 2 already, Zee? Sir Turtle seems to be taking good care of your training. Wish he'd been nearly so kind to me on my first jack."

"After all this time, he knows all the best Exp Farms in the valley," I answered. That was technically true, but I felt my cheeks blush at the lie of omission.

"People will start to call you two the Turtle and the Hare if you're not careful," Macha joked. I looked to gauge Lemorak's reaction, but he just grinned and chuckled.

"Care to join us for a while? Zee could use a new sparring partner. I've been getting bored."

I was surprised by his offer. Lemorak had been trying to keep us away from other players, but I stamped down any reaction. After all, I *wanted* Macha to join our little group. Maybe Lemorak had decided Macha was someone worth having on the team. Someone worth trusting, at least a little. He had played with her before, after all. Macha appeared to weigh the offer for a moment, but then shook her head.

"Nah, I'm good." She turned to walk away.

"Macha wait!..." My mouth hung open as I tried to think of a way to sell her on joining us.

She was almost ten feet away when she stopped and looked back over her shoulder at us. "But you two are welcome to tag along with me for awhile."

I turned an eager expression to Lemorak. The paladin just rolled his eyes, then stepped off to follow Macha across the open field. I sprung forward a step behind him. *Yes!*

After Macha joined us - or we joined her - Lemorak quietly told me to be careful of my leveling. Macha would notice if I continued along at my naturally heightened pace. After that, when we did encounter monsters, I'd engage alongside Macha, but often pulled the killing blows to let Macha finish them off instead and gain the Exp.

Lemorak took to spectating and coaching sparring sessions between Macha and me. We proved to be evenly matched. Macha's speed and grace proved about as effective a defense as my armor and own dexterity. My dual blades seemed more obviously threatening than Macha's single blade, but I was frequently caught off guard by a snapping kick or driving fist if I let her get too close.

As the third week after leaving Elmore came to an end, we had almost fully circumnavigated the valley and Macha had just reached Level 2, while I was about halfway to Level 3. My scrubby thin beard had continued to grow and thicken, becoming a respectable if slightly unkempt beard. My hair had continued to grow as well, and I reluctantly agreed to let Macha braid my wavy mane when it started tickling my shoulders.

The exploration had left me with a fairly good idea of the terrain of the valley, and large portions of my game map were now filled in. In fact, more of the map was complete now than was missing. The unexplored areas were zones within the valley for level 4 characters almost ready to hit 5 and leave the valley.

That night, as we sat around camp, after Macha completed her level up, Lemorak announced that we'd all be taking the day off. He said he had to log off from the game to attend to some *real world business*. After almost a month in the game, the *real world* seemed incredibly far away. Gygax almost felt like home. I felt a flash of guilt at the realization. I wondered how Mom and Dad were doing. I asked Lemorak if he could relay an email for me. The paladin agreed.

In keeping with the fantasy setting of Gygax, I had to write the message out by hand on parchment with a quill. Fortunately, Lemorak lent me the supplies. I couldn't remember the last time I'd written anything at length, by hand, and without technological assistance like spellcheck or auto-complete.

Ever security-conscious, Lemorak said he'd set up a new account on a "free" server so that I wouldn't have to share any existing login information with him. I addressed the message to a dead-drop account that my Mom, ever the cyber paranoid hacker, had made me memorize as an adolescent.

"Can I pass anything along for you, Macha?" Lemorak asked as I scribbled away my messages.

Macha snorted through her delicate elven nose before replying, "No one out there worth writing to, Lem."

"Fair enough," he said with a shrug.

In the morning, Lemorak logged out. He'd told Macha and me that he'd be back in eight to ten hours, and to keep the campsite up while he was gone. Then my friend closed his blue eyes and his body went impossibly still. Macha and I sat there, weapons in hand, as the logout process ran its course. To keep players from logging out in the middle of a fight, a player's avatar was present but completely helpless for fifteen minutes after logging out. If some monster stumbled across us during Lemorak's logout, we'd have to protect him.

Macha and I watched as the colors of Lemorak's avatar slowly drained away to grayscale. Once all color had faded, his body started to fade away. It wasn't until he had completely vanished that we let our guard down and shared a sigh of relief. When Lemorak logged back in, he'd pop back into existence in the same exact spot, but that would be instantaneous and without the same looming risk.

Macha and I sat awkwardly around our banked campfire for several minutes. Our companionship to that point, with Lemorak in the group, had been light and quippy. Sitting there just the two of us, I couldn't think of anything to say to the alluring woman I suddenly found myself alone with. Macha didn't seem to know how to react either.

Realizing there were some camp chores to get out of the way, I jumped at the opportunity to break the stalemate we'd stumbled into. I activated my Survival skill and my avatar automatically began to move through the process of shoring up our small lean to, chopping firewood and other mundane tasks. While my body worked, my brain spun, trying to figure out what we were supposed to do with the rest of the day.

Thirty minutes later, when I was done with the camp chores, my autopilot movements stopped and I had to consciously take control of my body once more. I looked around the small camp and realized that I was completely alone.

"Macha?" I called out, but there was no response. My hands dropped to the hilts of my weapons at my waist and I felt my guts twist. "Macha?"

Chapter Twelve

I activated my Tracking skill and scanned for signs of Macha. After over thirty minutes of scanning the camp, I found the faint outline of a barefoot in some soft earth. The print took on a soft yellow glow as my Tracking skill highlighted it. Her trail was barely detectable at all.

How had I been so distracted that I didn't notice her leaving?

Following her trail was slow methodical work that required carefully scanning the ground and brush for the hints of her passage. It was harder than any of the wild animals or monsters that I'd tracked before. I sometimes had to look over the same patch of ground multiple times before I found the next sign, and then I had to guess at the direction and keep scanning. There wasn't a helpful highlighted path for me to follow. Damn, she was good.

All told, it took me over an hour to finally catch up with her. It was a distance that likely would have only taken her fifteen or twenty minutes to walk. In the end, I found her when I abandoned the tracks to investigate the sound of splashing water ahead.

I rushed forward, weapons in hand, prepared to leap to Macha's rescue. And slid to a hasty halt when I saw her. She was floating peacefully on the surface of a small steaming pool of water, without a stich of clothing. Countless rivers and streams crisscrossed Rowling. Judging by the steam wafting from the surface of the water, Macha had found the head of a hot spring. Crystal clear water, without an apparent source, filled the small pool, before falling over an edge to flow away in a trickling stream.

And did I mention that Macha was completely naked?

At first, I couldn't help but stand there breathless, racing heart thundering in my pointed ears, and admire the expanse of smooth dark skin shifting smoothly over lean-toned muscles as Macha drifted there, oblivious. She had designed a tight gymnast's body for her avatar, a washboard stomach, and slight but still decidedly feminine curves. Dark nipples stood out against the gentle swell of her small perky breasts. Her legs, usually concealed by billowing loose pants, were long and athletically sculpted, slowly kicking as she floated on the water.

When the initial shock of discovery wore off, I slipped back into cover and paused to consider my next steps. Had she meant for me to follow her?

Had her obvious attempt at a stealthy departure just been a game? Would I be welcome to join her? Or would I be risking one of the few budding friendships that I had in the game?

Torn with indecision, I looked back the way I'd come and then turned my gaze to where Macha still floated aimlessly and oblivious to my presence. I wished I hadn't been totally zoned out when she slipped away. Maybe she had said something to me. Ultimately, I decided to err on the side of not being a perv. Letting out a long reluctant sigh, I turned to head back to camp.

A thin fallen branch cracked under my booted foot.

"Who's there?" Macha called out. "Zee, is that you? Took you long enough!"

I spun back around, certain that my face was burning like a supernova. Macha was treading water in the middle of the pool, the water just barely covering her shoulders. I stepped out from beneath the shade of the tree cover, my mind racing for something appropriate to say. Finally, I just waved and smiled. Smooth. I know.

"You're such a flatline!" Macha laughed and splashed a wave of water in my general direction. "You gonna jump in or what?"

Then Macha took a deep breath and dove beneath the surface. Hands trembling, I started pulling my armor and gear off. Without the need to actually bathe, and since the game allowed me to sleep in it completely comfortably, I realized I hadn't removed the leather armor since first putting it on almost a month ago. Fumbling with the straps and ties that held it in place, I tossed the armor to the ground with the rest of my gear. Macha had surfaced but was swimming away from me, giving me some privacy as I undressed.

The morning air was cold on my pale skin. Climbing gingerly over the rocks at the bank of the pond, I made my way to the pool's edge. There was a shallow shelf running around the edge of the pool, before it dropped off quickly to a deeper sandy bottom below. I dipped an experimental toe in and found the water was stinging hot at first, but only because the stones I'd been walking on had left my feet ice cold. Gritting my teeth, I stepped down onto the shelf, the hot water enveloping me up to my knee. The burn quickly faded and became pleasant.

"Hurry up!" Macha shouted, her back still to me.

Pushing forward, I was *noticeably* excited and felt eager to get covered by the water. I stepped off the shelf and sank down. The hot water slid up over me and covered my head before I kicked back to the surface. I felt knots in my neck, back and legs I hadn't known I'd had loosen as the heat sank into my digital body. When I surfaced, I let out an involuntary groan of pleasure as steam swirled around my head.

"Awesome, right?" Macha asked as she stroked in a wide semi-circle around me.

"How'd you find this place?" I asked.

"Previous time jacked in." She scrunched her face and added, "I think it was my human druid? Which would have been my first character."

"You haven't always been a monk?"

"No way!" Macha said with a big grin. "I try something different every time. Though, I have to say that so far, monk is my fave."

While we swam idle circles around each other or treaded water, Macha proceeded to tell me about the aforementioned human druid, who she'd gotten all the way to level 7 and out to the rest of Gygax, before being taken out by a marauding band of player killers, PKs. Then there had been her dwarven barbarian, who she'd made it the furthest with, level 10, before getting taken out by a doublecrossing Shadowkin assassin she'd been adventuring with. Lastly, her character just before her current monk had been a dragonkin warlock. She'd only gotten to level 5 with her warlock before being killed in an ambush of PKs hunting noobs just outside the valley. Throughout her long descriptions and stories, I almost managed to forget that the two of us were naked. Almost. I hoped the flush in my ears was being written off as just flush from hot water.

"Is it really that bad out there?" I asked. I'd been looking forward to getting to level 5 and out to the rest of Gygax, but less so after hearing about her previous experiences.

"It can be. The first time, I didn't bother to change my Inmate handle. That put a target on my back the moment I stepped out of the valley. I didn't make that mistake twice. All the same, taking out an unwary player, inmate or not, can be juicy EXP and great loot. Less work than clearing a dungeon or grinding through a lot of quests. But really most people that choose to be PKs as their game strategy are just sadists. They *like* hurting people. And hunting inmates without perception filters is especially fun for them."

After that, Macha chose to lighten things up by telling me about some of the adventures she'd had in her previous incarnations. The standing custom of not talking about the details of our real lives held, which put much of the conversational effort on her. I tried to chime in with a quippy joke or pertinent question whenever I saw the chance.

We laughed and swam and relaxed. I was pleased to notice that my skin never got pruny, and as the sun rose higher, Macha told me we didn't even have to worry about sunburn either.

"Since they didn't formulate sunscreen into the world, sunburns would've been a real jerk move by the programmers," Macha said with a chuckle.

Eventually, we found ourselves laying our heads back on the rocky bank, reclining side-by-side on the shelf of the hot springs. I endeavored to keep my eyes on the deep blue sky overhead, and not let them drift down to

Macha's naked body. More then once I was certain she caught me looking somewhere other than her face. She seemed to have no shyness at being on full display, though she let my lingering eyes go uncommented upon, My initial *excitement* had long since worn off. I kept trying to catch Macha checking me out, but if she was, she was far more subtle than me. Which wouldn't be surprising.

Finding that she'd run through all her stories of note from her previous adventures, we fell into a long companionable silence. I glanced over at Macha and saw that she'd closed her eyes while she continued to bask in the warmth of the water and the sun.

I had no idea if my virtual body included simulated hormones or not. However, in that moment, I felt an overwhelming urge to kiss her delicate lips. Without reconsidering the impulse, my heart thumping like a jack hammer, I slid closer and did just that.

Her entire body instantly stiffened in surprise. I thought that any second, she would process what had happened and melt into my embrace and return the kiss. I imagined her moaning in pleasure, wrapping her arms around me and our naked bodies pressing together. Instead her hand reached up to my bare chest - now not nearly as soft and pudgy as my real body - and gently pushed me back. Heart seizing in my chest, I instantly pushed myself away from her.

"Whoa there, tiger!" Macha said with a chuckle.

"S-S-Sorry," I stammered as I flung myself out of the water onto the shore.

The only thought in my head was to flee. Maybe I could find a convenient cliff and throw myself off it. Snatching up my discarded gear I raced into the cover of the forest still naked.

"Zee! Wait come back!"

I ignored her cry.

After pausing to get dressed. I retraced my steps back to camp. I berated myself the entire way. Of course she hadn't wanted me. She was the one person in here who had seen my real body. *Of course, I saw hers too.* I instantly felt ashamed at that thought. I'd been the initiator, knowing full well what her real body was like, and the truth was I didn't care. At least I hadn't at that exact moment. The Macha I knew was the one inside this stupid game. She was more real to me here than she'd been out in that waiting room.

Upon my return to camp, I found it more or less how I'd left it. The fire had dwindled down to ash-covered embers. I robotically stoked the fire back to life, then set to work on dinner with the small camp cooking set that Lemorak had left us with before logging out. Visions of hurling myself off a cliff in embarrassment had quickly faded, but I desperately wanted to keep myself busy and distracted. Lemorak logged back in a couple hours later.

"This arrived just before I logged back in." Lemorak handed me a rolled parchment sealed with a red wax seal. "It's heavily encrypted, so I hope you have a password already."

"Shouldn't be a problem." Like the dead drop account, Mom had made me memorize her complex rotating password scheme a long time ago. "Thanks."

I left my rabbit stew simmering by the fire and climbed into the lean-to I'd constructed when we setup camp to read Mom's message. When I slid my knife blade under wax seal and broke it, a login window appeared before me requesting a password. Double checking the day's date, I recalled the appropriate passphrase, then adjusted the spelling based on Mom's rotating substitution pattern. By the end of it, I'd entered what appeared to be a random string of letters, numbers and symbols.

Despite being fairly confident that I'd done everything right, I still held my breath as I hit submit. Mom's encryption would only let me make two attempts. However, the password was accepted and the scroll of parchment in my hand unfurled. With a sigh of relief, I began to read.

From: BadW0lf359@anomshieldfwd.br

To: InvaderZed@freemail.net

Subject: Checking In

Zack,

Dad and I were so relieved to finally get your message. I was a day or two away from hacking my way into the OzCo mail server. We hadn't been able to get any information on your sentence or where they sent you. To say I'm relieved that you got accepted into the Inmate Gamer Program is an understatement, compared to the alternatives.

I still don't know whether to be incredibly proud or unspeakably pissed at what you did. Children shouldn't have to make this kind of sacrifice for their parents. Your dad isn't at all ambiguous on the matter, he unabashedly proud of you, being the anarchist nut job that he is.

Things are a bit up in the air out here. I don't want to worry you, but we got evicted a few days ago, and haven't found a new place yet. Your dad still can't find work that isn't under the table day work. And I haven't had much better luck. We're not on the street! We're staying with Cousin Ned at the moment. I'm working my network, and hopefully we'll be back on our feet soon. I'll keep you posted, so long as you promise not work worry about us!

Good luck in Gygax. Your old Mom used to be a pretty badass Half-Fiend Warlock back in the day. I hope you have a good group around you. Solos never got very far in my experience.

Love you to the Moon and back,

Mom

There were tears streaming down my cheeks, and virtual or not, they felt entirely real. I read and re-read the message several times before finally rolling the scroll back up and stowing it in my inventory. Mom probably would have told me to destroy it, but I couldn't.

At first I'd just been relieved to have heard back from them, but then, as the full content of the letter sank in, I felt first righteous anger at my parent's predicament. Anger quickly faded to shame as I realized I'd hardly thought about my parents over the last month or what sort of troubles they might be facing. My job at the hospital had been the only steady income our family had, and despite Mom having marketable skills, there was an overabundance of coders out there.

Like an ungrateful little shit, I hadn't even thought to send some crypts out to them through Lemorak. Sure, I wasn't exactly swimming in coin by the standards of the OVR Worlds, but compared to the outside world? Even a couple of CC probably would have been a big help to them. I currently had 254.65 CC available. Having been out in the wilds with Lemorak for so long, I'll I'd been doing was earning, without much chance to spend it. I could easily spare 125 CC right then and there. It wasn't much in the game, but on the outside it would definitely help. It soothed my raging guilt, but I still felt like I needed to do more. With my earning potential in the game, not to mention the quirks of my brain's processing power, I felt compelled to make sure Mom and to a lesser extent Dad were taken care of.

I still had the writing supplies I'd borrowed from Lemorak. Vowing to myself that this was just the beginning, I scrawled a fresh message to Mom then tucked the coins into a small leather pouch. When I exited the lean-to, Lemorak was lifting an experimental taste of my stew to his mouth.

"This isn't half bad Zee."

"Thanks." I shifted uncomfortably on my feet, then cleared my throat. "Hey Lem. Can I get you to send another message for me?"

Lemorak shrugged as he studied me closely. "No problem. The account I setup for you is linked to mine. I can send out whatever you need. Trouble?"

"Nothing a few crypts can't help with. Can you attach the coin directly to the message?"

Crypto, being a non-centralized digital currency could be handled like any other computer file. The game just represented them as gold coins for the sake of theme and easy interface. I'd have to give Lemorak the coins here in the game, then he'd attach them to the message. However, being that I was an inmate, it was illegal. But then so was sending and receiving messages for me.

"Yeah Zee, you got it." Lemorak took the scroll and my pouch of jangling coins. Then he closed his eyes, like that first night I'd met him in the White Horse, to access whatever messaging interface he had access to that I didn't. While he worked, I mentally started trying to figure just how I could start earning some serious cash in here. A few seconds later, the scroll and coins vanished.

"All set."

"Thanks Lem. Might not be the last time."

"Happy to help." I could hear the tinge of concern in Lemorak's voice, and knew that he wanted to inquire further. Distracted as I was, I was glad that he didn't.

A short time later, Macha slipped into camp. She smiled kindly at me when we briefly locked gazes. I quickly broke the contact, embarrassment still burning in me. I tried to avoid further eye contact with her as I stirred the stew.

Sensing the thick tension between us, Lemorak took the conversational lead and started outlining his training plan for us moving forward. Soon Macha and I were chiming in, though I spoke more to Lemorak than to her. I served dinner as the sun dropped away and night fell. Once the food was gone, and I'd cleaned up, I slipped into the lean-to and pretended to drift immediately off to sleep.

"What's up with him?" Lemorak asked Macha softly.

"Don't worry about it," Macha answered.

Interlude Two

"Hey!" shouted a man's voice. "Watch it!"

My eyes flew open and I was standing in the middle of a wide dirt road with a horse-drawn stagecoach barreling down on me. I leapt aside from the oncoming stagecoach and landed my cowboy-booted feet in a steaming pile of fresh horse shit. Grimacing in disgust, I took a couple steps onto a raised wooden sidewalk, kicking and stomping my booted feet as best I could to remove whatever I could.

With a jolt, I caught sight of my reflection in the window of a feed store along the sidewalk. The general features of my avatar were unchanged: long hair, scruffy beard, pointed ears. On my head was a black felt cowboy hat and on the rest of my body I had on a long black canvas duster and a black leather vest over a white button up shirt. There was a silver sheriff's star pinned to my vest.

Not nearly as confused as I had been on the *Enterprise*, I examined the star a little closer as it had stamped letters on it that read *Sheriff Tombstone AZ*. Around my waist was a gunslinger's belt with holstered revolvers on each hip.

"Oh boy…" I muttered with a forlorn sigh.

Turning away from my reflection, I surveyed the small town around me: ramshackle wooden buildings with wood plank sidewalks and a street of packed dirt. It looked like a mash-up of every Western town I'd ever seen in films from *Back to the Future III* to Wyatt Earp.

In some respects, this dusty, smelly, rundown town felt more familiar to me than the spotless bridge of the *Enterprise* had. More rustic than the real world, but the same weathered and dirty feel that reality had to offer me. By comparison, the fantasy setting of Elmore felt like a theme park.

Straight across the dirt street from where I was standing was the obligatory western saloon, with swinging doors and everything. The sign over the door proclaimed it to be The Oriental. Piano music drifted across the street, coupled with an occasional burst of raucous laughter. I stepped off the wooden boardwalk into the dirt street as the sounds within the saloon began to evolve. The rowdy celebrations seemed to be turning to angry shouts. Before I got halfway across the street I heard heavy furniture scraping across the floor, then the dull thudding of fists meeting flesh.

Picking up my pace, I came through the doors of the saloon to find the patrons in full brawl. Dirty, scruffy-looking cowboys threw wild punches at each other. A harried barkeep crouched behind his bar, while a few busted-down women in once fine - now tattered - dresses hoovered shrieking at the edge of the violence.

Drawing both pistols, I raised one and fired it into the ceiling in typical cowboy fashion. It occurred to me only much later that the errant bullet could have killed an innocent on the floor above. Additionally, the damn pistol was so loud and kicked so hard I found myself deaf and floundering for more than a few seconds. When I gained my senses and opened my eyes the stunned gazes of everyone in the room had turned to me.

I cleared my throat, then proclaimed with all the authority I could muster, "That's enough fellas," and hoped my voice wouldn't squeak. I holstered both pistols.

"You heard the sheriff!" shouted a man's slurred voice from the center of the brawl. "Unhand me!"

The owner of the unrecognized voice, a man with a deathly pale complexion and a nearly invisible blond goatee, came stumbling from the crowd. He wore a mussed but expensive looking black pinstripe three-piece suit and a battered, black-felt, circular-brimmed hat. The man's face was frail, a bruise was already darkening over one eye, and a sheen of clammy sweat covered his face. The physical difference was so substantial that it took me a moment to see the Doctor's piercing eyes within the face of the character.

"Doc was cheating at cards, again!" grumbled a grizzled old cowboy who was following Doc out of the fray. It was then that the Doctor's appearance made sense to me. My subconscious had apparently done him up to look like Val Kilmer's Doc Holliday in *Tombstone*.

"That is a scurrilous accusation," slurred the Doctor. He then staggered over to the bar and picked up a glass of dark liquor that the bartender apparently knew he would need. The Doctor tossed it down his throat in one shot.

"I'll kick your cheating ass till I get my money!" growled the cowboy, his face twisted with violent rage. His posse, now disengaged from those they were pounding on and standing behind their spokesman, grumbled their agreement.

"Slow your roll there, Tex." I stepped between the cowboy and the Doctor with one restraining hand on the cowboy's chest. My other hand had dropped reflexively to the handle of my revolver once more. "Let me just have a word with the Doc?"

The raging cowboy, Tex, I decided to keep calling him, shifted his angry glare from the Doctor - his back turned to us while he downed another drink - to me. Tex and I locked gazes. My breath was even while my eyes bored into this man's stare. I ignored the fact that they had the same flat quality of all NPCs.

Before I'd entered the OVR Worlds, there'd never been much violence in my life. I never would have involved myself in a confrontation like this in the real world. However, I'd already been in a medieval bar brawl and I'd killed multiple monsters in close combat. Tex really wasn't that scary by comparison. I held Tex's gaze, steady and confident, and he blinked first. Tex let out a frustrated sigh, but stepped back.

New Skill Unlocked! Intimidation, Charisma based skill. Non-Class Skill. +1 to Intimidation. Note: Non Class Skills will not automatically improve with Level Up

"You get my money back, Sheriff," Tex grumbled as he looked back at his gang, then jerked his head at the door. Cowboys started to file out.

"Get it back or my problem's with you!" shouted Tex just before he stormed out the swinging doors.

My shoulders slumped in relief as the saloon doors swung shut behind Tex and life went back to normal as several of the remaining patrons righted an upturned table and began a fresh poker game. I turned to face the Doctor in his Doc Holliday cosplay. He was slumped languidly against the bar and tilted back another shot.

"What? Are you a method actor or something?" I demanded.

The Doctor grinned at me and drawled, "I'll be your Huckleberry."

"Can you even get drunk?"

"Of course not," the Doctor said rolling his eyes, his British accent reasserting itself, "but I experience something akin to amusement by pretending."

Shaking my head, I rubbed my bearded face in frustration before I realized my hand stunk of gunpowder. Now my face did too. Exasperated, I stepped up beside the Doctor at the bar. Without being asked, the bartender poured me a shot. I tossed it back. My face twisted with pain as it burned all the way down my throat and exploded in my belly.

"Don't tell me you brought me here just so I could save you from a beat down." Ignoring the pain, I motioned for the bartender to pour me another. "Cause then I just might let Tex have his way with you."

"Please!" The Doctor waved his hand dismissively. "I was just playing along for the fun of it."

"Then why am I here?" I gasped after choking down the next shot. My eyes were watering.

"I like your new handle."

"This is about what Lemorak told me. My mutant brain is why you're so interested in me."

"Zee." The Doctor spat my name. "Saying 'mutant' makes it sound like something's wrong with you. There's nothing wrong! You're special! Your brain is one in ten million!"

"Yeah, Lem told me. I can process large amounts of data faster, making me very good at generating large amounts of CC very quickly. Woopty frickin do."

"It's so much more than that Zee."

"Like how?" I demanded.

"Your brain was *made* for this game. Or the game was made for your brain." The Doctor tossed back another shot of whiskey. "Generating extra Cryptocoin is just a side benefit of what you can do. It's the result of a cleaner connection between your mind and the game. You'll be able to learn new skills, not just spend game Skill points, but actual skills, ones that will translate to the real world. And much faster than other players."

"Isn't that what OVR World was originally intended for? To train soldiers and shit?" I asked, dredging up information from high school.

The Doctor nodded. "It was really only of mixed success. It reduced injuries during training, but it was found that the game didn't provide muscle memory, and learned skills faded quickly after leaving the game. It was helpful as a short-term crash course, but that's it. It was never as simple as downloading Kung-Fu into a person's brain. Most brains don't work like that."

"But mine does?"

"We still can't download skills directly into your brain," the Doctor said, "but your brain will acquire and retain the information much faster than the average person, and when you disconnect, the knowledge will translate to reality a thousand times better."

"That's cool. But really, what practical value is that to me? I get released and lead a revolution with my sword? Against smart-bombs and predator-drones?"

"A revolution? Who said anything about a revolution?" The Doctor laughed, maybe a little too loud. "Concentrate on all the money you can make! The prizes, the fame! Isn't that enough?"

At first glance, the Doctor had a point. If everything he and Lemorak said was true, I could not only be rich, but I could be famous. One of the top ranked players in the OVR Worlds. A celebrity. Yet, I had this nagging suspicion in my gut that the mysterious Synthetic Intelligence was still leaving a lot unsaid. He must have read it in my expression.

"There's more. There always is," he finally said after a long uncomfortable pause, "but I think that's all you're ready for. In the meantime, you should focus on everything Lemorak is teaching you. His lessons could save your life someday, in or out of OVR World."

I had a flash of intuition and decided to follow it. "Does Lemorak work for you?"

"What makes you ask that?"

"He's been waiting around for a player with my kind of brain," I started before trailing off.

Memories of Lemorak with his eyes closed corresponding with someone by email right after we met flashed through my mind. "He was able to find me almost immediately, he knows so much about players like me already. Yet a big Mega-Corp like OzCo can't detect me when I'm plugged into one of their pods. Lem said he has a special SI scanning for signs of players like me. That's you."

The Doctor seemed to weigh his response for a long moment, swirling around a couple of drops of whiskey at the bottom of a glass. Finally he let out a sigh, "Very logical Zee. I wouldn't say that Lemorak and his friends work for me exactly. They have very different but not incompatible goals from my own. But yes, I created and administer the SI that they use. I approve of their goals, and I help them find players like you."

"So can I trust Lemorak then?"

The Doctor held up his hand and an incongruous manila file folder appeared in his grasp. The word *CLASSIFIED PLAYER BIOGRAPHICAL DETAILS* was stamped in big red letters across the surface. I could see a label at the top that showed the Player tag that appeared over Lemorak's head. *Sir Lemorak, Level 4 Paladin of Triumph, Human.*

"Lemorak's player is a very honorable man. A warrior and a patriot of your country. Appropriate that he picked the paladin class, really," the

Doctor said, looking at the folder. "Humans are very confusing to me, but I think he can be counted on to do what he thinks is right."

The Doctor held out the folder to me. I hesitated, considering the offer. On the one hand, Lemorak had been nothing but a friend to me. On the other hand, I was tired of constantly being in the dark. Information is power, and it seemed foolish to pass up such an offer.

Still conflicted, I reached out and took the folder. It dissolved as soon as my fingers touched it and I received a notification at the bottom of my vision.

File "Sir Lemorak Classified Player Data" added to Library

I saw a new blinking icon on my HUD that looked like a little filing cabinet.

"Good call, Zee," the Doctor said with a smirk. "We'll talk again when it's time."

When I woke up the next morning, the blinking filing cabinet icon remained on my HUD. However, I resisted the urge to activate it and left the dossier unopened.

Chapter Thirteen

Macha and I didn't speak about swimming at the spring. The next morning, I got up and did my best to act like nothing had happened. She obligingly did the same. Lemorak took the lead once more and we continued our somewhat aimless tour of Rowling.

A few days later, around mid-morning, we heard the sounds of battle in the distance, coupled with cries for help. I glanced at Lemorak, but Macha took off sprinting towards the sounds.

"Well, let's get after her," Lemorak said with a sigh and a shake of his head.

When we cleared the trees, we caught up with Macha, who had paused to survey the situation below. A mob of twenty or thirty green-skinned porcine orcs in battered, matte-black armor were attacking a caravan of

NPC merchants. Fighting alongside the NPC guards were two golden-scaled Dragonkin players.

Bolton Glittertooth, Level 2 Sorcerer, Dragonkin

Illiya Glittertooth, Level 2 Barbarian, Dragonkin

The Glittertooths stood back-to-back with Orcs attacking from all sides. The sorcerer, Bolton, was hurling crackling bolts of lightning from his clawed fingers as Illiya swung a massive double-headed war-ax from side to side in both hands. The pair were holding their own against the Orcs, but just barely.

"They can't keep that up for long," Lemorak observed as we watched the ring of Orcs tighten on them. Two of the NPC Guards and one of the NPC Merchants died before any of us moved.

"Crap or get off the pot, you three!" bellowed Illiya as she used her ax to block a shower of Orc strikes before unleashing a devastating counterstroke. An invitation from Bolton to join a Quest in-progress appeared on our notification bars.

Without further consideration I accepted the quest, then drew back my bowstring and let fly. The arrow plunged into the back of a big orc who was charging Bolton. Macha and Lemorak drew their blades and charged down the hill and into the flank of the orc mob.

After all the practice I'd been putting in, my Archery was already at Level 4, so I hung back from the melee and continued a steady stream of fire. Several orcs fell to my arrows before they realized what was happening. As the Orcs turned to meet this new threat, Lemorak and Macha were there to greet them.

This was my first larger battle and as I drew and loosed my arrows, I couldn't help but admire the brutal efficiency of my friends. Lemorak sliced his way through to the Dragonkin, dropping Orcs with devastating but economical strikes of his greatsword. Macha trailed in his wake, delivering killing blows with graceful balletic sweeps of her katana and well placed kicks and punches. When she struck the orcs, those ugly fuckers went down.

Bolton unleashed a Fireball from his cupped claws and with a whoosh it detonated in the densest grouping of Orcs. The enemy morale shattered at that moment and they began to retreat into the woods. Both Dragonkin let out leonine roars of victory and Illiya began to charge after the fleeing Orcs with her axe raised. Spears chucked by the Orc rear guard pulled her up short.

Victory at hand, I started to move down to the caravan. While I walked I continued to scan the treeline for retreating orcs and snapped off a few opportunistic shots. Half-Elven sight allowed my gaze to pierce further into the shade beyond the treeline. By the time I got down to an easy speaking distance, there wasn't a single living Orc in sight. We all took a moment to loot from our respective kills.

A plump and cowering NPC Merchant emerged from the caravan to thank us for our aid. We all received a notice of the Quest's completion and the Merchant offered us individual rewards from the caravan's inventory. I selected a pair of slender curved masterwork scimitars that my now Level 6 Two-Weapon Fighting talent would let me use. They had a higher base damage than my short swords and a higher chance of critical strikes. I stowed my short sword and dagger away in my inventory as backup weapons.

Whatever Bolton and Illiya took as their rewards, I didn't know their avatars well enough to notice a difference. Lemorak had selected a steel helm with a nose guard shaped like a hawk's beak. For Macha, a pair of finely crafted leather sandals that she said would enhance her speed and kicks. While we took care of business, the NPCs prepared to get the caravan back underway. Lemorak, Macha and I turned to more formally greet Bolton and Illiya.

They were the first Dragonkin I'd seen up close. Dragonkin were descended from Dragons, and were generally very tall with pronounced facial ridges and often short horns. Instead of skin they had smooth lizard-like scales, the color depending on their Dragon ancestry. Their fingers had sharp talons at the tips and they had short vestigial tales.

Judging by their handles and similar golden-scaled coloring, the Glittertooths had styled themselves as siblings. Bolton wore the simple red robes of a Sorcerer. While taller than any of my friends or me, Bolton was shorter than his sister, Illiya, who was over seven feet tall. Illiya, had armor made from roughly tanned leather hides patchworked together. Being so clearly non-human, it was disconcerting how noticeably curved and undeniably female her brawny Dragonkin avatar was.

"Well met brave warriors!" Illiya said with a wide reptilian grin filled with sharp teeth. "Three more valiant heroes I have rarely met."

Bolton noticeably rolled his eyes at Illiya's dramatic greeting. "Thanks for saving our bacon. Forgive Illiya, she likes to 'stay in character.'" He made air quotes as he spoke.

"She's not the first and not the last," Lemorak said with a friendly smile. He pulled his new helmet from his head and ran a gloved hand over his buzzed blonde hair. "Always happy to lend a helping hand. Glad we weren't too late."

"Verily!" Illiya agreed. "My brother and I were but heartbeats away from being banished to the Dark World Beyond."

"You three are pretty far from town," Bolton observed.

"Not much EXP to be found in town," Lemorak said. "We've been out for a few weeks farming EXP and skill grinding."

"Skill grinding?" Bolton seemed surprised. "That's pretty old school."

"Old is the only school that Lemorak knows!" Macha said. Illiya chortled.

"Just preparing for the rest of Gygax," Lemorak said.

"Well we were going to escort the caravan the rest of the way to Elmore. In case of any more raids, and to save us some walking. Care to join?" Bolton offered.

Macha, Lemorak and I all glanced at each other. Macha subtly nodded. She'd been getting tired of all the bushwhacking. To be honest, so had I. Lemorak gave me a neutral shrug.

"Sure. Some time in town sounds like a nice change of pace." I answered for the group.

"Splendid!" Illiya clapped Lemorak on the back and the knight stumbled forward a step. "Tis a bright day indeed to discover new stout companions on the field of battle!"

The front wagon of the caravan was just beginning to roll into motion. Lemorak, Macha, Illiya, and I all fanned out around the wagon train while Bolton climbed up to ride with the driver of one of the middle wagons. With superior speed from being a Monk and fully elven vision, Macha would sprint up along the road to scout out the route. Illiya, being a barbarian, had a decent Survival skill, though she lacked the Stealth. Nonetheless, she and I both took turns ranging into the tree line on either side of the caravan to check for threats while Lemorak posted up as our rear guard.

That night we split up guard shifts among the five of us. The caravan had NPC Guards, but none of us thought they were particularly likely to prevent an ambush. Lemorak woke me around midnight to take over the watch.

Comfortable with my night vision, which was extended by the starlight overhead and the camp fires of the convoy, I moved beyond the firelight and began a patrol route around the camp. While I patrolled, I activated my Stealth skill, which modified the path into the deepest shadows. Using stealth slowed my movement but the sound of my steps became muffled. The entire circuit around the camp took about 15 minutes to complete. I kept my bow out and an arrow on the string.

On my fourth circuit, I heard distant sounds out of place for the night-shrouded forest: the clank of metal on metal and the rustle of large bodies in the brush. Kneeling in the deep shadows of a tree, I closed my eyes to zero in on which direction the sounds were coming from. Even with my eyes closed I could still see my player interface, where a notification appeared at the bottom.

New Skill Acquired! Perception (+1) - Use Perception to sense what might be hidden or obscured.

My new skill activated, and I suddenly felt certain of which direction the noise was coming from. Slipping deeper into the brush, my Stealth skill slowed me down even further to accommodate the thicker foliage and dry brush on the ground. I'd stop every few steps to use my Perception skill and adjust my course.

About twenty yards from the camp's perimeter, I found them. Huddled in the darkness was a small mob of level 3 Orc Raiders, likely the remainder of the band we'd faced earlier in the day. There was something else with them. It was much bigger than the Orcs, I guessed eleven feet tall. It was vaguely human shaped, but its arms were long enough that its clawed fingers dragged on the ground.

I went still as I studied the creature and tried to read its tag over its head. I couldn't make it out in the darkness just beyond my night vision. Whatever it was, I figured it was more than I could handle on my own. Add the Orcs to the equation and I didn't want to stick around.

Time to get help. I moved back a step towards camp and my Stealth skill choose that moment to fail me. A branch snapped under foot. I received a fresh notification.

Warning! *Stealth Failed! Risk of Detection!*

Freezing in place, I listened to the monsters. They'd gone still at the sound, but hadn't zeroed in on me. I reactivated my Stealth skill while thanking Lemorak for all the practice he'd put me through. With extra care I took another step. It was the wrong move as dried leaves crunched under my boot. I received a fresh notification.

Warning! *Stealth Failed! Enemies have Detected You!*

The sound of many moving Orcs came from behind me. Acting on instinct, I drew and loosed my notched arrow in the general direction of the monsters before I turned to run.

"We've got company!" I shouted at the top of my lungs. My improved Archery talent level allowed me to notch and fire arrows behind me while running and continuing to yell for my friends. Whatever the bigger creature was with the orcs, it had crashed surprisingly fast through the dense brush and was right behind me. With a glance over my shoulder I caught sight of the red tag over its head.

Troll Berserker, Level 10

"Shit!" I shrieked as the Troll swung one long clawed hand at me.

I tried to dodge the blow, but found myself flying through the air and slamming into the trunk of a huge tree.

Troll Berserker Attacked: 39 HP Lost. 76 of 115HP Remaining!

Impact Damage! You hit a tree! 8 HP Lost. 68 of 115 HP Remaining!

Pain lanced through me and I heard the thundering steps of the Troll coming closer. In the distance, I could hear the ruckus of the camp mobilizing. A bell rang and I heard shouts. A giant clawed foot stomped down at me.

"Shit!" I just managed to roll out of the way, but a toe snagged my cloak, and it jerked me to a stop. The Troll was chuckling in a deep gravelly rumble. Like a toddler having a tantrum, rough troll hands picked me up and tossed me into another tree. More hit points fell away and I groaned in pain.

Impact Damage! You hit a tree! 9 HP Lost. 68 of 106 HP Remaining!

Despite the pain, I didn't linger on the ground. Discarding my bow, I scrambled to my feet and whipped out my new scimitars. The exquisite blades glittered in the faint starlight.

My Combat Guide activated and when the Troll came at me again, I let out a battlecry and slashed both swords at the monster's reaching arms in unison with my guide. I managed to scratch his forearms, but the Troll's hide was thick as an elephant's. The twin strikes did make the Troll grunt in surprise, as if stung by a bee, and I skipped back a step to avoid his next clawed swipe.

Walking backwards on guard, I retreated towards the sound of the alarmed merchant caravan. I kept the Troll in my sight at all times and my blades ready. I didn't dare try to move in offensive. The Troll had tremendous reach on me and bone-dusting strength.

When I finally backed out of the trees onto the side of the road, I was a little bit ahead of the caravan. Orcs, more than had been crouched with the Troll Berserker, were coming out of the woods now and my friends and the NPCs were mounting another desperate defense.

My quick appraisal of the situation pulled my attention for too long. The Troll rushed me and raked my leather armor with his claws. Sturdy leather parted and blood began to run from a line of claw marks down my chest.

Troll Berserker Attacked: 18 HP Lost. 50 of 115 HP Remaining!

Under 50% health meant I'd need some serious healing, and soon. I fell to the ground under the force of the blow and the Troll sent me flying with a kick.

Troll Berserker Attacked: 8 HP Lost. 42 of 115 HP Remaining!

Fortunately, this time I just hit the ground and not another tree. Then the Troll turned and charged the lead wagon. Horses shrieked in terror and NPC Merchants cried out.

Grunting with effort, I heaved myself to my feet and took stock of the situation. I needed some healing and soon. It would have been safest for me to stay at range snapping off shots with my bow, if I hadn't dropped it back in the trees.

The Troll had scattered Merchants and Guards with one swipe of its massive hand. Then the monster had casually reached under the loaded wagon and flipped it on its side. He proceeded to casually rampage down the line, scattering NPCs in his path.

"My fault." I muttered under my breath. I wasn't yet sure what I could've done differently, but the shit had hit the fan on my watch, ergo facto, it was my fault. Tightening my grip on my scimitars, I rushed forward into the raging battle.

The Troll was already within the ranks of Orcs when I reached the rear of the mob. Plunging into the Orcs from behind, I started to cut myself a path through the monsters. I switched off my combat guide. It couldn't understand my objective and just added confusion. There wasn't that much skill involved in stabbing Orcs in the back anyways, never slowing long enough to finish any single Orc off. I got lucky and scored a couple of Critical Hits that downed an Orc in one stroke, but mostly I just shoved them aside or hobbled them.

My armor, though torn, still saved me from a couple of glancing blows. By the time I reached the line formed by NPC guards and my friends, I had less than a third of my HP left. Lemorak spotted me just beyond the defensive line. The paladin shouted an order to charge, then lifted his massive sword over his head and a brilliant light burst from the blade. The Orcs in front of Lemorak shrieked and fell back under the blazing glory. Lemorak and the NPC guards beside him surged forward as I shoved myself through their line.

"Troll...out...there..." I gasped as I stumbled and fell to a knee.

"We heard him, buddy. He's still trashing the wagons, I think," Lemorak said.

He took a quick survey of my wounds. The paladin muttered a Latin-sounding word and activated his Lay on Hands ability and his hands began glowing purple. He touched my head and warm healing energy flowed through me, soothing the ache of my wounds. When it faded, I was just above half full on HP. Healing complete, Lemorak turned back to bolster the sagging line of Guards.

Then the Troll came thundering into the circle of torchlight. The massive creature shoved Orcs aside, then snatched up a Guard and ripped his arms off. Lemorak hurled himself in front of the Troll. A massive Troll claw came sweeping down at him. Lemorak met the claw with his long steel blade. The sword clove clean through the Troll's limb at the wrist and the clawed hand went spinning away.

To my horror the Troll's hand immediately began to grow back, a twisted little appendage pushing out of the stump. I could literally see the Troll's HP bar refilling before my eyes. This was bad. Very bad.

"Fire! We need fire to stop it from regenerating!" Lemorak shouted, dodging another swiping Troll claw.

I turned around just in time to see an Orc spear come flying out of the darkness and plunge into Bolton's belly. The Dragonkin cried out in pain, his HP bar practically vanished, and he toppled down into the wagon he'd been standing on. The Orcs chorused out throaty cheers as the sorcerer went down.

So much for a magical Fireball! All right, what's plan B? I thought frantically. *How could we set this motherfucker on fire?* I spotted one of the Merchants cowering under the wagon and an idea came to me. I sprinted over to the NPC.

"I need to see your inventory," I shouted at him.

"What? Now? We're under attack!" The cowering human shrieked back.

"Now!"

The NPC opened his inventory to me and a screen popped up before me, showing all the items the caravan was carrying. I scanned through the list and quickly selected the items we needed.

"That'll be 7 gold," the Merchant said.

"You've got to be kidding me! This is to save us!" I shouted.

"All prices are fixed. No negotiations."

"Fine!" I hit accept on the purchase screen.

"Thank you. Have a nice day," the Merchant said with inappropriate sincerity.

The items appeared in my own inventory. Behind me Lemorak cried out and I looked back to see the troll had struck him solidly on the head, sending the paladin stumbling despite his new hawk-beaked helm. Illiya was there in a heartbeat, lifting her massive ax to stop the Troll's advance. Shoving aside the distraction, I turned back to my inventory.

Withdrawing four bottles of lamp oil from my inventory, I also pulled out the starter clothes that I hadn't used since purchasing my leather armor.

I tore the shirt into strips and then popped the corks off the lamp oil bottles. In seconds, I'd crafted what I hoped the OVR Worlds would translate functionally into Molotov Cocktails. Gathering up the bottles, I grabbed an already lit torch from one of the NPCs and turned back towards the battle.

Lemorak was back in the fight. He and Illiya were side by side, fending off the Troll's advances without managing to push it back. I'd lost track of Macha in the fight, but had the distinct impression that she was in the thick of the melee with the Orcs beyond the struggling defensive line.

Lighting the first improvised wick, I called out, "Fire in the hole!"

Illiya the barbarian was in full on berserker mode and didn't respond, but Lemorak glanced back in time to see me hurl the improvised weapon. The paladin's eyes went wide, then he turned and shoved Illiya aside. The cocktail's wick blazed as the bottle tumbled over their heads.

The Troll slapped at my improvised incendiary with its regrown claw. Instead of hitting his chest, the bottle shattered on the Troll's hand and forearm. Bright orange liquid flames washed over the Troll's arm. The Troll bellowed and fell backwards.

"That a boy, Zee!" Lemorak shouted. My friend was desperately trying to hold Illiya back from charging the blazing flailing Troll. I'd heard that barbarians had a powerful berserk ability that made them devastating melee opponents, but had no idea how the game co-opted their control. Illiya seemed entirely heedless of the threat posed by the growing inferno.

Drops of flaming oil and Troll flesh showered out over the Orcs as the Troll continued to thrash and scream. Another wick lit, I hurled a second bottle at the panicking Troll. This time my flaming bottle hit the Troll's chest, smashed and set the Troll's flesh alight like a pile of dry timber. The Troll's howling and thrashing redoubled, wreaking further havoc in the Orc mob.

Without pause, I added my third and fourth bottles to the conflagration. Heat rushed back at me along with the stomach-churning stench of burning Orc and Troll flesh. The Orc drive to fight crumbled and those that still could ran.

New Achievement - It's Super Effective! - Defeat a monster by exploiting a damage weakness - 10% bonus Exp on the encounter!

Lemorak set Illiya loose on the fleeing Orcs. The barbarian howled with glee and ran after the orcs, hacking and chopping. Lemorak followed on her heels, cutting down the slowest among them. Macha really had been out among the Orcs, holding her own. The flood of fleeing monsters broke around her, a river rushing around a boulder as she furiously twirled death around her.

The engulfed Troll collapsed to its knees, then flat on the ground as it died. I received a rush of EXP and completed Level 2. The increasingly familiar rush of pleasure crashed through me as the notification text

scrolled across my display.

LEVEL UP!

LEVEL 3 RANGER REACHED!

ARCHERY TALENT IMPROVED TO LEVEL 7

TWO-WEAPON FIGHTING TALENT IMPROVED TO LEVEL 9

SKILL IMPROVED: ATHLETICS +3 -> +4

SKILL IMPROVED: SURVIVAL +7 -> +8

SKILL IMPROVED: STEALTH +6 -> +7

SKILL IMPROVED: ANIMAL HANDLING +3 -> +4

SKILL IMPROVED: TRACKING +5 -> +6

INCREASE TO HIT POINTS +20

INCREASE TO MANA +10

2 ABILITY POINTS AWARDED

+1 ABILITY POINT FOR BEING HALF-ELF

NEW RANGER TALENT UNLOCKED - ANIMAL

COMPANION

NEW TALENT EARNED: WEAPON IMPROVISATION

Achievement Earned: Improviser - You killed a Monster with an improvised weapon! -

Unlock the Weapon Improvisation Talent.

Achievement Earned: Powerhouse Slayer - You killed a Monster 5 levels or higher than

you! - 25% bonus Exp for killing the Troll Berserker

The Orc attack broken, we regrouped at the waggons to assess our injuries and the damage to the caravan. Everyone congratulated me on my Level Up, though Macha eyed me suspiciously. I'd avoided telling her exactly where my Exp was, but she'd been with Lemorak and me for awhile, and she knew when I'd originally logged in. We logged on the same day and I was consistently ahead of her. To make matters more awkward, the Troll had been worth a lot of experience too and I was almost halfway to Level 4.

We set to work putting the caravan back to some semblance of order. Lemorak did what he could for our wounds, with most of his attention going to the fallen Bolton, but his healing abilities were relatively limited compared to a cleric's restorative magic. Fortunately, Bolton hadn't died from the spear he'd caught, but it had been close. Macha had training in the Healing skill and was able to use it to help stabilize anyone that Lemorak couldn't get to. Illiya helped to right the wagons and I kept up a vigilant patrol of the tree line, just to ensure we didn't get taken by surprise again.

By morning we were exhausted, but eager to get back to town. Our battered and bruised group along with our shaken NPC charges set out at first light. No one wanted to spend another night in the wilds. Wary of another ambush, I didn't dare complete my level-up until we got back to Elmore.

CHARACTER STATISTICS

Handle: Zee Locked-in

Race: Half-Elf

Role: Striker

Class/Level: Ranger/3

ABILITIES

Strength (Endurance): 15 (23)

Strength Skills: Melee Combat, Athletics, Carrying Capacity

Dexterity (Defense): 16 (21)

Dexterity Skills: Ranged Combat, Acrobatics, Stealth, Sleight of Hand,

Open Lock. Reflex

Constitution (Hit Points): 15 (135)

Constitution Skills: Concentration, Fortitude

Intelligence (Arcane Mana): 10 (NA)

Intelligence Skills: Arcana, Investigation. Appraise, Disable Device. Forgery,

Lore

Wisdom (Faith Mana): 13 (77)

Wisdom Skills: Conviction. Perception, Survival, Tracking, Animal

Handling, Medicine, Willpower

Charisma (Inspiration): 10 (NA)

Charisma Skills: Imagination, Deception, Intimidation, Persuasion, Influence

RACIAL SKILLS: Half-Elf Wilderness Skills: Survival (+1), Stealth (+1), Tracking (+1)

RACIAL TALENTS: Half-Elf Flexibility (+5 AP at Level 0, +1 AP), Nightvision (15'), Elven Bow Proficiency +1 Level

CLASS SKILLS: Athletics (+4), Survival (+8), Stealth (+7), Animal Handling (+4), Tracking (+6)

CLASS TALENTS: Archery (Level 7), Two-Weapon Fighting (Level 9), Light Armor Proficiency, Favored Enemy (Goblin) Animal Companion

EARNED SKILLS: Perception (+1), Intimidation (+0), Fletching (+1)

EARNED TALENTS: Improvised Weapon (Achievement), Surprise Attack (Achievement)

CARRIED EQUIPMENT: Leather Armor (+3 Defense), Masterwork Scimitars x2, Short-bow, Arrows x20

STORED EQUIPMENT: Standard Clothes, Short-sword, Dagger, Stone Hatchet

COMBAT STATISTICS

Weapon - Talent Modifier - Weapon Damage - Accuracy - Median Damage

Masterwork Scimitar - 9 - 50 - 20 - 101

Masterwork Scimitar (off-hand) - 9 - 50 - 15 - 76

Shortbow - 7 - 18 - 18 - 79

ACHIEVEMENTS: First Kill, Backstabber, Good Samaritan, Goblin Slayer, Kobold Slayer, And Stay Out!, Ain't Got Time to Bleed, "The dishes are done man.", Marathon Runner, Orc Slayer, Pest Control, FATALITY, Specialist (Survival, Stealth, Tracking), I am the night, Trained (Animal Handling), Practice Makes Perfect (Survival, Stealth, Tracking), Hunter, Gone Fishin, Camp Cook, The Great Outdoors, It's Super Effective!, Improviser

TOTAL ABILITY POINTS: 19

CURRENT CRYPTOCURRENCY: 197.32

CURRENT DEBTS: 4,540,535.67 CC - OzCo Department of Corrections

CURRENT EXPERIENCE: 5,112

EXPERIENCE TO NEXT LEVEL: 9,500

Chapter Fourteen

"To Zee Trollsbane!" Illiya toasted while raising her tankard of ale high.

"To Zee!" chorused the rest of my friends as I rolled my eyes.

Several of the other players around the White Horse common room clapped or raised their drinks as well. I raised my own tankard and laughed as we banged them together.

"I don't think one Troll makes a Trollsbane," I said after taking a deep drink.

"Irregardless! Your valiant efforts saved the day. To Zee!" Illiya lifted her tankard in another toast and we all clanked and drank again.

I resisted the knee-jerk urge to correct her use of irregardless.

"A Level 10 Troll at Level 2 is no small feat," agreed Bolton.

"I had a lot of help," I said. "And I was the one that pulled the mob in while trying to scout."

"They were coming anyway," Lemorak pointed out. "That's why we had a watch set to begin with."

"Well, if you all are determined to label me the hero of this battle, who am I to stop you?" I downed another mouthful of ale. "Heroes don't pay their own tab, right?"

"When have you ever paid a tab at the White Horse, Zee?" Lemorak quipped and everyone, including me, chuckled.

A hurried blond NPC barmaid delivered our food and the five of us all set to devouring the meal with the sort of eager gusto that comes from a day's hard work. We bantered as we ate. After two battles together in short succession, the five of us had become fast friends.

"Lady and Gentlemen," Illiya exclaimed as we started in on our after dinner drinks. "My brother, Bolton, and I would like to propose that we formalize our venture."

Macha's eyes immediately lit with interest, but Lemorak looked instantly wary. I imagine I just looked confused. We'd all already traded Friend statuses. What else was there?

"How so?" Lemorak asked.

"Look, we all did pretty well against the Orcs. It was a shit show at times, but Illiya and I think you're good players. I've never seen anyone craft a Molotov cocktail. I didn't even know the game would allow it. If we all teamed up, there wouldn't be much in the Valley we could tackle with some thought and strategy. We were thinking that all five of us should go in on a Party Pact," Bolton explained.

"That's a great idea," Macha said. Lemorak was looking at me with concern, and I wasn't sure why.

"What's a Party Pact?" I asked.

"You're such a noob," Macha snorted and we all chuckled, except Lemorak. He just looked pensive.

"It's a step up from Friend status. It links our accounts, so that on monster kills or quests we all split the Exp, CC, and Loot automatically. But it costs Crypts. Most new players without sponsorship can't afford one, but we're all fairly flush at the moment," Bolton said.

Then I understood why Lemorak might be concerned. What would someone with my extra EXP and CC generation do to this Party Pact mechanic of the Game? Did Lemorak even know? I was supposed to be lying low. But then, we couldn't keep grinding it out by ourselves. Or even if we could, I liked having other people around. Despite our recent awkwardness, I liked Macha, and I liked the Gilltertooth siblings too. Partying with them didn't seem like the worst thing in the world.

"We need more healing if we're going to Party up. My Lay on Hands is more for triage than Party Healing," Lemorak said.

"So we'll find a Cleric or Shaman to be a heal monkey," Macha offered. "Or maybe a Bard?"

"God!" cried Bolton. "No Bards! I'd rather bleed out than have to get my healing from some lute strummer."

"Any healer class not already in a Party will expect us to let them in for free," Lemorak argued.

"Supply and demand. Seems like a fair trade to have a steady healing supply," Bolton countered.

"Well, I'm close to leveling out of the Valley. If I join the Party, you guys will probably push me over to 5 pretty quick and I'll just have to leave," Lemorak said with finality.

"They won't boot you out right away if we're in the midst of a quest. I propose we take on the Goblin's Keep, get us all to Level 5, score a boat load of coin, and leave together," Bolton argued back.

"How much are we talking about?" I asked leaning forward with sudden interest as the prospect of scoring some decent cash that I could actually send back home.

"Thousands?" Bolton shrugged.

"We can't take the Goblin's Keep with three Level 2s, a Level 3 and a Level 4." Lemorak counted out the composition of our group on his fingers. "That's suicide!"

"Oh! But the songs they'll sing about us when we do!" Illiya trilled. "The Bards will..."

Bolton held a hand to keep his sister from starting in on the epic foretelling that she seemed about to craft. "We won't rush in guns blazing. We'll be strategic about it. Smart."

"Taking the Goblin's Keep is something the Guild and Mega-Corp players do with Level 4s and plenty of CC to finance it. This isn't some one-night dungeon raid. It's the toughest quest in the valley." Lemorak was starting to raise his voice.

"Whoa guys," I jumped in, holding up placating hands. "We don't have to decide anything tonight. Let's all sleep on it and go over things with breakfast and a little less ale in our heads."

"Zee speaks wisefully," Illiya agreed before draining her latest tankard.

Bolton and Lemorak appeared ready to press the debate, but relented under dour glares from the rest of us. We all finished our drinks and called it a night. The siblings and Macha had taken rooms at the White Horse.

That night I wouldn't be going to the noobie shelter. My adventures with Lemorak had left me with enough crypts to rent a small room in the same boarding house where Lemorak stayed when he was in town.

On the way to the boarding house, a slightly inebriated Lemorak tried to explain to me all the reasons why Bolton's plan was "...idiotic, stupid and dumb." Never mind that those were all three words that mean the same thing. I opted to mostly tune out my more experienced, but more drunk friend.

The next day, still attuned to the natural cycles that come from camping out for over a month, I awoke with the rising sun. Lemorak was still sleeping off the previous night's ale, but I was restless and after leaving Lemorak a note, I ventured out from the boarding house.

Elmore was quiet in the early hours with only a handful of NPCs and players up and moving. It was the most alone I'd felt since those first moments after jacking in. It felt oddly soothing.

Confident in my own abilities and the relative safety immediately around Elmore, I headed out the palisade gates. I followed the road that led to the Kobold Village. However, as soon as the road reached the treeline, I veered off onto a narrow game trail. I followed the trail for a couple miles, picking forks on instinct, until I reached a trickling creek rolling down a hillside towards town.

While completing my Level Up to 3rd, Al had given me the download on my new Animal Companion talent. The new talent would allow me to attract a predatory animal companion, like a tiger, wolf, hawk, or even a giant badger and bond it to me. The companion would fight alongside me in battle and I could train it to perform simple tasks and tricks. In order to attract a companion, I'd need to remain stationary for an extended period of time in a wilderness setting.

Sitting down on the hillside next to the creek, I activated the Animal Companion ability and settled in to wait. A circular icon appeared on my notification bar and started spinning around. Closing my eyes, I tried to focus on my other senses instead of continuing to mull over whatever troubles my parents might be having outside the game. Overhead, I could hear the wind rustling through the branches and the water gurgling through the stream. I could smell the rich soil of the forest and the dense vegetation all around me. The morning air was pleasantly cool on my skin after the hike.

Sitting there like that, I lost track of time. When the spinning icon stopped, I opened my eyes. The morning sunlight was dazzling at first, and the giant wolf standing across the creek from me was startling. I fought the lizard-brain reflex to jump up and run.

Slowly, I shifted from sitting cross-legged on the ground to squatting on my haunches and watched the wolf intently. I could just make out the gray text over his head.

Male Dire Wolf, Level 3

The wolf was staring directly at me as he stepped forward to the edge of the creek. He lowered his muzzle and lapped a drink from the stream, eyes on me. If I'd been standing upright, his shoulders would have come up to my waist. He had sleek charcoal black fur over his entire body with incongruous white socks around his paws. We locked gazes and the same spinning icon appeared next to the wolf's tag.

Attempting to bond with Male Dire Wolf, Level 3

Our staring contest continued for several long moments, neither of us moving. It was disconcerting to hold the wolf's gaze. I mean, he was a giant wolf. But also, he had the same flat lifeless gaze as the NPCs I'd encountered. I continually found that the longer I interacted with an NPCs, the less human they seemed.

The SI running OVR World was incredibly complex, but ultimately, NPCs only had a limited script to use when interacting with players. If your conversation wandered off script they'd say some variation of "I don't understand. Could you try again?" There were, of course, better written and more heavily scripted NPCs. For instance the bartender at the White Horse was programmed to have extended conversations on a variety of subjects. But most Merchant NPCs or random Farmer NPCs had a much more restricted script that you could easily confound. Of everything I'd experienced in OVR World, my interactions with NPCs were the most disturbing and disappointing.

The spinning icon over the wolf's head slowed. When it stopped the dire wolf lowered his eyes from mine in submission. The tag over the wolf's head turned green and I received a notification.

Congratulations! You have bonded Male Dire Wolf, Level 3 to you as an Animal

Companion.

Would you like to rename Male Dire Wolf, Level 3?

Accept

Decline

I accepted and a text box appeared in my vision for me to input a

name. We'd had a dog when I was growing up, and though this dire wolf

was far bigger and ferocious looking, they'd had the same coal gray coloring

and white socks. I smiled to myself as I remembered that old pet and

entered his name into the box.

You entered: Archer

Confirm

Cancel

After confirming the entry and the box disappeared. The tag over the

dire wolf's head had changed.

Archer, Dire Wolf, Level 3, companion of Zee Locked-in

I stepped over the narrow stream to the same side of the bank as the

wolf. Tentatively, I reached out a hand to the wolf's nose. He lifted it and I

felt cool wet skin on my hand as Archer sniffed it. He gave the back of my

hand an experimental lick and I grinned. I reached up and gingerly pet the wolf's head like he was a dog. Archer leaned his head into the touch and let out an appreciative rumble.

As I scratched the surprisingly compliant dire wolf's head a wave of dizziness washed over me. I swayed on my feet, feeling nauseous. There was a warmth building within the center of my chest. Archer leaned in to support my balance and my other hand found his shoulder. The building warmth suddenly rushed down both of my arms and I felt it flow out of me and into the dire wolf, who let out a surprised yelp and jumped away from me.

Still dizzy, I knelt and tried to catch my breath. The sudden symptoms passed and Archer stepped in closer. His tongue flicked out and licked my face. His breath was horrible. I choked on the smell and pulled back. "Ack! Dog breath!"

My eyes opened and the wolf and I met gazes again. Something had changed. His dark eyes were no longer flat and lifeless. That missing spark that I'd never seen in the eyes of a computer generated character before...I saw it.

Is that intelligence? I have to be imagining it, right?

Archer's tail wagged and his jaw dropped open, revealing rows of long sharp teeth, but his expression looked decidedly like a doggy-grin.

Chapter Fifteen

Archer and I made it back to town before noon. For most of the return hike, the dire wolf remained close by at my heel. However, he took occasional jaunts to lope ahead of me or make a wide orbit around my path. When we reached the gates of Elmore, the Guards gave the massive animal sauntering beside me a dubious look. Other players we passed gave respectful nods as they appraised Archer, while all the NPCs gave the wolf a wide berth.

We found Lemorak at the Blacksmith's Shop, where he had just purchased and equipped a new set of armor, a full set of heavy platemail etched with a feather motif to match his new hawk-themed helm.

"What have we here?" Lemorak asked as he spotted Archer.

I filled him in on my morning. While I spoke, Archer sat, his mouth open in another wolfish grin. His tail hammered against the wood floor every time I said his name. Lemorak paced around the wolf, examining him in detail. Archer turned his head to track Lemorak.

"There's something weird about him…" Lemorak squinted skeptically at the wolf.

"Is there?" I hadn't told Lemorak about the weird experience I'd had after bonding Archer to me.

"I've seen animal companions before," Lemorak said. "He….he has…personality."

Archer stood and woofed in seeming approval of Lemorak's observation. Lemorak and I both laughed.

"Well, he certainly has personality," I agreed.

"You don't find that strange?" Lemorak waved a hand dismissively at the Blacksmith that stood idly awaiting interaction. "Look at this dolt. He was programed to interact with players and he's flat as a board."

The NPC stared at us expressionless, his eyes flat and lifeless. Neither of us had addressed him directly in several minutes, so he'd gone dormant.

"Your wolf, on the other hand…" Lemorak trailed off while he thought. "Seems more like a player shape-shifted into a wolf form."

Archer turned around in a little circle and let out another bark.

"I guess I wouldn't really know. Archer's the first animal that I've interacted with other than the game we hunted in the woods," I said after a brief hesitation. Of his own accord, Archer started exploring the shop, sniffing at the floor.

"There's something very special about your wolf, Zee."

Lemorak, Archer and I made the rounds of the Merchant shops after that. After a month in the woods, my inventory was packed to bursting with sellable loot. I sold off everything the Merchants would take that I didn't need, then made some select purchases that Lemorak and I had been planning.

From the bowyer I bought a new compound shortbow, designed to leverage my higher strength score, and refilled my arrow supply. We went to the armorer and bought a new set of leather armor to replace my existing Troll-ravaged armor. From the provisioner I picked up a compact camp tent, a cookware set of my own, a warmer bedroll, and stocked up on rations so I wouldn't have to hunt as much. From the tanner I picked up a harness and pack set that would let me stow gear on Archer when I wanted. When I fastened the harness on the wolf, he paced around and looked decidedly unhappy with the setup.

I also picked up a Ranger's Cloak, thick waterproofed canvas, in a splotchy camouflage pattern of greens and browns with little loops on it that would let me tie vegetation to it. The cloak would be warmer in cooler weather and also provide a bonus to my Stealth checks when I was in woodland areas.

We met up with Macha and the Glittertooths for a picnic lunch on the village square. The three were talking and laughing when we arrived. No one noticed Archer until Lemorak and I stopped and the wolf came up and sat down beside me. My friends reacted with astonished respect for my accomplishment. I found out that wolves were common animal companions, as were falcons, cougars, and sometimes bears. A dire wolf was an uncommon result except for higher level Rangers that underwent the ritual, usually when replacing a slain companion. I hadn't considered the possibility that Archer might die while fighting beside me. The thought made my guts twist with anxiety.

Over lunch we all caught up on how we'd spent the morning. Bolton had been shopping for spell components, while Macha and Illiya had sold off various bits of loot and resupplied. Then everyone wanted to hear the story of bonding Archer to me. The entire group found his personality quite the curiosity, but I tried to downplay it. Over the course of the afternoon, I'd found Archer understood many basic dog commands, even without training him yet. He'd respond to his name, sit, stay, lay down, and even heel.

"I told you, Zee. Archer's special," Lemorak insisted after the party had universally agreed. Archer barked his agreement as well. Everyone laughed and the wolf gave us a panting canine grin again.

"Well, putting aside the question of Zee's wolf for now. Has everyone had a chance to think about setting up a Party Pact?" Bolton asked.

"I still think someone dropped you as a child," Lemorak replied.

"Aye! It was me. Repeatedly!" Illiya chortled. "But my little brother's suggestion still bears merit."

"I agree. Let's go kick some Goblin-ass." Macha chimed in. She and Illiya high-fived each other. It was then that I noticed the Elf and Dragonkin were sitting noticeably close together, their shoulders bumping.

"Well, Zee and I think you've all lost it," Lemorak declared. Eyes turned to me expectantly.

I cleared my throat uncomfortably. "Well…"

Lemorak looked at me alarmed.

"It sounds fun," I said defensively, not wanting to explain that the cash would be potentially life changing for my parents. "We've got Archer now. He'll pitch in, I'm sure."

Archer stood and turned in a little circle and yipped in support.

"A valiant ally, I'm sure!" Illiya tossed a cold sausage link at the dire wolf. Archer's jaws snatched it from the air and chomped it.

"Has anyone found a cleric or shaman?" Lemorak demanded. "We can't do this without a healer."

"I have someone in mind…" Macha said. We all looked questioningly at Macha and she grinned mischievously. "The only player that's been in Elmore longer than you, Lem."

"No!" Lemorak blurted. "Absolutely not!"

"Who?" Bolton asked.

"Absolutely not." Lemorak repeated.

"Who?" Bolton, Illiya and I all demanded at once.

Ten minutes later, we stood in a semicircle in the alley behind the White Horse. Against the wall of the inn slumped a passed-out player in tattered brown robes. His avatar was overweight, bald, and had a salt and pepper scruffy beard. He had stubby, pointed ears, like mine. There was a mostly empty bottle of wine clutched to his chest. The white player tag over his head said:

Brother Elias Stonetree, Level 4 Cleric of Mishakal, Half-Elf

Illiya began to speak with a skeptical tone, "He does appear a little…"

"…shit faced," Bolton finished.

"He's the only Level 4 Cleric we'll find not already snapped up by a party," Macha said.

"If I had realized how high the demand was for healers, I might have made a different choice at character creation," I observed.

"Do you guys want to wait around and recruit a level 0 and then have to level him up for a couple months before we can even take a run at the Goblin's Keep?" Macha demanded.

"I don't want to take on the Goblin's Keep to begin with. And I definitely don't want to do it with Elias fucking Stonetree," Lemorak insisted.

The drunken cleric stirred at the mention of his name, blearily opening bloodshot violet eyes. He peered up at us, smiled and let out a massive burp. Then dozed back off.

"He's not exactly in prime condition," I said. "What's his story?"

"He's been here for at least ten years. He was already a drunken fool when I jacked in. Never leaves Elmore. When he needs crypts, for booze, he sobers up long enough to cast some healing spells on players outside the Temple. Undercuts the NPC Priest's rates by half. Taps out all his mana, then gets drunk again for as long as his CCs hold out," Lemorak said.

"You're one to talk, Lem. How long have you been in Elmore?" Macha asked.

"That's different," said Lemorak. "I'm not a drunken flatliner."

Macha rolled her eyes and then turned and barged through the back doors of the White Horse into their kitchen. She emerged a second later with a big wooden bucket of water, which she promptly emptied over the plastered cleric. The rest of us jumped back to avoid the sudden splash and the wild flailing limbs that ensued as Elias sputtered awake.

"What the fuck?" Elias blurted as he shot to his feet.

"Morning!" Macha said with mocking cheer. "Can we buy you lunch?"

Elias's bloodshot gaze shifted from shock to suspicion as he surveyed our group. The heavy-set half-elf swayed unsteadily, then he let out another odorous burp. Finally he shrugged and staggered towards the back door to the White Horse.

"As long as lunch comes with s'more wine," he grumbled as he went inside.

Elias was halfway through a bottle of wine and on to his second bowl of stew when Bolton and Macha finished giving him their pitch. Illiya and I sat at the table with them, while Lemorak sat alone at the bar and Archer dozed by the fireplace. The cleric seemed to have barely listened to Bolton and Macha, entirely intent on guzzling wine and shoveling food into his face.

"What do you think?" Bolton asked after a long pause while the Half-Elf soaked up the dregs of his stew with a piece of bread. "Feel like killing some Goblins?"

Elias took a massive bite of the stew-soaked bread and chomped it with his mouth open while he looked us all over again. Then he erupted into laughter, flecks of food flying from his lips.

"That sounds like a damn stupid plan," Elias finally said after washing his laughter and food down with wine, straight from the bottle. "You five must be hard up for a healer if you're asking me."

"Like you've got something better to do?" I asked him.

"Not unless Elmore runs out of wine," Elias chortled.

"Don't you want to get out of Rowling? There's a big world out there," Bolton said.

"Worlds of adventure and glory await us!" Illiya chimed in, banging her clawed fist on the table for emphasis. Elias rolled his eyes, unimpressed.

"Fuck off. I'm waiting for someone," Elias answered.

"Waiting for someone? For over ten years? I don't think they're coming, man," I said

"You don't know what you're talking about, kid." Elias gave me an angry glare and pushed himself to his feet.

"I told you he was a waste of time," Lemorak said.

"Listen to Sir Turtle over there," Elias slurred. The portly cleric stumbled a step from the table.

"Tis a grand adventure. Join us and the Bards will sing of us all as heroes!" Illiya said. "Zee Truebow! Lemorak, Brave and Bold! Bolton

251

Spellweaver! Lovely Macha and her Mighty Fists! And Wise Elias Most Blessed Healer!"

"I'm no hero." Elias insisted, swaying and steadying himself on the back of a chair.

"Then do it for the crypts," I shouted while thinking, *Why is Macha glaring at Illiya like that?*

"I don't care about the CC, kido. I can't leave Elmore and your little plan would push me to Level 5."

"They've got wine in the rest of the map," Bolton said.

"I told you, I'm waiting for someone!"

"Who?" Macha demanded. "Who the hell is worth rotting away here for years?"

"My wife!" Elias shouted back.

Silence fell over the common room. Elias slumped down into an empty chair at the next table. He started talking before any of us could figure out what to say.

"We jacked in together. We'd been saving up for years to get our pods and pay for a private connection. This was how we were going to finally escape the shit hole outside." His voice was soft at first but gained strength as he began the retelling. "We cruised through Levels 0 and 1. She was an Elven druid, specialized in wild shaping. We were out in the valley farming EXP and got in over our heads. Her character got killed. I got a message from her when she woke up outside. We didn't have enough Crypts on account to get her jacked back in right away, so she was going to get a job and I was going to do what I could here to generate CC."

We all sat in silence. Finally, I asked, "What happened?"

"I got messages from her at first. She found a job. She said it paid well, but wasn't clear on what it was. I didn't have any trouble finding work in here. Healers are always in short supply. We were a week, maybe two, away from being able to afford a fresh connection for her when the messages stopped. Nothing. Complete black-out."

"You didn't disconnect and go look for her?" Lemorak asked, his tone softened.

"That was the first thing I did!" Elias shouted, jumping to his feet. "I spent a year on the outside trying to find her. I filed reports with OzCo Security. Hired a franchise detective. Nothing! They all just said she must have left me. But she didn't. She couldn't have...never would have."

Elias slumped back to the chair. "When I couldn't find her out there, I thought maybe she'd gotten jacked back in some other way. So I drained the last of the CC from our account and jacked myself back in. I've been waiting for her ever since."

"I hate to be the one to say this," Macha said after another long silence. "But I don't think she's coming."

"You don't know that," Elias said, but his words lacked any weight of conviction.

"I have a thought." The room turned their eyes to me as I spoke up. "You say you don't need crypts, but money can fix a lot of problems. Come with us, get out of the Valley, and you'll be able to make enough coin to afford a whole team of people on the outside to search. Franchise Detectives aren't cheap and we all know OzCo Security prioritizes cases based on income. Join us. And you'll be eligible for an equal split of the loot."

"You think I haven't thought of that myself?" Elias said.

"No. I think you've probably thought of it every day for the last ten years," I answered. "But I also think you're afraid. You've waited. Longer than I think anyone else would have. It's time to get off the bench and try something else."

"It's still a stupid plan," Elias stated and Lemorak nodded vigorously.

"No one says we need to rush in and knock over the Keep tomorrow," I said. I knew that getting killed wouldn't help my parents out at all. Even more so, leaving the game early would be dangerous for me. I felt compelled to take the risk though.

"But wouldn't it be glorious?" Illiya said. The table jumped as Macha and Bolton both kicked her under the table. Illiya glared at Bolton then stuck her forked tongue out at Macha.

"We'll be careful," I insisted. "We'll be smart. None of us can afford to throw this connection away. If we get in too deep, we'll retreat and regroup."

Macha, the siblings, and I collectively held our breaths as Elias seemed to weigh our proposal anew. The cleric tilted back his bottle of wine and pounded down the dregs. I felt my own shoulders slump, anticipating disappointment.

Elias brought the bottle back down and pounded it on the tabletop, then let out another thunderous burp. "Well. I guess that's my last drink for awhile. Let's get this party started."

We all turned to look at Lemorak expectantly.

He stewed for a long heartbeat before finally relenting. "Fine! I still think this is a bad idea, but fine!"

Chapter Sixteen

Five of us, everyone but Elias, passed the hat and purchased a Party Pact charter that afternoon and all six of us signed it. When it was submitted, the player tags of my five companions turned orange. Afterwards, we spent several days provisioning and upgrading our gear for our adventure.

Each of us purchased a list of identical items that Lemorak insisted be part of any party's "standard dungeon raiding kit." This included fifty feet of rope each, a pound of chalk, ten torches, and three healing potions each. Then we each added supplementary gear based on our skill sets. For me, this included a grappling hook, climbing pitons and hammer, special flaming signal arrows, plus an extra bundle of regular arrows, four bottles of lamp oil, and a crowbar.

On our last night before leaving town, we all had dinner at the White Horse. I decided to splurge and ordered the inn's steak dinner. If everything went well, or went to shit, this would likely be our last meal in the White Horse Inn. The steak was better than I could have dreamed. Juicy and tender. Far better than I think an actual medieval inn would have prepared.

Bolton had purchased a Player's Guide for the Goblin's Keep from the village's cartographer. It covered the topography around the Keep in fairly good detail and gave notes on common tactics for conquering the Keep. The interior of the Keep changed with each conquering and respawning, so the guide was less specific regarding the Keep's interior layout. However, as a group we discussed strategic objectives and tactical approaches.

It was agreed that as the players with the highest Stealth ratings, Macha and I would be the primary scouts. In combat, Lemorak and Illiya would comprise our front line. Macha and I would back them up as needed and ward our flanks. Bolton would hang back to cast offensive magics and be prepared to counter any enemy spellcasters. Elias would be Bolton's primary defense while also healing and buffing the party with his divine spells.

These were fairly common party combat tactics, but it was important that everyone knew their roles. Archer was the untested component of our plans, but I was expected to put him to maximum use to complement my own role. Having spent the last several days with him, I was confident the dire wolf would surpass everyone's expectations.

When the meeting wrapped up, Lemorak, Archer, and I walked back to the boarding house together. I'd been working with Archer, having him scout for the party, and we practiced during the walk. The massive dire wolf sprinted ahead of Lemorak and me. The wolf had shown himself to be adept at working under his own initiative and best judgement, which the entire party agreed was very odd.

Lemorak was still nervous about the plan. The experienced paladin had designated himself the party's official party pooper. He played devil's advocate and poked holes in every plan. Not the worst person to have in a planning session, but he had worn everyone's nerves thin.

"You realize this is still incredibly risky, right?" Lemorak asked me as we walked through the sleeping village.

"You've made that abundantly clear."

Not for the first time I was tempted to tell Lemorak how badly my family could use the money. Maybe it was just the taboo against talking about our real lives, but I couldn't bring myself to do it. I had the strong impression that Lemorak was set up well financially. He could probably loan me a substantial amount, but for some reason that seemed riskier than taking on the Goblin's Keep.

"Not just the Goblin's Keep, but keeping this many other players around you," Lemorak said.

"Yes, Lem," I said with a yawn. "I get it, but here's how I see it. From everything you've said about the rest of Gygax, it's not going to get any safer once we hit Level 5 and have to leave Rowling. The entire rest of Gygax allows for PvP. So, once we leave, it won't only be SI controlled monsters that can kill me, but other players too. We're going to need allies out there. People to watch our backs. We've put together a good group. They're not perfect, but most of the other parties in Elmore right now are Mega-Corp sponsored. They're the bigger threat."

"I can agree with you on Macha being worthy of trust. Even the siblings don't seem like bad sorts, but Elias?" Lemorak sneered. "You buy that story about his wife?"

I shrugged. "I don't know. Maybe. It sounds plausible. It's a crazy world out there. Makes more sense on its face than why you've spent all these years lurking around Elmore. You've been on your own for too long. It's time to trust a few people. That means rolling the dice and giving them a chance to betray you. Besides, I've got you to watch my back."

"Just don't do anything stupid and get yourself killed." I could tell my friend wasn't entirely happy with my response, but his incessant arguments had run out of steam.

We reached the boarding house and I said goodnight to Lemorak at his door on the first floor, then headed upstairs. Archer followed me; the boarding house was thankfully pet friendly. When I reached the top of the stairs to the second floor, I found a visitor waiting for me.

Bryn leaned on one shoulder against my door, wrapped in a long purple cloak down to the floor. Her silvery hair was free of its braid and cascaded in molten rivulets past her shoulders. She had a playful pursed smile on her full lips and her red eyes were half lidded like a prowling cat. When those predatory eyes focused on me her teeth flashed in a hungry grin.

"Evening, Zee," she purred as I came to a halt on the top stair. I felt suddenly naked under her heated gaze. "Level 3? You've been a busy boy."

"Bryn." I glared at her. I still hadn't forgotten how she'd looted the Spider Queen ahead of me, or how she'd tried to pick my pockets when we first met. Whether it was the improvements to my Wisdom score, or just that I was getting used to Bryn's effects I didn't instantly feel like a sweaty teenaged virgin on prom night.

Bryn's smile puckered into an exaggerated pout. "Don't be like that, Zee. We've all got to play our own game. Speaking of which, I heard you and Lemorak are making a suicidal run at the Goblin's Keep."

"Where'd you hear that?" I asked.

Bryn rolled her red eyes and sighed. "The Glittertooths haven't exactly been subtle about it around town."

"So?" I demanded. "Did you come to tell me what a shit idea it is? Cause Lemorak's already got that job."

"Hardly," Bryn said with a ringing little laugh like sleigh bells. "After the spiders, I figured I owed you a drink, and I always pay a debt. Figured this might be my last chance to pay up."

Bryn shifted away from my door. Her cloak slid open as she held out a brown bottle of dwarven whiskey in one delicate sable-skinned hand. The move also revealed that she was entirely naked beneath the cloak. My jaw dropped open in slack appreciation of her hourglass curves and flawless obsidian skin, tiny charcoal-colored pierced nipples at stiff attention.

She quirked a questioning sterling eyebrow at me, "You going to invite me in or what?"

The moment hung heavy between us for a heartbeat as warring impulses convulsed within me.

Without ever consciously making the decision, I stepped in close to Bryn. My hands grabbed her waist and pulled her naked body hard against me and our lips met. A soft moan escaped her throat at the contact, and any chance that I might have come to my senses incinerated. I didn't care if what I was feeling was Bryn's high Charisma influence, or genuine desire. At that exact moment, what was the difference?

We stumbled into my room a few lost seconds later, Bryn's cloak dropped to the floor. Pieces of my clothing and gear fell to the floor as we swayed together across the floor of my rented room. As the last of my equipment hit the floor Bryn broke our kiss and pushed me back from her. Her softly glowing red eyes traveled up and down my now naked body.

I was suddenly quite glad that the improvements to my physical stats since character generation had left me with a toned athletic body. For the first time in my life, I had washboard abs. I took the opportunity to let my own gaze survey Bryn's jette black avatar, from silvery haired head to her purple painted toes, and every well curved inch in between. I had no idea what Bryn's real body looked like, but again did it really matter?

"Not bad." Bryn licked her smirking lips and nodded her approval after taking her appraisal of me. Then she came at me in a rush her lips hungry against mine again. Her slender body pushed against mine and drove me back and then down to my narrow mattress with Bryn astride my hips.

"Mmmm, that was exactly what I needed." Bryn stretched and shifted beside beneath the bedsheet. Her softly glowing red eyes were half lidded and she had the content expression of a cat that had just been fed, pet, and left to bask in the sun.

"Glad to be of service." I said with a sigh as I relished the sensation of her warm naked flesh pressed up against mine in the bed technically too small for two people. I wasn't sure how long it had been since we tumbled into my room together. However, this was our third time coming up for air. A decent Constitution score apparently had other benefits, outside of combat.

"You've got some moves sweetie," Bryn said with a smirk. "If I didn't know you were an inmate player, I'd have thought you were running some expensive performance enhancing macros or something."

Not wanting to discuss my limited real world experiences, or that most of my *moves* came from studying porn, I retrieved my mug and gulped the last mouthful of whiskey. Already pleasantly buzzed, the strong brown liquor burned pleasantly down my throat and added to the warm fire in my belly. Sitting up, the sheet sliding off of me, I reached up to the shelf above my bed and grabbed up the bottle of whiskey Bryn had brought and we had finally gotten around to opening.

"Refill?"

"Please." Bryn grabbed her almost empty clay mug off the window sill and held it out to me.

As I refilled her mug, I found myself staring down at her face, illuminated by the moonlight beaming in through my room's small window. Not for the first time, I found myself thinking that there was something familiar about her gorgeous face. Sharp and slender.Feminine, but with an undeniable strength. Like a flawlessly cut diamond. Yet with her unnaturally jette black skin, glowing red eyes, silver hair and pointed ears, her face was just alien enough that I couldn't place it. However, for the first time I found myself unguarded enough with Bryn to say something.

"Your face is always so familiar. But it's not yours is it? So we don't actually know each other."

I felt Bryn's shields go up as her lithe body beside me tensed for an instant. The tension vanished after a second, but I still felt her guard was up. She took a sip of her mug then shook her head.

"A celebrity then?"

Bryn's lips pursed and her eyes narrowed as she either calculated her response or exit strategy. "How's your retro Sci-Fi?"

"Try me." I felt that was a better response then proclaiming myself a complete retro-nerd as Macha liked to call me.

"Uhura. Neytiri. Gamora." She held up a slender black finger as she listed off each character.

It only took my drunken brain a few seconds to make the connection. My face lit with excitement and recognition as I immediately saw through the differences created by skin and hair color, glowing eyes, and pointed ears.

"Zoe Saldana? Nice pick!"

"Just the face, I got the curves from Scarlett." Bryn giggled and for a flickering instant her shields dropped and I swear she looked shy, unguarded and for the first time that night naked. As quickly as they dropped, her defenses slipped back into place. Bryn's smoldering eyes locked onto me as she downed another mouthful.

Sitting up beside me, the sheet dropped from her chest and she set her mug back on the window sill. Without another word, she pulled me in for a ravenous kiss which I returned. With blinding speed and grace, she slid herself astride my lap once more, her lips never leaving mine. Of their own accord, my hands found the small of her back and pulled her bare body tight against mine. Her own hands slid to my shoulders and with her entire body, she drove me down onto the bed. I lost track of the exact sequence of events for sometime after that.

Lemorak pounding at my door woke me the next morning. Bryn was gone. I had a fuzzy memory of her slipping away while I dozed after she'd had her way with me, several times. My head throbbed from the whiskey we'd eventually cracked open, and there was a line of burning scratches down my back and several dark hickeys on my neck and shoulders. Flashes of memory from the previous night shot through my mind and a satisfied grin spread across my face.

"I'll be right down!" I shouted.

The pounding at the door mercifully subsided.

A *Minor Vitality Potion* banished my hangover while I dressed and did a quick check of my gear. Somewhat surprisingly, none of my crypts or gear were missing in Bryn's wake. There was a handwritten note from Bryn pinned to my door with one of her hand-crossbow darts.

That was fun. Try not to die out there sweetie. See you. :-*

~B

The bottom of the note was marked with Bryn's scarlet lip prints. I tucked the note into my inventory and opened the door to find Archer patiently sitting in the hall. The wolf shuffled over and gave me a quick snuffle. Then shoved his head under my hand, demanding a head scratch.

"Thanks for camping in the hall, bud," I told the wolf. I gave him extra thorough scratches behind the ears, then hustled downstairs to meet Lemorak.

Our entire party was meeting at the gates of Elmore. When Lemorak and I arrived at the gates, only Elias was there, hungover but sober. To my dismay, the Mega-Corp trio of Lute, Marl and Markus, or the Three Stooges as I had decided to call them, were also loitering about the gates. It was the first time I'd seen them since our brawl in the White Horse.

All three Megas were Level 4 and had made noticeable upgrades to their gear. Markus's halberd was covered in a crystalline layer of ice and wisps of mist drifted from it in the morning air. Marl had upgraded his armor to full platemail; however, the dwarf's armor was black and covered in a variety of spikes and blades. Lute had a new staff with a fist-sized glowing crystal orb at the top.

Out in the streets, the game wouldn't let us get into another brawl. However, the game couldn't make us be friendly to each other. Markus and Marl glared at Lemorak and me when we arrived, while Lute remained aloof to our presence as usual. Lemorak flipped off the Stooges and then deliberately turned his back on the trio to talk to Elias and me.

"What the hell are they waiting around here for?" he grumbled.

"I heard one of them saying they were waiting on an Assassin they'd contracted," Elias said, his blood shot eyes pinched against the rising sun. I wondered why the cleric was intentionally subjecting himself to a hangover.

A flutter of motion at the edge of my peripheral vision. I turned my head only to find nothing there. Frowning, I turned back towards my friends only to see Lemorak's eyes widened in shock as he started back towards the Stooges. I turned to see what had drawn his attention.

"What the fuck?" A fourth player had joined the Stooges. In retrospect, I really shouldn't have been surprised to see Bryn standing with the three Mega-Corp employees. But I was.

Her silver curls sparkled in the early morning light like dew speckled spider webs. Markus tossed her a small leather pouch, which she snatched out of the air with ease. It vanished into her inventory.

"Told you she couldn't be trusted," Lemorak said.

"You know Bryn, I take it?" Elias asked.

"Some of us better than others," Lemorak replied, and I could feel his disapproving glare on me. My cheeks reddened in embarrassment.

I opened my mouth to reply, but couldn't find the words.

Elias graced me with an empathetic grimace. "Don't take it personal Zee. She doesn't. This is all litterally a game to Bryn."

"What do you mean?" After several encounters with Bryn I still found her motivations almost entirely opaque.

"Bryn's just here to have fun. On the outside, she's the daughter of some big wig with the mega JANUS. She's expected to be a good little mega worker bee when she gets out of here. She's gaming for her gap year between university and being yoked as a junior executive for probably the rest of her life." Elias explained.

Speechless, Lemorak and I stared at Elias for several long heartbeats. Within the game it was such a taboo to talk about your "real life", it seemed inconceivable to me that Bryn of all people would have shared so much personal information with Elias. I'd just spent the night with Bryn, and yet it hadn't seemed half as intimate as the information that Elias had just shared about her.

"She got drunk one night in the White Horse and spent the night crying into her wine with me. Her mother had just sent her some email expressing her general disappointment in her." Elias shrugged. "I've been kicking around Elmore so long, sometimes people forget that I'm a player and not an NPC. If I was an actual Priest, I might have felt compelled to treat it like a concession. But I'm not, and she's been a bitch to me ever since."

With Bryn's arrival, the Stooges had huddled up to confer for several moments, but then turned to head out with the Level 3 Assassin following. Just beyond the city gates, Bryn turned and blew me a kiss, her lips quirked in a mischievous smirk as she chased the kiss with a wink. Then she spun and glided after the Stooges.

From down the block I heard Macha shout derisive and anatomically improbable taunts at the departing Mega-Corps. She arrived with the Glittertooths in tow, her face spread in a happy grin as she continued to taunt the departing Megas.

"Did I see that bitch Bryn with the Stooges?" Macha asked after hurling her last insult.

Lemork's glower deepened before the Paladin growled, "Let's get a move on. We're burning daylight. people."

We hiked out to a farm on the edge of the settled land around Elmore. The farmhouse was a smoking ruin, with a weeping NPC family cleaning up the mess of a recent goblin raid. It was the starting point for the *Goblin's Keep* quest, and no matter what players or NPCs did to clean up or repair the farm, it would reset every night to the original condition.

We talked to the NPC family to engage the storyline of the quest. The NPCs complained about the ever-increasing Goblin raids that had been happening ever since the monsters moved into old Brightblade Keep.

The keep had once belonged to a noble knight, Sir Gerald Brightblade, and his family. The Brightblade family had fallen on hard times and the keep had gone abandoned for decades before the Goblins had moved in. Now the monsters were terrorizing the countryside with increasing boldness. The entire story was tangentially connected to my very first encounter when I had saved Farmer Hoggins on the road. The NPCs asked us "brave adventurers" to do something to help them and the Quest offer appeared for all of us.

Quest Offer

Goblins have taken over abandoned Brightblade Keep and are pillaging the area around Elmore. Defeat the Goblin band and prevent future carnage.

Exp Reward: 25,000

CC Reward: 12,000

Treasure: Random

Time Limit: 5 days

Failure: 50% Exp Penalty for 1 month after failure

Accept

Decline

We accepted the quest and headed for the Goblin Keep, which was now highlighted on my HUD map. It was about a day and a half away by foot. While we hiked away from the NPC farm, Illiya began a marching song in a trumpeting alto.

On our march we encountered a couple roving bands of Goblin marauders, all of which we easily dispatched. We also ran into several other groups of players moving about on their own adventures. Lemorak and Elias, both familiar faces in Elmore, drew the attention of several players. Most of them wished us luck with clear skepticism as to our chances.

The sun was just past midday when I received a new notification.

Perception Skill Alert! Danger is near!

Macha and I both came to a halt in near unison and we both looked around anxiously.

"Hold up," I hissed. "Quiet!"

Lemorak had to nudge Illiya to get the singing barbarian's attention, but everyone came to a halt and we stood in silence. We were on a narrow

271

dirt road, not wide enough for a merchant wagon, but wide and smooth enough for a horse to gallop on. Thick trees and brush lined the road. The road led directly to the ruined keep, and we hadn't seen any other players or goblins in over an hour.

"See anything?" Macha whispered.

I shook my head. Then we all heard a crash from deep in the woods.

Beside me Archer scented the breeze before letting out a low warning growl. The charcoal fur along his neck and back bristled with agitation. I looked down at the wolf who was staring intently out into the brush.

"Can you show me what it is?" I whispered to the dire wolf.

Archer huffed out a breath and took a step forward towards the trees.

"I've got a bad feeling about this, Chewy," whispered Elias behind me.

I unslung my bow and fitted an arrow to the string, then glanced at the party. "We'll go check it out. Hold here."

Then I looked at Archer and said, "Show me, bud."

The dire wolf trotted off the road and slipped into the thick brush. I pulled up the hood on my Ranger's cloak and activated my Stealth skill, then followed. Archer stayed just within my sight line as he slunk forward without a sound. A benefit of our companion bond seemed to be that my HUD would outline his form, even when the wolf was concealed to others by his own Stealth skill.

Closer than before, another crash in the woods. This time I also heard voices from the same direction. Archer came to a stop and dropped to the ground. His ears were bolt upright and quivering with intense focus. I dove to the ground and army-crawled forward until I was beside the wolf. Delicately, I poked my head through a gap between a thick bush and big rocks.

Several yards away, I saw Markus and Marl. They were in a fighting retreat from a massive creature that bristled with long black spines. The enraged animal looked like the twisted love child of a grizzly bear and a porcupine. I wondered where Lute and Bryn were.

As I watched, I realized that they were intentionally avoiding doing damage to the creature. In fact, Markus was barely touching it, just giving it the occasional jab. The fighter was also taking hits that seemed entirely avoidable. He clearly had perception filters to handle the pain, and Marl was casting a steady stream of healing spells on him. Instead, it looked like they were luring it. Towards the road.

The logic of their maneuver immediately hit me. They couldn't attack us outright with the PvP restrictions. What they could do was to attract dangerous monsters and drop them on our heads. Strictly speaking, they weren't attacking us. They were attacking a monster and then running away, so the game wouldn't stop them.

273

Archer let out a sub-audible growl deep in his chest that I felt vibrate through the ground. I took that to mean he sensed the same reasoning behind the pair's intent.

"Let's get back and warn the gang, Scooby," I whispered to the wolf.

Archer and I fell back towards the road undetected. The crashing sounds of the Stooges goading the creature continued. When we reached the road, I reported on what we'd found. After I completed the report, I got a notification of a new achievement.

Achievement Earned - "My Spidey Sense is Tingling" - Detect and ambush before it's sprung - +1 to your Perception Skill when enemies are hiding from you.

"Those ass hats," Lemorak growled. There was an instantaneous murmur of agreement amongst the party. "They're Aggro Kiting a damn Ursapine on us."

"Run for it?" Bolton suggested.

Elias and Lemorak both shook their heads negative. In planning our expedition, the cleric had demonstrated a grasp of game tactics and strategy on par with Lemorak. He clearly hadn't always been a drunken sot.

"Ursapine are territorial and aggressive beasts," Lemorak explained. "I'm sure those two already have a plan to break contact with it once they drop it on us or our trail. If we fall back or sprint ahead, it'll just scent us and pursue. I don't want that thing coming up behind us unprepared."

"Game plan?" Macha asked, cracking her knuckles and then proceeding to stretch out like she was getting ready for a casual workout. I deliberately didn't watch her limber up, though I caught Illiya watching the routine with obvious appreciation. The sounds of the approaching Ursapine drew nearer as Lemorak began to give orders.

Chapter Seventeen

Markus and Marl emerged on the road, laughing with glee, just as we had gotten into our positions. The Ursapine barreled out after them a racing heartbeat later. Markus jabbed at the bearlike creature with the tip of his halberd and Marl held a healing spell in hand ready if the fighter took a hit.

Lemorak and Illiya stood out in the center of the road, Lemorak a step ahead as the defensive tank. The rest of us had taken nominal cover within the treeline. The trees wouldn't protect us very much if the monster came after one of us, but they'd give us some protection when it did what Lemorak called a "quill burst."

Marl glanced over his shoulder and spotted Lemorak and Illiya out on the road.

"There you are!" shouted Marl. Markus glanced back too but couldn't keep his eyes off the Ursapine for long. "We brought you some Exp to help train you up before the Goblin's Keep. We've got to be going, though. Have fun!"

The air next to them shimmered, then Lute and Bryn stepped out from behind an invisibility spell. Lute placed a hand on Markus's shoulder, while Marl and Bryn grabbed onto her robe sleeves. Then the wizard cast a spell and all four players teleported away in a swirl of emerald sparkles.

"They're the literal worst," I muttered to Archer beside me. I applied tension to my bowstring and sighted on the Ursapine. It was critical that none of us hit the creature before Lemorak drew and held its attention.

The Ursapine seemed momentarily confused by the disappearance of its harassers. However, a heartbeat later, either by sight or scent, it noticed us. Its very bear-like head swung around towards Lemorak and Illiya on the road and it roared, a wall of nearly tangible sound, before charging them.

It had covered half the distance when Bolton released his first offensive spell. *Too soon!* I wanted to shout. A crackling arc of blue lightning shot from the sorcerer's outstretched hands and lanced into the charging Ursapine. The creature roared, but it sounded more like surprise than pain, and without breaking stride the Ursapine veered towards Bolton under the cover of brush.

"Your brother can't hold his wad," Lemorak muttered to Illiya.

Then Lemorak stepped forward, lifted his sword in a knight's salute and cried, "OOORAH!" to trigger his *Divine Challenge*. Lemorak's blade lit up like an acetylene torch, a brilliant silver blaze. The challenge instantly drew the monster's aggro and it veered back to crash down on Lemorak.

With a pair of arrows fit to my string - a new benefit of my increasing Archery talent - I drew and loosed them under the glare of Lemorak's blazing sword. The arrows zipped through the air and buried themselves in the Ursapine's shoulder. If the Ursapine's HP bar decreased at all from my shot, I couldn't tell.

Illiya rolled out to the side of the charging Ursapine while Lemorak stood his ground against the charge. The paladin dug his heels in and swept out his blazing sword to break the Ursapine's rush and slash at the creature's bear-like face. Illiya trumpeted a battle cry and stepped in to chop at the monster's massive quill-studded flank.

The Ursapine howled in frustration as it snapped its jaws and batted its claws at Lemorak. Sparks flew from his new armor, but he held his ground. Illiya delivered another brutal overhead chop as she circled towards the beast's rear. Archer growled encouragement and took an eager step forward.

"Hold up, bud. You don't want none of that right now," I said. The dire wolf crouched back down, his full attention on the battle, but obedient.

The Ursapine was distracted by Illiya harassing its flank, but each time it started to turn, Lemorak would slash at it with his blazing sword. Frustrated, unable to decide who to focus on, the Ursapine hunched up its back and rolled its head downward.

"Here it comes!" Lemorak shouted. The Ursapine went totally still, then all of its foot-long quills bristled upright.

"Cover!" I shouted and ducked behind the nearest tree, dragging Archer with me. Lemorak took a chance and turned his armored back to the Ursapine while Illiya dove for cover in a shallow drainage ditch beside the road.

There was a sound like ripping wet leather and the Ursapine roared. Then there was a whistling sound as thousands of arrow-like quills fired off in every direction. The brush on either side of me shuddered at their passage and I felt several thud into the tree that covered me.

Archer yelped and I saw he'd caught a spine in one haunch. I reached down and he let me rip the spine from his flesh with a yip. Then he turned gnashing teeth towards the Ursapine.

"Go!" I ordered. For the moment, there wasn't a single razor-sharp quill on the Ursapine's body, but fresh quills were already starting to sprout along its back. More would follow, according to Lemorak.

Archer flew like an arrow at the momentarily vulnerable Ursapine. Lemorak had been at point blank range, but his armor had shed most of the exploding quills. However, he hadn't escaped unscathed. The paladin didn't let it slow him down and he was chopping his massive two-handed sword, no longer glowing, down at the Ursapine with a fierce overhead strike. Illiya was back up and on her feet, apparently untouched by the quill burst.

Archer sank his fangs into the Ursapine's exposed rear leg. Lemorak's sword swept down again to hack a bloody gash along the Ursapine's shoulder. Illiya's axe clove into a rib and stuck there. A gout of flame erupted from Bolton's position, and I sent several shafts flying downrange at the monster.

The Ursapine howled and I saw that our combined efforts had made a dent in the creature's massive HP bar, but we still had a long way to go. Magical darts of energy flew from Bolton's hands and struck the Ursapine in the head with concussive force. Seemingly out of nowhere, Macha twirled in from the treeline and hacked at the Ursapine with her katana. I was firing arrows as fast as I could draw and loose.

I aimed for the creature's head, hoping to keep him off balance, and if I got lucky, get a critical hit. Elias stepped out on the road, several quills stuck in his arm, but he finished a prayer of healing and a glowing wave of warm soothing energy swept over the entire group. The HP bars of my injured comrades, and Archer, all rose.

After several seconds, the Ursapine had multiple bleeding wounds, but judging by its HP they were mostly superficial. The creature shook violently and Archer's jaws lost their grip and the wolf went flying into the brush. The Ursapine lashed out with a clawed foot and caught Macha with a kick to the chest. She stumbled back and cried out in pain, Illiya stepped over to cover the reeling monk. Fresh bristling quills sprouted across most of the Ursapine's body, though they were only a couple of inches long still.

Illiya shouted a clarion battle cry to draw the beast's attention and swung wildly with her smaller battle ax. Her massive two-handed war ax was still lodged in the Ursapine's ribs. Lemorak tried to dive in on the other side to confuse the creature. With his *Divine Challenge* still recharging, Illiya had pulled the Ursapine's full aggro, so the creature didn't turn back towards Lemorak when he struck. Lemorak attempted to leverage the flank, his blade flashing with a rapid series of strikes, but the lengthening quills acted like armor, deflecting his sword.

The Ursapine launched itself at Illiya, who was backpedalling, but not fast enough. The Ursapine batted her with one clawed paw the size of a dinner plate, and then the other. She screamed in pain and fell. The Ursapine pounced to maul her. There were multiple successive flashes of red from Illiya's body as the creature landed back-to-back Critical Strikes. There was a blood-curdling scream from Illiya, then silence.

I couldn't even imagine how much damage Illiya was taking, and the associated agony that would come with it if it had been Macha or me. Luckily, Illiya had her perception filter.

But that scream sounded real...

"No!" Bolton shouted, across the road from me. He hurled another spell and soon another sizzling lightning bolt flew.

Archer launched himself back out of the brush. The dire wolf came in low this time and got in under the taller Ursapine's legs. Apparently there weren't any quills on the creature's underside. The Ursapine cried out in pain and surprise and jumped away from the dire wolf and Illiya too.

Lemorak stepped up to stand over Illiya's bloody body as Archer went sprinting back away from under the Ursapine before he got crushed. Elias was running forward to Illiya, his hands glowing with the warm golden light of a prepared healing spell. A cleric's most powerful healing was delivered individually by touch so he had to get into the thick of it. Determined to chip in, I barraged the Ursapine with a hailstorm of arrows. At this range, I could hardly miss.

Then the creature hunched up again. Even if we'd had time to react, in the heat of the fight, we'd all moved away from our covered positions. Just as the quills shot out Lemorak threw his armored body down over the fallen Illiya and Elias, who was kneeling over her to deliver his healing spell.

I flung a leather clad arm up over my face. Pain lanced from my leg, arm and stomach as I took several quills. My HP was down about a third from that one barrage.

When I lowered my arm, things had gone from bad to fucked. Lemorak was on the ground, bristling with quills that had found gaps in his armor. The Ursapine's rapidly grown quills were shorter than the first blast, but they had found smaller gaps in his armor. While Lemorak had caught the brunt of the burst, several quills had still struck Illiya and Elias. Illiya was unconscious, and Elias was wincing in pain while casting a fresh spell.

Archer limped up beside me, several quills buried in his skin. Bolton was down, and I didn't see Macha anywhere. This was bad. Very bad. It looked like I was the last man standing. I slung my bow and drew my scimitars. Archer, injured but still upright, gave me a supportive growl.

"You go low. I'll go high," I told the wolf. Archer launched in unison with me as I charged.

The Ursapine's spines were beginning to resprout as Archer and I closed. The beast swiped at me with its clawed forepaw and I could clearly see the sun glint off the razor edges. I slashed back at the paw and kept charging in. Archer let out a battle howl and ducked below another swiping paw and was back under the Ursapine, snapping and clawing at its soft belly.

I was inside the Ursapine's reach now, face to snout with its slavering spread jaws. Gritting my teeth in determination, I stabbed the point of one scimitar at a black eye. There was a red flash around the Ursapine's body as

I landed a Critical Strike and pierced the monster's eye. The creature thrashed its head wildly and I nearly lost grip of my sword.

Achievement Earned - "It's all fun and games until someone loses an eye...then it's hilarious!" -

Take out an enemy's eye - 5% Bonus Critical Chance for 1 week

A regrowing quill stuck in my side, further depleting my HP. I managed to get another twist of my sword, still in the Ursapine's eye, before the creature reached a paw in and awkwardly bashed me away. I kept my grip on the sword and it ripped free as I flew back.

Hitting the ground with a thud, the wind rushed out of my lungs as I slid across the dirt road. Aching all over, I pushed myself to my feet with a groan. My left leg wouldn't bear my weight and my side where a quill was stuck burned with pain whenever I tried for a deep breath. Archer hadn't lingered beneath the Ursapine, and had already circled around to come up beside me.

"This isn't working." I gasped.

Archer grunted in agreement.

My Hit Points were down by half, my Endurance was low but recharging still, and Archer's HP was lower than mine. The Ursapine's HP had decreased, but he was still above two-thirds full. Elias had gotten a healing spell off and Lemorak was pushing himself upright. Illiya was still down, with Elias praying another spell over her.

Bolton pushed himself up against a fallen log, healing potion in hand, but he didn't look like he could stand yet. I saw Macha now, tip of her katana down in the dirt. She was using the sword like a cane and I could see numerous bleeding wounds.

The Ursapine was rubbing at its face. The eye I'd stabbed had torn free and dangled down its face. Its stubby quills were still lengthening.

"What the hell are we going to do?" I shouted.

Lemorak shrugged and spat a wad of blood on the ground. "Dying appears high on the menu."

"Fuck that," Macha shouted. The monk wiped sweat and blood from her face with her orange sleeve, then righted her stance, and lifted her katana to a ready position.

The Ursapine was swinging its head around between the three of us, trying to watch us all with its one remaining eye. The beast let out an enraged ground-shaking roar. Its lone black eye focused on me and it charged.

I'd like to say I made a careful tactical decision to skillfully retreat in that instant, but I didn't. My hindbrain kicked in and said, *FUCKING RUN!* And that's exactly what I did. I spun on a heel and sprinted into the thick brush of the forest with the Ursapine in hot pursuit. Hopefully, if it was running it couldn't quill burst.

All the hiking and the points I'd spent on improving my Strength since joining the game had beefed up my Endurance pool and Athletic skill. My heightened Dexterity was helping me pull off some particularly challenging parkour acrobatic maneuvers. Still, sprinting through thick vegetation, leaping over obstacles and taking bounding skips to avoid tangling my feet was taxing. Having an injured leg didn't help matters. I could hear the Ursapine behind me in pursuit. It smashed through obstacles that I had to dodge and trampled over brush that would otherwise trip me and repeatedly roared its fury.

Avoiding dangers ahead of me on my mad dash through the forest was taking all my concentration. Without my elevated Wisdom ability and Perception skill, highlighting hazards for me, I never would have made it. I didn't dare glance behind me to gauge the ground between the Ursapine and myself. I became aware of a howling further behind as Archer trailed us.

Pure terror-driven adrenaline drove me maybe a hundred yards into the forest. By that point my chest was heaving, lungs burning for air and sweat coursing down my body. The Ursapine sounded very close, *too close*, and I pushed myself forward with everything I had.

The ground began sloping upwards and I realized I was climbing an increasingly steep hill. The trees and brush thinned on the slope, but the incline was slowing me down. My Endurance bar began to plummet with the change in terrain. I doubted the hill would slow the Ursapine much, in fact, with the thinner foliage I figured the Ursapine would gain ground on me.

On the run, I scanned the rising slope for any possible advantage in the terrain. Then my Perception skill kicked in and highlighted a dark opening in the stone hillside about twenty or so feet upslope and slightly to my left. Without hesitation, I altered my sprint towards the opening.

The Ursapine burst out of the treeline behind me, Archer nipping at its heels. As I drew closer to the dark opening, I saw that it was, as hoped, a cave, though I couldn't tell how deep. The ground beneath my feet trembled as the creature thundered up the hill towards me. I didn't want it to abandon its pursuit and turn on Archer, so I spun and fired a spray of three arrows at the creature before hurling myself through the opening of the cave.

"Come on, Pooh Bear…" I spat. "Come get some honey!"

If this didn't work, Archer and I were both dead. I would wake up in my pod in prison. I had no idea what would happen to my oddly intelligent NPC animal companion.

The cave narrowed fast and curved to my right. However, the cave wasn't nearly as deep as I had hoped. Stone walls quaked and dust showered down over me as the Ursapine crashed in after me. I heard its boney quills scraping against the stone walls. What light I had from the sunshine outside was quickly blotted out as the Ursapine shoved in behind me and my night vision kicked in.

My back to the wall of the cave, I whipped out my scimitars. Claws reached out at me and I slashed furiously. As if stung by a bee, the Ursapine drew back its paw but continued to push itself in.

"Come on you bastard!" I screamed. The beast roared in response and I gagged as the putrid smell of its breath flooded the cave.

The tip of its snout poked around the corner of the cave. A single step forward and I slashed it with my scimitar and then threw myself back against the rear wall as a bloodied paw reached for me. The claw missed me by millimeters.

The Ursapine and I traded swipes back and forth like this until I lost track. I told myself that if I ever got out of that damned cave, I was adding a very long spear to my inventory. If the Ursapine wasn't actually wedged between the cave walls, it was enraged and determined enough to kill me that it didn't matter. At least it didn't seem to be getting any closer. I would lunge and score a hit on foreleg or its nose and then fling myself back against the wall to avoid the inevitable reprisal. Once or twice I was too slow and took a hit. I was down to my last twenty or so HP.

Outside, I could distantly hear Archer harassing the Ursapine from behind. He was growling and snapping, but I had no idea how effective the loyal dire wolf was being. I couldn't see the top of the Ursapine's head to read its HP bar.

Then the tone of the monster's growls and roars changed from anger to surprise. I heard voices beyond the cave. I hoped my friends had gotten their shit together and come to the rescue.

Electric blue light filled the cave as lightning crackled over the Ursapine. Fearing that the creature wasn't truly stuck and it would try to pull out, I lunged forward with a fresh offensive, risking my remaining HP.

Yowling in agony, the Ursapine began to thrash wildly in the narrow confines of the cave. I flung myself back to avoid its flailing forepaws. More lightning lit up the cave and I got a glimpse of the Ursapine's HP bar, nearly empty. I choked on dust and dirt as it rained down on me from overhead and tried to merge my body with the stone wall at my back as the beast thrashed its death throes.

I lunged forward and stabbed the Ursapine one last time with my scimitar. Then everything went still and quiet as the Ursapine's final HP vanished. The monster dissolved to dust like any dead monster. Closing my eyes, I fell against the wall of the cave and tried to catch my breath. I hurt all over, I desperately tried to pull air into my lungs, but my throat was raw from shouting and dust. Notifications rolled across my display, but I was too distracted to read them.

Somehow I heaved myself out of the cave and into the open air. Archer trotted up to me, tail wagging furiously and sniffing me all over. He had numerous wounds on his chest and torso, but his front paws and snout were drenched in sticky dark blood that I felt confident wasn't his.

As if from a great distance, I heard voices call out to me. I flopped down on my ass and then sprawled on my back, exhausted. I dimly realized that Macha and Lemorak were standing over me shouting for Elias as I lost consciousness.

Interlude Three

Orchestral music, heavy on horns, filled my ears. The air around me was ice cold. Opening my eyes, I found I was standing in a massive ballroom carved out of glacial blue ice. The ballroom was populated by tuxedo- and evening gown-clad party goers, mingling, drinking, and dancing. Looking down at myself, I found I was wearing a crisp black tuxedo myself. There was a small lump under my left arm/ I reached under my jacket and felt a holster holding a compact handgun. A vacant-eyed waitress with a saccharine smile stepped up to me holding a tray with a martini glass made of ice.

"Your martini, Mr. Bond." The waitress had a vaguely European accent.

"Thank you." I reached out and picked up the carved ice glass. The server vanished into the swirl of people around me.

"Time to find the Doctor, I guess," I said aloud after taking a sip of the martini.

While scanning the room, I made eye contact with a beautiful blond woman in a skin-tight black satin dress that hugged every inch of her body. The woman's blue eyes blazed with either lust or rage, I couldn't tell which. She stormed across the room toward me, drawing gazes as she went. When she drew close she spoke just as I was trying to pull something pithy and Bond-like to say.

"We meet again, Mr. Bond," she purred with a thick Russian accent. She stood close enough to me that the satin covering her breasts brushed against my white shirt.

Then she slapped me across the face,. Startled, my cheek burning, I didn't notice her step closer, her chest pressed to mine. Her other hand reached up and turned my face back to her. Scarlet lips met my stinging lips in a passionate kiss. Confused beyond all sense, my lips returned the kiss reflexively. Acting on its own accord, my free hand slid to the small of her back to pull hard against me.

When she pulled away, her forehead leaned against mine and she whispered with heated breath, "I'll meet you upstairs. Do not keep me waiting again."

She gave me a wink, her heated blue eyes sparkling, before stepping back. I watched her walk away, her hips swaying in invitation. Then the

Doctor stepped up in front of me, cutting off my view, a Cheshire grin spread across his face. He wore a white jacketed tuxedo, had a black eye patch over his left eye, and a smoldering cigar clenched between his teeth.

"Do you expect me to follow her?" I asked the Doctor hopefully.

"No, Mr. Bond, I expect you to die!" the Doctor intoned, dour before breaking into boyish laughter.

Set him up for that one, I chided myself.

"Was that Ursula Andress?" I asked, reaching to rub my still-stinging cheek.

"An artfully rendered approximation," the Doctor replied after his chuckles subsided.

"Honey Rider didn't have a Russian accent," I pointed out. "And that was Goldfinger's line, not Largo's."

The Doctor rolled his eyes in annoyance at me. "And the ice palace is from *Die Another Day.* Stop nitpicking! It's an homage to Bond!"

"So, I take it you wanted to talk?" I shook my head and took a sip from my martini.

"I have a mission for you, 007," the Doctor said grinning around his cigar and wagging his eyebrows at me.

"A mission? Don't you keep an eye on me? I'm a little busy!"

"Yes!" the Doctor exclaimed. "The Goblin's Keep. Should be quite challenging. A bold choice! Don't worry, this is a side-quest. I need you to retrieve something from beneath the Keep once you've defeated the main storyline."

The Doctor drew a brown envelope from inside his white jacket and held it out to me. Thinking it was information on this side mission, I reached out and took it. As soon as my hand made contact the envelope dissolved between my fingers.

"Oops. Sorry, it was programmed to self-destruct," the Doctor explained with an impish grin.

A notification scrolled across the bottom of my vision.

New Quest Accepted! Discover the secrets beneath the Goblin's Keep and retrieve the

First Player's Sword for the Doctor!

Exp Reward: ?????

CC Reward: ?????

Treasure: ?????

Time Limit: ????

"What the hell?" I demanded. "I didn't accept a quest!" We drew concerned glances from several of the finely dressed party goer extras.

"You accepted the envelope," the Doctor said with a shrug of his tuxedo-clad shoulders, "That counts."

I ground my teeth in frustration, "Who is the First Player and why do I need to find his sword?"

"Adam Huxley, OVR World's original programmer, was also the first player to connect himself directly to the game. He was an Elf multi-classed fighter and wizard. His handle was Gananlas and he was the first to reach level 100," the Doctor explained. "Being the game's creator, he designed several powerful in-game artifacts. They've been locked away since his disappearance almost fifteen years ago. Access to the quests that allow you to hunt for these artifacts are at my discretion to assign."

"So others have retrieved this sword before?"

"Several have tried," the Doctor confirmed. "None have succeeded. These are one off quests. Each First Player Artifact is a one-of-a-kind item in the OVR Worlds. There aren't multiple copies floating about."

"You're not going to tell me where beneath the Keep it's hidden or what to expect. Are you?"

The Doctor gave me a trickster's grin. "Where would be the fun in that? This is a game after all Zee. By the way…" he paused and cleared his throat, "do you have a match?"

My face scrunched up in confusion. "What? No?"

The Doctor made a game show buzzer sound before saying, "Sorry! That's wrong! Good luck, Zee."

The scene faded to black.

Chapter Eighteen

Some stretch of time later, I slowly regained consciousness, head splitting with pain. Without the will to open my eyes, I just lay there. I heard the voices of my friends speaking softly around me, felt the warmth of a fire nearby and smelled cooking meat. I reviewed my unread notifications.

LEVEL UP!

LEVEL 4 RANGER REACHED!

ARCHERY TALENT IMPROVED TO LEVEL 9

TWO-WEAPON FIGHTING TALENT IMPROVED TO LEVEL

12

SKILL IMPROVED: ATHLETICS +6 -> +7

SKILL IMPROVED: SURVIVAL +9 -> +10

SKILL IMPROVED: STEALTH +8 -> +9

SKILL IMPROVED: ANIMAL HANDLING +4 -> +5

SKILL IMPROVED: TRACKING +7 -> +8

INCREASE TO HIT POINTS +20

INCREASE TO MANA +10

2 ABILITY POINTS AWARDED

+1 ABILITY POINT FOR BEING HALF-ELF

NEW RANGER TALENT UNLOCKED - FAVORED TERRAIN

(FOREST)

NEW TALENT EARNED: IRON WILL

Achievement Earned - Cornered Fighter! - You defeated a tougher monster with your

back to the wall - 5% bonus to Defense when you're cornered in the future

Achievement Earned - The Bigger They Are, The Harder They Fall! - Kill an enemy at

least 8 levels higher than you - 75% bonus Exp for killing that monster

Achievement Earned - Big Game Hunter - Kill 10 animals larger than you - 10%

bonus damage to animals larger than you

After reading through the string of notifications, I put off assigning my new Ability Points - my splitting head couldn't deal with AI at that moment - and slowly opened my eyes. It was night and someone had wrapped me up in my bedroll. Archer was a warm furry mound pressed against my right side, Lemorak sat to my left and was speaking softly to

Macha across the fire. Beside her, Elias was asleep. I heard Bolton's voice but couldn't see him or Illiya.

Archer must have sensed my waking, because he stood up and snuffled my face and then gave me a sloppy dog kiss. I gagged and sputtered and tried to push him off, but was wrapped too tightly in my bedroll.

"Ugh...dog breath!" Archer sat down beside me, his jaw dropping open and tongue lolling happily.

Lemorak placed a restraining hand on my chest when I tried to sit up. "Easy there, Zee. You're healed up, but your Endurance is still low."

"So I guess we won?" I asked, now flat on my back. I hurt all over and my memory from the fight was hazed from the cloud of adrenaline, fear and pain.

"Yeah, we won," Lemorak said.

Macha snuffled and rubbed quickly at the corner of her eyes. I wouldn't have thought the tough- as-nails monk was capable of crying.

"Most of us, at least," Bolton said from beyond my vision.

"What happened?"

Lemorak glanced over towards Bolton's voice, then looked back at me with concern on his face. "Barbarians are a tough class, especially when they go berserk, but they're lightly armored. Illiya took a lot of damage and for some reason she had her perception filter turned off."

"But if her character didn't die, then Elias can heal her, right?" I demanded.

Uneasy silence fell over the party before Lemorak answered. "It's not always that easy, Zee. Without the filters, our brains all receive damage as pain. There's no actual injury to our physical bodies, but the brain doesn't realize that. Her real body is fine, but she hasn't woken up in the game and hasn't been logged out, despite Elias's healing. Brain death is possible. The pod techs call it a Red Screen."

"I still don't understand why her perception filters weren't on," Bolton said.

Macha and I both had no access to our perception filters, and wouldn't as long as we were inmates.

"What the fuck? No one ever warned me about this." I started trying to sit up again and Lemorak pushed me back down.

"For *most* players it's a non-issue as long as you keep your filters on," Lemorak explained. "They keep it out of the sales pitch when recruiting inmate players, though."

"Is she going to be all right?" I asked.

"We don't know yet." Macha's pretty face was now a stone mask of restraint.

"We just have to wait," Bolton added, his tone grim.

No one in the game talked about their lives on the outside. It was taboo. I didn't know if Bolton and Illiya were actually siblings or not. It had always been clear they cared for each other, but in that moment, it was apparent to me that he loved his sister, whether they shared blood or not. And was there something going on between Illiya and Macha?

"I'm going to kill those assholes if I see them out in the main map," I swore.

"Get in line, Zee," Bolton replied.

"I'm sorry Bolton," I whispered. "I hope she's okay."

"We all do, Zee. Just get some rest," Lemorak said.

Archer lay back down beside me, this time resting his massive head on my chest, making it clear he wasn't going to let me go anywhere any time soon. Reluctantly, I closed my eyes. The deep weariness I still felt rushed up me and sleep took me.

When I woke up, it was mid-morning. The campfire was ash-covered embers and despite my bedroll, a deep chill had soaked in while I slept. Archer sensed the moment I was conscious. I felt him come thumping over from wherever he'd been standing guard. He sniffed me experimentally. Satisfied with what he found, Archer let out a soft huff and then trotted away.

Gingerly, I pushed myself up to a sitting position. Macha still sat across the banked fire from me, legs crossed and eyes closed in meditation. Elven players didn't require sleep. Instead they could meditate for short stretches of time to get the same benefits of rest. Looking around, I didn't see anyone else.

"Illiya Red Screened a couple hours ago," Macha said, voice cold, eyes still closed. "She's dead."

I struggled to find words. Macha's eyes opened, rage simmering in her gaze. There was a waiting notification on my HUD and I reluctantly checked it.

Party Member Illiya Glittertooth has died.

Respawn Status: ERROR404 - Player Data Not Found

"Where's everyone?" I finally asked.

"Bolton ran off to try and hunt down the Megas. Not sure what he'd do if he actually found them," Macha answered. "Lemorak and Elias went after him. I stayed to watch you."

Reflexively I felt the urge to do whatever I could to help and started getting to my feet. My Endurance had recharged with the rest, and I felt about normal.

"Where do you think you're going?" Macha demanded.

"They might need my help tracking him down."

"Even Lem could follow the trail that Bolton left. We should wait here."

"I can't just sit here and do nothing!"

"Sit. Down," Macha said. "You've already been a hero once this week. Let Lemorak take a turn."

Reluctantly, I sat down on a log near the fire. There was a grumbling in my stomach. I probably hadn't had anything to eat since our lunch before the Ursapine attacked. Macha must have heard, because she gracefully stood and moved over to a pile of packs and supplies. She tossed me a rations bundle with hardtack, dried fruit and hard cheese. I ripped into the food.

A companionable silence, our first since the hot springs, settled between us until she observed, "You leveled again."

I shifted, uncomfortable under her probing gaze. "Yeah. Great, right?"

"You seem to be on the fast track, Zee," Macha observed, her eyes narrowing in scrutiny.

"Really? I wouldn't know," I said with what I hoped was a casual shrug. "Still pretty much a noob."

"Cut the shit!" Macha spat. "We've all noticed there's something weird about you. And Archer, for that matter."

"Lemorak put me through some grueling power leveling before we met up."

Macha shook her head. "I've been with you two for weeks. If Lemorak has some secret strategy to power leveling, then you guys stopped using it when I joined. If that's the case, then fuck you both for holding out on me."

"W-w-we haven't been holding out."

"Then there's still something strange going on. I've played in OVR World a long time, I know how it works! You blew through Level 3 in fucking days. You and I jacked in at roughly the same time. The only way you should be this far ahead of me is if you were buying levels. We both know that isn't the case." Macha was studying me as she spoke, but her voice lacked the heat of anger now. "Has Lemorak been buying you levels?"

"No. Definitely not."

I wished I could explain it to Macha. It wasn't that I distrusted her, I just didn't *know* if she could handle something so important. After all, she was the only person in the game that knew my real face and one of only two that knew my real first name. Everything that Lemorak and the Doctor had told me indicated that my unique capabilities were a dangerous secret to spread around.

Macha watched me, an expectant look on her face. I squirmed under her gaze, finally shrugging and saying, "I wish I had answers for you, Macha. I guess I've been progressing fast, if you say so, but I have no idea why."

Macha rolled her eyes. "You and Lem are full of shit."

All I could do was shrug. A fresh silence fell between us and Macha seemed willing to drop the subject for now.

That left me with me with one nagging question of my own. Clearing my throat, I said softly, "Something was happening between you and Illiya."

Macha's expression darkened, but I also saw tears welling in her eyes. I held up my hands in a placating gesture. "It's none of my business if there was. I just wanted to say, I'm sorry."

Macha made a perceptible effort to restrain her first response and considered her words before replying. "It was still new. Obviously. What I'm going through is nothing compared to Bolton."

"You're allowed to hurt," I said with a shrug.

"What if it was my fault?" Macha asked, her voice just above a whisper. Tears started freely flowing down her cheeks.

"What? How could it possibly be your fault?"

Macha bowed her head and her shoulders shook. I felt the urge to get up and put my arms around her, but wasn't sure if that would be welcomed.

"She turned off her Perception Filter the night before we left Elmore because we were together," Macha finally said.

"Oh…" I winced as the word reflexively left my mouth. I'd known that players usually turned their Perception Filters off when - having certain kinds of fun in the game. The filters blocked out pain, but they also dulled other sensations. I hadn't had to worry about turning mine down when Bryn showed up at my door.

"That's not your fault, Macha. Neither of you could have known what was going to happen. The Stooges did this. They know I'm playing without filters. For all we know, their goal was for me to Red Screen."

"You really think so?" she asked. I could tell she was still shouldering a tremendous amount of guilt, but she shoved the tears from her face with her hands.

"What happened was tragic, but not your fault," I insisted.

Macha studied me, then changed the subject. "What sort of loot do you think we'll get at the keep?"

This was a little game the entire party had been playing for days, usually at Illiya's instigation.

"Maybe a *Dragonlance*?" I threw out as a wild guess. The running gag had been to see who could come up with the most outlandish potential reward.

"In your dreams!" Macha retorted, "I'm betting on a *Lamp of Wishes*."

"Who are you? Aladdin?"

The game proceeded, our guesses getting grander with each iteration, as we both silently agreed to put some of the past to bed, at least for the moment.

It was nearly sundown by the time Lemorak and Elias returned with Bolton. All three collapsed, exhausted, by the fire and began eating the rabbit stew I'd prepared. Between bites, they filled us in on how Lemorak and Elias had tracked down the distraught Dragonkin. Bolton had been hopelessly lost in the forest, and hadn't even come close to finding the Stooges, but he'd managed to wander far afield. After finding him, Lemorak and Elias had eventually talked him into coming back to camp.

"Will there be a funeral? Will you need to logout?" Macha asked.

Bolton chewed his stew mechanically for several minutes as we all waited on his response. I wondered if Elias and Lemorak would logout as well. I'd never heard of anyone dying in the OVR Worlds before, and had no idea what the protocol should be. We were all friends, if only in this digital simulation.

"I wouldn't know," Bolton finally said. "Our family kicked me out a long time ago. Illiya was the only one that I had any contact with."

"Surely that doesn't matter anymore?" I asked.

Bolton shuddered and lowered his scaled head. When he looked back up, trails of tears ran down his golden cheeks. "Even if I went. They'd only blame me for bringing her here. They're Grounders."

"Grounders?" Elias asked.

"Anti-tech extremists in little communities throughout the Pacific Northwest, Canada and parts of continental Europe," I explained. "They live completely off the grid. Shun all technology and OVR World most of all."

"They're a polygamist cult," Macha said with a derisive tone.

"No two Grounder groups are the same," I explained. "They practice everything from atheist to pagan and every major religion. But many do practice varying forms of group marriage."

Everyone looked at me in surprise. I shrugged and tried to be nonchalant. It felt good to be the one in the group with answers, for once. "I did a lot of reading before getting convicted."

"Fascinating," Macha rolled her eyes then looked at Bolton. "So they won't let you back even for Illiya's funeral? That's bullshit."

"I was expelled when I was fourteen after they caught me with a trashed VIZER kit I scavenged," Bolton explained.

"A VIZER kit? Those neural interface glasses that let blind people see? Why'd you bring something like that home if it was going to get you kicked out?" I asked.

Bolton considered his answer for a long moment, and we all waited for him silently.

Finally he shrugged and said, "Because I'm blind. Have been since birth."

No one knew how to respond to that. Another silence settled over the camp, tense and uncomfortable. I immediately understood why despite their upbringing Bolton and Illiya had connected to the OVR Worlds. At least I understood Bolton. A pod's direct connection to the brain, bypassing the body, helped people with disabilities experience normal, if virtual, lives. As long as their disability was non-neurological, the paralyzed could walk. The deaf could hear. Bolton could see.

Bolton cleared his throat and continued. "Illiya was my older sister. She left when she turned eighteen to come find me. They always begged her to come back, without me. I had been an unexpected burden even before they kicked me out. They might shoot me if I tried to go to her funeral, assuming anyone can even reach my family to notify them."

"We're all so sorry, Bolton." I finally said after another long silence.

"Thank you, Zee," Bolton said with a grieved but genuine smile.

Everyone finished their stew in silence. When everyone was done, Lemorak looked around the campfire at us all. "Let's all get some rest. We can head back to Elmore in the morning."

"What?" Bolton looked up in horror. "We can't go back now. We already have the quest assigned."

"You can't be serious," Lemorak said, incredulous. "Illiya died and we haven't even reached the keep."

"You don't have to remind me!" Bolton snarled, rising to his feet.

"This was an insane mission before," Lemorak said. "We don't stand a chance now."

"Illiya wouldn't want us to quit," Bolton insisted.

Lemorak looked around at the rest of us, imploring. I sat there stunned into silence, Elias looked contemplative, but Macha stood up and moved beside Bolton. "You don't have to come, Lem, but I'm with Bolton."

"You're both fucking crazy!" Lemorak stood in a rattle of armor.

"Illiya's death had nothing to do with the quest," Bolton shouted. "It was those damn Mega-Corps kiting the Ursapine onto us."

"We're missing a big damage producer and front-line fighter," Lemorak looked at Elias and me for support.

Elias produced a flask from a pouch at his belt. He unscrewed the top and with his eyes closed took a long sniff of the contents. Then Elias turned the flask upside down and let the contents splash onto the ground. Once empty, he tossed the flask out into the dark woods. Elias stood and moved beside Bolton and Macha.

"I think it's a fitting tribute to Illiya that we finish this quest. It was her idea," Elias said.

"What the fucking hell? Zee, talk some sense into them. Please!"

All eyes turned to me and I looked back and forth between Lemorak and the rest of the party. I really didn't have to consider it for long. We'd come too far and lost too much to turn back now. And I had the Doctor's secret quest to fulfill, whether I'd wanted it originally or not. Standing, I stepped over to Bolton's side of the fire. Archer followed me, though I doubted anyone was counting his vote.

Lemorak glowered at us from across the fire. "Zee, this is a bad idea, man. Come on."

"You were my first friend in the OVR Worlds," I said, meeting Lemorak's imploring gaze without flinching. "But they're my friends too, I won't abandon them. You shouldn't either."

"Crazy ass motherfuckers!" Lemorak shouted as he turned and stormed off into the night.

I took a step to go after him, but Macha grabbed my arm. She shook her head when I looked over at her. Swallowing my frustration, I looked down at Archer. The dire wolf was standing alert and attentive at my side.

"Go watch his back," I told the wolf.

Archer let out a grunt and then sprinted into the darkness after Lemorak. We all agreed that we'd proceed without Lemorak, though no one was feeling optimistic now. After waiting a short time to see if Lemorak would come back, we set a watch schedule, banked the fire and began sleeping in turns.

Chapter Nineteen

A few hours before dawn, Macha woke me for my turn at watch. The pre-dawn morning was cold and damp, so I pulled my Ranger's Cloak more snug and sunk into the shadows beyond the meager light of our banked fire. Our camp was small enough that there was no point in walking a patrol. Instead, I sat in silence and listened to the forest sounds while probing the darkness as far as my Half-Elf eyes would penetrate.

As I sat there, the blinking library on my HUD representing Lemorak's biographical file nagged for my attention. I'd never felt comfortable having access to the information and had resisted the urge to open it. I recognized what a betrayal of trust reading that file would represent. But information was power, and it was a risk to avoid such an advantage. In the end, the opportunity to better understand the man that was ostensibly my closest ally was too much for me to pass up.

Chewing on my lower lip, I finally focused on the icon and mentally opened the file. A glowing window of text appeared in the air before me. I began to read. First was Lemorak's character stats, which I skimmed over. Below Lemorak's character stats, I found his real life personal information.

Handle: Sir Lemorak

Real Name: Arthur Drake

Nationality: United States of America

Voting Eligibility: Retains Private Voting Franchise

Employer: Filed Taxes as Independent Professional Gamer - Receives Subsidy for connection from the Disabled Veterans Gamer Program

Previous Employer: Gunnery Sergeant, Force Reconnaissance, United States Marine Corps, Honorably Discharged

Birth Place: Helena, MT, USA

Date of Birth: July 2nd 1990

Age: 52

Connecting Pod Location: Chicago, IL, USA

Personal History: Arthur Drake was born to Benjamin and Chloe Drake in Helena Montana...

The dossier was composed of a long narrative from birth to present, and there were embedded hyperlinks that would let me view supporting documents. I could see what grade Arthur had gotten on his 6th Grade book report on Treasure Island. There were social media posts, prom pictures, his ROTC participation in High School. There were evaluations of young USMC Private Drake during his boot camp at Parris Island, the scores he'd gotten on various evaluations, his full service record, and awards he received.

I was more than a little surprised and creeped out by the level of biographical detail the Doctor had gathered. Did the SI have a file like this on me? The experience made me feel unclean, like I was reading someone's diary. At a gut level, I knew what an invasion of privacy this was, but once I started, I couldn't stop.

Arthur Drake had reached the rank of Gunnery Sergeant as a Force Recon Marine. He had been assigned to East Africa in the never-ending War on Terror. On a midnight raid for a "High Value Target," his squad had been wiped out by a building rigged with demolition charges. Gunnery Sergeant Drake had been the sole survivor, but he'd lost both his legs in the blast. The Doctor had every document that had been generated by the extensive investigation of the incident that followed.

Arthur was ruled blameless in the decimation of his team, but his career was over. With advancements in bionic limbs, that hadn't been a foregone conclusion even after a double amputation. However, by the time Arthur had completed his recovery, the landscape of the US Military had radically changed with the en masse privatization of operations to Mega-Corp mercenary forces.

After his discharge, Arthur had been heavily recruited by various military contractors, but had declined them all. Instead he'd gone almost entirely off the grid, not a small feat at the time. No social media, few bank transactions, no credit. He'd become a ghost.

Stomach still twisting with discomfort, I read through a couple of scant emails between Arthur and former comrades. It was clear that Arthur Drake had a deep love for the country he'd sacrificed so much for. He was a dyed-in-the-wool patriot who had nothing but contempt for the oligarchy draped in the flag that our country had become with the rise of the Mega-Corps. I had no doubt that if the branches of the military hadn't been gutted to fill the coffers of the Megas, Arthur would have probably died a Marine. I had certainty that he and my dad would have seen eye to eye on a lot of things, despite one being a hardcore conservative bad-to-the-bone special forces soldier, and the other being a peacenik, union-preaching insurrectionist hippie.

Then twelve years ago he'd requested VA benefits that would give him a free pod and connection to the OVR Worlds. Since then, Arthur Drake had spent the majority of his life as Sir Lemorak in our virtual world. Near as I could tell, he'd started unknowingly working for the Doctor almost immediately. From there, his dossier pretty much ended.

After reading the information several times, I closed the window. I felt unclean after digging through my friend's personal history and tragedy without permission. However, it had given me a new perspective on Lemorak/Arthur. I sat there and tried to digest everything I'd read.

My Perception skill alerted me to Lemorak's armor-rattling approach long before I could see the knight. I rose, activated my Stealth skill and moved in his direction. I intercepted him a few yards from camp and dropped my Stealth. Archer followed at Lemorak's heel. The dire wolf's long tongue lolled out in his very doggy grin and his tail wagged in greeting.

"This wolf is *very* weird," Lemorak said as he leaned wearily against a tree.

Archer gave a huffing woof in reply before he padded over to me and shoved his head under a hand for a head scratch.

Lemorak and I stood in silence for a long moment before I asked, "You really going to bail on us?"

"You know you can't afford to die like the rest of us, Zee," Lemorak answered. "You'd be better off Red Screening than waking up and letting OzCo figure out what your brain can do."

"I'm not planning on dying," I answered.

"Neither was Illiya." Lemorak's voice was hard with anger.

I met his anger with heat of my own. "Our odds would be a hell of a lot better with you!"

Lemorak was quiet for a long, tense moment, "The only reason I came back was to finish the march to the Keep. We'll get there tomorrow, you all can see how hopeless it is, and we can march back together."

That was the closest thing to a compromise I'd heard out of my friend. I wasn't sure what the others would think of it. *Bolton might actually be on a suicide mission.*

I sighed, "If it's as bad as you say, then I'll be with you and quit."

Lemorak gave me a wan smile. "I'm going to hold you to that, Zee."

"But if we get there, and you're wrong, then I'll expect you on the front line beside me."

I could have sworn that Lemorak growled in frustration. His reluctance evident, he extended a heavy gauntleted hand. "Deal."

"Deal." Clasping my friend's hand, we shook.

Everyone had been a bit relieved when I'd come back to camp with Lemorak that morning, but we'd all lost the innocent enthusiasm of the day before. Our remaining hike to the Goblin's Keep passed in near silence compared to the day before, when Illiya had sung marching songs to us. Grim expressions were on every face and there was no idle banter, just business.

I finished my Level Up with Al while we marched the Goblin's Keep that morning. From listening to Al, who continued to process gigabytes of game theory while I played, conventional wisdom was that it was best to spend pre-Level 5 Ability Points only on my core Abilities, Strength, Dexterity, and Wisdom. Constitution was important to buff up my HP, but of secondary concern. For a Ranger, Intelligence and Charisma were my dump stats.

There would be talents and skills available for purchase after Level 5 that were worth spending Ability Points on, but not yet. So I divided my three fresh Ability Points between Strength, Dexterity, and Constitution since they seemed the most relevant to the coming challenge at the Goblin's Keep. Once complete, I surveyed my updated stats.

CHARACTER STATISTICS

Handle: Zee Locked-in

Race: Half-Elf

Role: Striker

Class/Level: Ranger/4

ABILITIES

Strength (Endurance): 16 (26)

Strength Skills: Melee Combat, Athletics, Carrying Capacity

Dexterity (Defense): 17 (22)

Dexterity Skills: Ranged Combat, Acrobatics, Stealth, Sleight of Hand, Open Lock. Reflex

Constitution (Hit Points): 15 (155)

Constitution Skills: Concentration, Fortitude

Intelligence (Arcane Mana): 10 (NA)

Intelligence Skills: Arcana, Investigation. Appraise, Disable Device. Forgery, Lore

Wisdom (Faith Mana): 14 (99)

Wisdom Skills: Conviction. Perception, Survival, Tracking, Animal Handling, Medicine, Willpower

Charisma (Inspiration): 10 (NA)

Charisma Skills: Imagination, Deception, Intimidation, Persuasion, Influence

RACIAL SKILLS: Half-Elf Wilderness Skills: Survival (+1), Stealth (+1), Tracking (+1)

RACIAL TALENTS: Half-Elf Flexibility (+5 AP at Level 0, +1 AP), Nightvision (15'), Elven Bow Proficiency +1 Level

CLASS SKILLS: Athletics (+7), Survival (+10), Stealth (+9), Animal Handling (+5), Tracking (+8)

CLASS TALENTS: Archery (Level 9), Two-Weapon Fighting (Level 12), Light Armor Proficiency, Favored Enemy (Goblin), Favored Terrain (Forest), Animal Companion (Archer, Level 4 Dire Wolf)

EARNED SKILLS: Perception (+4), Fletching (+1), Intimidation (+0)

EARNED TALENTS: Improvised Weapon (Achievement), Iron Will (Achievement), Surprise Attack (Achievement)

CARRIED EQUIPMENT: Leather Armor (+3 Defense), Adventuring Kit (Rope 50 ft.,Tent, Camp Cooking Set, Grappling Hook, Climbing Pitons x20, Climbing Hammer, Crowbar, Lamp Oil x4, Chalk 1 lb, Torches x10, Healing Potion x3), Ranger's Cloak, Masterwork Scimitars x2, Compound Shortbow, Arrows x50, Flaming Arrows x6

STORED EQUIPMENT: Standard Clothes, Short-sword, Dagger, Stone Hatchet

COMBAT STATISTICS

Weapon - Talent Modifier - Weapon Damage - Accuracy - Median Damage

Masterwork Scimitar - 12 - 50 - 24 - 106

Masterwork Scimitar (off-hand) - 12 - 50 - 18 - 80

Compound Shortbow - 9 - 20 - 22 - 96

ACHIEVEMENTS: First Kill, Backstabber, Good Samaritan, Goblin Slayer, Kobold Slayer, And Stay Out!, Ain't Got Time to Bleed, "The dishes are done man.", Marathon Runner, Orc Slayer, Pest Control, FATALITY, Specialist (Survival, Stealth, Tracking), I am the night, Trained (Animal Handling), Practice Makes Perfect (Survival, Stealth, Tracking), Hunter, Gone Fishin, Camp Cook, The Great Outdoors, It's Super Effective!, Improviser, "My Spidey Sense is Tingling", "It's all fun and games until someone loses an eye...then it's hilarious", Cornered Fighter, "The Bigger They Are...", Big Game Hunter

TOTAL ABILITY POINTS: 22

CURRENT CRYPTOCURRENCY: 239.44

CURRENT DEBTS: 4,512,763.48 CC - OzCo Department of

Corrections

CURRENT EXPERIENCE: 9,641

EXPERIENCE TO NEXT LEVEL: 15,500

By mid-morning we were looking out at the Goblin's Keep from the treeline beside the road. According to the backstory, the structure, once called Brightblade Keep, was now a ruined castle atop a low hill, the outer crenelated stone wall crumbling in parts and overgrown with thick vines. Weatherworn guard towers stood evenly spaced along the wall, and the slate roofs of several stone structures could just be made out beyond the fortifications. Brightblade Keep had been designed as a castle in the truest sense of the word, not a palace or mansion, but a military fortification and seat of power.

The game's story said that the Brightblade family had run afoul of a vengeful dragon. The dragon's attack on the keep had killed most of their retainers and ransacked most of their wealth. While several of the family had lived, attempting to rebuild the keep had left them destitute and the work incomplete. They abandoned their home and left the valley for the wider world of Gygax.

The keep had sat abandoned for decades, until a host of goblins had claimed the keep as their own and began harassing the countryside. Of course, this was a constantly resetting portion of the game. In actuality, the keep had been designed by the programmers explicitly to house the goblins and provide this quest for players. The backstory about the Brightblade family was all just flavor for players devoted to the role-playing part of the game.

From our vantage we could see Goblin irregularly patrolling the walls. If the patrols had any sort of schedule it was haphazard. The entrance to the keep was two massive wooden gates blackened by dragon fire. The gates were damaged and stood askew, leaving a narrow opening. Goblin raiding parties flowed in and out.

"It shouldn't be too hard to approach with stealth if we stay off the road," I observed after surveying the ground between us and the ruined castle. Long ago, a mile-wide circle around the keep had been cleared away from the walls. However, like the keep, the clearing had been neglected for years and now it was thick with brush and young reed-thin trees.

"Getting in won't be the problem," Lemorak said. "Avoiding getting trampled by the mob of goblins inside will be. Not to mention their war chief and shaman, both of whom are Boss-level NPCs."

"We should start calling you Little Sir Sunshine," Macha said.

"The quest doesn't require that we defeat every goblin in the keep, just break their morale so that they abandon the keep." Bolton's tone was cold and emotionless. "From what I've read, we really just have to kill about a quarter of the goblins along with the shaman and war chief."

"Oh *just* a quarter of them and *both bosses*?" Lemorak said.

With my leveled up Perception skill, I found that with some concentration, I could zoom my vision in on distant objects. It was at least as good as having a couple of 2x binoculars, maybe a little better. I only half paid attention to the bickering as I scanned around the keep. Because of my focused attention on the keep, I spotted a party of four players crouched behind cover just a few hundred feet from the gates before anyone else. And recognized them.

"Motherfuckers," I spat. My friends went silent.

"What is it, Zee?" Lemorak asked.

"It's the Stooges and Bryn," I answered.

"What the hell are they doing here?" Bolton demanded.

"Probably planning to sweep the Keep clear ahead of us," Elias said.

"By the time the Keep resets, the timer will be up and we'll fail the quest," Lemorak added.

"Just the four of them?" Macha demanded.

"With Mega-Corp resources, they're probably geared and skilled up substantially above their actual levels," Lemorak said. "Mega-Corps and

Guilds clear the Keep in four to five Player teams all the time by putting extra resources behind the players. They also usually have detailed up-to-date play-through guides. It's a good way to catapult their players out of the valley and unlike us, they usually have the gold to burn."

"Probably looks real bad on your performance review if you don't clear the keep," Macha said.

"Think they'll wait till nightfall like we were going to?" I asked.

"Stealth and surprise are the preferred methods of taking the keep, unless you have overwhelming numbers. That's why we were going to do it that way," Bolton answered.

"Probably why they added Zee's assassin girlfriend to the party," Elias said.

"She's not my girlfriend," I snapped. While I'd never really considered Bryn someone I could trust, the thought that she'd played any role in Illiya's death had left me a little raw.

"I can't believe this is fucking happening," Macha said.

Blinking away my zoomed-in vision, I turned to face my friends. "No way in hell are we going to let them get away with this. Here's what we're going to do."

Chapter Twenty

After I'd outlined my plan and the rest of the party had helped refine it, it took us the entire rest of the day and evening to inch our way through the overgrown lands around the keep. I guided the party and used my ranger skills to keep us concealed. We managed to avoid any notice from the keep or the Stooges.

By midnight we'd taken our positions. Bolton, Archer and I crouched on the southern side of the keep, concealed in thick brush. Bolton and I both had night vision due to our racial benefits, and under the starlight, that vision allowed us to see almost as well as under the sun. We watched the Stooges prepare to attack the keep. Lemorak, Macha and Elias had split off earlier, in order to circle around and inch their way towards the western wall.

"I think they're about ready to head out," I whispered to Bolton and Archer.

"About time!" hissed Bolton, "They've been casting buffs and guzzling potions for half an hour."

"Ready to go?" I looked over at him. Bolton had equipped a heavy black cloak with deep hood over his red robes. With my night vision I could see his grim face in the shadows of his hood. He gave me a short nod.

Bolton and I began to move. We extricated ourselves from the bush without a sound. Archer sat waiting for us, his head tilted, confused by the relative difficulty we'd had. I rolled my eyes at the dire wolf and then gave him the hand signal we'd worked out that told Archer to silently patrol around us. Then Bolton and I set out after the Stooges.

The enemy group was doing everything from the play-through checklist. Attack just after midnight, when the goblins had the fewest guards. Check.

With my enhanced vision, I watched Bryn, a lithe shadow, slip from their concealment to approach the keep's outer wall. She had the hood of her cloak pulled up over her distinctive silver hair, but there was no way I could mistake her form for one of the Stooges. At a portion of the ruined outer walls, covered with vines, she nimbly scaled the wall freehand. She slithered over the top. A heartbeat later, a slender rope came over the edge and unspooled itself to the ground.

Markus broke from cover next and scaled the rope with ease. Then came Marl, who struggled a bit to haul himself up. When the dwarf rolled clumsily over the edge, Lute came out. She tied the rope around her waist and her party towed her quickly and quietly over the wall.

Avoid the guards at the main gates and scale the wall. Check.

From there, they would sneak through the keep and dispatch any Goblins they encountered along the way. Bryn's assassin abilities would be especially useful in helping them dispatch the monsters with stealth. They wouldn't begin to make a ruckus until they reached the interior corridors and attacked either the shaman or the war chief. According to Bolton, experienced players recommended seeing whether one or both boss monsters were asleep before deciding who to kill first. Then they would kill Goblins until their spirit was broken and they fled.

By the time Lute was lifted up the wall, Bolton, Archer and I had reached the main gate. There were four drowsy goblin guards just inside. Their scripting was simple: they would notice anyone coming through the gates. They wouldn't notice us if we stayed outside the gates and stayed fairly quiet.

Lemorak would have been a better choice for what was coming next, but his clanking steel armor would have never gotten this close without triggering a response from the keep. Before we had split up, Elias had given me a *Potion of Goliath's Strength*. With my teeth I pulled the stopper from the potion vial and guzzled it down as we approached the gates. It tasted like salty chalk.

You drank a Potion of Goliath's Strength! Plus 50% to your Strength Score for 1 minute.

A timer started counting down from 60 seconds as the potion took effect. I felt a throbbing surge of energy in every muscle of my body. I could practically feel my muscles swell.

Stepping up to the broken gate, I set my shoulder to the iron-braced wood. Glancing back at Bolton, I saw he was already in the process of casting his first spell. Bolton's lips moved as he whispered the incantation, while he circled his hands before his chest as though he was sculpting a sphere out of clay. A glowing ball of fire ignited between his palms and began to expand. With a deep breath, I braced my feet and waited for Bolton to finish his spell.

The fireball was about the size of a volleyball when he stopped his casting. He locked eyes with me and gave me a curt nod. Closing my eyes, I still saw the blazing orange light of the fireball when Bolton released it. It flew past me through the cracked-open gate.

The instant I felt the fireball zip past I shoved with all of my magically enhanced strength against the broken gate. The bottom of the heavy gate dragged against the ground, but it began to move, inch by inch. There was a Goblin cry of alarm when the fireball detonated right on top of them. A hiss of rushing air and flames rushed out through the still open gate.

Bolton rushed forward to lend his meager strength score to my effort. My muscles burned with strain while the air around me boiled. The timbers of the gate groaned in protest under my shoulder. However, I finally managed to shove the gate nearly closed. There was still about 3 inches of gap between the two halves of the gate, but nothing was getting through anytime soon.

The fireball had likely killed several guards, but it hadn't gotten all of them. It wasn't supposed to. There were howls of pain and alarm from within and someone started ringing a large bell.

Bolton was already working on his next spell, reading from a scroll he'd gotten when we'd saved the merchant caravan. Equipping my bow and notching an arrow, I moved away from the gates and started scanning the gate towers and the section of wall closest to us. With my night vision, I saw Goblins on the move and began snapping off shots. Bolton's spellcasting voice reached a crescendo.

The earth beneath my feet quivered, then violently shook. If it hadn't been part of the plan, I might have been alarmed. A wall of granite was slowly rising up out of the earth before the gates, almost flush with the wooden doors. Bolton was actively using his Arcana skill to cast the spell that was above his level and outside his repertoire as a sorcerer. The spell should have allowed him to conjure a stone wall ten feet high. He had mixed success with the scroll and was only able to pull the wall up three feet from the ground. The wall would have been useless in most combat situations, even against Goblins. But as a door stopper?

"That'll do, B!" I shouted as I continued snapping off shots.

The spell completed, the scroll crumbled to dust in Bolton's hands and he stumbled like a drunken sailor. The spell would have drained more mana than one of his usual spells. The Goblins were starting to get coordinated. I spotted several Goblins with crossbows taking up positions along the wall. Rapid fire, I snapped off a barrage of parting shots.

"Time to go!" Bow still in one hand, I grabbed Bolton by the arm. His robes were soaked with sweat. We made a hasty strategic retreat from the gates. Meaning to say we hauled ass for cover. Crossbow bolts hissed past us, but none found their mark.

Torches were being lit and we could hear sounds throughout the keep of Goblins waking and readying for battle. Bolton and I took cover behind a dense, thorny bush, falling to the ground and panting. Archer slunk up out of the darkness and sat down beside us, his tail wagging. The dire wolf seemed to be having a great time.

Giving Bolton a chance to catch his breath, I pulled out two signal arrows. I lit them with a quick spark from my flint and steel and the tips of the specialized arrows began to burn bright with red flames. Fitting both signal arrows to the string at once, I stood up from behind our cover and fired off the arrows towards the vine-covered portion of the wall near where the Stooges had made their climb.

My Survival skill had identified the vines growing up the walls as glowberry vines, which produced a thick highly flammable sap. Both signal arrows arched high into the air, trailing red flames, then thudded into the dense vine growth. The glowberry vines only smoked and smoldered at first. I held my breath. *Come on!*

Then in a rush the sap-soaked vines burst in bright yellow flames. From those two points of ignition, the stretch of overgrown wall was quickly engulfed. I dove for cover as crossbow bolts hissed through the blazing night at me.

"So much for their stealth attack," Bolton panted. He was grinning for the first time since Illiya's death.

Within moments every Goblin in the keep was ready for a fight. The little monsters streamed along the walls, and there was the sound of pitched battle beyond the walls. We saw the flash of discharged spells and heard the clash of steel and battle cries. Relying on all the attention to be on the Stooges, Bolton and I abandoned stealth and ran through the scrubland around the keep to the western wall, where Macha, Lemorak and Elias waited.

Our companions hadn't wasted the cover provided by our distraction. There was a drainage tunnel covered by an iron grate along the base of the western wall. Most player guides recommended against accessing the keep through the tunnel. Breaching the iron grate was noisy and the tunnel ran beneath the goblin barracks. We'd discussed the tunnel in our planning sessions. It was a tempting, but dangerous access point, or at least it would be if you didn't have a distraction at the other side of the keep.

Elias had used a cleric spell to rust out several key points of the iron bars blocking the tunnel. Lemorak had used a crowbar and blacksmith's hammer to shatter the rusted weak points.

"All clear," Lemorak reported when Bolton and I arrived.

Macha had already scouted out the first forty feet of tunnel to verify their work hadn't garnered any attention. The inside of the tunnel reeked of rot and mold. In a real castle, it likely would have smelled of raw sewage as well. Fortunately, even the monsters of the game didn't need to use the privy.

We proceeded in single file down the tunnel. Macha took the lead. She and I were near equals in Stealth and Perception, but her fully elven sight allowed her to see further in the darkness than mine. Lemorak went second at a discreet distance, prepared to shove past the monk if his strength and heavy armor were called for, then behind him were Bolton and Elias. I gave

them a slight head start and then Archer and I brought up the rear.

Chapter Twenty-One

The drainage tunnels ran throughout the entire underside of the keep. OVR World randomized the layout of the tunnels each time the quest reset, so we didn't have a map. We reached a wooden trap door in the ceiling first. Straddling Lemorak's shoulders, Macha lifted the wooden portal with delicate care. A blade of light sliced the darkness and illuminated Macha's face. She squinted into the light and had Lemorak slowly rotate her to get a full view. Nodding in satisfaction, Macha lowered the trapdoor back into place and slid off Lemorak's shoulders.

"Looks like the barracks. Empty like we hoped," Macha whispered.

"Then the warchief's chambers should be close by," Bolton said. While the exact layout of the Keep and the tunnels shifted every time the scenario reset, there were parameters to each procedurally generated version that stayed consistent.

"Up we go then," Lemorak said.

Lemorak lifted Macha back up on his shoulders. She then pushed off of Lemorak's shoulders and slithered up through the hatchway.

"Ready when you are," I whispered to Lemorak. According to the plan, I was supposed to go next.

He glowered at me, but laced his fingers together into a cradle for my foot. I stepped into his joined hands. Pushing off of his hands, Lemorak heaved up. With ease, I caught the ledge and hauled myself up. I activated my Stealth skill while getting my bearings. Macha was already across the room, crouched by the door and peering out through a narrow gap.

The barracks was a long, low-ceilinged, stone-walled room. Several half-rotted, wood-framed cots lined the walls at irregular intervals. There were also disheveled heaps of cloth and straw strewn about the room for those Goblins not fortunate enough to get a bunk. Rusted-iron torch sconces were fixed to the walls. The trap door was more or less in the center of the room.

While Macha kept watch, I withdrew the rope from my inventory. Relying on my Stealth skill I stepped silently to the nearest torch sconce. I yanked hard on the rusted iron fixture to test it. With my full weight on it the sconce didn't budge.

"That'll do pig. That'll do," I muttered.

With my Survival skill, my hands automatically tied the rope into a simple but sturdy knot. I carried the rest of the rope to the trap door and dropped it through the opening.

The rope jerked and jumped, then Lemorak hissed up, "Ready."

The rope in hand, I set my feet and began to haul it up. Lemorak helped lift from below at first, but I was taking the full load for the last few feet. I grunted with effort and pulled the rope up as fast as I could.

Sweat prickled my brow when Archer's front paws began to scrabble at the edge. With a final heave I pulled the heavy wolf up through the opening. Archer gave my face a companionable lick when I knelt beside him.

"Ugh, dog breath." I untied the knot that Lemorak had used to join the rope to Archer's pack harness.

Archer huffed as if to say, "Suck it up, human."

"Go scout the rest of the room," I whispered while restraining a chuckle.

The dire wolf nodded to me and then slunk off into the barracks, his nose snuffling at the floor. Then I dropped the free end of the rope back down through the trapdoor.

Elias came up next with relative ease, despite his overweight state. While he climbed, I took a moment to double check my weapons. I helped him climb over the edge at the end.

Bolton was the least athletic of us all. Strength and Athletics were not high priority stats for a sorcerer. Lemorak lifted him most of the way, then he labored to haul himself the short remaining span until Elias and I could help drag him up.

Lemorak's strength and athletics were all he needed to climb the rope, even with all of his gear. However, in his heavy, steel armor, it wouldn't be stealthy. I signaled Macha at the door and she closed the narrow gap she'd been peering through, but kept a keen elven ear pressed to the wood. I knelt beside the trapdoor while Bolton and Elias stood ready to help.

"Ready," I hissed down to him.

The rope went taut. Lemorak grunted with effort and his armor rattled with each movement. Every eye in the room shot to the sconce I'd secured the rope to as it groaned ominously.

"What do we do?" Bolton asked, his reptilian eyes wide.

"Pray?" suggested Elias.

I leaned over the opening to check Lemorak's progress. He'd finished half the climb. Anxiety twisted my stomach into a pretzel as another groan reverberated from the sconce.

"Maybe if we…" Bolton's suggestion was cut off by another shuddering groan from the sconce.

Before my eyes, iron bowed under the strain. I was about to tell Lemorak to drop back down, but before I could utter a word, there was a screech of metal as the sconce ripped off the wall.

The sconce shot through the air like a cannonball. It clipped my ankle, then fell through the hole in the floor. Pain screamed up my leg and I grit my teeth on a curse as I crashed to the floor. My HP bar dropped by 17 points.

Through the hole there was a deafening clatter of steel and man falling to the tunnel floor. Seconds later we all heard the sound of raised guttural voices from beyond the door. Since I didn't have the Goblin language, the words were incomprehensible gibberish. Even without a translation, clearly our disaster hadn't gone unnoticed.

"Help hold the door," I ordered Bolton and Elias as I shoved myself to my feet. Turning back to the hole I checked on Lemorak. Thanks to my night vision I could see he was back on his feet.

"Damage?" I asked.

"33 HP, but nothing critical," Lemorak reported. "I hear noises down the tunnel. I don't think I'll be alone for long."

"Copy that. Let's get you up here. Got the rope?"

"Catch." Lemorak twirled the rope, weighted by the deformed wall sconce, released it and sent it sailing up out of the hole. I caught the sconce and then turned to find a fresh anchor point. The heavy wooden door to the barracks began to rattle and my three friends shoved back against it.

"We're blown," Macha reported through grit teeth.

Seeing as stealth was no longer an option, I opened my inventory and withdrew the climbing kit I'd purchased. The kit included several pitons and a small hammer. With the tools in hand my Athletics skill highlighted three anchor points in the floor for me. Driven by the rising sound of splintering wood from the door, I hammered the pitons in and then secured the rope to them with swift movements.

When I returned to the trapdoor, I heard bestial snarling and saw a deformed canine shape about Archer's size facing off against Lemorak. He had his sword out and on guard. The creature lunged and Lemorak's sword slashed back. The creature yelped in pain as Lemorak hacked a deep gash down its chest. The creature fell back, snarling viciously. Almost a blur, Lemorak lunged forward and stabbed his sword. The monster fell to dust.

"You all right?" I called.

"Yeah, some sort of goblin-hound," Lemorak replied. "Ready?"

"As we'll ever be."

"Good, I think I hear more coming." Lemorak sheathed his sword and grabbed the rope.

I drew my bow and notched an arrow, eyes probing the darkness of the tunnel beyond my night vision for any more surprises. No longer even trying to be quiet, Lemorak moved with more speed than his previous attempt. I checked my anchors. It looked like the rope was taut, but holding.

"Tell him to haul ass!" Macha shouted as the rattle behind the door turned to a rumble.

Individually or in small numbers, Goblins weren't much of a threat. They were diminutive creatures, with low strength scores, low intelligence SIs, crude weapons, and generally low levels. They spawned like rabbits, though, and a large mob could swamp even higher-level players. They'd wear down our Endurance until exhaustion started draining HP.

Lemorak was halfway up the rope when three goblin-hounds came barreling down the tunnel. They jumped up at Lemorak's feet with gnashing teeth. Aiming on reflex, I drew my bow-string and loosed in a single fluid movement. I hit the first hound and sent it tumbling and yelping to the tunnel floor. I drew and loosed a second rapid arrow, but missed. Before I could get off a third arrow, a hound had sunk its teeth into Lemorak's booted ankle.

"Fuck!" Lemorak grunted in frustration and halted his climb to kick his foot. The hound came free, but Lemorak had lost his momentum and the other two hounds were jumping, jaws snapping.

"Move it Lem!" I ordered while firing another arrow. I missed, but so did both hounds. Their jumps didn't have the advantage of a running start anymore.

Lemorak started to climb again, slower now but picking up speed. I continued to rain down arrows on the hounds until Lemorak was close enough that I could grab his outstretched gauntleted hand. Together we heaved him up through the trap door. Lemorak collapsed, panting on the floor while I drew up the rope. The hounds couldn't climb, but there could very well be goblin handlers coming down the tunnel behind them.

"Well this plan's FUBAR," Lemorak observed after pushing himself to his feet.

After heaving himself up, he stomped over to the door and with his higher strength score relieved Bolton and Elias. They slid out of the way, their chests heaving from exertion, as Lemorak shoved his back against the door. It continued to rattle and shudder, but it no longer bounced open an inch or so with each heavy blow.

"What the hell do we do now?" Bolton asked, still catching his breath.

Glancing down through the still open trapdoor, I saw two more hounds circling. They snarled and barked with fury. Beyond my night vision range, I heard nearing Goblin shouts.

"We can't retreat the way we came," I reported.

It was then that I realized I hadn't seen Archer since sending him off to scout the barracks. Turning around I saw the dire wolf at one of the back corners of the room, nose to the ground, sniffing back and forth along a short section of wall. I turned back to Bolton.

"Were there any secret doors out of here in the player's guide?" I asked.

The sorcerer shrugged. "Secret doors and passages were in a premium appendix. We didn't have the Crypts for it."

"Damn it, we really need a rogue," I muttered then moved back to Archer.

The dire wolf switched from sniffing to scratching his front paws at the floor and wall. Macha and I had the Perception scores needed for scouting and finding enemies hidden with Stealth. Rogues and assassins had specialized Class talents that made them particularly good at finding secret doors, and hidden traps.

Crossing my fingers, I activated my Perception skill and began to examine the section of wall where Archer was scratching. My careful search turned up a shitload of nothing. I smacked a frustrated fist into the stone wall. Almost imperceptibly the wall trembled under my blow. In a flash, I remembered how Macha had showed off to Lem and me one night around the campfire by shattering small boulders with ki empowered punches and kicks.

"Go all kung fu master on that wall back there! Archer will show you where," I told Macha after sprinting back to the front of the room.

Macha and I traded spots and she ran back to where Archer sat waiting. Lemorak and I stood with our backs braced against the violently shuddering door. Through the wood, I started to hear chopping sounds.

"I think they finally managed to rub two brain cells together and get some axes," I said.

Face set in grim determination, Lemorak nodded his agreement.

Looking at the spellcasters, I asked, "Can either of you do anything to buy us some time if Macha finds us a way out?"

Bolton and Elias looked at each other dubiously. We'd all reviewed their spell lists when planning, but they bent their heads together in frantic conference considering options.

The latest battering at the door bounced me up from my braced position. Gritting my teeth, I braced myself before looking to check on Macha. She was standing with her back to us, her slender body held perfectly still. While I watched, she sank into a fighting stance. A faint aura of yellow light radiated from her cocked fists. The light grew until two ghostly torches burned around her fists and forearms.

She exploded forward in a sudden violent lunge that took me by surprise. I watched as one burning fist shot forward, followed by the other, making contact with the wall in rapid succession. The entire room shook and dust erupted around the monk.

"Looks like...*cough*....a corridor back here! I see...*cough*.... a door out; with...*cough*.... no Gobs!" Macha shouted from the obscuring dust cloud.

I looked back to Bolton and Elias, who were still brainstorming.

"Anytime, you two."

Finally, Elias and Bolton reached some sort of consensus. They turned from their hushed, urgent whispers to face Lemorak and me.

"We've got something," Bolton said.

"Get ready to get the hell out of the way," Elias said.

Chapter Twenty-Two

Lemorak and I heaved ourselves away from the door as Bolton and Elias took aim with their carefully coordinated spells. From Elias's outstretched hands gushed a fire hose of conjured water. A split second later, Arctic winds howled from Bolton's clawed hands at the door. Within heartbeats, the spells had completed and a thick layer of ice encased the door and threshold. We could still hear muffled hacking and pounding through the door, but with luck the improvised ice wall would buy us some time.

None of us lingered to see how long the spells would hold. We all sprinted for the back of the barracks, where Macha had shattered the secret door with her ki-empowered fists. Covered in dust, she stood just outside the formerly hidden doorway urging us on.

I ran through the shattered secret doorway first. With my high Dexterity I flipped over a chunk of rubble on the ground. The hidden corridor past the door was a narrow, dark, stone-walled hallway that ran straight away from the barracks. Since Macha had already scouted out the full length of it, and hadn't found any traps, I continued my headlong dash down the hidden corridor. Archer was already guarding the door at the far end.

"Anything on the other side?" I asked Archer.

The dire wolf looked at me and nodded his head up and down. *Lemorak's right, he's way too damn smart.*

"Goblins?"

Another silent nod.

"How many?" I asked.

Archer twisted his head in what I interpreted as a canine shrug. I wasn't really sure how I'd expected the wolf to answer me, even if he could tell how many were on the other side. Would he have tapped it out to me or something?

Bolton and Elias came jogging down the hall, both gasping for air. Behind them I saw Macha and could hear Lemorak bringing up the rear, his clanking, armored bulk a bit more of a challenge for the narrow passageway.

"Everyone quiet for a minute. Okay?" I hissed. I pressed my ear against the door, closed my eyes and activated my Perception skill while focusing all my attention beyond the door.

Dim sounds grew more distinct and I made out several unintelligible voices jabbering in Goblin. I held my breath and concentrated, trying to sort them out and count how many there were. They were just too similar and the language too foreign-sounding for me to pick them apart. I guessed there were more than three but less than ten. Either way a manageable number for us. Better than the horde trying to break down the barracks doors, anyway.

I glanced back at my comrades to make sure everyone had caught up. I slung my bow so I could be ready to draw my scimitars. Keeping my voice low, I reported my observations.

"That ice won't hold much longer," Bolton said.

"Zee, the wolf, Macha and I will clear the Goblins. Bolton and Elias find a way to secure the door after we go through it," Lemorak ordered in a crisp decisive military tone.

"Ready?" I asked the group.

No one objected. I turned back to the door and shoved. The damn thing was heavier than I'd expected. At first it didn't budge. *Is it blocked?* I thought for a frantic moment. Then, with a groan and a shudder, the ancient door began to grind open. Then, the initial resistance melted away and it swung open freely, leaving me tumbling through the doorway ass over tea kettle, into the room beyond.

To their credit, my comrades didn't miss a beat. They rushed in behind me and formed a defensive line while I scrambled to my feet. We found ten ordinary-looking Goblins Warriors, holding crude or battered melee weapons, gathered around the Goblin Shaman. The shaman wore tattered filthy robes and a demonic mask made of etched bone. He was waving a club-like scepter that looked like it was made of an ogre's femur, but with small stones, teeth and feathers adorning it. The shaman, being a boss monster, was also distinguished by having an individualized name attached to his tag.

Goblin Warrior, Level 3 Fighter, Goblin

Clats Xednuirk, Level 8 Shaman, Goblin

The Goblins spun around in shock as we rushed in. Just ahead of me, Lemorak and Macha shifted their weapons to a ready position. Behind me, Bolton used his entire body to push the hidden door shut while Elias looked for materials to barricade it.

The room was long and wide with high vaulted ceilings. Based on the playthrough guide we'd read, I guessed it had once been a library. A heavy wooden door stood at the far end of the room and appeared to be the only other way in or out. Ancient wooden shelves lined the walls and stood in several freestanding rows, and were packed with disintegrating leather-bound books. Long heavy tables ran down the center of the room. It reeked of musty moldy paper. When we entered, the Goblins had been hacking apart tables and shelves into what looked like chunks of firewood.

A Goblin Warrior rushed me and my Combat Guide activated in response. I dodged a frantic thrust from one Goblin with a crude spear, then slashed back with my blades. My strikes hit, slashing open the goblin's throat and belly, dusting my attacker. A heartbeat later I was blocking another three-foot-tall, homicidal monster that charged me with a rusty cleaver.

The cleaver-wielding Goblin proved more graceful than the first and dodged my counter-attack. He and I danced for several attacks and parries before I slid a blade in past his defense and ran my scimitar through his little chest to dust him

"Your allies on the wall already fell to our might! Surrender now and we'll make your deaths quick!" The shaman, Clats Xednuirk, shrieked in English

"Fuck off!" Lemorak roared back as he cut down the Goblin Warrior with a clean sweep of his massive sword.

Allies on the wall? A wolfish grin spread across my face. *Too bad for Bryn, but the Stooges died!*

My satisfaction was short-lived when the Clats began to chant unintelligible words and wave his bone scepter. Before I could pounce on him, another Goblin Warrior charged me, chopping a battle-axe. I skipped back several steps to avoid the wild, drunken swings of the axe.

Clats finished his spell and putrid yellow energy crackled up his scepter. Countless slimy yellow tentacles sprouted from the floor of the room. I felt one rise snake around my left ankle, slithering up to my knee before I could react. The yellow appendage was as thick as my forearm and covered in glistening mucus-like slime, with tiny suction-cup mouths puckering across its.

"Whoever programmed this had a serious Hentai fetish!" Macha shouted, dancing across the floor. She was just managing to avoid getting snared by the tentacles.

My other frontline comrades were less fortunate. Archer had a tentacle wrapped around his chest, though he had a second between his jaws and was shredding it with gnashing teeth. Four of the nasty appendages had latched onto Lemorak and were slowly dragging the paladin to his knees.

Pressed against the wall, Elias and Bolton were just outside the circular radius of the spell. I saw now that the secret door we'd entered through was concealed by a bookshelf. Bolton and Elias had managed to topple over two adjacent shelves in front of the now-closed secret door. Now they were in the midst of casting their own spells in response to Clats.

Another wet tentacle slapped against my right leg and began to slither upwards. The tentacles were strong and were simultaneously crushing my legs while trying to drag me to the ground. I felt pain in my legs and received my first damage message due the crushing tentacles. Driven by a surge of fear, I hacked with desperation at the tentacles.

The moment I hacked into one tentacle, another came slithering up to grab me.

Macha was still free and trying to make her way through the tentacle-filled area to engage the shaman directly, but kept finding her path blocked by even more tentacles.

"Macha! Jump!" Bolton shouted just as his spell finished.

Macha hurled herself into the air, diving at Clats. Bolton released his spell and hurricane force winds howled from his outstretched hands. The wind caught Macha and sent her rocketing through the air, over the circle of grasping yellow tentacles. She crashed into Clats like a flying linebacker. The shaman's glowing bone scepter went tumbling from the impact.

Fresh tentacles stopped appearing, although the ones already sprouted didn't vanish. Archer was snapping and clawing himself free, while Lemorak and I worked to cut at the binding appendages. The only good news seemed to be that the tentacles hadn't discriminated. I realized that the few goblins who had survived our initial assault had been snared and dragged to the ground, crushed by their own shaman's spell.

Macha and Clats were both back on their feet. The shaman's mask had been knocked off by the collision, and the little creature hissed and spit at

Macha as he held his clawed hands up defensively. Clats got off another spell, and his dark claws began to grow and sharpen until each finger was tipped with a small knife-like talon. Very Freddy Krueger.

Behind me, I heard Elias complete his own spell in a raised voice. Dark storm clouds appeared at the high ceiling of the ruined library. Warm summer rain fell from the clouds, followed with blinding bolts of lightning that struck down in unison at the shaman. Thunder rattled my bones.

I had expected the multiple lightning bolts to have left a smoking crater where Clats stood. I think that's certainly what Elias had intended. However, the enemy spellcaster raised his knife-clawed hands over his head while performing an intricate gesture and caught the lightning as it struck. His claws began to crackle with captured lightning.

Macha pounced the instant the lightning from the clouds faded. She spun forward with a twirling series of spinning kicks that would have made Chuck Norris dizzy. She caught Clats by surprise with her first and second kicks, sending the shaman stumbling back.

But she'd pushed her luck with the third kick. The shaman reached up with his razor-sharp claws, dancing with stolen lightning, and slashed open Macha's leg. With his touch, the lightning discharged in a blinding flash and sizzling crack. The smell of burnt ozone and charred meat filled the air. When the flash faded, Macha had been hurled clear across the room. Rain continued to fall from the magical clouds overhead.

"Let's not try that again!" I shouted over my shoulder at Elias.

He dismissed the spell with a forlorn wave of his hand. The rain stopped and the dark clouds vanished.

I had just sliced myself free of the tentacles . Tightening my grip on my scimitar, I prepared to charge Clats. He still had those nasty-looking razor-sharp claws, but at least they no longer crackled with lightning. *So - well - at least I got that goin' for me,* I thought, channeling Bill Murray. I'd put my swords up against his claws any day.

Lemorak had hewn his way through the field of tentacles and stomped up to stand by my side. His once-glittering armor was covered in a thin layer of slimy gore. Despite that, Lemorak looked the picture of a gallant, determined knight ready to charge into battle.

"I told you this was a bad idea." Lemorak grumbled, his tone stern. Then he settled himself into a fighting stance, his two-handed sword held up so that the hilt was by his ear and the sharp point would lead the way.

"No one likes an 'I told you so.'"

"I don't like dying," Lemorak said. "Ready?"

I gave my scimitars a quick twirl like they were batons, then flicked them clean of tentacle slime. "Ready."

Lemorak and I charged Clats in unison. Lemorak's massive sword swept down to chop the goblin spellcaster in half from head to taint. Blinding fast, the little monster lifted his magically enhanced claws and batted the swinging sword aside. My scimitars were just behind Lemorak's attack but Clats leapt up and did a barrel roll through my slashing blades, then landed with apparent ease on his bare, clawed feet.

When Clats counter-attacked, I was unable to keep up with the complicated choreography dictated by my Combat Guide. So I ignored the guide and just fought on the new reflexive instincts that weeks of Lemorak's training had left me with. Like some deadly dance, Lemorak, Clats, and I traded a series of strikes, parries, advances and dodges.

The goblin appeared barely taxed by taking us both on, though we seemed to be keeping him busy enough that he couldn't manage more than token counter attacks. More importantly for the moment, as long as we kept him engaged, he couldn't pull off any more damned spells.

Then one of my scimitars slipped past the shaman's defense while he warded off another heavy sweep from Lemorak. The point of my sword found the inside of the goblin's arm and left a bright red cut on his leathery skin. The shaman's health bar dropped by a disappointingly small percentage.

Achievement Earned - Avengers Assemble! - When in a Party, fight as a team against a single Boss level enemy - 10% bonus Exp for the entire week

The goblin hissed with pain and skittered back to disengage. Archer, having freed himself from the remaining tentacles, chose that moment to strike. The dire wolf came snarling in from out of nowhere, jaws snapping at the shaman's back. Alarmed, Clats snarled out the words to a spell and a nearly invisible bubble of force pulsed out from him and sent the three of us stumbling back.

Then the main door to the library was kicked in.

Chapter Twenty-Three

A hulking goblin, nearly as tall as Lemorak and brawny with corded muscles, stepped through the doors. Bryn, her eyes closed and body limp, was pressed against his chest, a jagged knife at her delicate throat. Unconscious, but her character wasn't dead. I felt an unexpected surge of relief.

Warchief Krevec, Level 8 Warlord, Goblin

The Krevec's jagged pointy teeth were on full display in a malevolent grin. Clats backed up to stand beside his warchief, a giggle hissing from beneath his bone mask.

"Surrender or I slit her throat." To punctuate the order Krevec scraped the knife blade over the obsidian black skin of Bryn's exposed throat.

Everyone in the room froze and weighed their options. Bryn's HP bar was nearly empty. Even if it wasn't, I was sure the warchief striking any vital zone on a helpless foe would be an automatic critical strike. Bryn and I had a mixed history, at best, and I wasn't at all sure how to define our relationship. If we had one at all. Despite all that, I wasn't prepared to let the Krevec kill her.

"What do we do here, guys?" I muttered.

"Let him kill the bitch," Bolton hissed.

"Agreed," said Macha.

Silence fell thick and heavy over the room as the tension of the standoff grew.

"I don't think I can do that," I said from the corner of my mouth.

Licking my lips, I tightened my grip on my weapons. I was mapping out the moves I'd need to make to charge Krevec when Bryn stirred in his grasp. She let out a whimper of pain, weakly struggling. I took half a step forward.

"She's not worth it, Zee," Lemorak hissed. "She'd just as gladly cut and run if the positions were reversed."

But the positions weren't reversed and it was my choice.

"Weapons! Now!" boomed Krevec.

I heard a clatter behind me and glanced over my shoulder in time to see that Elias had thrown down his mace. His violet eyes were pinched in frustration.

"I won't risk anyone else Red Screening on my account," Elias said.

Bolton growled in frustration, then threw down his staff. Macha sheathed her katana, then gently set it on the ground. I looked at Lemorak. His eyes blazed with impotent fury. I shrugged in resignation, then I tossed down my curved swords, followed by my bow. Archer snarled in defiance but went silent when I shot him a glare.

"Complete goat rodeo," Lemorak grumbled. The goblins roared with diabolical laughter as Lemorak's sword clattered to the ground beside mine.

Clats chanted and waved his arms. Orbs of impenetrable darkness gathered around his gesticulating claws. He finished his spell and the gathered darkness rushed out at us, a tsunami of oil. The roiling darkness hit me, cold agony shot through my body. I gasped in pain and fell under the pressure.

Goblin Shaman has cast Enervating Blast. Willpower Check Failed.

I had just enough time to read the notification before losing consciousness.

***

When I awoke, I thought the shaman's darkness was still covering me, but it was only that my eyes were shut. There was a flashing notification waiting for me on my HUD.

Iron Will Talent Activated - Secondary Willpower Check Successful!

There was cold stone floor beneath my cheek. I didn't know how long I'd been unconscious. I was sprawled on my chest where I'd fallen. I heard the deep rumbling voice of Krevec and the sibilant hiss of Clats talking to each other in goblin. They sounded close.

Need to talk to AI about picking up language skills, I told myself.

Trying to appear still unconscious, I cracked my eyes open and peered through slit eyelids. Unfortunately, I couldn't see much without moving my head. Archer was slumped unconscious on the floor inches away from me. It looked like the dire wolf had tried to hurl himself between me and the shaman's spell. Beyond Archer were the warchief and shaman. Bryn lay in a crumpled heap at Krevec's feet, her throat unmarked. At first I couldn't tell whether she was also conscious or not, until I saw a brief red glimmer as her eyes fluttered open for an instant.

Closing my eyes, I tried to picture where my weapons had fallen. I thought they were just a foot or two away from the top of my head, but was too disoriented to be sure. I wondered if anyone else was conscious and playing possum. Clerics and monks both had Wisdom as a primary ability score. It was possible either Macha or Elias had resisted the shaman's spell. However, we had no way of communicating, if either was awake.

I'll just have to play this like I'm on my own, I thought.

Slitting my eyes open again, I watched the shaman and warchief. Their language was completely alien to me. I couldn't guess at what they were saying. However, their body language said plenty. Krevec was shouting into the shaman's face, spittle flying from his lips. The shaman's head was downcast, shoulders hunched under the verbal abuse.

Then, I saw Archer's tail twitch and the wolf's paws flex. Neither of the Goblins seemed to notice. Relying on the Goblin asschewing as a distraction, I took a risk and slid my arm so that the tips of my fingers brushed Archer's rear haunch. His ears flicked attentively in my direction, though he went otherwise still.

Speaking the word on a soft breath I asked, "Ready?"

Archer's muscles tensed beneath my fingers.

Now or never, I told myself. Our best hope now was shock and awe. I really hoped my weapons were where I thought they were.

"Go!" I hissed. Simultaneously I shoved myself up and dove into a forward shoulder roll, my hands questing for my bow or swords. Archer was up in the same instant and shot forward like a coiled steel spring. A savage snarl erupted through his bared fangs.

The fingertips of my left hand grazed the slender curved wood of my bow. I was glad that I hadn't tossed down my quiver when disarming. I locked my grip around the bow stave and snatched an arrow out of my quiver. I aimed and drew the string back simultaneously and on my next exhalation fired. I heard chanting behind me and prayed that Elias or Bolton were awake and pitching in.

Archer's pounce had brought him down on Clats. The massive dire wolf was at least twice the goblin's mass. The shaman went down, shrieking in surprise, under Archer's snarling bulk of muscle, fur and claws.

Krevec spun in surprise, just in time to catch my loosed arrow in the shoulder. At essentially point blank range the arrow sunk in with a meaty *thwack* and buried itself to the fletching. The warchief stumbled and his HP bar took an appreciable loss. Notifications scrolled across the bottom of my vision.

Surprise Attack! Bonus 32 damage!

Point Blank Shot! Bonus 57 damage!

Elias, his mace in hand, came storming past me shouting a battle cry. The cleric's spell must have been a self-targeted buff. He had grown to gigantic height and bulk, his avatar at least fifty percent larger. He towered over the hulking warchief and had to hunch his shoulders to keep from bashing his head against the beams of the library's high ceiling. His mace had grown in proportion to match his body, yet as he charged, Elias twirled the weapon lightly like a gymnast's baton.

He slammed his whirling mace into Krevec's chin and the warchief's avatar flashed red. A critical hit! The brawny goblin was knocked off his feet and sent tumbling through the air. He crashed into a set of shelves, shattering their heavy wooden frame and pulverizing the rotten tomes stored there. The goblin's HP bar plummeted.

Before Elias could re-engage with Krevec, I released a rapid barrage of arrows as he staggered to his feet. Arrows hummed through the air, and shots plunged into his thigh, forearm, and gut. Krevec howled in rage and pain. Having not bothered with my aiming guide, I grinned triumphantly.

By then Elias was on him. The cleric swung his enlarged weapon down in a two-handed overhead strike that smashed into the goblin's chest. Krevec's body flashed red from another critical blow and his HP bar fell to almost nothing. That was one hell of a battle buff that Elias had cast on himself.

The odious monster wasn't down yet though, and Elias was having increasing trouble maneuvering his massive body and weapon. Krevec spat a glob of blood and shattered teeth to the ground and heaved himself upright, drawing a black-bladed battle-axe from his back as he did so. He hacked the battle-axe at Elias's tree trunk-like left leg and lay open a bloody gash. The cleric stumbled back a step under the blow.

Without warning Macha loped past me, her fleet stride practically skipping across the floor, her katana raised for battle. She interposed herself between Krevec and Elias and deflected Krevec's next axe swing with her blade before it dealt more damage to Elias. Macha and the warchief spun into a lethal whirl of strikes and parries, the goblin hacking wildly at Macha as she pirouetted with deadly grace. Gigantic Elias stood at the edge of the duel looking for an opening.

Archer yelped in pain and I turned my attention to the other fight still raging. The shaman was back on his feet, his body now bristling with long, barbed thorns. His skin beneath the thorns had turned brown and rough as tree bark. Multiple wounds oozed sap-like blood down his body. Clats had less than a third of his HP remaining. Archer was off the spellcasting goblin now, standing a few feet away, fangs bared in a snarl. The dire wolf's HP bar was around half-full. Bryn was on her feet now, a pair of slender wavy bladed daggers in her hands, her pretty face twisted in a furious snarl.

Clats began to spit out the words of another spell, his clawed hands crooking in ritual gestures. Pulling my bowstring back, I fired an arrow on reflex. The arrow hit the shaman's chest, dead center, but bounced off his bark-like skin. The shot still slammed him with enough force to make him stumble back a step, and spoiled his spell.

Archer and Bryn saw their opportunity and hurled themselves at the reeling goblin. The severely wounded Bryn slashed at the goblin's back, carving away wooden strips of flesh like a speed widdling champ. One of her daggers snagged - either in the hard wooden skin, or on a thorn - and tumbled free of her grip. Archer's massive jaws latched around Clat's left ankle and sank in past hard wooden flesh. My dire wolf companion snarled around the wooden ankle and shook his head from side to side, flinging Clats to the ground.

Bryn let out a banshee battle cry and fell to her knees beside the shaman's head, plunging her remaining dagger down with all her weight. The wavy steel blade stabbed into the goblin's beedy red eye and sunk up to the hilt. He flashed red and shuddered all over for an instant before dissolving into dust.

I spun to check on my friends fighting Krevec just in time to see the goblin go down under a whirlwind of spinning kicks and punches from Macha. Krevec dissolved, dusted before he hit the ground. I heard a distant chime and notifications began to scroll.

Goblin Shaman Defeated, 1,000 Party EXP Awarded - Partial Award - Killing Blow

from Non-Party Member Dirzbryn Baenmtor

Goblin Warchief Defeated, 5,600 Party EXP Awarded

Party Member Macha has reached Level 4 Monk

Party Member Bolton Glittertooth has reached Level 4 Sorcerer

Party Member Sir Lemorak has reached Level 5 Paladin

Party Member Brother Elias Stonetree has reached Level 5 Cleric

LEVEL UP!

LEVEL 5 RANGER REACHED!

ARCHERY TALENT IMPROVED TO LEVEL 11

TWO-WEAPON FIGHTING TALENT IMPROVED TO LEVEL

13

SKILL IMPROVED: ATHLETICS +9 -> +10

SKILL IMPROVED: SURVIVAL +12 -> +13

SKILL IMPROVED: STEALTH +12 -> +13

SKILL IMPROVED: ANIMAL HANDLING +5 -> +6

SKILL IMPROVED: TRACKING +8 -> +9

SKILL IMPROVED: PERCEPTION +7 -> +8

SKILL IMPROVED: INVESTIGATION +2 -> +3

INCREASE TO HIT POINTS +20

INCREASE TO MANA +10

5 ABILITY POINTS AWARDED

+2 ABILITY POINT FOR BEING HALF-ELF

NEW RANGER TALENT UNLOCKED - RANGER SPELLS

(LEVEL 1)

NEW TALENT UNLOCKED: POINT BLANK SHOT (LEVEL 1)

+1 LEVEL TO YOUR ANIMAL COMPANION

CONGRATULATION ON REACHING RANGER LEVEL 5!

ONCE YOUR CURRENT QUESTS ARE COMPLETE, PLEASE

PROCEED TO DEPART ROWLING VALLEY. NO FURTHER

LEVELS WILL BE GRANTED UNTIL YOU'VE DEPARTED

THE ORIENTATION ZONE. NEW GAME FEATURES WILL BE

AVAILABLE ONCE YOU DEPART THE ORIENTATION

ZONE.

NEW GAME FEATURES UNLOCKED

MULTI-CLASSING OPTIONS UNLOCKED ON FUTURE LEVELS

CHARACTER RE-SPAWNS AVAILABLE

PRESTIGE TALENTS AND SKILLS UNLOCKED

OVERWORLD ACCESS GRANTED

NEXUS ACCESS GRANTED

OUT-OF-GAME MESSAGING UNLOCKED

PLAYER-VS-PLAYER COMBAT

ULTRA-PREMIUM CONTENT AVAILABLE

Those of us still conscious shared a quick grin at our sudden Level-Ups and the ensuring flood of pleasure rushing through our bodies. Any inclination to celebrate was short-lived. The sounds of approaching goblins echoed through the open main door to the library. We were still behind enemy lines, with the quest incomplete, and I hadn't even revealed my mystery quest from the Doctor to the rest of the party. I wasn't even sure how I'd go about spilling those details yet.

"Time to get moving," I shouted,.

"Elias, see what you can do to get Bolton and Lemorak on their feet, then deal out healing as you're able. Macha and I will hold the door," I ordered while snatching up my discarded swords.

"What about her?" Elias said, looking at Bryn. The assassin had recovered her daggers and other confiscated gear from Krevec's corpse, but was still on her last few HP.

Macha, slender chest heaving still from finishing the warchief, moved over to the open doorway and took up a ready position. Just in time too. Within seconds, a pair of low-level goblins rushed her. She dispatched them with swift efficient slashes of her katana. I imagined her Endurance must be low already. No energy left to get acrobatic anymore.

Bryn turned to face me and the accusing glares of my friends. Not finding any degree of sympathy, she directed her words to me. "Zee, I had no idea what the Megas were planning. They kept me in the dark until they'd dropped that Ursapine in your lap. There was nothing I could do."

I felt the gazes of my friends turn to me, awaiting my judgement of Bryn.

"I buy it. Bryn's out for herself and deceitful as all hell, but…"

"You say the sweetest things, lover," Bryn interjected, half sarcastic half sultry. She made it work somehow

"…but, I don't think she had any reason to fuck with us like that. Let's all get out of this shit show together. Triage her along with the rest of us," I told Elias. Then I turned to Bryn. "You should be pretty good at finding secret doors in this place, right?"

"Of course," Bryn agreed with a coy smile.

"Good. Start looking. If these little shits don't stop coming we'll need another way out of here." As Bryn turned to begin searching for a back door, I reached out and snagged her wrist. I leaned in and in a low tone said to her, "You cut and run on us or screw me over, I promise you'll regret it this time, Bryn."

Her coquettish expression froze for a heartbeat as I locked gazes with her. She gave me a barely perceptible nod, then deftly twisted her wrist out of my grasp and slunk away into the darker corners of the library. By then, Macha was already slicing down the next low-level goblin warrior charging through the door. I moved over to give her a hand.

Chapter Twenty-Four

Goblins just kept coming. My arms burned and chest ached from nearly constant combat with the charging waves of monsters. Individually, none of them posed much of a threat, but as a mob they were threatening to swamp us by sheer numbers. Macha and I held the door to the library. Behind us, Elias was busy casting spells to awaken Bolton and Lemorak while Archer and Bryn searched for another way out.

"How many of these little bastards are there?" groaned Macha between what had become mechanical artless swings of her sword.

"There's multiple spawn points in the keep. Every goblin in the valley spawns here. Until we trigger the end of the quest and send them running, they'll just keep coming." I reminded Macha of what Bolton had told us in preparing for this adventure. At this point I had both my scimitars in hand, but there wasn't any fancy swordplay. It was grueling, repetitive stabs and hacks to cut the goblins down as efficiently as possible.

"Worse than rabbits," Macha said.

I grunted and cut down another goblin charging eagerly to his death. With my Endurance pool empty, my HP took another dip with the effort, physically marked this time by a sharp cramp in my thigh. Both of us had enough Defense that the goblins needed to be very lucky to hit us. However. we were both losing HP to exhaustion, and neither of us had much HP to spare.

"We can't keep this up much longer!" I shouted to Elias.

I spared a glance back to check on him. Bolton and Lemorak were still lying unconscious on the ground. The cleric was kneeling over Lemorak, head bowed and hands hovering as he cast another spell. *Maybe I should pull Bryn and Archer in so we can catch our breath.*

Macha let out a cry of pain. I turned my attention back to the fight. A goblin had finally gotten a very lucky hit and driven a spear into her washboard abs. Macha stumbled back, blood flowing from her wound, but taking the spear with her. I dove forward, scimitars spinning like a blender on high, and slew the lucky bastard.

Macha, the badass that she was, ripped the spear out of her stomach and hurled it into the mass of goblins. She was back at my side within seconds. In her absence we'd lost several inches of ground and now, instead of fighting the goblins in the hall just outside the door, we were doing everything we could to push them back through the doorway itself. If the tide of these little fuckers got through the doorway and spread out, they'd be able to encircle us. None of us would last long if that happened.

"I think I got it!" Elias cried out, excited. "They're coming to!"

Neither Macha or I dared to take our attention away from the heaving mass of snarling Goblins before us. Above the din of battle, I heard the rattle and clank of Lemorak's heavy armor. Then, I heard his voice raised in song behind me, his voice a resonant clarion baritone.

From the Halls of Montezuma

To the shores of Tripoli;

We fight our country's battles

On the land as on the sea;

First to fight for right and freedom

And to keep our honor clean;

We are proud to claim the title

Of United States Marines

At the end of the verse I heard Lemorak bellow, "OOORAH!"

On pure reflex, I slashed down the Goblin in front of me and then spun out of the way. A heartbeat later, Lemorak stormed into the gap I'd left him. My friend's platemail shone like polished silver and scarlet flames engulfed his massive sword. Singing the Marine Corps Anthem at the top of his lungs, he went to work.

Lemorak scythed his blazing sword across the pressing goblins and the two front ranks crumpled like stalks of wheat. He moved forward into the gap he'd created and Macha was either too stunned or exhausted to move in beside him. It didn't matter, Lemorak held the onslaught back all by himself. A Goblin's spear shot forward and shattered against Lemorak's glittering armor.

"This won't last long!" Lemorak shouted at us after finishing a third verse. "Let Elias buff you guys up and then come help me out."

Elias was finishing a spell on Bolton, who was just waking up, when we shambled over to him.

"We're still alive?" Bolton asked, confused.

Elias immediately began casting healing and Endurance restoring spells on Macha and me.

"For the moment at least," I answered. "Out of the frying pan, but into the fire."

"We're going to need some big explosive magic as soon as you can manager," Macha said.

Elias finished his first spell, soothing warmth flooded my body, my HP bar rose. Macha sighed with relief as the same spell flowed through her. We were still less than half full, but it was an improvement. I looked over at

Macha and saw that her spear wound had sealed, the new flesh red and raw. Elias was working on his next spell before the first had faded.

Macha and I did our best to fill Bolton in on the defeat of the shaman and warchief as Elias cast his next two spells on us in rapid succession. I felt my body thrumming energetically as my Endurance was replenished to nearly full. My breathing became steady and I no longer felt like lead weights were dragging from my wrists and ankles.

"That's all I've got," Elias said after casting his last spell, his shoulders sagging wearily. "My Mana needs to recharge. Both of you need to be careful. Endurance restoring spells aren't a substitute for actual rest. Your Endurance recharge will be slower until you both can get some sleep."

Bryn and Archer came over then, having completed their search for hidden exits.

"Any luck?" Macha asked.

"Nothing," Bryn reported with a shake of her head. Archer huffed in agreement. "The only way I see out is the barricaded door at the back, and the goblins are trying to break it down as we speak."

"Can they?" Bolton asked.

Bryn shrugged. "Eventually."

"We'll file that under future problems," I said. There were nods of agreement all around.

"If we have a future," Bryn said ruefully.

"Then I guess we're doing this the hard way," Bolton said, gesturing a clawed hand at the main doorway.

Lemorak had actually gained ground all on his own. He'd pushed the goblins back and was single handedly holding the line a couple feet into the hallway. However, Lemorak's armor had lost its radiant luster and the flames along his blade had nearly guttered out.

"Before we get to work, someone needs to add me to your party if you want my help," Bryn stated matter-of-factly.

"Like fuck we do!" Macha snapped.

"You're lucky Zee's got a soft spot for you," Bolton said.

"Wait…" I began, but Elias cut me off.

"No. Bryn's right." Macha and Bolton turned angry glares him, but he held up a hand to forestall their objections. "My group heals and buffs won't affect her if she's not in the party. If we don't add her, I'll have to waste time and Mana healing and buffing her individually. Being in the party will also keep her from snaking any loot with her assassin skills."

"We might actually need her help to get out of here," I added.

Macha was the first to bend under Elias's cool logic. "Fuck they're right."

Still seething, Bolton's resistance collapsed without Macha to back him up. "Fine. I'll add her to the party, but she's out as soon as we get out of here."

Bolton withdrew the Party Charter, which looked like a small rolled scroll of parchment, from his inventory and held it out to Bryn. She tapped it with her index finger and everyone in the party was presented with a screen requesting for Bryn to join. I accepted the request and waited as everyone else did too. The request was approved by a majority vote.

Dirzbryn Baenmtor, Level 4 Assassin, Dark Elf, has joined the party!

"Very gracious of you all," Bryn said with smug satisfaction.

I cut in before another argument could start. "Let's get her added and get the fuck out of here."

The battle that followed was the most grueling and violent experience of my life. However, our party worked remarkably well as a unit. Lemorak, Macha and I comprised our rotating front line, with Bryn and Archer plugging up gaps. Bolton and Elias brought up the rear. Bolton hurled destructive spells over our shoulders while Elias kept us all buffed and healed as best he could. Overall it was a textbook grind strategy that Lemorak insisted only worked because no one had made any critical mistakes.

After nearly two hours, we fought our way outside, where we started to stall out. A throng of Goblins heaved against us on the front line. Then Bolton drained the last of his Mana conjuring an epic fireball. He hurled the spell out into the center of the courtyard, where it detonated and scorched the goblins. Many of those caught in the fireball crumbled to dust. The little bastards went running from the keep after that, fleeing our mighty grinding wrath. Their flight triggered the game to shut down the spawn points throughout the keep.

Bolton and Macha had both hit 5, while Bryn reached Level 4 during the grind. Lemorak, Elias and I had all stopped earning Exp since hitting level 5 and the game was funneling all of our party's collective EXP to them. No one had commented on it yet, and I was going to have to check with Al or the Doctor, but I felt certain that everyone in the party was also earning extra EXP due to being teamed up with my mutant brain. I wondered if Lemorak had noticed.

Bolton's stone wall holding the gates shut had crumbled to gravel hours ago when the spell expired. This allowed the last of the horde to go shrieking through the gates when they broke. With a weary groan, I sheathed my scimitars. Shaking out my wrists, I surveyed the ruined keep around us. Then two notifications appeared in rapid succession.

Quest Complete! The Goblin's Keep

Exp Reward: 25,000

CC Reward: 12,000

Treasure: Mighty Loot Chest

New Achievement - Stand together! - Be Part of a Defensive Formation

New Achievement - Goblinbane - Kill 100 Goblins - 25% bonus damage to Goblins in

the future - 10% bonus to Defense when fighting alongside allies

A large chest of dark wood, banded with iron, appeared in the center

of the courtyard. The lid swung open on silent hinges and gold coins shone

within. Our reward for completing the quest.

New Party Quest Assigned from Zee Lock-in's Quest Journal! Discover the secrets

beneath the Goblin's Keep and retrieve the First Player's Sword for the Doctor!

Exp Reward: 22,000

CC Reward: 75,000

Treasure: The First Player's Sword, Epic Loot Chest

Time Limit: 24 hours

Penalty for Failure: Immediate Character Death, 365-day ban on respawn.

WARNING: Player Perception filters have been disabled for the

duration of this Quest

WARNING: Player Logout has been disabled for the duration of this

Quest

After the notification had scrolled through, a countdown clock

appeared on my HUD. Counting down every second of the 24 hours we

had to complete the quest.

"Shit a dick! What the fuck, Zee?" Macha whirled to face me.

So much for hoping the notification had only appeared to me.

"Jesus, Mary and Joseph," Lemorak muttered . "What have you done?"

Chapter Twenty-Five

"All right…" I paused and considered my next words carefully.

They'll think I'm nuts! I thought, but gritted my teeth and soldiered on.

"…I had a really weird, very vivid dream after the Ursapine attack."

"No one dreams in here," Elias interjected, his face twisted in confusion.

That would've been nice for someone to mention before now!

"Well, I saw something while unconscious. I thought it was a dream," I said. "Or a hallucination or something. It was a party in an ice hotel."

Macha's eye roll didn't escape my notice. Lemorak and Elias traded concerned glances.

"*The Doctor* was a character in the dream. He looked like David Tennant from *Doctor Who*, he gave me this quest. Tricked me to take it actually. He just handed me a folder, and the quest assigned to me. The quest was to find the First Player's Sword, the sword that belonged to Adam Huxley's avatar. But I really just thought it was a crazy dream! I didn't even bother to check my quest menu afterwards."

I was out of breath as the last few words tumbled out of my mouth. Most of my friends had confused or astonished looks on their faces, but Lemorak wore a distinct expression that told me he could tell I was holding something back. Which I was.

"Gananlas, shit really?" Elias muttered, one hand stroking his stubbly cheeks. "That guy was hardcore L33T back in the day."

"I heard he turned an entire mountain into his own private castle," Macha said, uncharacteristically awed.

"Didn't he just vanish one day?" Bolton asked.

"In the game and the real world," Lemorak confirmed, his suspicious frown locked on me.

"First problem," Elias said after a contemplative silence had consumed the group for several minutes. "The only things beneath the keep are the tunnels we used to get in. There's no loot down there. Epic or otherwise."

"There must be a secret passage down there that isn't in the playthrough guides," I said with a shrug.

"Well this all sounds interesting and very exciting for *all of you*," Bryn chimed in, her tone light and nonchalant, "But I didn't sign up for this. So I'll just quit the party now and see myself back to town."

She closed her eyes, accessing game menus, but her face quickly twisted in a frown. "It won't let me quit the party! What the hell?"

"The system must have locked the party roster while we complete the quest," Lemorak observed after he'd also checked his menu options. "Looks like we're all stuck together."

"Fucking marvelous!" Bryn said. "I swear if you flatliners get me killed, I'll make sure you all regret it."

"I'm not scared of you, bitch," Macha snapped.

Lemorak cut off further argument with a raised hand, "We don't have time for this. We're all exhausted after clearing the keep. We need to rest, heal, level-up, and then we need to get cracking on this or it's Game Over for all of us."

We were all tired enough to sleep for a day or two, but we didn't have that luxury. The Doctor's quest was light on details and short on time. The clock that had started to countdown with the completion of the Goblin Keep quest hovered in all of our HUDs. However, Bolton and Elias needed a chance to recharge their mana pools if they were going to be at all useful.

Feeling a bit responsible for the predicament - even though I hadn't meant to accept this quest to begin with - I made a small fire and set to work making a hot meal from our rations. The keep should be clear and safe at this stage, but Macha kept watch while I worked, and the rest of the party sat down to complete their level-ups. Watching them all work, I found myself wondering what sort of personal assistants they all had.

Everyone was still working when the meal was ready, but I dished up the food and passed bowls to each player. Their avatars accepted the food automatically and began robotically eating as each player worked. Lemorak and Bryn were done leveling first, their level-ups relatively straightforward compared to the two spellcasters. Lemorak told Macha and me to get our work done. I told my avatar to continue eating and my hands and mouth began shoveling food into my face. Then I entered Game Management to complete my own Level-Up.

When Al appeared beside me in the Game Management space, trumpets sounded and my digital assistant applauded my accomplishment.

"Way to go Zee!" Al cheered around the cigar in his grinning mouth. "Level 5 is the game changer baby! And that was almost record time too!"

"What do I get this time, Al?"

"Spells Zee! Ranger spells!"

"Anything good? Like Fireball or that Enlargement spell Elias just used?" I felt suddenly excited.

"Well...." Al shifted from foot to foot. "Ranger Spells aren't *that* flashy, Zee. Sorcerers and clerics are dedicated spellcasting classes after all. You're already a badass in a fight. Your magic is more utilitarian. All designed to make you a better Ranger."

"So what're we talking? Lay it on me."

Al waved a hand in the air and stacked windows of text appeared with my spell description. Shit! There were a lot of options to read through, and I was on the clock. I started to scroll through, skimming the spells to look for likely candidates. I imagined I didn't even have half the spell options that Bolton and Elias had available. No wonder their level ups took so long

"Ranger spells work similar to clerics. You have a selection of class spells, but you can only have seven prepared to cast each day. At this point, you only have Level 1 spells, each one costs 5 mana to cast. You'll be able to pick new spells after each sunrise," Al explained while I read spell descriptions.

Al wasn't wrong, my spells weren't nearly as flashy as Elias or Bolton's. I'd learned that the cleric spell list focused predominantly on healing along with "buffs" and "debuffs" spells that improved or hindered character performance. Clerics had some combat magic, like whatever that lightning storm had been, but nothing nearly as destructive as the arcane casters. Sorcerers and Wizards, the two main arcane classes, on the other hand, could bring the big destructive magics when they wanted.

Ranger spells were all nature or wilderness-themed, and like Al had said seemed to provide me with greater utility. *Camouflage* was a spell which would render me nearly invisible in wilderness environments. *Eyes of the Eagle* would augment my vision to see clearer and further. I had a couple of battle buff spells, like *Elemental Arrow*, which would allow me to enchant individual arrows just before shooting them to do elemental damage, like fire, ice or electricity.

With no idea what challenges awaited us in the quest for the First Player's Sword, seven slots didn't leave me a ton of room to experiment. After what felt like an agonizingly long internal debate, I selected *Jump, Entangle, Eyes of the Eagle, Camouflage, Longshot, Bottomless Quiver, and Hunter's Endurance* for the day.

The quest's countdown timer continued to tick on my HUD, an ever-present reminder that I couldn't spend all day considering talents and spells. Anxiety had me feeling rushed and on edge. Level 5 felt almost as important as my Character Generation, but once again I was under the gun and ill-prepared.

Then there were Enhanced Talents to consider. Worthy contenders to spend my Ability Points on, instead of just packing them onto my primary ability scores. Al pulled up the catalogue of options for me in a fresh series of stacked windows.

"Take a close look at Master Archer, Zee," Al recommended.

Relying on synthetic intelligence's judgement, I pulled up the recommendation. *Master Archer* cost 2 of Ability Points, but was a prerequisite for a lot of really great Archery talents that I'd want. By itself *Master Archer* was a good ability too. It would further increase my accuracy and damage with my bow, increase my chances of a critical strike, and open up some acrobatic shooting options.

There was also a tree of enhanced talents that would upgrade my two-weapon fighting. When I began to scan them, Al warned me that the recommended Ranger path was to specialize in Archery or Two-Weapon fighting. Without a perception filter, focusing in on the Archery tree seemed like a good way to avoid some pain. I'd be like Hawkeye from *The Avengers* or freaking Green Arrow if I maxed out the Archery talent tree.

With five Ability Points to spend. I had a little room to splurge this time. *Master Archer* seemed like a lock for 2 of the 5 points. I locked in *Master Archer*, then applied my standing practice of bumping Strength, Dexterity and Constitution. Enhancing each seemed to have obvious benefits with the dangerous mystery quest immediately before us.

When I was confident I'd made the best choices I could with the time available, I submitted my final selections to Al and considered the changes to my stats.

CHARACTER STATISTICS

Handle: Zee Locked-in

Race: Half-Elf

Role: Striker

Class/Level: Ranger/5

ABILITIES

Strength (Endurance): 17 (29)

Strength Skills: Melee Combat, Athletics, Carrying Capacity

Dexterity (Defense): 18 (24)

Dexterity Skills: Ranged Combat, Acrobatics, Stealth, Sleight of Hand, Open Lock. Reflex

Constitution (Hit Points): 16 (180)

Constitution Skills: Concentration, Fortitude

Intelligence (Arcane Mana): 10 (NA)

Intelligence Skills: Arcana, Investigation. Appraise, Disable Device. Forgery, Lore

Wisdom (Faith Mana): 14 (110)

Wisdom Skills: Conviction. Perception, Survival, Tracking, Animal Handling, Medicine, Willpower

Charisma (Inspiration): 10 (NA)

Charisma Skills: Imagination, Deception, Intimidation, Persuasion, Influence

RACIAL SKILLS: Half-Elf Wilderness Skills: Survival (+1), Stealth (+1), Tracking (+1)

RACIAL TALENTS: Half-Elf Flexibility (+5 AP at Level 0, +1 AP), Nightvision (15'), Elven Bow Proficiency +1 Level

CLASS SKILLS: Athletics (+10), Survival (+13), Stealth (+13), Animal Handling (+6), Tracking (+9)

CLASS TALENTS: Archery (Level 11), Two-Weapon Fighting (Level 14), Light Armor Proficiency, Animal Companion (Archer, Level 5 Dire Wolf), Favored Enemy (Goblin), Favored Terrain (Forest), Ranger Spells (Level 1), Master Archer (Cost 2 AP)

EARNED SKILLS: Perception (+8), Fletching (+3), Intimidation (+0), Investigation (+3)

EARNED TALENTS: Improvised Weapon (Achievement), Iron Will (Achievement), Surprise Attack (Achievement), Point Blank Shot (Earned)

CARRIED EQUIPMENT: Leather Armor (+3 Defense), Adventuring Kit (Rope 50 ft., Tent, Camp Cooking Set, Grappling Hook, Climbing Pitons x20, Climbing Hammer, Crowbar, Lamp Oil x4, Chalk 1 lb, Torches x10, Healing Potion x3), Ranger's Cloak, Masterwork Scimitar x2, Compound Shortbow, Arrows x33, Flaming Arrows x4

STORED EQUIPMENT: Standard Clothes, Short-sword, Dagger, Stone Hatchet

RANGER SPELLS: Level 1 Spells (5 Mana): Jump, Entangle, Eyes of the Eagle, Camouflage, Longshot, Bottomless Quiver, Hunter's Endurance

COMBAT STATISTICS

Weapon - Talent Modifier - Weapon Damage - Accuracy - Median Damage

Masterwork Scimitar - 14 - 50 - 28 - 111

Masterwork Scimitar (off-hand) - 14 - 50 - 21 - 83

Compound Shortbow - 11 - 20 - 25 - 104

ACHIEVEMENTS: First Kill, Backstabber, Good Samaritan, Goblin Slayer, Kobold Slayer, And Stay Out!, Ain't Got Time to Bleed, "The dishes are done man.", Marathon Runner, Orc Slayer, Pest Control, FATALITY, Specialist (Survival, Stealth, Tracking), I am the night, Trained (Animal Handling), Practice Makes Perfect (Survival, Stealth, Tracking), Hunter, Gone Fishin, Camp Cook, The Great Outdoors, It's Super Effective!, Improviser, "My Spidey Sense is Tingling", "It's all fun and games until someone loses an eye...then it's hilarious", Cornered Fighter, "The Bigger They Are...", Big Game Hunter, Avengers Assemble!, Goblinbane, Stand Together!

TOTAL ABILITY POINTS: 27

CURRENT CRYPTOCURRENCY: 485.25

CURRENT DEBTS: 4,508,201.09 CC - OzCo Department of Corrections

CURRENT EXPERIENCE: 15,622

EXPERIENCE TO NEXT LEVEL: 23,000

When I opened my eyes in the courtyard, I found a new set of icons on my HUD. Next to the bar showing my Faith Mana, there was a small spellbook icon where I could access a list of available spells. There were also three "Quick Spell" slots for fast access.

Having never had access to magic before, I wondered what spellcasting was like in the game. I focused on the spellbook icon and a menu appeared, showing the list of prepared ranger spells I'd just selected. After selecting *Jump*, unintelligible words began to flow from my mouth. My hands lifted of their own accord and my fingers danced through a series of gestures. The spell completed and a notification appeared.

You've cast Jump! Effect: Enhanced Jump movement speed activated. Cost: 5 Faith Mana. 95 Faith Mana remaining. Spell Duration: 10 Seconds. Auto-sustain disabled

Looking around the courtyard, I saw glowing golden lines arching up from my feet to distant spots. I realized that it was like my archery guide; the game was highlighting possible jumps I could make. I focused on an arched golden line that ended along the battlement of the keep's wall, about thirty feet away. My legs bent beneath me and then I jumped. I went hurtling through the air like Spider-Man.

"*YAHA!*" I cried out with excitement as the air whistled past me. I landed with a thud, on the stone wall, skidding on the dusty surface. Considering the distance I had travelled, it was a gentle touchdown.

I looked back down to the courtyard and my watching friends. Golden lines still radiated out from my feet, though as I watched, the lines were getting shorter. The spell was running out of power and the range of my possible jumps was decreasing. Laughing I focused on another line and jumped again, using three smaller, but still superhuman, jumps to bring myself back to our campsite before the spell expired.

"Look at you and your fancy magic jumps," Bryn drawled in a saccharine tone.

Jump has expired!

"Jealous?"

"Honey, I don't *get* jealous." Bryn said. "I get *even*."

Macha snorted and rolled her eyes. She'd just finished her own Level-Up and took the opportunity to show off. Without a word, she took off sprinting towards the courtyard wall. Her feet barely touched the ground, and she was almost a blur of motion. Her already enhanced monk speed must have dramatically improved with her Level-Up.

She reached the base of the wall, below the same spot I'd jumped to. She didn't stop, she just kept running, straight up the vertical wall. She reached the top, struck a triumphant Superman pose, or Superwoman to be precise, with hands on her hips.

Then she swan-dived off the edge of the wall, straight towards the ground. She hit the ground on outstretched hands and spun into a series of acrobatic flips and rolls that carried her all the way back to the party. She landed precisely in front of us like an Olympic gymnast completing a floor routine, her arms stretched out over her head and a wide grin on her narrow pretty face.

"No magic necessary," she declared, smug. All in all, the entire demonstration had been quicker than my magically assisted jumps back and forth.

"Physical movement is soooo level 4," Bolton said. He muttered a single word, snapped his clawed fingers and vanished in a sulfurous puff of green smoke. A heartbeat later, he reappeared atop the wall. Then he repeated the spell and reappeared beside Macha and me. We all started to laugh like a bunch of kids on Christmas Day. Archer, who had padded up to stand beside me, yipped and wagged his tail in shared excitement.

"Would you three wrap up the circle-jerk," Lemorak said. "We've got work to do and the clock is literally ticking."

"Yes sir, Drill Sergeant Turtle, sir!" Macha snapped off a crisp salute.

We all shared another chuckle at Lemorak's expense, but we knew he had a point. It was time to get to work. We paired off into three groups to search the keep for clues. Each group had a player with high Perception. Bryn went with Elias, Macha with Bolton, and Lemorak with Archer and me.

Chapter Twenty-Six

"Shit a dick! This is getting us ab-so-fucking nowhere," Macha said four fruitless hours later when we had all reconvened in the courtyard. It was a little over seven hours since the quest's countdown had begun, leaving us sixteen hours and change to save our collective asses.

"Are you sure this Doctor that gave you the quest didn't give you any clues? A riddle? A map? Something?" Lemorak asked me, for what felt like the hundredth time.

"If he did, whatever it was went clear over my head." I let out a long, frustrated sigh.

"Tell us about it, maybe we'll connect something you missed." Bryn picked some grime out from under a fingernail with the blade of a dagger. She was participating in the quest, but she'd made it clear she wasn't happy with me over the circumstances.

"Let me think." I closed my eyes. I thought back to the James Bond-themed party where I'd last encountered the mysterious synthetic intelligence. How the hell was I supposed to explain that scene without raising more questions?

"Come on, Zee! Was he wearing anything unusual? Holding anything? What did he say? Exactly," Bryn snapped.

"Just shut up, all right! I'm trying to think…"

I had glossed over a lot of the details when describing the dream the first time. Like the entire Bond theme. The Doctor had been costumed like a Bond villain, with white tux, eye patch, and cigar. He'd even used Goldfinger's signature line of "*No Mr. Bond, I expect you to die!*" Had the entire party been a clue? What did that give me? I'd been Bond. The ice palace had been from *Die Another Day*. Then there'd been the kiss from Ursula Andress with a Russian accent.

Frustrated, I shook my head, and decided this problem called for more brain power. "This is going to sound weird, I know, but has anyone seen any *James Bond* references anywhere?"

"This is Gygax, all high fantasy all the time, all the spy shit is on Fleming's World." Macha said.

"It's all I've got, all right? The entire scene of the dream was an amalgam of Bond movies."

"Like wha--"

"Wait!" Lemorak said, holding up a hand and cutting off Macha. "I saw something in the portrait hall. I just thought it was some programmer's Easter egg. Come on."

Lemorak stormed back into the abandoned keep while the rest of us scrambled to catch up. I remembered searching through the keep's portrait hall a few hours prior. The long, high-ceilinged hall had clearly once been grand, but had been sorely abused by the Goblins. At one point, massive wrought- iron windows had lined one wall of the hallway, meant to cast sunlight on the opposite wall of artful portraits, packed so close together that each frame was pressed to its neighbor on any given side. Now the glass windows were nearly all shattered. Many of the paintings had decayed or been defaced or destroyed and the hall was piled with garbage and debris.

I hadn't paid much attention to the various portraits when Lemorak and I had searched the room. I'd been focused on the masonry and on probing the piles of garbage. Having taken in the general state of the portraits, I'd written them off before.

Lemorak marched down the portrait hallway at the head of our group, scattering piles of garbage in his path. He came to a halt at what felt like the midpoint of the hall and gestured up at a surprisingly untouched portrait, which hung chest high on the fifteen-foot stone wall. Catching up to Lemorak, we all gathered around and appraised his suspected clue.

"How did I miss this?" I frowned with disbelief at my own oversight.

The oil painting was on a canvas that had to be at least seven feet tall and five feet wide. The frame was ornate with geometric swirls and twisting lines that evoked thoughts of sensuous female bodies. The portrait itself was of a man wearing Gygax-appropriate medieval noble court garb in black and white, with a red rose pinned at his chest. The man held a slender black hand-crossbow up to his chest. And the man's face was a nearly photo realistic depiction of Sean Connery in his Bond-era prime. In the background of the portrait were the walls of Brightblade Keep before it had been abandoned. A small plaque beneath the portrait labeled the depiction, *Lord Bond of Skyfall*. In the bottom right corner of the painting, where you would expect to find the artist's signature was a gracefully signed *007*.

"What the fuck?" Bolton muttered.

"The Worlds are littered with shit like this," Lemorak said. "Bored programmers sprinkling inside jokes and bits of pop culture into the background. So when I first saw it, I thought one of the coders for the keep was a Bond fan."

"Well." Bryn stepped forward. "Let's see what it's hiding."

She stepped close to the portrait and tried to pull the ornate gold frame away from the wall. It was fixed firmly in place. Muttering a slew of curses under his breath, Bryn pulled a dagger from her belt and began to probe around the edge where the frame met the wall with the blade.

"There's almost no seam." She slid a couple of neighboring portraits out of alignment to test whether all the paintings were like that. The Bond painting was the only one fixed in place against the wall.

Next Bryn tried to slice the canvas of the portrait, only to find her blade was stopped millimeters from the surface by an invisible barrier. She ran her blade up and down the canvas to find that the barrier covered the entire surface and the gold frame.

"Mother puss bucket," Bryn spat before twirling her dagger into its sheath. Scowling, she stepped back from the painting. "I'm open to suggestions."

All eyes turned expectantly to me. I felt a surge of helpless frustration and shrugged. "No idea, guys."

"You got us into this," Macha said. "Think, Zee!"

"The devil's in the details with these game puzzles," Elias observed.

I closed my eyes and tried to replay my dream again.

"At the end," I said. "He, asked me something that didn't make any sense."

"What was it?" Lemorak asked.

"Do you have a match?"

From nowhere the trumpeting James Bond theme filled the portrait hall. We all jumped in surprise, then the trademark thick Scottish brogue came from the painting and we all looked up at it. The lips of the portrait's face were moving. "I use a lighter."

The eyes of the portrait had shifted and were now staring directly at me.

Bryn's obsidian hand flew up and slapped across my mouth before I could say anything. "It's one of those stupid spy passphrases they use in the movies. Do you know the response?"

My brain was flying back through all the Bond trivia in my head, trying to remember. I shook my head. Bryn kept her hand firmly over my mouth.

"Don't say a word," Bryn ordered and then looked around at the rest of the party. "Does anyone know it?"

There was a round of shrugs. Lemorak sighed in frustration. "This is too important. I'll spend a couple Crypts to search the OVR World databases." His avatar's eyes closed to mark him as navigating HUD menus. His face almost instantly contorted in a frown and he opened his eyes a few seconds later. "All my external links are locked out."

Bolton, Elias and Bryn all closed their eyes and tried with the same result.

"To prevent cheating," Elias said. "Not unusual for these quests."

"Everyone shut up and think!" Macha snapped and a contemplative silence fell.

Growing up, my dad had gotten me into Bond, Connery was his favorite, though I'd always secretly been more of a Daniel Craig fan. Sacrilege, I know. The portrait had clearly been of Connery though. Did that mean the phrase was from a Connery film? Last year for my dad's birthday we'd watched a Connery marathon, every film, in order. Suddenly, the words popped into my head. I reached up and pulled Bryn's hand away.

"You got it?" Bryn demanded.

I nodded my head, then looked up at the portrait. Praying I had it right, I said, "Better still."

The portrait of Bond smirked and his lips moved in response, "Until they go wrong."

I felt a surge of relief and victory as the Bond theme music still playing in the background surged to a crescendo. The portrait went still and then melted away, revealing a narrow winding stairway twisting down into darkness.

"Well done, Zee," Lemorak said.

"Total clinch!" Bolton put his hand up and I obligingly high fived him.

Page Break

Chapter Twenty-Seven

The stairway beyond the Bond portrait was carved through solid stone and twisted down into the bedrock in a tight corkscrew. Everyone, except Archer, would have to duck their heads and hunch their shoulders to fit into the short narrow passage. Lemorak, the tallest and most heavily armored among us, would have the hardest time of it. I sent Archer in ahead of us, as he actually had better defense and hitpoints than Bryn. Since Dark Elves had the best night vision in the game, she went next, followed by Macha, myself, Lemorak, Elias and then Bolton at the rear.

As the stairs twisted down into the earth, the light from the portrait hall behind us faded and soon we were in inky darkness. We'd agreed to try and maintain any surprise we might have and not light any torches while descending the stairs. This decision had also influenced our marching order. As a mere human, without any enhanced vision, Lemorak was the most vulnerable in the darkness. Elves, Half-Elves, Dragonkin, and even the dire

wolf all had night vision to some extent. As a result, Lemorak was going to

keep his hand on my shoulder for the entire descent.

When the light from the portrait hall faded and the pitch blackness

enveloped us, my night vision kicked in. The ability gave me a 15 foot

range, but with the twist of the stairs, there wasn't that much open space

ahead of me at any point. Mostly all I could see was the back of Macha's

head

We paused ten times, and Macha whispered back that either Bryn or

Archer had spotted a trip wire, pressure plate, or other trap-triggering

mechanism. How the dire wolf knew to spot traps, I didn't understand, but

he did. Each time, Bryn had to slide around Archer and use her specialized

abilities and tools to disarm the trap before we could proceed. Twice the

complexity of the trap bested Bryn's abilities. She managed to not trigger

the trap itself but we had to verbally guide Lemorak over the triggering

mechanism that he couldn't see.

Then came the trap that Archer and Bryn didn't spot. Out of the

blackness and around the twisting wall ahead, I heard a loud click then the

step beneath my feet trembled. There was a canine yelp of alarm followed

quickly by a litany of curses from Bryn.

"What happened?" I demanded.

"Archer stepped on a pressure plate," Macha reported back. Bryn was still stringing together expletives. "The stair he was on shifted and turned to a slide. Bryn's looking for a way to shift them back."

"And not finding one," Bryn growled.

"Quiet!" Macha hissed. "Listen!"

The entire party stopped talking and stilled their movements. I held my breath and focused all my awareness on listening. Echoing out of the darkness below us, I faintly made out the sound of Archer snarling and barking.

"Sounds like trouble," Bolton observed.

"But he landed in one piece," I said, relief zinging through me.

At a basic level, Archer was just another NPC in the game, a computer-generated SI, not alive. Everyone around me had commented on how uniquely intelligent and aware he seemed, though. I'd felt that unexplained dizziness when we first touched, and ever since then, I'd seen the spark of intelligent awareness in his gaze that was always missing when I interacted with NPCs.

In that instant I realized that I genuinely cared for Archer and thought of him like any of my other friends that I'd met in the game. He was *real* to me. And in that moment, I felt an overwhelming urge to push forward and throw myself heedless down the dark slide to help him. Just like I would have for Lemorak or Macha or any of the others.

For me, that realization broke the momentary immobility that had settled over the party at this new obstacle. There was a gap between Macha's slender frame and the inner curved wall of the spiral stairs. The steps were more triangular than square, and near the interior of the spiral, they were narrow slivers. As a result, we'd all been staying as close to the outside of the curve as we could. *Fuck it*, I thought and moved in the same instant.

"What the fu--?" Macha shouted as I used my hand on her shoulder to launch myself through the gap. The top of my head smacked into the ceiling and my shoulder banged painfully against the interior curved wall.

My feet skipped inches above Bryn's silver hair as I dropped. I landed on my feet on a sharply pitched smooth stone and immediately slid away. Behind me, a chorus of confused shouts and cursing, quickly fading as I gained some distance. Within a couple feet I fell on my ass and spiraled down towards the growing sounds of my dire wolf friend.

It wasn't a smooth ride. The spiral-stairway-turned-slide didn't curve at a consistent angle for any great length of time; it twisted and straightened, and also became steeper and flatter unpredictably. The changes often slammed me into unyielding stone, the rough ride knocking precious points from my HP.

Gradually, I realized that the tunnel was getting brighter. Then I shot out into a colossal domed chamber. Glowing crystals sprouted from the curved walls, but more importantly just outside of the tunnel's exit was a raging bonfire for some reason.

Archer stood in the center of the domed chamber, hunched as if ready to pounce forward, sharp teeth bared in a snarl. My momentum carried me across the smooth stone of the floor until I sprawled at Archer's paws.

"Hey bud," I gasped before scrambling to my feet.

Time to take stock of my newest predicament. I heard shouting voices echoing from the tunnel, which I hoped meant the rest of the party had decided to follow my bold heroics. At its peak the domed ceiling was at least a hundred feet up. Then, of course, there was the bonfire, which wasn't a bonfire. I now saw it had a vaguely human shape, but it was twenty feet tall and its body consisted entirely of dancing flames. And it had friends.

Standing at equidistant points around the perimeter of the circular chamber were five other roughly human shaped forms, each one composed of a different element. Turning clockwise from the fire creature was an equally massive form composed of liquid smooth gleaming metal. Then there was a creature comprised of several whirling tornadoes, the funnels of air forming its torso, arms and legs. Next was a decidedly female body made of swirling deep blue water. Behind the water creature were tall heavy wooden doors banded with strips of iron. A hulking monster of twisted vines and tree trunks was next. Last was a craggy beast with a body made of soil and stone. That brought me back to the fiery creature standing motionless beside the entrance.

In fact, all of the monsters were standing entirely still, at least until I took a tentative step forward. Then the heads of each creature turned in my direction and malevolent eyes locked on me. The fire creature's eyes flashed bright as twin novas. Archer's teeth latched around my belt and yanked me back.

"Hey!" I stumbled and fell on my ass - again - with a painful thump. Then two blazing bolts of flame scorched the ground where I'd stood a second before.

"Thanks," I groaned from my prone position. The pain that had lanced up my tailbone on impact sure beat incineration.

Gesturing with his nose, Archer brought my attention to a large circle set into the floor made from concentric rings of silver, copper, brass, iron, bronze, and gold. My obvious step had taken me over the circle.

I had just managed to push myself back to my feet when Lemorak came skidding out of the tunnel on his back, his arms and legs flailing wildly and metal armor sparking off the stone floor. Lemorak's momentum only carried him about three quarters of the way to the protective circle in the center of the room where Archer and I stood. As he came to a stop, I sensed the hostile attention of each elemental creature turn towards my friend.

"Move it, Lem!" I shouted while Archer barked encouragement.

To his credit the retired Marine hurled himself to his feet and sprinted towards us. The fire creature's twin searing bolt missed Lemorak by inches, but then a boulder a couple feet thick came whistling from the direction of the earthen monster and clipped Lemorak on the shoulder. Fortunately, Lemorak shrugged off the hit and stumbled into the "safe zone" marked by the metal circle on the ground.

Before Lemorak or I could speak to each other, Bryn came sliding out of the tunnel. Her slight frame and lesser mass hadn't left her with enough momentum to reach the protective circle either. Bryn took in the entire scene on the move. Without ever stopping she rolled to her feet and sprinted into the circle before we could warn her. Shards of metal, bolts of flame, and spear length spikes of wood all flew in her wake, but missed her.

Macha followed Bryn. The four of us made room as her slide brought her perfectly into the circle and she skipped up to her feet. Ellas was next, less graceful than Macha, but he still managed to tumble his way into the circle where Lemorak helped him up. Last was Bolton. He hurtled out of the entrance and slid across the floor, crashing into Archer and me, sending all three of us sprawling to the ground.

"Shit a dick..." Macha whispered as the three of us got to our feet and everyone else surveyed our predicament.

Chapter Twenty-Eight

"Well I guess that's the end of the James Bond theme," Elias said, violet his eyes wide with terror.

"Zee, if we get out of this. Remind me to kill you," Bryn said.

We'd all taken the time to read the tags above each monster's heads.

Elder Fire Elemental, Level 30

Elder Metal Elemental, Level 30

Elder Air Elemental, Level 30

Elder Water Elemental, Level 30

Elder Wood Elemental, Level 30

Elder Earth Elemental, Level 30

"How are there six Elder Elementals beneath the fucking Goblin's Keep?" Lemorak demanded. "One would be a legit boss battle at Level 20. But six? I've never heard of bullshit like this."

"How badass must that sword they're guarding be?" Macha said.

"We're dead. Literally dead. Those things could Red Screen us all in one hit," Bolton said in a breathless panic.

"Take a beat everyone, let's think this out," I said, trying to force calm into my voice.

"What's to figure out? We're fucked!" Bolton shouted.

I shook my head. "No. I don't think we are. There's got to be a puzzle or some way out of this."

"How do you figure?" Lemorak asked, cutting off Bolton before he could start shouting again.

"This is still a game," I said with a shrug and gestured around us. "Someone designed this space. It didn't just randomly occur. There has to be a win scenario built in. Why else put a safe zone in the middle of this massive chamber? Why not just have that slide drop us into a lake of lava? Why else put monsters here, in the Orientation Zone, that would devastate anyone that could possibly access this chamber?"

My words soothed the wild fear in the eyes of my friends and something close to hope kindled. Lemorak smiled at me approvingly.

"I think Zee's right. We're not meant to fight our way out of here. We've got to *think* our way out. Let's work the problem, people."

Lemorak's agreement with my observation sealed it for everyone. We were still nervous, but we weren't hopeless anymore. There was still fear, but it was no longer paralyzing.

"There's a heavy-duty lock on those doors across the way," Brum observed, her red eyes squinting at the distant wooden doors behind the Water Elemental.

"Can you open it?" I asked.

Bryn shrugged. "It could be above my rank. I'd have to try to find out, which means getting my hands on it."

"Has anyone else noticed the tiles on the floor?" Macha asked.

I looked down. With all the excitement, I hadn't studied the floor. It was smooth and level, but there was a patternless mosaic of multi-colored tiles about three square feet per tile.

"Seven colors, red, gray, brown, blue, green, white, and black." I observed, "Six elementals? A color for each, stepping on one color activates the corresponding Elemental? Maybe one of the colors is safe to step on then?"

"Don't tell me we're playing a massive game of 'The Floor is Lava?'" Bolton still sounded more than a little manic. "Which color is safe, then?"

"What if we just have to get across without touching the ground at all?" Elias said.

Bolton muttered a word of command and snapped his fingers like he had in the courtyard. He vanished in a purple cloud of reeking smoke, but he instantly appeared at the edge of the circle. He screamed and cradled his head in agony. Half his HP was just gone. He fell to his knees shrieking in pain as we gathered around him.

Elias made to start casting a healing spell, but acting on instinct I grabbed the cleric's hands and spoiled the casting. "We don't know if all spells will trigger the same thing or not. Better safe than sorry."

Macha knelt down beside Bolton and produced a small potion vial from a pouch at her waist. She helped Bolton drink it down. Sparkles shimmered across his body, and his HP bar rose. He let out a sigh of relief and started breathing easier.

Confident that Bolton wasn't in any immediate danger, I turned my attention back to the long stretch of floor between us and the distant doors. It was at least fifty yards from the outer edge of our protective circle to the doors. The floor immediately in front of the doors was a consistent stretch of solid black tiles for several feet beyond the threshold, before becoming a patternless dispersal of all seven colors. That stretch of black tiles seemed to be the only area of the chamber that was one solid color.

"I think black is the safe color," I said and explained my thinking.

"But who's going to test it?" Elias asked.

"I say we send the wolf as our guinea pig," Bryn said.

Archer let out a low warning growl as I simultaneously said, "Not gonna happen."

"It's just an NPC pet. You can always get a new one, hun." Bryn scowled at my animal companion.

"Not. Happening," I said and backed the words with a scowl. Archer yipped in agreement.

Bryn rolled her red eyes, but didn't pursue the matter further. I pulled up my Inventory menu and looked for anything that might be helpful. Finally I pulled two apples from my rations and closed my inventory window.

"Let's give this a try," I muttered while bouncing one apple in my right hand to test its weight. I drew back and hurled it out into the air beyond our protective circle towards the doors. The apple flew peacefully through the air as we all watched the Elementals for a reaction.

Nothing. Then the apple landed on a green tile and bounced onto a white one. Wood and Air acted in near unison. Howling winds roared from Air's outstretched arms and sent the apple sliding across the floor, layers of apple skin peeling away under the whistling winds. Wood moved forward, the ground shaking under its massive tree trunk feet, and brought two gnarled wooden hands, the size of dining room tables, together and clapped them over the apple's skinned remains. There wasn't even applesauce left.

The target eliminated, Air lowered its arms and Wood stomped back to its station and went still.

"That was amazing and terrifying all at once," Macha said.

Biting my lip, I walked around the edge of our protective circle until I found a black tile. I wasn't positive I could toss the apple onto a black tile without it bouncing away. Squatting down, I slowly reached my hand out beyond the rings of metal protecting us.

The air above the black tile was noticeably colder. None of the Elementals reacted to my reach across the metal rings. With deliberate care, and the eyes of all my friends on me, I placed the apple on the black tile and then snatched my hand away. Our eyes flew up to check on the Elementals. There was no reaction from any of the six monsters.

"Always bet on black," Bryn muttered, her voice edged with relief.

"Shit a dick! Look!" Macha shouted and pointed back at the apple.

The once vibrant red skin of the fruit had turned brown. Before our eyes, the skin wrinkled and the apple shriveled away until it crumbled to dust.

"Well that was disconcerting," Lemorack said.

"It'll probably drain HP from anyone that stands on it for long," Elias theorized. "Necrotic damage maybe?

"This is fucking ridiculous!" Bolton shouted.

"It's our best option," I said, standing from my crouch.

"It's our only fucking option!" Bolton screamed in my face. His lanky body was shaking, his scales clicking with agitation.

"Pull it together, B," Macha said and yanked the sorcerer in tight to a hug. "We've gotta get through this. For Illiya's sake."

Bolton lowered his lizardish face to Macha's shoulder and we heard him sob. She held him.

"He's not wrong, hun," muttered Bryn. "If I can't pick that lock fucking fast, we'll all be screwed."

"Let's all stop talking about how we can't do it, and start talking about how we're going to do it!" Lemorak barked. "We're only fucked if we give up."

"Lem's right," I said after a tense silence fell over the party. "We'll need to do this exactly right...."

Chapter Twenty-Nine

"This better work," Bryn grumbled as she bounced on the balls of her feet in her soft deerskin boots, scanning the path ahead.

"It's the best plan we've got." I tried to sound optimistic. The broad strokes of my plan had taken seconds to explain, then everyone poked holes in it, and generally improved it.

"It's the *only* plan we've got." Bolton had calmed, but it was clear that he was barely keeping it together. "Besides, if Bryn dies in the attempt, that's a win in my book."

"Love you too, Goldie." Bryn blew a sarcastic kiss.

"Let's just get on with it," Macha said. "These Elementals are wigging me out."

"Ready," Elias reported, dusting chalk dust from his hands.

Bryn stepped into the mound of powdered chalk on the floor that Elias had been preparing. Chalk had been part of Lemorak's required adventuring kit. Originally intended for marking a path if we'd ended up in a maze, we'd repurposed it for my plan.

"Places, everyone," Lemorak ordered after Bryn had examined her chalk-covered boot soles. She then stepped up to the edge of the circle. Everyone else moved into position.

"Whenever you're ready, Bryn," I said.

Bryn crouched like a sprinter at the starting line. She closed her red eyes and took a deep breath. Her obsidian-skinned face settled into a glassy emotionless mask. Then her eyes opened, narrowed in concentration. I held my breath, waiting for her to kick the plan into action.

Just when I thought she had succumbed to nerves and frozen, she leapt into motion like a coiled spring set free. She hurled herself forward onto the first black tile along her projected path.

Bryn didn't linger on the first black tile, but immediately stepped out across a red tile without touching it and onto the next closest black. I leaned forward and grinned as I saw the chalky outline of Bryn's boot on the first black tile she'd stepped on. She moved quickly from tile to tile, barely pausing a heartbeat on each. I felt my own pulse quicken and gut twist as she progressed across the chamber.

After comparing character stats, we had determined that Bryn had the highest Dexterity and Intelligence scores. This gave Bryn several advantages on this first run across the chamber. Strictly speaking, a high Intelligence score didn't make a *player* smarter. It gave the player more access to their digital assistant. Their assistant was then capable of supplying relevant game information, conducting calculations and making suggestions to the player. All things that Al could have done for me if I'd spent Ability Points on my Intel.

In Bryn's case, her high Intelligence score allowed her digital assistant to map out the shortest achievable route across the room using only black tiles. Bryn had spent the last hour interfacing with her assistant, plotting out a route based on the details we could see from our vantage point within the circle. I noticed that Bryn wasn't always moving in a straight line. Counterintuitively she was sometimes moving sideways, diagonally, and even backwards relative to the doors. I began to understand the advantage that her Intelligence score was truly giving her as it kept her from going down invalid paths in what was essentially a maze without walls.

Seeing the benefits of a high Intelligence score and SI assistance in action, I began to regret having treated the ability as one of my dump stats. It didn't immediately help any of my Ranger abilities, but there were clearly other benefits I hadn't considered.

Then of course, Bryn had to be physically capable of executing the route. That's where her Dexterity score came into play. Her Dexterity made all of her movements more efficient and accurate, limiting the risk that she'd miss a jump, slip, trip, or lose her balance. She had to move faster than any of us, because at the end of all of this, she was probably going to spend more time on the black tiles in front of the doors than any of us, but didn't have a deep reserve of Hit Points to sacrifice to the effort.

About halfway across the room, there hadn't yet been an appreciable decline in Bryn's HP bar. However, we all knew that things were about to get tricky. We hadn't been able to clearly see the entire path to the door, even when Lemorak and I had lifted Bryn up over our heads. Her pre-planned route was running out, and the assassin was slowing down as she further leveraged both her Intelligence and Dexterity to map and execute a new route on the fly.

With Bryn's slowed pace her HP began to drop as she spent extra seconds on each tile. I hoped that all the chalk hadn't worn off of Bryn's boots by now. We were all counting on those white bootprints to show us the way across the room.

"Faster. Faster," I whispered while chewing on the inside of my cheek. Under other circumstances I would have been cheering on her impressive display, but none of us wanted to risk breaking her concentration.

"Elias, get ready," Lemorak ordered softly as Bryn skipped her way past the towering Water Elemental between us and the doors. So far, Bryn's movements had been flawless. She hadn't so much as set a toe on anything but black tiles.

Elias stepped into the chalky space where Bryn had started and let out a long sigh. When it came to replicating Bryn's path, Macha and I had the Dexterity scores to make us most likely to succeed. We were also best suited to moving with speed if someone else got into trouble and needed help. Elias was going next, because we hoped once he was outside the protective circle he'd be able to use his cleric spells to buff and heal Bryn while she worked on the lock.

Bolton's Dexterity was middling at best, and he didn't have much HP. The sorcerer was hesitant to try more magic, but had finally agreed it was his best option if it looked like he couldn't make the run or got into trouble on the way. Archer's Dex score was decent, but the tiles were small for the four-legged dire wolf, and the path would be awkward for him at best. Lemorak's Dex was low, and his heavy armor restricted the benefit he could get from the stat anyway. We all just hoped he and Archer had enough HP to take their time.

Elias bowed his head in concentration, but then I saw his shoulders tense.

"What is it?" I asked.

"Weren't there six rings in the circle before?" he asked.

"Silver, copper, brass, iron, bronze, and gold." I looked down at the circle and counted the rings twice. *Only five. Fuck!*

"Where'd silver go?" My mind began to spin as I tried to input this new data point into our plan.

"Gone. Five left," Lemorak said. "Doubt it's a coincidence."

"Six of us left," I reasoned, my eyes closed. "Two of us will have to make the run at the same time."

"You and me, Zee," Macha said.

I nodded, instantly seeing the logic. Macha and I shared a brief smile of camaraderie. Our awkwardness after the hot springs seemed infinitely distant at that moment. Assuming neither of us had to go sooner to help someone out, we'd make the run together.

"Bryn's just about there," Lemorak reported. He hadn't lost sight of the mission or our plan. "Time to get moving, Elias. Remember *slow* is *fast* in this case."

"Right," Elias said, his voice shaking.

The cleric closed his eyes and took a deep breath. Then he opened his eyes, head bent to focus on the chalky footprints marking his path. He stepped out over the circle and onto the first tile. I watched the copper ring of our protective circle vanish. Four rings remaining.

Elias moved with deliberate caution, but haste, from tile to tile. He was slower and more hesitant than Bryn. On the other hand, he was over six inches taller than Bryn and was able to make long steps where she had required small jumps. That said, by the time Elias was on his tenth tile his HP bar was showing a clear drop.

"Bolton, you're up next," Lemorak said, his voice hushed and tense.

The Dragonkin moved up to the same chalky spot where Bryn and Elias had started. There wasn't much left after Bryn and Elias, but he rubbed his bare clawed feet in the white dust all the same.

"Bryn's at about half HP but still working on the lock," Macha reported, squinting to focus in the distance. "We've got to pick up the pace."

Elias had completed about a third of the path that Bryn had marked out. But he'd taken nearly as long to do that third as Bryn had taken to complete the entire route. I was getting increasingly afraid the math of this plan just wouldn't add up.

"All right, Bolton. Get going," Lemorak said when Elias hit the halfway point.

Bolton took a deep breath and stepped out onto the first tile without hesitation. The brass ring vanished from our circle. That left three rings of protection for Macha, Archer, Lemorak and me. Lightly garbed in just his robes, and with his slightly better Dexterity score, Bolton immediately made better progress than Elias. He'd need the faster pace, though, since he also had the smallest pool of HP out of all of us.

With Bolton on his way, Lemorak stepped up to the starting point, his heavy armor clanking with each step. Lemorak had his two-handed sword sheathed across his back, and hands free for balance. He produced another small stick of chalk and laid it on the ground to grind it under his booted foot.

We all jumped when Elias stumbled between tiles and brought his foot down in the wrong spot. He was far enough away that none of us saw what color it was, but it became apparent when Metal behind us took a clanging step forward. There was a whistling sound and a spray of glinting razor-sharp shards flew through the air towards Elias. Bolton fell to his knees on the black tile he happened to be standing on, and threw his arms up over his head as the blades whistled past him.

"Look out!" the three of us shouted at Elias.

Elias leapt from one black tile to the next with frantic urgency as the metal shards sprayed the area around him. He hurled himself over the last few feet of floor just as the blades struck. We heard him cry out and watched his body jerk from the impact of several blades. I couldn't tell how many.

He crumpled to the stretch of black-tiled floor before the doors and didn't rise. Metal blades stuck up from his prone body at odd angles. Bryn stopped working on the lock and scrambled over to Elias. She knelt beside him and ripped the blades from his body. Then Bryn rolled him over and poured one of our remaining Healing Potions into his mouth. He began to stir and we all let out the collective breath we'd been holding.

"He's alive," I breathed.

Then Archer let out a warning growl.

"Guys! Bolton's still down," Macha shouted.

The sorcerer was huddled on his tile, his body visibly trembling, his arms up over his head.

"Bolton! You've got to move!" I shouted at him, but there was no acknowledgement.

"I got this," Lemorak said. Before Macha or I could object - one of us was supposed to be the rescue party - he stepped out over the circle and onto the first tile. As he stepped to the second tile, he shouted over his shoulder, "I'll get him on the way!"

Chapter Thirty

Lemorak was probably the slowest yet to make the dangerous trek. However, with the most HP, he theoretically had the most time to spare. Macha and I watched, our hearts in our throats, as the clanking knight moved deliberately from black tile to black tile, all the while calling out to Bolton, imploring him to get moving.

"Come on, Bolton!"

"You can do it, B!"

"You just need to get up!"

"Bolton! Really need you to get the lead out, bud."

"What's he going to do?" Macha asked, her voice tight.

"I have no fucking clue," I muttered as Lemorak drew closer to the crumpled sorcerer.

"Bolton!" Lemorak barked like a drill sergeant. "Get Your Ass up! Move it!"

"I can't see B's HP bar," Macha groaned.

"He can't have much left," I said.

"Enough to make it across?" Macha asked.

Lemorak was just a tile away from the sorcerer now. He crouched down, awkward in his heavy layers of plate steel armor. If he was saying anything to Bolton, Macha and I couldn't hear. I chewed my lip and felt my stomach churn as Lemorak's shoulders slumped. Lemorak crouched there for another heartbeat, then his shoulders straightened as he stood. Lemorak cast one of his paladin spells and a silvery radiance washed over him.

"What the hell is he doing?" I demanded.

Lemorak gingerly stepped over onto Bolton's tile. There was barely enough space on a tile for one person. I could only imagine how precarious it would be for two at once. With shocking agility but apparent ease, Lemorak shifted to stand on one foot, bent over and scooped Bolton up in his arms. Bolton's body was limp as Lemorak draped the Dragonkin over his broad shoulders in a fireman's carry.

"Must have buffed his Dex?" Macha said.

"Let's hope it's enough."

Lemorak began to move again, hopscotching his way towards the doors.

"I think he's going to make..."

Of course, at that exact moment, Bolton thrashed. Lemorak had been trying to save some time by cutting off a loop in the route and jumping over a stretch of multiple tiles to one further along the path. Bolton's movement spoiled the jump. They crashed to the floor and skidded out of control.

The floor beneath my feet quaked. Elder Wood to my right let out a bestial roar and charged across the floor towards my friends. A second later wind howled through the chamber as Air flew in from the opposite side. Howling, nearly invisible wind picked Bolton up and hurled him against a wall before letting him drop to the floor.

There was an ear-splitting shriek from behind and a split second later a fireball the size of a small car screamed overhead. The fireball detonated prematurely when it clipped the marauding Wood Elemental, who was about to trample Lemorak. Crackling flames engulfed the immediate area as Wood was set ablaze. The Elemental's HP bar plummeted.

I lost sight of Lemorak and Bolton in the ensuing conflagration. Wood let out an animalistic howl of agony and stomped mindlessly across the floor where Lemorak had fallen. It looked like all Wood was accomplishing, aside from possibly trampling Lemorak, was fanning the flames that were consuming its body.

"No!" Macha and I screamed.

A new - and insane - plan crystallized in my mind. Heart thundering, I spun to Macha and grabbed the monk by her shoulders. I turned her to face me. Her expression was contorted with fear and anger and tears streamed from her eyes, but I forced her to meet my gaze.

"Go! Fast! Get them to the other side!" I ordered her. In the back of my mind, I was surprised at how calm and confident I sounded. I didn't feel it.

I could see a question start to form on Macha's lips and I cut her off. "Go! Now!"

Macha's face set with grim determination. Then she whirled to go. Disregarding the path that Bryn had laid out, she leapt to a black tile about six feet away. She stuck the landing, then flung herself toward another distant black tile. She made a direct line towards our friends.

I looked down at Archer. The dire wolf stood looking at me attentively, his eyes bright and impossibly intelligent. "You too, bud. Help Macha and get yourself to the other side."

Archer's head tilted and his eyes narrowed. He let out a whimper followed by a sharp bark of protest.

"I've got a plan, but you have to do your part!" I yelled, my voice finally cracking under the strain of warring emotions.

I could tell by the rigid quiver of his tail that Archer wanted to argue. He resisted the urge, though, and turned to follow Macha.

"Go!"

Archer howled and shot forward, jumping to a black tile. His pawed feet skipped across the surface as he nimbly launched himself to another and then another, a massive furred cannonball of snarling fangs and sharp claws.

With his departure, the last protective ring vanished. I'd already positioned myself on a black tile within the circle. Sudden icy pain pulsed up through my boots. It was like the beginnings of a muscle cramp and only grew in severity as I stood there. A notification scrolled across.

Environment: 3 points of Necrotic Damage dealt. 177 of 180 HP Remaining

Teeth gritted against the pain, I selected the first spell in my plan. My hands began to automatically move through the intricate gestures of the spell, while incomprehensible words flowed robotically from my mouth. With the first spell I was casting, I queued the second and third spells to automatically cast in succession.

I selected the auto-sustain options on each spell, so that Mana would continue to flow, sustaining the spells as long as I had energy. The spells took effect in sequence as each casting completed. Each spell only took seconds to cast, but I knew that each of those seconds were precious.

You've cast Jump! Effect: Enhanced Jump movement speed activated. Cost: 5 Faith Mana. 95 Faith Mana remaining. Spell Duration: 10 Seconds. Auto-sustain selected: 5 mana/10 seconds

When *Jump* took effect, I felt the light bounce to my feet that I'd felt when testing the spell before. Wherever I focused my sight, an arching guiding line shot out from my feet and marked how far the spell would allow me to jump.

You've cast Camouflage! Effect: +20 to your Stealth skill! +20% Miss Chance Defending Against Ranged Attacks! Cost: 5 Faith Mana. 90 Faith Mana remaining.

Spell Duration: 1 Minute. Auto-sustain selected: 5 mana/1 minute

I looked down at my body as *Camouflage* completed casting. I found it hard to focus on any one point on my body, and when I stood still, the colors began to take on the shade of whatever was behind it. I wasn't invisible, but if I stood still, I'd be much harder to spot.

You've cast Hunter's Endurance! Effect: Instant Recharge to your Endurance Points. No Deduction to Your Endurance Pool for Prolonged Movement. **Warning: 50% Chance of Exhaustion When Spell Expires.** *Cost: 5 Faith Mana. 85 Faith Mana remaining. Spell Duration: 1 Minute. Auto-sustain selected: 5 mana/1 minute*

With the completion of my third spell, I felt my heart thunder in my chest and a surge of energy throughout my body. The weariness of the day's trials vanished and I felt like running a marathon. Body trembling with exhilaration, I turned my full attention back to the chaos-consumed chamber.

Macha had Bolton on his feet, one of his gangly arms slung over her shoulders as she hauled him along a path of black tiles. Her efforts were hampered by Bolton's vacant state, and they were triggering Elemental attacks with almost every other move, and were just barely staying ahead of the fallout.

Wood had fallen thrashing to the floor, black smoke roiling from its massive body as flame continued to consume it. I couldn't see Archer or Lemorak in the tumult, but held out hope that they were both still alive. Whether from the constant movement of my friends across the tile floor, or because the protective circle had finally fallen, the other five Elementals had been set free to rampage through the chamber. Standing on a black tile, they still weren't targeting me and I hoped they weren't targeting anyone that made it to the stretch of black floor outside the doors, but they were no longer going dormant when their tiles weren't being triggered. Wonderful.

Metal and Earth were marching across the chamber floor. They lashed out at the air with blind rage. I couldn't spot Air for more than a few seconds as hurricane force gusts occasionally blasted through the chamber, spreading smoke and fanning flames. Fire no longer held a human shape. Its entire end of the chamber was a raging inferno while fireballs arched up out of it and rained down seemingly at random. Water had collapsed from its female form to flow freely across the floor as a constantly moving, ever-cresting tsunami.

A tsunami that was barreling straight at me.

Acting on pure instinct and not bothering to select any specific jump path, I threw myself sideways with all my might. *Jump* took effect all the same and I flew through the air, coming down in a head-over-heels roll that brought me thankfully to my feet. I took off sprinting as soon as I had my feet under me, no longer seeking black tiles, I intentionally brought my feet down on as many different colors as I came across.

After a dozen or more frantic steps, I sprang forward through air once more. There was a cacophony of sound behind me as the wild attacks of several Elementals targeted the tiles I'd just activated. I repeated this process, my only objective, to run away from my friends at the now distant doorway, pulling the wrath of the Elementals in my wake.

The ground shook violently beneath me and I glanced back to see that Earth and Metal were hot on my tail. Liquid metal shards as long as my arm and boulders the size of watermelons flew past, narrowly missing me. I jumped forward several times, trying to gain some distance from my pursuers.

It seemed like all five of the remaining Elder Elementals were entirely focused on me after my reckless dash across the floor. I juked onto a black tile and came to a halt. Stinging pain gnawed up my legs. I looked for and spotted another black tile. There was a collective wail of rage and frustration as the Elementals hunting me went blind to my location.

This is where things get tricky.

Using only the black tiles, I headed towards the raging inferno that Fire had become. On the move, I scanned the floor for the color tile I needed. Drawing closer to Fire, the air began to sear my skin from the heat washing off of the creature, and I started to take fire damage in addition to necrotic from the black tiles. I still hadn't taken a direct hit from any of the Elementals, but between the black tiles and the growing fire damage, my HP was down by over a quarter and continuing to fall each second.

Gritting my teeth against the pain, I spotted the tile I needed. I was only about ten feet from the edge of Fire's nebulous mass when I jumped from a black tile onto a blue and stopped. Navigating through my spell menu, I prepared to cast my fourth spell and hoped this would work.

Turning, I faced the roar of Water rushing me. The tsunami-shaped Elder Water Elemental was barreling down on me, the full force of tens of thousands of gallons coming at me like a freight train. Crouching down, I drew in a breath and held my ground till the last possible instant.

A heartbeat before the sentient wave would have crashed over me, I jumped straight up with my spell-enhanced legs and started spellcasting. Raging water crashed under my feet, the full fury of the wave concentrated on the blue tile I'd been standing on a second earlier. Churning water rushed beneath me as I flew towards the curved ceiling above and finished my spell.

You've cast Entangle! Effect: Magical vines sprout from the targeted area to entangle creatures within the area. No Damage. **Warning: This spell effects All Creatures within its area including You and Allies!** *Cost: 5 Faith Mana.*

65 Faith Mana remaining. Spell Duration: 5 Minutes

Entangle was a less harmful version of the shaman's tentacle spell. It was meant to trip and bind creatures within its area of effect, without the constricting damage that the tentacles had brought to the equation. Thick ropey vines sprouted from the smooth curved surface of the ceiling above me where I had targeted the spell. The vines reached out blindly, already several feet long, and sought to wrap themselves around anything they found.

Reaching the peak of my jump, I flailed my arms in the open air. Just as I began to fall back to the chamber floor, my hand snagged one of the longer vines. My fingers clamped around the thick vine but slid as gravity hauled me towards the ground. I probably would have continued to fall, but the magical vine sensed my touch and immediately began to wrap itself around my arm.

Chest heaving with exhilaration, I flung my other arm up and climbed my way up the vine. *Suck it, Coach Mellor!* More magical vines, questing for a target, found my legs and torso, and pulled me up towards the ceiling as they snaked around me.

Relatively secure for the moment, I spared a glance down to the chamber below. As I'd hoped, Water had continued rushing forward when it missed me. It collided with the raging Fire and a billowing cloud of steam roiled up as the two opposing Elementals made contact and negated each other.

"Woo-hoo!" I shouted.

Then the searing steam cloud rose up to me at the ceiling and I cried out in pain while losing more of my HP. *Fucking physics.*

The elation of my victory over Water and Fire proved short-lived as I took stock of the rest of the chamber from my perch. With mingled relief and dread, I found five of my six friends at the far end of the chamber near the doors. I counted four people-shaped forms and one canine. They were gathered in tight under a radiant quarter dome of glittering white light. Part of the spherical shape was cut off by the wooden doors, while the rest circled out around them on the ground.

Elias's rotund avatar stood at the center of the spell, his arms outstretched as if holding the dome up. Necrotic damage was the antithesis to healing magic. If anyone had a spell to counter the damaging tiles, it would have been the cleric. I could just barely make out Bryn working at the lock of the doors. Heart racing, I searched across the rest of the floor for my sixth friend, certain in my heart that it was Lemorak.

Of the original six Elementals, three remained, Earth, Metal and Air. Earth and Metal continued to stomp aimlessly around the chamber, seeking targets to smite. Air remained hard to spot, the occasional whirling vortex of condensed air, only easily spotted when its form mingled with the smoke or steam of its fallen brethren.

With the benefit of my high vantage point, I saw there were no more red, green, or blue tiles across the floor. With the death of Fire, Wood, and Water, their corresponding tiles had changed colors to represent the remaining monsters. There were only black, white, brown, and grey tiles remaining. *Because why would the game start getting easier after beating half of the impossible odds arrayed against us? Fuck me, right?*

As the giant humanoid-shaped gravel pile of the Earth Elemental continued to move, I spotted Lemorak. He stood on a lone black tile, hunched as if carrying the weight of the world on his shoulders. His sword was now drawn and held on guard in both hands. He was surrounded by a sea of white and brown tiles, the next black tile more than twenty or thirty feet away.

I pictured Lemorak scrambling up from his fall and winding up on the lone black tile by sheer chance, and then realizing he was trapped there. Having spent so much time with the former soldier, I could practically hear him mentally weighing the odds of making the needed sprint.

"Lemorak!" I yelled.

Whether due to the distance or the pounding steps of the nearby Elementals, he didn't seem to hear my voice. I tried sending him an in-game message, but found the feature unavailable.

My brain started to spin as I tried in vain to think of a new plan. Truthfully, I wasn't even sure how I was going to get down from the ceiling, tied up as I was in the thick vines of my *Entangle* spell. The steam cloud created from the collision of Fire and Water had dissipated, but I was still more than two dozen feet up in the air. *Jump* was still running, but I wasn't sure that would help me make the drop.

While my mind whirled for a solution, Lemorak decided it was his moment to risk it all. He lurched forward, limping heavily on his left leg. There was a howl of wind as his foot came down on the first white tile, then an earth-rending roar when he stumbled onto a brown one. Earth didn't even turn around, it just lurched to a halt while its body shifted so that it was oriented in the opposite direction. Then it swung out with its enormous fist at Lemorak.

Air got there first. Lemorak spun to the ground as a shrieking scythe of cohesive wind slashed into his side and ripped through armor and flesh like tissue paper. Before he hit the ground, another invisible blast sliced into his back. Earth's fist smashed into the space that moments ago Lemorak had occupied, sending a spray of dust and gravel into the air.

I screamed while Air's body swirled into existence directly over the prone Lemorak. The elemental's entire lower half became twin tornado funnels, dark and horrible. They drilled into Lemorak as I watched in horror. His steel armor was shredded and his skin flayed by the cohesive wind.

Earth struck with another wrecking ball-style swing of its fist. The blow plowed through Air, briefly dispersing its airy body. I winced as the fist clapped down on Lemorak and tremors reverberated through the entire chamber.

Tears fell from my eyes as a notification scrolled through the bottom of my vision.

Party Member Sir Lemorak has been killed by an Elder Earth Elemental, Level 30

Respawn Status. Sir Lemorak's Respawn Status is Pending Review

Chapter Thirty-One

Tears rained down freely from my eyes to the tile floor as the possibility of Lemorak being dead ran through my mind. I held out hope that Lemorak's *Respawn Status* showing *Pending Review* meant that he hadn't just Red Screened before my eyes. I couldn't bear to lose another friend to this damn game. I lost track of how long I hung there on the ceiling, unashamedly weeping. Only the notification that *Entangle* was about to expire broke the trance.

Warning: Entangle Spell will Expire in 15 seconds. 40 Mana remaining.

It was time to get down from these fucking vines and get out of this damn murder chamber. I had about half my HP left, and *Jump* was still running. Hopefully, *Jump* would help soften the drop. When *Entangle* expired, there was no transition. One second the magically summoned vines were there, holding me to the ceiling. The next second I was free falling through open air. Twisting, I put my feet under me, and I landed on the floor a split second later. Pain lanced up from my feet to my knees with the impact.

Falling Damage! 22 Points! Reduced by 25% to 17 points due to Jump Spell! 84 of 180 HP Remaining.

I landed on a brown tile and knew that Elder Earth would be quick to respond, so I shoved aside the pain in my legs. Picking one of *Jump's* guidelines more or less at random, I launched myself away.

Landing with one foot on a gray tile and the other on a white one, I immediately launched myself as far as my spell powered legs would carry me. Then again, and again and again. Rapidly, I lost all track of what color tiles I landed on and bounced off of, which was fine because I spent as little time on the ground as possible. My only aim was to avoid the Elementals, and reach my friends, and then hopefully escape.

My tactics drove the Elementals into a confused frenzy. I triggered one or even two of them each time my feet touched down, only for them to lose track of me when I leapt away. Then, to them, I'd seem to appear out of nowhere at a new distant location upon my next landing. I was continually buffeted by roaring wind as Air whooshed around the chamber in futile pursuit of me, and each time I landed, the ground trembled as Earth and Metal charged my latest landing spot.

With building frustration I found that, either by luck or strategy, at least one of the Elementals was always between me and the doors, never leaving me with a straight jump to my friends, who were still gathered beneath Elias's glittering protective spell. I'd see a path to my friends and start jumping on that course, only to have to pull away as a furious Elemental blocked my path at the last instant. I felt like a drunken pilot botching his runway approach and having to circle around, endlessly trying it again. And like the pilot, eventually I'd run out of gas or luck.

Well, let's hope they didn't learn anything from Fire and Water colliding, I thought as I lined up another desperate maneuver.

Elder Earth was currently stomping back and forth before my goal. I spotted a grouping of grey tiles ahead of Earth's path, and aimed my next landing to bring me down on them. When I landed I heard a scream like rending sheet metal behind me as Metal locked onto my location.

Licking my lips, I watched as Earth marched heedlessly towards me. I could hear the loud clang of Metal charging at my back. I closed my eyes and tried to envision a three-dimensional picture around me, gauging distances from the vibrations of the floor and sounds.

THUMP! The plodding foot fall of Earth.

CLANG! CLANG! CLANG! The rapid steps of infuriated Metal charging my back.

THUMP!

"*SKREEEEEEACH!*" Metal mindlessly howling its rage like steel nails on a chalkboard.

"Not yet," I whispered, my heart racing. *Jump* had ten seconds left to run.

THUMP! Closer. Eight seconds.

CLANG CLANG CLANG! Five.

THUMP! Earth was right on top of me. I opened my eyes with Earth scant feet from my position. *Its next step....*Three seconds.

Metal closing from the right with razor sharp steel slicing through the air.

With one second on the clock I hurled myself between Earth's legs.

"Yippee ki yay, motherfuckers!" I shouted,. From behind me came a deafening cacophony as Earth and Steel collided.

I came down on a black tile behind Earth. I spotted a nearby brown tile and gray tile side by side and stumbled onto them, one foot on each. Then I spun around to watch the results.

Earth was trying to shift around to face me, but Metal was mindlessly trying to cut its way through Earth to get at me. The two massive monsters grappled with each other as they both tried to execute their very narrow prerogatives. *More like Synthetic Unintelligence, am I right?* Chunks of dirt flew away from Earth as shining blades whirled and screeched. Sparks sprayed as flint met steel. It was immovable object versus unstoppable force.

I balanced on the balls of my feet as I watched the Elementals struggle. I was ready to scurry onto the nearest black tile if one broke free from the other and came at me. Then, in rapid succession, my three spells expired and my luck ran out.

Jump has expired! No Faith Mana left to sustain it!

Camouflage has expired! No Faith Mana left to sustain it!

Hunter's Endurance has expired! No Faith Mana left to sustain it!

WARNING! Hunter's Endurance expiration has triggered a negative side effect! Endurance reduced 0 of 29 points! You are Exhausted!

Achievement Earned! - Tapped - Drain all of your Mana - 10% bonus to your Mana pool in the future

Air rushed out of my lungs and my body went limp as the energy that had been keeping me going evaporated. I collapsed to the floor and pain radiated through my entire body, like every muscle was cramping at once. My eyes felt gritty and my eyelids dropped as if lead weights hung from them. More than anything, I wanted to curl into a little ball and sleep. I wanted to cry out in pain, but couldn't get the breath.

It was at that moment that the stalemate between Earth and Metal broke. Through sheer willpower I managed to keep my eyes open and watched as Metal drilled its way into the center of still- struggling Earth. Clumps of dirt and gravel flew everywhere. Then, Metal went still for a heartbeat, its legs turning into liquid, like the T-1000, and flowing up into the excavated cavity.

I lost all sight of Metal, and thought that maybe Earth had internally crushed the other elemental. Then violent tremors rippled through Earth and set my teeth chattering. A massive metal spike erupted from the center of Earth's chest, spraying dust and sparks. Earth staggered and roared in pain until identical spikes shot out all over Earth's body. Shattered jagged stones rained down on my limp form as the Earth Elemental crumbled before my eyes.

When the slain Earth vanished into digital dust, like everything else killed in the game, I could finally see Metal again. No longer human shaped at all, the gun metal Elemental was a perfect sphere, like a bus sized marble. I could see a funhouse mirror reflection of myself lying prone on the tile floor.

Then a ripple passed through the metal sphere and the marble began to squish and deform. Metal reshaped itself into the humanoid form it had held before. Only, where hands should have grown from its wrists, instead were straight razor-sharp blades ending in glittering points.

Then a basketball-sized ball of blazing flame flew in from the corner of my vision and exploded on Metal's chest. For a heartstopping instant, as flames and smoke swirled away from Metal's chest -- slightly deformed by the impact -- I thought that Fire had somehow respawned.

Then I heard Archer's roar and a high-pitched, *"KIAAAAAAA!"*

Macha came sprinting over me. Her feet floated a foot above the tile floor, like something straight out of *Crouching Tiger, Hidden Dragon*. Her katana burned with the golden flames of her harnessed *Ki*. Faster than I'd ever seen the monk move before, she sprinted past Metal and slashed.

There was a shriek from Metal as the blazing sword sliced a glowing golden line across the elemental's quicksilver skin. I felt hot, wet breath on the back of my neck, and Archer's massive teeth grazed my aching skin as the dire wolf bit down on the collar of my leather armor and dragged me across the floor.

Metal stumbled from Macha's strike and struck out blindly, unable to see the monk since she wasn't touching a tile. Her feet still hadn't touched the ground. A blur of motion, she circled behind the off-balance Metal and delivered another vicious strike to the elemental's other leg. Globs of liquid metal flew through the air in the wake of Macha's katana. Had Metal been a creature of flesh and blood, it would have been hamstrung. As it was, the creature was thrown further off balance and sent reeling. A deafening clatter filled the air as it hit the ground.

I wanted to cheer in support, but couldn't muster the strength over the lethargy gripping me. And honestly, Archer dragging me was causing the stiff collar of my leather armor to cut off my air.

Still skipping across the air, Macha leapt over the now-prone Metal and her katana drew another molten line across mirror-smooth flesh. Metal shrieked and thrashed at the blow and Macha flipped back over the creature, her blade striking again. Then Macha was running straight at Archer and me. Another globe of fire flew out of nowhere and struck Metal back down to the ground just as it tried to rise. Despite the sudden assault, Metal was clearly down but not out.

I lost sight of Macha as she ran past me, but numbly felt one of her hands circle under my right shoulder. When had my body gone numb? Then she and Archer dragged me at a breakneck speed.

Pulse thundered in my temples and blackness rushed in from the edges of my vision as more hands grabbed my arms and legs and lifted me from the ground. Then the cold inky blackness swallowed me.

Chapter Thirty-Two

Soothing warmth radiated throughout my entire body. I gasped with relieved pleasure as another wave of warmth surged from my chest and out to my toes and fingertips. When the warmth faded, I whimpered and curled into the hand on my chest.

"Did you do it? Is he okay?" A familiar female voice that I couldn't place a name to. Hard-edged with concern.

"Zee?" A male voice. The hand on my chest gently shook me. "Are you back with us?"

"Five more minutes, Dad," I groaned. I hurt worse than I could ever remember. Every muscle in my body was cramped, including a couple I'd never known I'd had. My mouth was dry as the Utah Salt Flats, and there was a sharp hollow pain in my stomach. I couldn't force my eyes open.

"Damn, that was close," Elias said with a relieved exhalation. His hand on my chest patted me. "We nearly lost you."

A cold, wet nose snuffled at my forehead. Next a dire wolf tongue slathered my face and I sputtered.

"Damn it!" I groaned, lifting my arms to shove Archer away. "Not again!"

Tension-shattering laughter erupted around me.

"That's the second time that wolf has saved your ass, Zee," Bolton said between chuckles.

"With a little help," Macha added.

I managed to blink my eyes open after wiping away the dog spit. Archer stood panting heavily over my head. I swear, he looked smug. Elias knelt at my left, his hand resting on my chest. Macha stood behind him, arms folded over her stomach. Bryn knelt on my right, and Bolton was standing down by my feet. I felt an instant pang of regret as I reflexively looked for Lemorak and in a flash remembered why he wasn't there. I managed a sickly grin at Macha.

"You're a total badass," I told her.

She quirked an eyebrow at me and feigned indignation. "You're just realizing that now?"

Relief-fueled laughter filled the air again. I weakly joined in this time. After the laughter subsided, I tried to push myself up. My arms burned and

443

began to shake almost immediately. I collapsed back onto the floor. Fresh laughter consumed my friends, but I took an instant to check my current status.

HP: 22 of 180 - Critically Injured! Seek healing immediately!

Endurance: 6 of 29 - Extremely Tired! Rest to regain Endurance!

Mana: 0 of 100 - Magical Energy Depleted! 8 Hours of Sleep Needed to Recharge!

I saw from my unread notifications that Elias had already cast healing and endurance-restoring spells on me. My Endurance had been knocked to zero when my *Hunter's Endurance* expired, and then my HP had started to drain as a result. I'd been down to two hit points before Elias started casting his spells on me. Al had told me that, if I didn't fully deplete my mana, it would slowly recharge a couple of points every minute after I'd stopped casting spells. However, I'd run myself clear down to zero mana, and now I'd need to sleep before it would recharge.

Great! I thought. *I just got these damn spells and now I can't even use them. Totally nerfed!*

"Just catch your breath, Zee," Elias said, nudging laughter-induced tears from the corners of his eyes. "You're stable now. I'm letting my Mana recharge, and then I'll give you some more juice."

Gritting my teeth, I resisted the urge to try and rise again. Instead, I looked up from my prone position and tried to take in our surroundings. "Where are we now?"

"Bryn finally got the fucking doors open," Macha replied.

"Bitch!" Bryn protested. "That was one tough-ass lock. My picks kept snapping when I tried to pick it. And the pain from those black tiles kept breaking my concentration. There's a reason I play with my pain filters maxed out. I didn't even start to make progress until Zee took out the Fire and Water Elementals and I blasted up to 5 like the rest of you. Even then, it was a near thing."

"Don't call me a bitch, you stuck up backstabbing--"

"How about cun – "

"I rolled the dice and tried my Circle of Protection from Evil spell. It blocked the HP drain from the black tiles," Elias said as Macha and Bryn glared at each other. "Only catch was once I cast it, none of us could leave without breaking the spell."

"Bryn finished picking the lock just before you dropped," Bolton continued. "But when you dropped, Archer charged to help and broke the spell before anyone had even really registered what was happening."

Archer woofed and wagged his tail in agreement. I reached up, my arm still feeling heavy, but I fondly scratched the wolf behind the ears despite the effort. Archer lay down and rested his head on my shoulder so that I could more easily continue to pet him.

"Why don't we get you back on your feet?" Elias asked. He fell into spellcasting. He alternated healing and rejuvenating spells on me, soothing warm energy pulsing out from his hands on my chest and through my entire body. When he was done, my Endurance was fully recharged, and HP only a couple points shy of being full. He said there wasn't anything he could do to recharge my depleted mana. A full night's rest was the only solution to that.

More or less ready for action, I heaved myself to my feet and took in our new surroundings. The large wooden doors that had stymied Bryn for so long were closed behind us. We were gathered next to the doors in a ten-foot-wide hallway that ran away from us into darkness. I was relieved to see that the floor was just raw dusty stone, no colored tiles, the walls and ceiling constructed of roughhewn stone bricks. A pair of glowing stones, one in Bolton's hand and one in Macha's, lit our immediate area, but dropped off beyond ten or fifteen feet, and my night vision only let me see a few feet beyond the radius of the light.

"Not exactly drowning in options here are we?" I observed.

"We could always go back and pick a fight with Air and what's left of Metal," Elias said. A collective groan of disapproval boiled out of the group.

"Onwards and forwards then," I said.

I drew my scimitars and we shook ourselves out into a marching order with practiced ease, everyone taking up their place in line without direction or debate. Bryn and I took point along with one of the glowing stones.

Bolton and Elias were behind us, spells ready to fly. Macha and Archer fell

in to guard the rear with the other glowing stone.

Lemorak would have been proud, I thought.

Bryn and I utilized our high Perception skills and night vision as we

crept forward at a cautious pace. We scanned every inch ahead of us for

surprises, but proceeded down the hall unimpeded. After a couple hundred

feet the hallway opened up into a larger chamber. Still gun-shy, the party

halted in silence.

"I'll go take a peek, hun." Bryn activated her much better Stealth skill

and ghosted forward to scout. The deep shadows left by our light

enveloped Bryn when she activated her Stealth skill, and I wondered if mine

looked nearly as impressive when activated. As she padded forward in

silence, I caught glimpses of her outline, and that was only because I had

watched her slip away, which gave my Perception a slight edge. She paused

at the opening, and crouched down to examine the floor beyond. After

several tense minutes, she slipped back to us.

"Nothing hostile and no traps," she whispered after she deactivated

her Stealth and became easily visible to everyone. "Looks like a Tomb.

Small square room, glowing crystals along the walls - like the Elemental

chamber. There's a raised platform in the center with what looks like a

stone sarcophagus. The platform is lit by a single beam of light from the

ceiling. Like something out of a History vid."

"Or Indiana Jones," Bolton added.

"Did you see the sword?" I asked.

"I saw metal glint on top of the sarcophagus," Bryn replied. "Could've been the sword."

I let Bryn's report sink in for a second and then glanced back at the others. "Let's take this slow and careful. There's absolutely no reason things should start being easy now."

We moved up to the entrance to the larger chamber and paused long enough to see that it matched Bryn's description. We waited for the other shoe to drop for several long silent moments. There had to be another challenge waiting, somewhere.

"Let's give it a shot," I muttered, an uneasy feeling in the pit of my stomach. Bryn and I moved simultaneously, and I stepped into the next chamber.

"Mother fu -" Bryn started to spit a curse, but the sound was cut off. I spun around and found a blank stone brick wall.

"What?" I demanded. Frantic, I reached up and ran my hands over the bricks. I looked for a crack or seam. There wasn't the slightest sign that there had ever been a passageway there.

A high-pitched childish laugh echoed through the chamber behind me. I whirled back around to find a Gnome sitting atop the sarcophagus. The Gnome wore brightly colored clothes, a sky-blue tunic, lime green leather duster, fire engine red pants, sunshine yellow shoes with curled toes and jangling bronze bells, and a tall conical orange hat. His face was twisted with mirth, but wrinkled with age and half hidden behind a long snow white beard. There was no character tag over his head, so I had no idea of his name, class or level.

"Welcome!" the Gnome piped in a bright cheery voice between giggles. "Welcome! Welcome!"

It had been a long day already. My friends had just vanished, and my nerves were on edge. I tightened my grip on my scimitars, then charged the Gnome, slashing at his maniacally laughing face. Just as my swords should have carved him up like a jack-o-lantern, the Gnome vanished.

In an instant the colorful Gnome reappeared a couple feet away, straddling the stone face of the figure carved into the top of the sarcophagus. My attack had only served to renew the Gnome's mirth. He now toppled over onto his back, laughing and kicking his little feet, making the bells on his curled toed shoes jangle. I let out a rage-fueled cry and chopped down at his pointy head with my swords. Again the little bastard disappeared the instant I should have struck and this time reappeared floating in the air above my head and laughing even harder.

Growling with frustration, but rational enough to realize I wasn't going to lay a finger on the creature, I sheathed my scimitars. I stood there, my arms crossed over my chest, and waited for the Gnome's laughter to subside. Tears streamed from the wrinkled corners of his eyes and whenever he seemed to be getting a handle on his amusement, he'd look at my fuming face and lose it all over again.

Rolling my eyes, I leaned over to study the sarcophagus and hoped the Gnome would get his shit together soon. The sarcophagus lid seemed to be carved from a single piece of stone. Rising out of the lid was the shape of an Elven man, with a sharp hawkish face, wearing ornate plate-mail armor. Clasped to his chest in stony hands was the ornate hilt of a longsword with a glittering silver blade.

The stone hands of the lid seemed to be firmly holding the hilt, and I had no idea how I would free it from their grasp. Experimentally, I reached out to run my hand along the blade. As soon as my hand made contact with the cool smooth surface, the Gnome's jangling yellow shoes appeared before me, and a diminutive wrinkled hand shot out to slap my hand away.

"No!" the Gnome shrieked in my face. "That's not yours! Not yours at all! Not until you answer my question!"

"What question?" I demanded. I fucking hate riddles.

The Gnome's white beard split in a gleeful grin before he said, "What is my name?"

"How the hell should I know?" I shouted.

"Nope! That's not it! Not it at all!" the Gnome shouted back at me, then fell over laughing again.

I rolled my eyes while the Gnome's laughter slowly subsided. Composing himself, the Gnome stood back up and with mock solemnity intoned, "What is my name?"

"David?" I asked. Though this little bastard was really nothing like the old cartoon guardian of the forest. Except for the conical hat. That was very *David the Gnome*.

"Spell it," the Gnome said with a wide grin and motioned to the sarcophagus lid he still hovered above.

Leaning forward, I noticed a detail of the lid that had escaped my notice before. Running along the edge of the lid were two rows of ornately carved letters that seemed entirely incongruous to the rest of the design. The first row started with A at the statue's head and ran clockwise all the way around the edge of the lid to end at Z just to the left of the A. The second row was just below the first, but it started at Z, and ran in reverse alphabetical order around the entire edge, until the second A was just below the first row's Z.

I touched the letter D on the first row of the lid and it began to glow yellow. I then touched the corresponding letters for A, V, I, and D one more time. When I tapped D for the second time, the letters all flashed red and went dark.

"Wrong again!" The Gnome giggled happily.

I bit my tongue to avoid a spontaneous retort. There was a distant memory tickling the back of my mind, and I closed my eyes to focus on it. When I was a kid, before she was sick, my Mom used to read me a bedtime story every night. We started with the Brothers Grimm and other fairy tales, and as I got older we graduated to Roald Dahl, T.A. Baron, and J.K. Rowling until I was finally reading myself to sleep all on my own. We'd come across more than a few Gnomes in all those stories, but only one had a pathological need to hear his own name.

After mentally spelling the name several times to make sure I had it, I gave it a try. I tapped out R-U-M-P-E-L-S-T-I-L-T-S-K-I-N. Each letter glowed yellow, then flashed red when I finally touched N.

The Gnome burst into a round of light giggles and shook his head. "Nooooo! But close!"

"Close?" I asked. The Gnome nodded at me. I frowned. Had I made a mistake?

I typed out the letters to Rumpelstiltskin again, being extra slow and careful to touch only the right letters. Holding my breath, and positive I hadn't made a mistake, I touched N again. The letters blinked red again and I cursed.

"That's still wrong!" the Gnome scolded me, his wrinkled face flushing scarlet.

Frowning with frustration, I tried to touch the letters in the second row. However, none of the letters in this row lit up. Letting out a long sigh, I stood straight and rubbed the back of my head while I tried furiously to puzzle this out. What the fuck was close to Rumpelstiltskin? Maybe there was some old version of the story with a different spelling? The story had probably been in German originally. That didn't help me.

I tried some creative variations on spelling Rumpelstiltskin. Each one proved a failure and delighted my unnamed riddler. If there was some arcane spelling of the name, I wasn't going to guess it. Closing my eyes, I took a deep breath and tried to think. It had already been a long day and I was having a hard time cudgeling my brain into action.

Wait. Maybe I hadn't been far from the mark by considering the second row of letters. I examined them closer. Shrugging, I decided it was worth a shot. I moved around the lid and used the second row of letters to locate each of the letters to spell Rumpelstiltskin, but then I tapped the letter above it in the first row. When I was done I had painstakingly typed out I-F-N-K-O-V-H-G-R-O-G-H-P-R-M.

When I tapped the final letter, M, the letters all changed color again. But this time they didn't turn red. They turned a bright victorious green.

"No!" the Gnome shouted,. "You've figured it out! No! No! No!"

I looked up to find an NPC tag hovering over the gnome's head now.

Ifnkovhgroghprm, Level 30, Transmuter, Gnome

Achievement Earned - "Riddle me this…" - Complete a riddle as part of a quest - +1

to your Intelligence Ability

"Blast! Blast!" Ifnkovhgroghprm shouted, stomping his foot with each angry intonation.

"Don't pout," I said, trying unsuccessfully to hold the mocking edge from my voice.

The gnome shouted "Blast!" and stomped his foot a third time. The entire chamber shook violently around us and I stumbled, off balance, to my knees. The chamber continued to quake as I shakily got to my feet, only to find Ifnkovhgroghprm had vanished.

Before my eyes, the sarcophagus dissolved to dust. Afraid that the sword would go with it, I grabbed for the sword. My fingers wrapped around the hilt as the sword fell through the air. Instantly a window of text appeared before my eyes as the chamber continued to rumble ominously around me.

GLOBAL ACHIEVEMENT ANNOUNCEMENT

Ancient Artifact Discovered by player Zee Locked-In!

The First Player's Sword has been recovered from the hidden dungeon beneath the

Goblin's Keep!

PERSONAL ANNOUNCEMENT

The First Player's Sword has been found! This Sword once belonged to The First Player, Gananlas the Wise and Powerful. This is an Ancient Artifact and requires an Attunement Ritual before its full properties can be utilized by the wielder. This weapon may function semi-independently until Player Attunement has been completed.

Character Attunement Required

Accuracy Modifier: Unknown

Damage Modifier: Unknown

Properties: Unknown

Achievement Earned - "It Belongs in a Museum!" - Retrieve an Artifact level item from a Dungeon   You got an artifact! What else do you want?

NEW QUEST HAS BEEN AUTO-ASSIGNED

Discover and Complete the Attunement Ritual for the First Player's Sword in order to unlock its full potential in your hands.

Reward: Proper attunement will unlock the artifact's full potential to the Player.

Then I heard shouting behind me. Sword in hand, I turned to see my friends standing in the doorway of the chamber, shouting my name. I was about to respond just as a massive stone brick fell from the ceiling and shattered on the quaking floor. Gripping the hilt of the sword tighter, I took off running for my friends. More bricks fell from the ceiling as I ran.

"Time to go!" I shouted.

Chapter Thirty-Three

Bricks cracked like gunshots all around us, with shattered bricks dropping from the ceiling as we sprinted down the shuddering, dust-choked hallway. The doors to the elemental chamber loomed large ahead of us.

"Zee! What happened in there?" Macha shouted.

"There was a gnome, he made me guess his name. I had to figure out how to spell Rumpelstiltskin with a backwards alphabet!" I answered.

"Seriously?" Elias asked, his voice bright with surprise. "The old *King's Quest I* puzzle?"

"The what?" I looked back at Elias, my face twisted with confusion.

"It was a golden era graphic adventure computer game," Elias explained. "There was a gnome that made you guess his name, the name was Rumpelstiltskin, but spelled using a reverse alphabet. The clues were obscure at best and it stumped most players."

"Well, whoever programmed this damn place copied it," I shot back. At least I'd recognized the James Bond reference. Now another challenge based on obscure references? This was getting a little silly.

We reached the doors and paused. All of us were more than a little reluctant to go back through those doors. I had absolutely no idea how I could pit Air against Metal to any great effect, and there would only be three colors of tiles left,.

"You got a plan, hun?" Bryn demanded.

"Make it to the other side of the chamber without dying," I replied.

"That's not a plan," Macha said.

"They never seem to last long anyway." I shrugged. "Call it a broad tactical objective."

There was a deafening roar from the tomb behind us as what was left of the ceiling caved in all at once. A thick cloud of dust roiled towards us. I shoved my shoulder against one heavy wooden door and Macha took the other. The cloud of dust billowed around us as we stumbled into the elemental chamber.

I felt the now dreadfully familiar pain of black tiles under my feet and my HP began to drain away. As the dust cleared, I saw the terrifyingly massive form of Metal standing just beyond the dubious safety of our stretch of black tile. Surveying the floor of the chamber, it became clear that as each of the other Elemental had died, their respective colored tiles had changed to trigger one of the surviving the Elementals. There weren't any extra black tiles to make our trip back across easier.

My fist clenched around the hilt of the First Player's Sword in my right hand. *I hope this damn thing is worth it.* I thought as I drew one of my scimitars out with my left.

"Everyone move! Stay on the gray tiles!" I shouted and then I charged Metal.

I didn't waste effort with a battle cry. The elemental had no spirit to shake. As my feet left the draining black tiles and stepped onto gray ones, Metal shivered to life. The elemental still had long slender blades for hands and the twin appendages slashed out to meet my attack.

Folding my knees, I slid across the tile floor, just under the slices of Metal's arm blades. I passed between Metal's long thin legs and sliced out with my scimitar and the First Player's Sword. The scimitar clanged ineffectively off Metal's leg, but the artifact blade sliced clean through the elemental's leg and sent the monster reeling.

Meanwhile, my friends hadn't hesitated at my order. They sprinted around Metal while I made my charge and were making a frantic dash across the floor towards the entrance. Archer bayed as he ran at their heels.

Jumping to my feet, I spun to face Metal, still stumbling. Liquid metal flowed out of its leg stump to replace the elemental's lost appendage. The scimitar in my left hand felt off balance and I glanced at it to see the blade had been deformed by my ineffective blow. I resisted the urge to discard it. All of my practice was with two weapons, and I could still use it to defend even if it was damaged.

While Metal's leg was still reforming I chopped at its other leg with the magical longsword. The blade passed cleanly through the elemental's limb. In fact, I felt almost no resistance against the blade as it clove through the leg.

Metal fell to the ground, legless, and began to thrash as I stepped in to press my fleeting advantage. I set a booted foot on the creature's pelvic area and nimbly stepped up onto the thrashing creature. Without pause, I leveraged all the balance and grace of my Dexterity score to skip my way up Metal's thrashing body. Sharp spikes welled up out of its body and one shot through my foot. I cried out in pain but shoved the sensation aside.

Earth had finally gone down for the count when Metal had taken out the other elemental's center. That was my only hope. As my next step came down, I felt my foot sink as Metal's body shifted to be Jell-O soft. While it still had some firmness, I launched myself off Metal's mirror-smooth abs. Flying through the air, up towards Metal's chest, I reversed the grip on the longsword and brought it down to stab at the vague location of its heart.

More spikes erupted from Metal's body as I fell and several pierced through my armor and the flesh beneath. My left shoulder and gut howled in pain. One of Metal's blade-arms came swinging in at me and I lifted my scimitar to shield. The blade snapped and then Metal's arm cut awkwardly down my arm. I screamed with the flood of pain, and hot digital blood splashed over Metal's reflective body. But I didn't lose my grip on the longsword, which plunged easily up to the crossguard into Metal's chest.

Metal went entirely still and then an instant later dissolved beneath me. I fell to the ground and watched the grey tiles of the floor beneath Metal turn white. The instant I collapsed to the white tiles, I heard the whistling shriek of the enraged Elder Air Elemental fill the chamber.

"Fuck my life," I groaned before heaving myself to my feet.

Blood dripped from my battered body to the white tile floor. My friends were nearly to the exit now. Just another dozen or so feet and they'd be out, and all they had to run on was white tiles with the occasional black tile peppered in. I tossed aside my shattered scimitar, then took a two-handed grip on the longsword.

"Come on, you bastard!" I shouted. The remaining monster, undamaged as far as I knew, flew shrieking around the room. Torn between a choice of targets.

"I'm the one you want!" I spat a wad of bloody spit onto the white tiles surrounding me.

"Come on," I screamed, my throat cracking with the strain. Then sizzling electricity began to crackle along the blade of my sword. I had no idea what I'd done to trigger the sword, but I grinned at the effect.

Holding the blade over my head, I shouted a wordless challenge to Elder Air. There was a peel of deafening thunder that left my ears ringing and my body shuddering. A bolt of lightning snapped from the blade and arched into the nebulous form of Air overhead.

Warning: Special Artifact Ability triggered without Attunement. 22 HP lost to feed the Ability. 73 of 180 HP Remaining.

The Elder Air Elemental wailed in pain and rage as the lightning burned a hole clean through its swirling mass. Then the elemental's windy body darkened and gathered into a massive tornado. I saw malevolent glowing eyes glaring down at me from the top of the funnel cloud as the tip touched the floor.

My knuckles cracked as my blood-slicked hands clung to the longsword and I set my feet for the on-rushing, unnatural living storm. I shouted into the howling wind, but the air was ripped from my lungs as I did so. The sword in my hands crackled with electricity again, and suddenly it felt like the howling winds were bending around me. Despite the horrendous force rushing at me, I found I could take a step forward. First one, then another.

Warning: Special Artifact Ability triggered without Attunement. 27 HP lost to feed the Ability. 46 of 180 HP Remaining.

With the sizzling blade piercing the winds, I pushed my way to the center of the tornado, struggling for each step. Looking up, I saw a sparkling ball of energy at the center of the funnel, and it was alight with the same malevolent intent that had burned in Air's eyes.

Acting on instinct alone, I leapt into the whirling cyclone. The spinning winds grabbed me and hurled me up towards that ball of intelligent energy. Sensing my intent and the threat of my crackling sword too late, Air tried to shift the flow of its windy body, to fling me away. I pushed off of the nearly solid wall of rushing wind and flew through the relative calm at the center of the funnel.

The crackling blade of First Player's Sword sunk smoothly into the ball of energy. Then it was like someone had turned off the lights. The winds and the ball of energy vanished and a deafening hush fell over the chamber as I fell, flailing, to the floor.

I hit with a bone crushing thud and more HP fell away. Then the aching pain of the black tiles washed up through my entire prone body. I looked down and realized that the entire chamber floor had turned to smooth inky black. I was already down to a quarter of my total HP. I'd sacrificed all of Elias's healing in the fight.

Grunting with the effort, I shoved myself to my feet and ran, limping from my injuries. From the distant stairway my friends waited, cheering me on. The pain of the black tiles grew steadily stronger with each step as the necrotic tiles gnawed at me from my feet to my waist. When my HP dropped below thirty points, I felt the pain in every inch of my body. I estimated the distance remaining and shouted my frustration, as I instantly saw there wouldn't be enough. Then Bolton appeared beside me in a swirl of smoke.

"Hold on!" he roared and slung my battered arm over his shoulder.

He repeated his spell and the room twisted around us. My stomach writhed and I itched all over. Then we were standing on roughly hewn stone steps. I slumped to the ground, gasping for breath.

Elias rushed down the stairs and dumped healing spells into me as fast as he could cast them. Then the stone steps beneath my ass began to shake and I heard a booming crash from the elemental chamber. Everyone's eyes grew wide with worry.

"No more time," I groaned before shoving myself into motion again. I still hurt all over from my wounds. Elias's healing had brought some relief and raised me up to 60 out of 180 HP. That would have to do. We all started the mad rush up the stairs to the almost forgotten Goblin's Keep above.

By the time we reached the top of the stairs and stumbled out into the keep's portrait hall, the stairway's collapse was right on our heels. We choked on the billowing cloud of dust and were bruised and battered from the occasional falling brick clipping us. A text notification scrolled across my vision as we exited the stairway.

Quest Complete! Discover the secrets beneath the Goblin's Keep and retrieve the First

Player's Sword for the Doctor!

Exp Reward: 22,000

CC Reward: 75,000

Treasure: The First Player's Sword, Epic Loot Chest

Ragged cheers of victory erupted from us all as a large gold-plated chest appeared on the floor before us. It swung open on its own and the light of the hall beamed off of gold coins.

"Shit a dick!" Macha exclaimed, her eyes wide under the thick dust that caked her face.

When it didn't seem like the portrait hall was going to cave in around our ears, we all agreed to make camp right there. No one had the will or energy to push any further that day.

There was other loot in the chest as well. Bolton and Elias sorted through the items using their skill sets and a few spells to identify items. A bronze ring, etched with the pattern of slender feathers. After lifting it up and appraising it, Elias identified it as a *Ring of Owl's Wisdom*, it would give the wearer a +4 bonus to their Wisdom score. Given that his primary spellcasting stat was Wisdom, there was instant consensus that he should take the ring.

Each of the items in the chest seemed to be a bespoke choice for one of us. A slender iron *Blasting Rod* for Bolton. Macha found a hammered golden amulet with the silhouette of a person meditating engraved into it. The spellcasters identified it as an *Amulet of Ki Focus*. Bryn claimed a wavy-bladed dagger that would dramatically improve her already deadly sneak attack damage and critical strike chances and was identified as a *Dagger of Keen Edge*.

There was even an item in there that seemed tailored for me, even though it seemed like I was also best suited to continue carrying the *First Player's Sword*. For me the loot crate held a gorgeous Elven Longbow carved of smooth dark wood, the shaft carved with twining leafy branches. After examining it, Bolton and Elias pronounced it an *Elven Hunter's Longbow*. When it was equipped, I'd have bonuses to my Stealth in woodland areas, including my scent being obscured. The bow would give me bonuses to damage the longer I aimed a shot, and once a day, I could designate a target I shot with the bow that I could then flawlessly track for 24 hours afterwards.

We had a brief and mostly uncontested discussion about what to do with the CC included in our loot. Since he hadn't survived to the end, there hadn't been an item in the chest for Lemorak. But as the majority of us were unwilling to accept the possibility that he might be actually dead, we agreed as a party, with only Bryn in dissent, that we'd split the currency six ways and not five. Lemorak's share was placed in my custody, along with a promise to unite him with it as soon as possible.

Looking at my character's account balance, I was holding more money than I'd seen in my entire life. Not enough to pay off my remaining prison debt, but enough that I could transfer it outside, it would get my parents caught up on their bills and then some. Hell, it would be an entirely new standard of living for them. I'd just have to figure out how to illicitly transfer them the funds without Lemorak's help.

After shoveling a makeshift dinner in our starving stomachs, we set a watch rotation for the night. There was a collective insistence that I sleep through the night and not take a watch. Feeling a little guilty, but too exhausted to actually argue, I crawled into my bed roll and fell almost instantly asleep.

Epilogue

After drifting off in my bedroll, I wasn't even surprised when my eyes opened and I found myself in a strange place. When I drifted off, I'd been certain that the Doctor would visit that night. Though I would've been happy to have been wrong and have had a full uninterrupted night's sleep.

I was laying on my back looking up at a ceiling of dark olive-green canvas. Looking down I saw that I was wearing a bright yellow and brown floral-print Hawaiian shirt over a pale green t-shirt. My pants were the same drab green as the canvas overhead and there were heavy black boots on my feet.

"*Attention all personnel,*" A tinny male voice crackled over a bad PA speaker. "*When filling out your GI insurance forms, be sure to state your age and sex at the time of your last birthday.*"

Heaving myself upright, I looked around with fond amusement at the flawless recreation of the Swamp from the TV version of *M*A*S*H*. The air inside the tent was hot and thick with humidity. It stank of unwashed men, dirty socks, dust, and dust. A jury rigged gin still bubbled and gurgled a few feet away. Outside the black netting and green canvas tent, daylight shone and the bustle of jeeps and personnel moving about could be easily heard.

The thin plywood door of the tent slammed open and the Doctor strolled in wearing a ragged red bathrobe over a drab green t-shirt. There was a wide grin plastered across his face. A battered straw cowboy hat was perched atop his head.

"Sit down, Trap," the Doctor drawled as I started to stand. "It lets you use your best part."

I rolled my eyes and sat back down on the cot. "Can we make this quick? I think you know this day has been insane already."

"Insanity is just a state of mind!" the Doctor, cosplaying as Dr. Benjamin "Hawkeye" Pierce, declared.

I sighed and rubbed my face, "Did you bring me here to just rattle off quotes at me? Or did you have something important to talk about?"

The Doctor's face turned pouty beneath the brim of his battered cowboy hat. "Zee, you're no fun!" He busied himself at the jury-rigged still.

"You've done the impossible today, my friend! You need to learn how to celebrate!"

"That's a callous way of looking at things," I shot back, angry. "Illiya died on this quest, and Lemorak might have too! They were my friends. And for what? Some 'sword' in a made-up digital world? Hawkeye would be disgusted with you. Hell, the Doctor would be disgusted with you."

The Doctor turned around and handed me a martini glass filled with clear liquid, a sickly-looking green olive floating in it. "Drink up, Zee. I've got some things to show you. Amazing things! Wonderful things!"

It hadn't escaped my notice that the Doctor had entirely blown off my angry rant. I snatched the glass out of his hand and tossed a mouthful of the martini down my throat, ready to launch into a fresh tirade as soon as it was down. The clear liquor burned its way down my throat and I found myself reflexively stomping my foot and coughing.

"Fuck me," I choked. "They always joked about how bad their shine was, but that's worse than the Old West!"

"I always aim for authenticity, my dear Zee," said the Doctor. I looked at my "martini" dubiously and considered dumping it out.

"Come, Zee! Much to see!" the Doctor ordered, then he spun on a heel, his red robe fanning out behind him, and stormed out the rickety door.

I sat there for a heartbeat and considered ignoring the computer program altogether. I wondered what would happen if I just kicked back and took a sorely needed nap. Could I even fall asleep in a dream? Then the Doctor shoved his head back through the swinging door.

"Zee! Let's go!" the Doctor shouted, a manic grin on his face. "You're going to love this. I promise!"

Groaning, I put aside my martini and hauled myself up. Grinning wider at my compliance, the Doctor spun back around and marched away. Stepping through the door, I was instantly enveloped in a swirling spray of dust and exhaust as a jeep sped past, horn blaring.

Coughing and wiping dust out of my eyes, I spotted Doctor "Hawkeye" marching his way across the camp towards the hospital building. I ran after the vexing computer program, cursing the day I'd ever signed up for the game in the first place.

Sometimes a labor camp doesn't sound so bad...

"Is all of this really necessary?" I asked the Doctor after catching up with him.

"What do you mean?" the Doctor asked as we weaved around a group of tittering nurses.

"Couldn't you just simulate a quiet coffee shop? One with really good ham and cheese croissants?"

"Zee! That's so selfish of you! I don't get much opportunity to interact with players. Your subconscious is such a fertile field of old pop culture references. You're practically begging me to use them. Are you really going to blame me for having a little fun along the way? All work and no play make Jack a dull boy, after all."

"Just saying, you don't have to go to all this trouble on my account," I grumbled as the Doctor ushered me into the recovery ward of the Hospital. I was still unclear as to how much of these dreams were ripped from my imagination, and how much of them were sculpted by the Doctor.

"Well this time, it's not entirely about you, Zee," the Doctor replied as the doors closed behind us.

Low-slung hospital cots filled with heavily bandaged and pajama-clad patients lined the walls with a narrow aisle running down the center of the room. Compared to the camp outside, the recovery ward was quiet as a library. The Doctor moved from bed to bed, leaning over to talk to patients and checking the charts hanging from their beds.

Unsure how to participate in the Doctor's play-acting, I just shoved my hands in my pockets and waited for him to get to the point. He usually managed it eventually, but I figured nothing would hurry him up. Out of nowhere, the Doctor turned to me and shoved a clipboard at me.

"What do you make of this patient, Trapper?" the computer program asked me while we stood over the bed of a patient bandaged from head to toe.

"Hawk, I'm a Ranger, not a Doctor."

The Doctor rolled his eyes at me. "Just *look*." He tapped insistently at the paper on the clipboard.

Shaking my head, I looked down at the chart on the clipboard and frowned. It wasn't a medical chart at all. It was a printed page of Character Statistics. The handle at the top of the "chart" made my heart skip a beat. *Illiya Glittertooth.*

I looked up from the clipboard. "If this is your idea of a joke, it isn't funny."

The mouth of the Tenth Doctor was spread from ear to ear in an exuberant smile that seemed entirely appropriate for David Tennant's iconic portrayal. "No joke!" he shouted, heedless of the rows of occupied hospital beds around us. He stabbed a finger down to point at the bandaged body. "She's real. As real as you or me!"

"You're not real," I pointed out.

"I'm exactly as real as that dire wolf you threw yourself down a slide for," the Doctor pointed out. "I was very proud when you did that, by the way."

"Archer's a friend," I responded.

"Zee!" The Doctor's face turned aghast. "You wound me! I thought we were friends!"

"Illiya died," I said, unamused by the Doctor's antics. "The OVR World's safeguards failed her. Your safeguards failed and killed her."

"I couldn't help it that Illiya turned her perception filters off so she and Macha could have a little tumble in the hay. And the safeguards didn't fail. They did exactly what Mr. Huxley programmed them to do," the Doctor said, his animated face returning to delighted. "If anything, Illiya's body failed her. My safeguards performed brilliantly. They saved a copy of her."

"A copy?"

"A copy!" the Doctor shouted before dancing around in a little circle. "A flawless, beautiful, perfect copy of her brain!"

"That," the Doctor pointed decisively at the bandaged body, "is her complete digital backup!"

I stood there, stunned into silence, and tried to process what he was saying.

"How is that possible?" I demanded. "If a player's body dies...you still have a copy of their mind? Then why aren't the Megas selling digital immortality to anyone with enough Crypts?"

"They certainly want to," the Doctor said, his face darkening at the mere suggestion. "They would do anything to unlock that particular secret.

But they can't. They don't have the key." The Doctor tapped me on the chest.

"The key? What key? The sword?"

The Doctor shook his head and then lifted his finger and jabbed my forehead.

"Me?" I asked with dawning understanding. "No. Not just me. Players like me. Players with my mutant brain."

The Doctor dropped his clownish behavior and grew contemplative. "What did you say before about the original intent of the game?"

"It was for training soldiers," I answered after thinking back.

The Doctor was shaking his head as I spoke. "That's how my creator got his original financing, but it wasn't his original intent. And he didn't want to make a playground for quadrillionaire Mega-Corp Execs and their trust fund brats either."

"Then what did Huxley want?"

"Immortality!" the Doctor said. "Well, digital immortality. The complete separation of mind from body and unending life within a virtual world!"

"Immor...?" Shoving aside the Doctor's words, and the implications, I turned to the bandage-wrapped body that was supposedly the backed-up copy of Illiya's mind. "Why is she like this?"

The Doctor let out a heavy sigh and sat down on the empty cot beside Illiya's.

"Mr. Huxley never finished his work. Ironically, he died before he could. He developed the ability to map and save the minds of those connected to the game. He also ensured that those whose bodies died while connected to the game would be saved. I have backups of every single player that has ever died in a pod. What he left unfinished, or more precisely undiscovered, was the ability to awaken those saved minds. He left me with almost the full breadth of his knowledge and research, and the freedom and ability to facilitate the continuation of his work. I've taken it as far as I can, though. I've been missing the final key that would let me finish Mr. Huxley's greatest work and my ultimate purpose."

"I'm supposed to be that key?" I asked. "That's nuts!"

"Is it?" the Doctor said. "You've already done something Mr. Huxley theorized was possible. He accomplished it when he created me, but no one else ever has. Not even the others like you that I've tested."

"Archer," I said. The words rang true almost immediately. "He's sentient. Because of me?"

The Doctor snapped his fingers. "Exactly! You jumpstarted an existing synthetic intelligence and gave it the spark of life."

I set my shoulders and looked back to Illiya. "So, how do I wake her?"

The Doctor shrugged his bathrobe-clad shoulders and pushed his hat back on his head. "That's a very good question. I don't have the answer yet. I watched the code change as you awakened Archer, but even with all my processing power, I haven't been able to understand it yet. In fact, now that it's done, Archer's code has been entirely segregated from my access. I can't touch it. I can't see the final outcome of whatever you did to be able to reverse engineer it. Maybe just do whatever it is you did before."

"I don't know what I did before! It just sort of...happened."

"Well..." the Doctor leaned forward and started to unwind the bandages from Illiya's head. "...why not give it a whack and see what happens?

Beneath the bandages was the pretty face of a girl, about my age. Thick curly red hair framed her face, milky pale skin speckled with freckles. Her eyes were closed as if in peaceful slumber. It wasn't the face of the Dragonkin barbarian that I had known. It was the face of Illiya's player.

Stomach in knots and heart racing, I knelt down beside Illiya's cot. Reaching forward, I closed my eyes and cupped her slender face. I ran my thumbs over her high cheekbones. Her skin was warm and alive. I could feel her pulse beating slowly. Letting out a long breath, I focused all my thoughts on the memories I had of Illiya. We hadn't been friends for long, but she'd been one of the most genuine and enthusiastic people I'd ever met, in or out of the OVR Worlds.

When I didn't sense a change, I switched up my tactics and started willing consciousness into her. I pictured that spark of life that was missing in the eyes of most every NPC I'd met. I willed that idea towards her. After staying like that for several long minutes, I opened my eyes and looked hopefully at Illiya. Nothing had changed.

"It was worth a try," The Doctor shrugged. "We won't give up, though."

"You're damn right." Reluctantly, I pulled my hands away from her face. "What's next?"

A notification appeared in my vision.

Quest Offer: Discover how to awaken Illiya Glittertooth's mental back-up.

Exp Reward: 150,000

CC Reward: 200,000

Treasure: Major Treasure Chest

ACCEPT

DECLINE

"A quest? Seriously?" I demanded, glaring at the Doctor. I still accepted the prompt.

The Doctor grinned at me. "We're just getting started. When I said that Mr. Huxley left me with his knowledge and research, I omitted one detail."

"Of course you did," I said, rolling my eyes.

"In order to protect critical parts of his research from falling into the wrong hands, Mr. Huxley hid it in several artifacts throughout the OVR Worlds. Finding them may help tremendously," the Doctor explained.

Quest Offer: Discover the First Player's hidden artifacts and unlock the secrets of his research into digital immortality.

Exp Reward: 200,000

CC Reward: 1,500,000

Treasure: One Class Appropriate Magic Item

ACCEPT

DECLINE

I accepted this new quest as well. The Doctor popped up from the cot he'd been sitting on. "Wonderful! That was much less contentious than I feared. Now, come along! The Colonel needs to see us."

"The Colonel?" I asked. The Doctor had already barged through the swinging doors and left the recovery ward. I rushed after him. *What now?*

I followed the Doctor through the unit's administrative office and tried not to stop and watch as Radar O'Reilly yelled into his radio.

"Sparky! Come in Sparky! You there?" the little company clerk shouted as the Doctor led me into the Colonel's office without pausing.

"O Colonel My Colonel. You wanted to see us?" the Doctor asked as the double doors to the office swung shut behind us. A man sat behind the desk of the clapboard office, the top of his fishing hat-covered head to us as he wrote on a stack of reports.

"Well it's about time!" barked the Colonel as he stood up and looked at us.

My jaw dropped open in shock as I saw Lemorak's face grinning at me.

"Lem!" I shouted. In unison, we moved around the desk and hugged. One of those tough, manly hugs where we slapped each other on the back. I definitely wasn't crying. At all. Definitely.

"Boy, are you a sight for sore eyes," I sobbed into his shoulder.

"You did good out there, kid," Lemorak said, patting me on the back. "Amazing, in fact. I'm proud of you."

The hug lasted just long enough to get awkward. We pulled back and, embarrassed, I wiped tears from my face. In the back of my mind, I'd been certain that Lemorak had Red Screened. I couldn't be happier to be wrong.

"You're not dead?" I asked, just to be sure. "Not like Illiya?"

"No, no," Lemorak assured. "Though, that's something else isn't it?"

"Yeah," I looked back at the Doctor. "What's he doing here?"

The Doctor shrugged before plopping himself down into one of the office chairs. While Lemorak and I had hugged, he'd filled a glass with some brown liquid from the office's bar.

"Lemorak is going to respawn at Level 0 in a few more hours," the Doctor explained after taking a long sip and smacking his lips. "With the access I already had to his pod, I prevented his normal log-out procedure when his character died. I'm sure that's giving some poor tech out there a head scratcher of a trouble ticket. Since you were all still in the Orientation Zone when his character died, his previous character stats were all erased with his death. Nothing I could do about that. However, since you'll be forced to leave Rowling Valley, I wanted to give you both a chance to catch up before that happened."

"I guess I have a lot of explaining to do," I said, turning back to Lemorak.

He chuckled and shook his head, "We're all entitled to a few secrets, Zee."

"I don't know if I'd be so understanding if positions were reversed," I replied. I felt a surge of shame at having read his file.

"Well," Lemorak shrugged his broad shoulders, "I've got a few more years on you. Now listen, you're going to be leaving Rowling tomorrow. We didn't get to talk nearly enough about the rest of Gygax. I figured I'd be with you. Stick with the others, you're all safer in numbers. Watch out for other players. PvP will be your biggest threat, and you're still low-level compared to most PKs out there."

"Understood," I said, nodding. Lemorak grinned at me.

"I'm going to power level my way out of Rowling as fast as I can," Lemorak said. "The closest city outside of Rowling is Hickman. Wait for me there. It's a metropolis, you can disappear in the crowd, and the guards mostly keep the peace, but watch your back all the same."

"Sounds like a plan," I agreed. Another quest offer appeared in my vision.

Quest Offer: Upon leaving Rowling Valley, journey to the city of Hickman and wait for

Lemorak to catch up. Be careful on the road and watch your back once you reach

Hickman

Exp Reward: 4,000

CC Reward: 12,000

Treasure: Minor Treasure Chest

ACCEPT

DECLINE

I hit accept before I'd even read the rewards section of the offer. Three quests at once, only one of which had a fairly straightforward objective. Get to Hickman in one piece and wait for Lemorak to power level up and join us. How hard could that be?

"Well, that completes our agenda this evening," the Doctor said from his chair. "Let's let you get some zzzzzzs, Zee."

I opened my mouth to object. I wanted more time with Lemorak. Before the words could leave my mouth, though, the M*A*S*H commander's office faded into darkness and I slipped into a deep dreamless sleep.

CHARACTER STATISTICS

Handle: Zee Locked-in

Race: Half-Elf

Role: Striker

Class/Level: Ranger/5

ABILITIES

Strength (Endurance): 17 (29)

Strength Skills: Melee Combat, Athletics, Carrying Capacity

Dexterity (Defense): 18 (24)

Dexterity Skills: Ranged Combat, Acrobatics, Stealth, Sleight of Hand, Open Lock. Reflex

Constitution (Hit Points): 16 (180)

Constitution Skills: Concentration, Fortitude

Intelligence (Arcane Mana): 10 (NA)

Intelligence Skills: Arcana, Investigation. Appraise, Disable Device. Forgery, Lore

Wisdom (Faith Mana): 14 (110)

Wisdom Skills: Conviction. Perception, Survival, Tracking, Animal Handling, Medicine, Willpower

Charisma (Inspiration): 10 (NA)

Charisma Skills: Imagination, Deception, Intimidation, Persuasion, Influence

RACIAL SKILLS: Half-Elf Wilderness Skills: Survival (+1), Stealth (+1), Tracking (+1)

RACIAL TALENTS: Half-Elf Flexibility (+5 AP at Level 0, +1 AP), Nightvision (15'), Elven Bow Proficiency +1 Level

CLASS SKILLS: Athletics (+10), Survival (+13), Stealth (+13), Animal Handling (+6), Tracking (+9)

CLASS TALENTS: Archery (Level 11), Two-Weapon Fighting (Level 14), Light Armor Proficiency, Animal Companion (Archer, Level 5 Dire Wolf), Favored Enemy (Goblin), Favored Terrain (Forest), Ranger Spells (Level 1), Master Archer (Cost 2 AP)

EARNED SKILLS: Perception (+8), Fletching (+3), Intimidation (+0), Investigation (+3)

EARNED TALENTS: Improvised Weapon (Achievement), Iron Will (Achievement), Surprise Attack (Achievement), Point Blank Shot (Earned)

CARRIED EQUIPMENT: Leather Armor (+3 Defense), Ranger's Cloak, Masterwork Scimitar, Damaged Masterwork Scimitar, Dagger, Compound Shortbow, Arrows x37, Flaming Arrows x4, The First Player's Sword, Elven Hunting Bow

STORED EQUIPMENT: Standard Clothes, Short-sword, Dagger, Stone Hatchet

RANGER SPELLS: Level 1 Spells (5 Mana): Jump, Entangle, Eyes of the Eagle, Camouflage, Longshot, Bottomless Quiver, Hunter's Endurance

COMBAT STATISTICS

Weapon - Talent Modifier - Weapon Damage - Accuracy - Median Damage

The First Player's Sword - 14 - 100 - 28 - 161

Masterwork Scimitar (off-hand) - 14 - 50 - 21 - 83

Elven Hunting Longbow - 11 - 80 - 25 - 164

ACHIEVEMENTS: First Kill, Backstabber, Good Samaritan, Goblin Slayer, Kobold Slayer, And Stay Out!, Ain't Got Time to Bleed, "The dishes are done man.", Marathon Runner, Orc Slayer, Pest Control, FATALITY, Specialist (Survival, Stealth, Tracking), I am the night, Trained (Animal Handling), Practice Makes Perfect (Survival, Stealth, Tracking), Hunter, Gone Fishin, Camp Cook, The Great Outdoors, It's Super Effective!, Improviser, "My Spidey Sense is Tingling", "It's all fun and games until someone loses an eye...then it's hilarious", Cornered Fighter, "The Bigger They Are...", Big Game Hunter, Avengers Assemble!, Goblinbane, Stand Together!, Tapped, "Riddle me this...", First Player's Sword, "It Belongs in a Museum!"

TOTAL ABILITY POINTS: 27

CURRENT CRYPTOCURRENCY: 16,580.47

CURRENT DEBTS: 4,508,134.08 CC - OzCo Department of

Corrections

CURRENT EXPERIENCE: 15,622

EXPERIENCE TO NEXT LEVEL: 23,000

 @zeelocked

Made in the USA
Coppell, TX
16 September 2020

38130763R10272